# PRAISE FOR SIM

## The Elias Network

"Secrets, lies, and wall-to-wall action! *The Elias Network* is a master class in globe-trotting, international intrigue. Simon Gervais brings his A game and then takes it to an entirely new level. Absolutely riveting!"
—Brad Thor, #1 *New York Times* bestselling author of *Shadow of Doubt*

"Simon Gervais is a true master of action and intrigue—NOBODY does it better!"
—Mark Greaney, #1 *New York Times* bestselling author of *The Chaos Agent*

## The Last Protector

"A thrill ride from the first page to the last! Simon Gervais is coming in hot with *The Last Protector*. Looking for action, intrigue, and suspense? This is your novel! Move it to the top of your list!"
—Jack Carr, #1 *New York Times* bestselling author of *The Devil's Hand*

"*The Last Protector*, by Simon Gervais, is a perfectly built, spellbinding thriller with true heart and depth woven into the blood-soaked and bone-crunching action. Relentlessly paced, authentic, and utterly engrossing, *The Last Protector* knocked me off my feet."
—Mark Greaney, #1 *New York Times* bestselling author of *The Gray Man*

"Simon Gervais writes with an insider's knowledge, putting us in the shoes of someone working close-protection assignments. Tightly plotted and lightning fast, *The Last Protector* is a must read."
—Marc Cameron, *New York Times* bestselling author of *Stone Cross* and *Tom Clancy's Code of Honor*

"Gervais's brisk series kickoff, which jumps around the world, is built on the tension underlying the tenuous alliances among the sort of power-hungry villains who will stop at nothing. Well-modulated action scenes alternate with showdowns that reposition the pawns."

—*Kirkus Reviews*

"[A] solid thriller from Gervais."

—*Publishers Weekly*

"Gervais has already cemented himself as one of the supreme writers in the genre, and this newest novel only adds to it. This is a book that thriller fans won't want to miss."

—Stuart Ashenbrenner, Best Thriller Books

## *The Last Sentinel*

"The numerous action scenes are depicted with precision and authority, including technical details of armaments and vehicles. Gervais's action-packed odyssey of a righteous American Everyman continues in fine fashion."

—*Kirkus Reviews*

## *The Last Guardian*

"[Clayton] White's third thrill ride spans the globe, unfolding in Monaco and Switzerland as well as China and Washington, and benefiting as much from its numerous surprises as from its expertly choreographed action scenes. A brisk globetrotting thriller with abundant tension and a timely premise."

—*Kirkus Reviews*

# Hunt Them Down

"In *Hunt Them Down*, Gervais has crafted an intelligent and thoughtful thriller that mixes family dynamics with explosive action . . . The possibilities are endless in this new series, and this will easily find an enthusiastic audience craving Hunt's next adventures."

—Associated Press

"[An] action-packed series launch from Gervais."

—*Publishers Weekly*

"Nonstop action meets relentless suspense . . . The blood flows knee deep in this one as Gervais uses his background as a drug investigator for the Royal Canadian Mounted Police to bring a gritty authenticity to his latest thriller."

—The Real Book Spy

"Gervais dishes out lavish suspense to keep a reader glued."

—Authorlink

"Superbly crafted and deceptively complex . . . This is thriller writing at its level best by a new voice not afraid to push the envelope beyond traditional storytelling norms."

—*Providence Journal*

"Another simply riveting read from author Simon Gervais, *Hunt Them Down* showcases his mastery of narrative-driven storytelling and his flair for embedding his novels with more twists and turns than a Coney Island roller coaster."

—Midwest Book Review

# THE
# ELIAS
# NETWORK

# ALSO BY SIMON GERVAIS

*Robert Ludlum's The Blackbriar Genesis*

## CLAYTON WHITE SERIES

*The Last Sentinel*

*The Last Protector*

*The Last Guardian*

## PIERCE HUNT SERIES

*Hunt Them Down*

*Trained to Hunt*

*Time to Hunt*

## MIKE WALTON SERIES

*The Thin Black Line*

*A Long Gray Line*

*A Red Dotted Line*

*A Thick Crimson Line*

# THE ELIAS NETWORK

A CASPIAN ANDERSON THRILLER

# SIMON GERVAIS

THOMAS & MERCER

Text copyright © 2024 by Simon Gervais Entertainment Ltd.

Published by Thomas & Mercer, Seattle

www.apub.com

Amazon, the Amazon logo, and Thomas & Mercer are trademarks of Amazon.com, Inc., or its affiliates.

ISBN-13: 9781662518539 (paperback)
ISBN-13: 9781662518522 (digital)

Cover design by Damon Freeman
Cover image: © vichie81 / Shutterstock; © Shelley Richmond / Arcangel

Printed in the United States of America

*To Lisane, Florence, and Gabriel.*
*You are the pillars of my world and the heartbeat of my*
*inspiration.*

# CHAPTER ONE

*Zermatt, Switzerland*

Exactly ninety-one minutes after he'd started his surveillance detection route, Caspian Anderson emerged from the belly of a dark alleyway and turned left onto Bahnhofstrasse—Zermatt's main thoroughfare—where he joined the swarms of tourists casually strolling past the lively potpourri of restaurants, bars, ski shops, bakeries, and trendy boutiques that lined both sides of the street. Ninety minutes wasn't considered lengthy for a surveillance detection route. Caspian's SDRs were often two, sometimes three times longer. But Zermatt wasn't a large city. Compared to Kowloon, where his last operation had taken place, Zermatt was like an oasis of peace. In Kowloon, which was located north of Hong Kong and across Victoria Harbour, the sidewalks were always flooded with pedestrians no matter what time of day it was. It had seemed like every establishment at street level stayed open round the clock, which was thankfully not the case in Zermatt.

Careful not to lose his footing on a hard patch of gray frozen slush, Caspian increased his pace and crossed the busy pedestrian street before entering a café. The luscious scents of roasted coffee beans and freshly baked breads and pastries filled his nostrils, but he dismissed the pleasant aromas, his focus already on the dozen or so customers inside the establishment. Through the warm light emanating from the vintage bulbs of the five chandeliers that hung from the ceiling, Caspian surveyed the room while he brushed the freshly fallen snow off his ski jacket and knit cap. His eyes stopped on a group of three men seated together at a six-person table. One of them, a broad, flat-nosed man, made brief eye contact with Caspian.

For a covert operative, even one like Caspian who understood the tactical environment, the balance between awareness and paranoia was a hard one to keep. In the back of his head, a little voice kept whispering questions into his ears.

*Have I seen these three guys before? Weren't they two tables away from me last night at dinner? And why is Flatnose still wearing his coat when nearly everyone else has theirs hung on the back of their chair? Is he dissimulating a knife, maybe even a firearm?*

After cataloging the faces and the reactions of the rest of the patrons, he headed to the counter and ordered an espresso and an almond biscotto. Glancing toward the table where Flatnose was seated, Caspian noticed the men were about to be joined by three women carrying shopping bags from high-end clothing stores. By the way the six of them interacted, it was evident they knew each other well. The massive diamond rings the women were sporting on their fingers hinted they might even be more than friends, which was enough for Caspian to dismiss them as immediate threats.

Curious to see if one of the two people he had identified as potential watchers during his SDR would follow him inside the café, Caspian kept an eye on the entrance while the barista prepared his drink.

It would be a bold, risky move for a watcher to come in—and a clear indication that Caspian had somehow royally screwed up, since he hadn't shared his plan to travel to Switzerland with anyone outside of Onyx, the black program buried deep within the International Operations branch of the Department of Homeland Security's Investigations Division that had been Caspian's employer for the last ten years.

Caspian thanked the barista for the coffee and the biscotto and made his way to the café's covered, heated terrace. Most tables were occupied by groups of three or four people scattered around the tables, chatting among themselves and sipping their drinks. No one paid him any attention. Very few people ever did.

Onyx had trained him well.

An inch under six feet and weighing slightly less than 180 pounds, Caspian didn't have a diminutive physical presence, but neither did he evoke a spontaneous and feral fear in a potential adversary's gut. This was by design.

One thing Caspian's instructors had hammered into his head during his training was that in his line of work, it was better to be underestimated than to be feared.

Ten years and thirty-three sanctioned kills later, Caspian hadn't forgotten the lesson.

*Better to be underestimated.*

He still lived by these words, to the great chagrin of Liesel, Caspian's first real long-term girlfriend. Thinking about her, he felt a pinch in his heart. He really liked that girl. Liesel Bergmann was an active, super attractive, and incredibly smart German expat who was two years his senior.

He missed her, even though the last hour they'd spent together prior to his departure hadn't ended on a high note. Apparently, apart from his delightful expertise in the bedroom, he was *boring as hell* and *dull*. While Liesel had apologized twice to him on the phone about what she'd said, Caspian had a bad feeling about where their relationship was headed. Her words had hit a chord. He had wanted to fight back and defend himself by telling her he was neither boring nor dull, and that he had to work very hard to maintain that monotonous facade, but he didn't. He couldn't. He had a persona to keep up.

*But I'm not boring in bed, so I guess there's that.*

If anyone was to take a closer look at his day-to-day life, they'd only see what Caspian wanted them to see: a generally happy, if somewhat dissatisfied, midlevel employee of the United Nations. His two-bedroom apartment, although nicely furnished and kept as clean as a once-per-two-weeks, forty-five-minute-long cleaning lady's appearance could manage, wasn't walking distance from the United Nations headquarters in New York. His car, which he barely drove since he took the subway to work, was an older-model Toyota Camry.

*Very* boring.

It was the same for his appearance. Although his muscular frame tilted more toward endurance than raw strength, Caspian often downplayed his physique by wearing jackets that were a size too big.

Caspian Anderson was a wolf in a sheepskin.

He chided himself for letting his mind wander about Liesel and took a seat at one of the available tables. He stirred his espresso with his biscotto before taking a small sip. From the café's terrace, which had a wide opening onto Bahnhofstrasse, he had an excellent view of the Hotel Schweizerhof. Caspian looked at his watch.

*A quarter of an hour, give or take five minutes,* he thought.

The people he had dispatched since he'd joined Onyx hadn't been honorable, law-abiding citizens. Quite the contrary. Mid- to high-level drug cartel members, foreign politicians trying to influence American elected officials, and crooked start-up entrepreneurs had all made the list.

In Caspian's honest-to-God opinion, the world was a better place without them, and it was a true privilege to have been given the opportunity to make such an impact for the greater good, even if it meant using methods more extreme than those acceptable to the general public. It was hard, dangerous work, but it had to be done.

And Caspian was good at it.

His target for this op, an American named Leonard Aldrich, was a banker with direct ties to a human trafficking ring. He was also a man of habits. Having observed Aldrich's routine every night since his arrival in Zermatt six days ago, Caspian fully expected the banker to stop by Le Fumoir—the Hotel Schweizerhof's opulent smoking room—where he would purchase a cigar he would later enjoy on the large balcony of his suite at Le Clarion—a luxurious owner-operated hotel, located near the Zermatt-Sunnegga funicular, where Aldrich stayed with his wife and three daughters.

Tonight, though, would be different. Leonard Aldrich wouldn't enjoy his cigar; he'd be dead long before he had the chance to light it.

# CHAPTER TWO

*Zermatt, Switzerland*

Edgar Augustin entered his hotel room and locked the door behind him. He wiped the perspiration off his face using the white towel wrapped around his neck, then headed to the bathroom. He let the sweaty towel fall to the floor and turned on the shower. While he waited for the spray of water to run hot, Edgar lifted his T-shirt and angled his body in a way that allowed him to inspect the wound on his flank.

"Damn," he swore.

Barely an inch below his left kidney, the thick scab that covered the cut where Sebastian—his schizophrenic seventeen-year-old son—had stabbed him the month before had pulled away during his workout. Edgar's wife, Juliette, a stay-at-home mom who used to be a nurse in the French Navy, had done a good job fixing the wound, but clearly Edgar had pushed himself too hard during his early evening workout. A cup of green tea and a solid workout had been his go-to method for relieving stress since he'd left the French Foreign Legion eight years ago, but he was forced to admit that the last set of dead lifts had been one too many.

Yesterday, after a challenging overseas operation, Edgar had been on his way back to Paris to try to fix things up with his wife and son when one of his contacts, a former Algerian army general named Bilal Amirouche, who was now living in Andorra la Vella, the capital city of the Principality of Andorra, had offered him the Zermatt job.

"It's a quick one, Edgar," Amirouche had promised him. "You and your team will be in and out in thirty-six hours, forty-eight at the most. And the client pays top dollar."

Edgar had almost declined before he had even heard the specifics about the mission. He was exhausted from a difficult weeklong operation that had started in Port-au-Prince, Haiti's capital, and ended in the port city of Durrës in Albania. He'd gotten less than thirty hours' sleep during the entire week. He was tired and irritable, and it was vital for him and his five-man team to get some well-deserved rest before their next big contract, which was set to begin once again in Port-au-Prince ten days from now.

But when the former general told Edgar how much money he would make for the two-day job, greed had taken over. Again.

His wife, furious, had yelled at him on the phone, threatening to throw him out of their lavish penthouse in Paris's sixth arrondissement if he didn't come home to help her deal with their son. Apparently, Sebastian was threatening to mutilate himself if he wasn't allowed to join his friends and party with them in Ibiza.

"Ibiza? I didn't know he had friends in Ibiza," Edgar had said.

"Damn you! He doesn't!" Juliette had screamed, losing it. "That's the whole friggin' point, Edgar. He's imagining things and talking to people who don't exist. You'd know that if you were around more often."

"I'll be back in two days. I promise. It's a job I can't . . . listen, the money is—"

"I don't care about the fucking money! I need you now, Edgar, not in two days."

"I understand, but I already—"

"If you won't do it for me, will you at least do it for Sebastian?" Juliette had pleaded one last time.

"I can't. I already accepted the job."

"Then cancel it!"

"That's not how it works, Juliette."

"*Crève, enfoiré!*" his wife had spit back at him before hanging up. Die, piece of shit!

Edgar didn't blame his wife for being pissed at him. How could he? He'd made a habit of breaking almost every family engagement he'd made since he'd become an independent contractor. The money he was bringing in was exponentially more than what he'd made as a commandant—the French Foreign Legion's rank equivalent to major—but his hectic work schedule was wreaking havoc on his relationship with his wife and son. Still, despite the threats she'd made to the contrary, Edgar knew his wife would take him back. She always did.

As he stepped into the shower, Edgar pushed aside his personal problems and focused on the task at hand. His five-man team hadn't wasted a minute since they had arrived in Zermatt earlier that day. They were already in position in and around Le Clarion, the hotel where Leonard Aldrich, an American banker who had blackmailed someone he shouldn't have, was staying. Whoever that *someone* was, he, or she, had contacted a conduit who in turn had reached out to Edgar's contact in Andorra. Over the years, General Amirouche had sent more than twenty very lucrative contracts Edgar's way. This one was no different. An impressive €75,000 was on its way to Edgar's account in the Cayman Islands. Even better, that represented only half of what he'd get for the operation. The rest of the money, plus expenses, would follow once Aldrich was dead.

There were only three small caveats. No big deal, really, but operational challenges nonetheless. Before Edgar could kill the banker, he was to dial an overseas number and pass the phone to Aldrich. A series of questions would be asked, and if the person on the other end of the line thought Aldrich answered truthfully, he would instruct Edgar to give the banker a quick death. Edgar was convinced the number was assigned to a burner phone belonging to whoever was footing the bill for the operation. The second condition—not a very hard one—was to acquire Aldrich's laptop, and the third, also not difficult, was to bring Aldrich's wife and three daughters to a specific apartment at the other end of Zermatt, where two contractors who weren't part of Edgar's team would take possession of the surviving members of Aldrich's family.

Although he was still waiting for the final message that would green-light the operation, Edgar had made good use of his time in Zermatt. In order to expedite the process, he had tasked his team with staking out the hotel the banker and his family were staying at. They were to inform him the moment Aldrich headed out for his evening walk. Knowing in advance that Aldrich would go for a walk was a critical piece of intelligence the client had shared with them and one that Edgar had used to plan his operation. Once the banker was out, Edgar's team would abduct Aldrich's wife and his three daughters and take them to the secondary location.

Edgar didn't expect his team to run into any problems. It wasn't their first time doing such work. They had become experts at this sort of mission. That's why the former general kept contracting Edgar's team to extract women and children out of Haiti and escort them to Europe. Edgar knew he was breaking international laws by smuggling people out of Haiti, but at least they would get a chance at a better life.

Maybe not a good life, but a better one.

While most of Edgar's team would be busy with Aldrich's family, Edgar would tail the banker and follow him back into his suite at Le Clarion. Edgar, with the help of his brother, Laurent, would then subdue the banker and follow the procedure.

Edgar didn't consider himself a monster. He played by a certain set of rules. Rules that he often bent to accommodate his needs, but rules nonetheless. He hoped Aldrich would understand it was in his best interest to cooperate. He wasn't in the mood to torture anyone tonight. He just wanted to go home to his wife—who loathed him—and his son.

Edgar dried himself and got dressed. He was in the process of adjusting the tactical holster at the small of his back when his phone chirped. It was a message from Laurent, who had taken position inside Le Clarion's lobby. Aldrich had just walked past Laurent and was about to exit the hotel. Edgar typed a short reply to acknowledge the message, then grabbed his red-dot-sights-equipped FN 509 Tactical pistol from the room safe. He inserted a seventeen-round magazine, racked the slide, then stuffed two spare magazines and a suppressor into his coat pockets.

It was time to earn his keep.

# CHAPTER THREE

*Zermatt, Switzerland*

The resort town of Zermatt, at an elevation of 5,276 feet above sea level, lay at the foot of the mighty pyramid-shaped Matterhorn peak. Since there were no motor vehicles spewing diesel or gasoline smoke in Zermatt—only electric vehicles and horse-drawn carriages were permitted—Caspian had had to leave his rental car in Täsch, a small village five kilometers away, and board a train for the twelve-minute ride to Zermatt. From the Zermatt railway station an electric taxi had transported him to the studio apartment he had rented for two months through a popular online marketplace.

Caspian looked at the no-vehicle policy through the eyes of a local inhabitant. An inconvenience, for sure, but he thought the slightly longer travel time was well worth it if it meant Zermatt avoided the fumes that plagued many cities and small villages alike. While Zermatt was home to only six thousand residents, it attracted more than two million tourists annually and could never accommodate the sheer number of vehicles usually associated with that many people. As with the rest of Switzerland, the local populace had long ago understood that their region's natural wonders were the greatest assets they possessed and were willing to take the necessary steps to safeguard them. Caspian had to salute the effort.

Zermatt was popular year round among hikers, climbers, and skiers alike. The vacation village was a true outdoor lover's paradise and exactly the kind of place he knew Liesel would fall in love with. Perhaps he could invite her to spend a week with him over the summer? If not in Zermatt, there were plenty of other charming places in Switzerland where two people could reconnect.

Catching himself, Caspian rolled his eyes. Never had he let someone occupy so much prime real estate in his head. He would have to do something about this. Liesel was getting in the way of his work.

Taking a bite of his biscotto, Caspian saw a man and a woman entering the terrace. They were both well dressed. The man was in his late fifties, but the woman didn't appear to be a day over thirty. Each was carrying a teacup in one hand and a small plate with a croissant in the other. Caspian recognized the man instantly, which prompted his heartbeat to spike, but his relaxed demeanor didn't change. He angled his face away from the new arrivals, hoping the man wouldn't notice him. But it was a lost cause. Since Caspian had sat down at his table ten minutes ago, the terrace had filled up considerably, and only two tables remained available. One of the two was near a mixed group of loud American and British teenagers, and the other was next to Caspian's. It was clear which of the two tables the couple would choose. There was no point in pretending otherwise.

*Shit. This is going to be a problem,* he thought, preparing himself mentally for the inevitable conversation that would come next. When he was ready, Caspian looked in the man's direction and made eye contact. For the briefest moment, a panicked look flashed across the man's face. Then it was gone, replaced by the generic smile politicians and diplomats around the world were famous for. An instant later, the deep voice of Ambassador Claus Eichberg, the permanent representative of the Federal Republic of Germany to the United Nations, boomed from the table next to Caspian's.

"Caspian, is that you?"

Acting surprised, which wasn't difficult in this situation, Caspian said, "Ambassador Eichberg? I . . . I can't believe it."

Caspian rose to his feet. Not doing so would have seemed rude to anyone watching.

Eichberg was a very tall, slim man with a broad forehead and wavy white hair that had just started to thin. His blue eyes, small and narrow, were, in Caspian's opinion, set way too close together.

"An unexpected surprise, but so very pleasant," Eichberg said in perfect but heavily accented English.

As much as Caspian wished he could make up an excuse and simply walk out, it wasn't really an option. It would be out of character for him to do so, and something Eichberg might remember and question later. Prior to his being named to his current position by the German chancellor, Eichberg's occupation at the United Nations had been as the high commissioner for human rights, a prominent appointment that had conferred on Eichberg vast powers and an unlimited access to the secretary-general.

Though the timing couldn't be worse, Caspian had no choice but to make small talk with the ambassador and the lady standing next to him. At least for the next few minutes.

"Would you like to join me, Ambassador?" Caspian said in German while shaking Eichberg's outstretched hand.

"*Danke schön*, Caspian. But we wouldn't want to impose."

"Not at all."

"May I introduce you to my wife, Catharina?" Eichberg said.

Catharina was shorter than her husband, but still tall for a woman. She had long black hair, big brown eyes, and flawless skin and was elegantly dressed in expensive après-ski wear. She offered Caspian a gloved hand.

"Very nice to meet you," Caspian said, continuing in German, his lips brushing the soft leather of the glove.

"Caspian is a senior translator and interpreter at the United Nations—"

"I'm sorry. A translator, you said?" Catharina appeared surprised that her husband, the great ambassador, would be friends with someone as low on the diplomatic totem pole as a mere translator.

"Yes ma'am, that's correct," Caspian said, unfazed. Like most interpreters working at the United Nations headquarters, he was used to being snubbed by top-tier diplomats. Ambassador Eichberg's open attitude toward lower-level staffers like Caspian was an exception to the rule, not the norm. Caspian's first impression of Catharina was that she didn't quite share her husband's down-to-earth approach.

He couldn't care less.

"Caspian is truly gifted when it comes to languages, Catharina," the ambassador explained once they were all seated. "For a couple of weeks at the end of last year, Caspian assisted me on a delicate file—"

"Did he now?" Catharina quipped, raising an eyebrow.

"Yes. He's one of the best people I've had the pleasure to work with in New York."

"Thank you for saying that, sir, but I assure you the privilege was all mine," Caspian said.

"What are you doing in Zermatt, Mr. . . . ?" Catharina asked as she slowly removed her gloves, one finger at a time.

"Anderson, ma'am. Caspian Anderson," he replied. "A friend of mine, who is a much better skier than I'll ever be, told me this was the greatest ski resort in Switzerland—"

"In the world, dear," Catharina said, interrupting him, her tone grave, as if she was discussing something of vital importance. "Zermatt is the greatest ski resort *in the world*."

Caspian gave Catharina his best smile and said, "I'll admit that after spending a few days exploring the mountain, I agree with you. And what about you? Are you here on vacation?"

"I am, but *His Excellency* is working," Catharina said, pointing a delicate finger toward her husband. "Or at least he's pretending to. Sometimes I'm not sure what my husband does. Take today, for example. He's been checking his phone—"

"Please, Catharina, Caspian doesn't need to be bored to death hearing you complain about my work schedule." Eichberg interrupted his wife, his deep voice cutting and sharp. "He's here on vacation. We should respect that."

The ambassador's tone wasn't one Caspian remembered him using while working with him.

A plastic smile instantly appeared on Catharina's lips. "Of course. You're right."

"Where are you staying while you're in Zermatt, Caspian?" Eichberg asked.

"I was lucky enough to find something not too far from the Matterhorn Express," Caspian replied.

"Oh. How nice," Catharina said, clearly uninterested. "You have your own bathroom, I hope?"

"It's small, but it fits my limited budget. And rest assured, I don't have to share a bathroom with anyone. I'm sure you and the ambassador have found something much nicer. Though I couldn't afford to stay in any of them, I heard Zermatt is home to some of the nicest hotels you'll find in Switzerland." Caspian found the passive-aggressive treatment he was getting from Catharina entertaining.

"Oh, but we're not staying at a hotel, Mr. Andrews," Catharina said, stirring her tea with a spoon. She eyed Caspian, a condescending smile appearing on her thin-lipped mouth. "We have our own place in the village."

Caspian suppressed a smile. He didn't bother correcting her about the incorrect last name, but he did wonder why the ambassador's wife felt the need to constantly assert her imaginary superiority over him. Catharina's behavior screamed loneliness and insecurity, but he wasn't buying it. Not entirely, anyway. It felt forced.

Eichberg, though, didn't seem amused by his wife's apparent flexing. He shot Catharina what Caspian thought was a look of pure annoyance. The ambassador swallowed the piece of croissant he had in his mouth, then said, "It's a small three-bedroom apartment. Nothing too fancy."

"I'm sure it's lovely."

"It's quite charming, yes," Eichberg admitted. "But we barely use it. Three, maybe four weeks per year if we're fortunate enough."

"A real shame at the price we paid for it," Catharina said through pursed lips. "Real estate prices in Zermatt are through the roof."

"I take it you would like to spend more time in Zermatt, Mrs. Eichberg?" Caspian asked, finishing the last of his biscotto.

"Of course she does. Who wouldn't?" Eichberg said before his wife could come up with an answer. "But my duties at the United Nations are keeping us away, I'm afraid. With that in mind, Caspian, and to show my appreciation for all the hard work you put in while we worked together, Catharina and I would be delighted to let you stay at our modest apartment if you were to find yourself in Zermatt again."

Caspian heard Catharina gasp as she almost choked on her tea.

"Are you all right, dear?" the ambassador asked, pulling a white handkerchief from an inside pocket of his winter jacket and handing it to his wife. "Was it something I said?"

Caspian wasn't sure what to think of the dynamic between Eichberg and his wife. Though he had never rubbed shoulders with Eichberg outside of work and didn't know him personally, Caspian was taken aback by the ambassador's harsher-than-usual attitude. Eichberg was more guarded than Caspian ever remembered seeing him, and less jovial too. His body language portrayed a sense of anxiety.

*And there was that terrified look on his face when we first made eye contact. Then again, maybe I'd be pissed off, too, if I had to share my life with someone as petulant as Catharina.*

Then Caspian's eyes caught the figure of a lone man walking on the street across from the terrace. The man wore a black Burberry trench coat, a woolen hat, and black winter boots. His hands were shoved deep into the pockets of his coat. And then Caspian saw his face. It was Leonard Aldrich. The banker's pace was brisk, and he was heading straight for the Hotel Schweizerhof's entrance.

Caspian ignored the ongoing bickering between Eichberg and his wife, focusing instead on the individual faces of the people in Aldrich's vicinity. Caspian compared the faces to those he had memorized over the last four days. Nothing registered. He spent a few seconds on each person, searching for an earpiece, a radio, or anything that could identify someone as a possible watcher. He didn't see anything.

*Nothing obvious, anyway.*

Most of the pedestrians looked like wealthy tourists. They were wearing expensive ski coats and designer jeans and walking in groups of two or three. None of them seemed to pay any special attention to Aldrich.

On the table, Eichberg's phone chimed once. The ambassador's hand shot forward to fetch it, almost knocking over Catharina's teacup in the process.

It was time for Caspian to go.

"I have a video call scheduled in a few minutes," Caspian said, getting to his feet. "I can't thank you enough for your generous offer to stay at your place, sir, but this ski trip is a once-in-a-lifetime experience for me. The airfare alone was a stretch this time around."

The relief on Catharina's face was evident, but Eichberg, who was typing a message on his phone, didn't bother looking up, his only acknowledgment a barely perceptible nod. Caspian couldn't be sure, but he thought he saw a slight tremor in the ambassador's hands as he held his phone. Caspian thanked the ambassador one more time and wished him and his wife a great end to their stay in Zermatt, then grabbed his belongings and left the terrace, puzzled by how the whole encounter had gone down. Caspian pushed whatever thoughts he had about Eichberg and his wife out of his mind. He had a more pressing issue to deal with.

He had a man to kill.

# CHAPTER FOUR

*Zermatt, Switzerland*

Ambassador Claus Eichberg locked his screen and put his phone back in his pocket. His eyes caught the departing figure of Caspian Anderson as the UN translator exited the loud, busy terrace.

"You're offering our apartment to strangers now?" Catharina asked him.

"I knew he was going to say no," he said.

"Were you? I'm not so sure."

"What game were you playing, being a pain in the ass like that?" Eichberg snapped but kept his voice to barely a whisper.

"Me? Oh, I thought we were just having fun."

Eichberg shook his head. He didn't mind the role-playing in the bedroom, but he was getting annoyed with Catharina's constant changing acts when they were with other people. She'd tried to explain it to him once, saying that destabilizing people during a first interaction was key to understanding who they were and their true motivation. Eichberg wasn't sure he understood. But he was the dealmaker. Catharina was the spy.

"Well, tone the fun down a few notches, will you?"

"I was just trying to make conversation," she said. "But you, my dear, your hands were shaking holding that phone of yours, and I think your friend Caspian noticed."

"Don't worry about Caspian," Eichberg said, reaching for his cup of tea. "He's irrelevant."

His cup was halfway to his lips when he felt his wife's hard gaze boring into him. He exhaled loudly.

"What is it?" he asked.

"You've never been good at reading people, Claus," Catharina said. "Mr. Anderson isn't fazed easily. He's not one of your regular UN staffers."

Eichberg was barely listening to his wife. His mind was occupied by the new offer that had just come in. But he knew he had to respond to Catharina. If not, she would keep going on and on until he did.

"I told you, Catharina, Caspian is good. He knows his stuff, okay? And he gets things done. A rare commodity at the UN. Can we move on now? There are more important things to discuss than a UN translator with whom I worked for two weeks."

"You still offered him our apartment to stay at. Should I be worried?"

"Oh, for Christ's sake. I did that to annoy you," he said with a smirk. "And it seems to have worked even better than I had hoped."

Catharina eyed him over the rim of her teacup, then took a sip.

"So, what got you so excited that you didn't even notice your friend was leaving?" she asked.

"I got a new deal going."

"To replace the last shipment, the one you lost in Albania?"

Eichberg's jaw tightened at the rebuke. "I didn't lose the shipment, Catharina, my forces on the ground were overwhelmed by the Albanian mob. I'll have to deal with these assholes eventually, but my priority was to restore Amirouche's confidence in my ability to provide the goods."

"And?"

"It's almost a done deal. And the broker is pleased."

"What's the new offer?"

Eichberg looked around him. The terrace was nearly filled to capacity. He was confident the background racket more than covered the sound of his voice, but he still leaned toward his wife and whispered, "Two million euros. Eight kidneys. One heart. Two lungs."

Catharina's mouth opened wide in surprise, but she caught herself rapidly, and she whispered back, "Two mil? Who do you think is behind the purchase? A Chinese buyer?"

Eichberg shrugged. "You know as well as I do that isn't how it works. The buyer places the money in an online escrow that is administered by Amirouche. Once the funds clear, I receive the offer. I'm never told who the buyer is. And I don't care."

"Is there a penalty? You know, for what happened in Albania?"

"Apart from the financial loss, no," Eichberg said. While this wasn't a lie, he had received a dire warning from Amirouche. But he wasn't about to admit that to Catharina.

His wife's eyes narrowed. "How's this possible?"

Eichberg sighed. Sometimes he forgot his wife was smarter than he was.

"Because the organs aren't being harvested from malnourished Haitians this time but from four rich, healthy Americans."

Eichberg smiled. For the second time in less than a minute, his wife was looking at him with a bewildered expression. He enjoyed baffling Catharina. It hadn't happened often in the six years they'd been married to each other.

"How . . . how did you manage that?" she asked.

Eichberg remained silent, waiting for Catharina to reach her own conclusion. It usually didn't take her long to catch up, but he remembered that she was missing some crucial information. He'd been so damn busy in the last three days that he hadn't thought about bringing her up to speed.

"I won't meet with Leonard Aldrich tomorrow," he said.

"What? Isn't that why we're here? And what does it have to do with what we're talking about?"

"Everything."

"But you must meet with him, Claus. The little shit blackmailed us, and I received specific instructions from—"

"Catharina," Eichberg said, reaching across the table for her hand, "I have this under control."

"You do? How?"

Eichberg knew the wheels were spinning fast in Catharina's head.

"Mother of God," she said between tight lips a moment later. "You'll have him killed."

Eichberg didn't react. He didn't say anything. He wanted his wife to continue her thought process.

"Mother of God," she said again, "you sold his family."

"A healthy mom and her three daughters," he said. "For two million euros."

There was a sparkle in Catharina's eyes, and her cheeks were flushed. Eichberg could tell she was as excited as he was about the prospect of a big payday. It took a moment for his wife to regain her composure.

"Healthy Americans or not, that's about three times the rate we got on the last deal. What's the catch?" she asked.

"It has to happen tonight," Eichberg said. "Amirouche said the timing isn't negotiable."

"Tonight? But that's impossible," Catharina said, shaking her head, suddenly looking defeated.

Eichberg, who was still holding on to his wife's hand, squeezed it gently.

"It's happening as we speak, my dear," he said. "I have a team in place."

Catharina nodded slowly, taking everything in. "Okay. What's next?"

"I suggest we get out of Zermatt," Eichberg said, pulling his phone out of his coat. "The last message I received confirmed that the team is in place and ready to go. They just need the final go-ahead, which I'm about to send to my contact."

"Where are we going?" Catharina asked, getting up.

Eichberg glanced at his watch and considered his options.

"I think we should go check out Andorra. I heard the mountains there are terrific."

# CHAPTER FIVE

*Zermatt, Switzerland*

Caspian donned his knit cap, zipped his coat, and stepped out of the café, noticing at once the change in temperature as his breath clouded the air in front of his face. The fluffy, low-hanging clouds that had been present earlier, and the snow flurries that had come with them, had given way to a high, moonlit sky and a knifing wind that bit into his bare cheeks. A sensation he welcomed and savored. The cold helped to keep his mind sharp.

Caspian reached into his left pocket and wrapped his hand around a small plastic device that resembled a syringe but worked like an EpiPen. The injector contained 150 milligrams of a lethal venom, the same toxin Caspian had used to eliminate a high-ranking member of ISIS who had sought medical care in Pakistan two years ago. After he had stealthily gained access to the private room where the ISIS man had been hospitalized, Caspian had witnessed firsthand the toxin's efficiency. Seconds after he had pricked the terrorist under the nail of his left toe, a yellowish foam had started to come out from the man's mouth. A minute later, the ISIS man had stopped breathing. During the mission debrief, Caspian had learned that, although the poison's preferred method of delivery was through injection, the toxin could be equally fatal if enough of it was ingested—a concept he was willing to test on Aldrich if the right opportunity presented itself.

Thirty meters away, the American banker entered the Hotel Schweizerhof. Caspian fidgeted with the injector to make sure he could pop off the cap that covered the device's needle at a moment's notice. He was about to follow Aldrich inside the hotel when something drew his attention. Across the street from him, a lone man had slipped on a patch of ice. The man was agile and had caught himself quickly without losing a step, but his right hand had immediately shot to his lower back. To most people, this gesture would have gone unnoticed, but to a trained assassin like Caspian, this was something worthy of his attention.

*Strike one.*

In Caspian's world, the motion was often attributed to an equipment check. In this case, it looked as if the man had verified that whatever he kept in the small of his back was still properly in place.

*Something like a pistol.*

Aware that the gesture could mean many other things—maybe the man had somehow strained the lower part of his back when he had regained his balance—Caspian didn't want to jump to conclusions, but he opted not to alter his trajectory. Instead of changing direction and heading toward the Hotel Schweizerhof, he kept to his side of the street and approached a group of three similarly dressed men who were finishing off a shared cigarette a few steps away. The people in the group were all in their early twenties and sported identical black winter coats with the name of a nearby restaurant printed on the back. Caspian drew a pack of cigarettes from a pocket and made a show of searching for a lighter.

"You guys have a light?" he asked in German, positioning himself in a way that allowed him to spy on the suspicious man across the street while keeping an eye on the hotel's entrance.

One of the workers lit Caspian's cigarette using a well-worn silver-colored Zippo. Caspian nodded his thanks and shook a few cigarettes out of his pack and offered them to the three men, who readily accepted. Though he wasn't a smoker, he had long ago figured out that keeping a pack of cigarettes handy—especially in Europe, where tobacco consumption was higher than in North America—was a sound practice if one wanted to blend in. Using his newfound friends as shields, Caspian took a moment to study the man who had caught his attention.

The man was dressed in black jeans and wore a dark jacket and a black ball cap pulled low, which cast a shadow over most of his face. He was tall and fit, and he was strolling in no particular hurry and with no obvious destination. The man didn't look stressed, either, and, if it hadn't been for the half second Caspian had seen him react when he had nearly lost his balance on the patch of ice, Caspian doubted he would have given the man a second look. Caspian observed the man walk past the Hotel Schweizerhof's entrance and noted that he didn't even glance inside through the lobby's large glass panel doors, nor did he look back or scan his surroundings.

Caspian laughed at a joke one of the restaurant employees made, but internally he was beginning to regret his decision not to follow Aldrich inside the hotel. Then, half a block past the Schweizerhof's entrance, the man stopped at a little hole-in-the-wall crêperie. There were two customers in line in front of him waiting to place their orders. The man angled his body in a way that allowed him to keep the hotel lobby in sight without making it obvious he was doing so.

But Caspian caught the movement.

*Strike two,* he thought, already looking for the man's associates while planning his next move.

Caspian was a third of the way through his cigarette. It would look out of place for him to linger at the same location once he was done with his smoke. Though he spent the next two minutes chitchatting with the restaurant workers, his senses were on alert, keeping track of the movements of those around him and searching for any additional watchers. If his assessment of the man was correct and he was indeed a surveillance operative, the man patiently waiting in line for his turn to order a crêpe was very good.

Which was cause for concern.

Could Aldrich have hired a crew to conduct countersurveillance? Caspian dismissed the idea. The man wasn't positioned to provide any type of cover for Aldrich.

*No. Like me, he's watching him. But why? What's his end goal?*

Another possibility was that Aldrich's criminal activities had been uncovered by a law enforcement agency. If that was the case, Caspian had to accept the man he had spotted could be a police officer. But by the way the man operated, Caspian doubted he was from the local cantonal police office. He was too smooth for a regular cop.

Caspian would have to be careful and might even need to take a step back until he figured out exactly what the man's intentions were. Whether he was a police officer or not, his presence had heightened the mission's level of difficulty.

But was slowing down even an option? If the police—or an intelligence agency, for that matter—was onto Aldrich, would Caspian's superiors be pleased if the American banker was taken into custody and questioned? Probably not. If Onyx had thought that arresting Aldrich and bringing him in front of a judge was the best course of action, they wouldn't have assigned Elias—Caspian's code name—to kill him.

He swore under his breath. At some point, he would have to check in with his handler, Laura, to update her. There was no way around it.

*But not yet. Not while I'm standing next to these restaurant workers.*

He glanced at his watch. Aldrich had been inside the hotel for just under five minutes, a few minutes short of the length of his last two visits.

Across the street, it was the man's turn to order, but just as he seemed about to take a step toward the take-out window, he looked back, his gaze locking onto Caspian.

# CHAPTER SIX

*Zermatt, Switzerland*

Over the course of his career, Edgar had developed an acute sixth sense. Identifying incoming trouble before those around him did had kept him alive, so, when a sudden feeling of being watched registered in his subconscious, he checked over his shoulder, his eyes moving left and right, searching for whatever had triggered the warning in his brain. To his relief, Edgar didn't spot an immediate threat to his safety, but that didn't quiet his concern completely. He'd been careful since he had started trailing the American banker, but he hadn't put much emphasis on countersurveillance, instead focusing on confirming that Aldrich didn't have some sort of covert security detail assigned to him.

At this hour, Bahnhofstrasse was filled with tourists looking for a place to get dinner or a drink. Edgar hadn't observed anyone jerk their head in another direction when he had looked back, but he couldn't be sure. Across the street, four men smoking cigarettes stood in a loose circle a few feet away from a small Italian restaurant. Three of the men wore identical black winter coats. Printed on the back of their jackets was the name of the trattoria they were standing next to. The fourth man, though, wasn't wearing the same winter coat. Not a big deal, but Edgar's instinct was to catalog the man's face for future reference. Unfortunately, one of the restaurant employees had just moved in front of him, obscuring a large portion of the man's features.

"Sir, it's your turn. Can I take your order?" the long-haired clerk working the take-out window asked before Edgar had the chance to alter his position.

"Yes, thank you. I'll have the sugar-and-lemon one," Edgar replied, fishing a ten-franc note from his pocket and placing it in front of the clerk.

"I'm sorry, but we're out of lemons," the clerk said. "The dulce de leche is my favorite, if you're interested. And you can add a scoop of homemade vanilla—"

"Fine, fine. I'll take it," Edgar said, his mind occupied by the smoker across the street.

"With ice cream?"

"No. Just the crêpe."

"Would you like a coffee or hot chocolate? They're only three Swiss francs with the purchase of a crêpe."

"Just the damn crêpe," Edgar snapped, starting to get flustered with the clerk's questions.

The clerk, who couldn't be older than eighteen, raised his hands. "Hey, not my fault, man. My boss wants me to push the beverages, okay?"

"Right, sorry," Edgar said.

"Anyway, here's your change," the clerk said, pushing a few coins in Edgar's direction. "Please step to the side. Someone will let you know once your order is ready."

Edgar left a small tip and pocketed the rest of the coins before moving to the side and resting his back against the brick wall of the building.

*Shit. He's gone.*

Edgar barely moved his head as he searched for the fourth man, but his eyes were a flutter of constant movements. Less than a minute later, the three remaining men of the group entered the restaurant, one after the other. When his order was finally called, Edgar gave up on finding the man and grabbed his crêpe. Returning to the brick wall, he resumed his surveillance of the Hotel Schweizerhof's entrance but couldn't shake the feeling someone was watching him.

# CHAPTER SEVEN

*Zermatt, Switzerland*

Caspian made his move the moment the man turned around to place his order. After a quick nod to say goodbye to the three men with whom he had shared the last few minutes, Caspian hurried east for fifteen meters and turned left onto the first side street he encountered. A few steps away, a green neon sign advertised an Irish pub. He pulled the door open and entered the pub. The establishment was busy but not yet full, and Caspian was met with the smell of beer and fried food. The floor was made of dark wood and was already sticky underfoot despite the evening's early hour. Still, the place did have a cozy feel, and Caspian could see why the pub could be appealing to ski bums after a hard day on the slopes.

A busboy walked past him, holding a tray of empty and not-so-empty half-liter beer mugs. Caspian grabbed a quarter-full mug on the fly and headed toward an available table located next to one of the three windows with a direct view of Bahnhofstrasse. But before he could reach the table, three young couples coming from the bar with drinks in hand sat around the high-top table Caspian was aiming for. Forced to find another vantage point from which he could keep an eye on the Hotel Schweizerhof's entrance and the hole-in-the-wall crêperie, Caspian spotted a nearby pool table where two women were playing a game of eight ball. Pretending to be interested in the game, Caspian moved around the table until he could see out the window. The angle and the lighting were far from optimal, but from where he was standing, he was able to monitor the entrance of the Hotel Schweizerhof.

The crêperie, though, was too far down the street.

Caspian's internal clock told him he'd been inside the pub for approximately one minute. Aldrich could exit the hotel any moment, and it was essential that Caspian be able to watch the reaction of the man at the crêperie when he did so. He looked around for a solution.

*There. At the back of the room.*

Cordoned off with a black velvet rope at its entrance, a narrow staircase led upstairs. Careful not to spill his beer, Caspian casually stepped over the rope and began to climb the stairs, only speeding up once he was out of sight. The second floor appeared to be only half as wide as the first, and there was barely any light. The only illumination came from a blue neon beer sign located behind the long stool-lined bar that occupied the back wall. There was just enough light for Caspian to see that the room was empty of patrons.

On the opposite side, the one with the windows, were two doors leading to small offices. Both doors were ajar. After a cursory check to ensure no employees were in either of the offices, Caspian stepped inside the one that was farther to his right and closed the door behind him. He left the lights turned off so as not to silhouette himself against the window. Careful not to disturb any of the numerous boxes stacked on the floor or the papers piled on the desk, Caspian slowly approached the window but refrained from getting too close to it.

He'd been inside the pub for just over two minutes.

He looked out. His reward was immediate. From his new observation post, he had an unblemished view of the Hotel Schweizerhof and the crêperie. The man with the ball cap was still there, munching slowly at his crêpe.

By moving one floor up, Caspian had made the right call, and not a minute too soon. He had been at the window for less than fifteen seconds when Aldrich stepped out of the hotel. Caspian looked at the man with the ball cap, gauging his reaction. The man was in the process of taking another bite of his crêpe but stopped midway. He, too, had seen Aldrich. The banker paused for a moment, fumbling for something in his pocket. The man in the ball cap stiffened, and Caspian watched him take a few steps toward a pregnant woman with a baby stroller who was waiting in line to order—a move Caspian himself would have done to go unnoticed among the small crowd that had gathered near the popular crêperie despite the cooling temperature.

Then a chill ran up the back of his neck as he thought about another reason why the man with the ball cap might have moved next to the woman. *He wants to use them as a shield in case Aldrich pulls out a gun.*

After a few tense seconds, Aldrich pulled out a pack of cigarettes and a lighter from his pocket. Caspian breathed a sigh of relief as Aldrich lit a smoke. Cigarette in hand—and as he had done the previous nights—Aldrich began to walk and soon strolled past the crêperie. Only then did Ballcap step away from the expectant mother and return to his previous position against the brick wall. The man's head didn't move much, but Caspian knew he was scanning his surroundings—including gazing at the windows of nearby buildings—for threats or watchers. Caspian had time to count until thirty-five before the man threw away his half-eaten crêpe in a nearby garbage can. Then, instead of following Aldrich, Ballcap turned one last time to scan his rear.

And that's when the light over Caspian's head came on, flooding his entire world in bright white.

# CHAPTER EIGHT

*Zermatt, Switzerland*

Confident Aldrich hadn't hired a protective detail, but still wary that he was missing something, Edgar discarded his crêpe and glanced one more time behind him. Out of the corner of his eye, he caught a flash of light coming from a second-floor window across the street. He caught the upper silhouette of a man standing a few feet away from the window, but only for an instant before the man retreated deeper into the room and out of Edgar's sight.

It was impossible to say if the man at the window was the same man he had spotted earlier. And even if it was indeed the same person, wouldn't it make sense that the man knew the people working at a nearby restaurant? Smokers tended to hang together, and often at the same spot, didn't they?

*Shit.*

There was nothing unusual about what he had just seen.

*Is my mind playing tricks on me? Am I imagining things, just like Sebastian?*

An image of his son flashed across his eyes with his wife's pleading in the background.

*I need you now, Edgar!*

He sighed, suddenly feeling tired and hopeless. The fatigue he had accumulated during the last operation was starting to weigh on his mental and physical abilities. That wasn't good. He had an entire team counting on him to guide them safely through the operation and bring them home alive, including his younger brother, Laurent, whose wife had recently given birth to a set of twins.

*Get a grip!* Edgar told himself, forcing out of his mind anything that wasn't related to the mission.

In his chosen profession, anything less than peak performance was simply not acceptable. And that was especially true for a leader. This was something he had learned long ago when attending Saint-Cyr, the French military academy.

After one last look at the window across the street, Edgar started after Aldrich.

The American banker had a seventy-meter lead. That was fine. Anyone tasked with Aldrich's protection would be operating at a much closer range than that, which would give Edgar another opportunity to detect them. But based on what he had observed so far, Edgar doubted Aldrich had anyone watching his back. He would have identified them by now.

Edgar pulled out his phone's Bluetooth earpiece from his pocket and slipped it on. After performing a radio check with each member of his team, Edgar updated his brother on Aldrich's location.

"We can't move now; we'll draw way too much attention," Laurent said. "Two of the kids are in the heated outdoor pool with the wife. We should wait until they return to their room. Shouldn't be too long now. They've been at it for a while."

"Agreed," Edgar said. "Let me know once they're out of the pool."

Worst-case scenario, they could try again the next day if the kids and the wife weren't back in their room by the time Aldrich reached the hotel. Though it would prolong the operation by an extra day—not an option Edgar was particularly keen on since his contact had insisted the op needed to be done that night—it was better than botching the job.

The bigger threat came from his wife. Juliette was going to throw a fit if he didn't get his ass back to Paris as he'd promised. But what was he supposed to do?

# CHAPTER NINE

*Zermatt, Switzerland*

Caspian didn't know if he had moved fast enough to get away from the window in time not to be seen by anyone on the street, but he couldn't afford to think about that now. He had a much more urgent matter to take care of.

Someone was behind him.

Caspian had two options. The first was to fling his beer mug toward whoever had surprised him, hoping to create the second and a half he needed to draw the SIG Sauer P229 pistol he had in an inside-the-waistband holster. The second option was to play dumb. His brain computed the data, analyzing the pluses and minuses of both options in less time than most people would need to find the solution of two times two.

Going for the second option, Caspian, acting drunk, turned around while he brought the half-liter mug to his lips, making sure to spill some beer on the floor. A tall, wide-shouldered man in his midthirties stood in the doorway, muscular arms crossed against his chest. The man didn't look amused, but he didn't seem surprised either. Caspian took it as a win that the man wasn't holding a gun to his face and guessed it wasn't the first time a customer who'd had a few too many had made his way to the second floor.

"What are you doing here?" the man asked in German as he closed the distance with Caspian. "Didn't you see the stairs were blocked off?"

"I . . . I needed to pee. I'm s-sorry," Caspian slurred as he wobbled to his right and then to his left, his left hand reaching for his pants zipper.

The man's eyes opened wide. "What? You . . . you peed in my office?"

Caspian shook his head and steadied himself against the desk to his left.

"I'd . . . I'd prefer . . . not to, but . . . would it be okay?" he said, raising the mug to his lips once more.

One of the man's big hands closed around Caspian's wrist in a viselike grip.

"All right, pal. You've had more than enough," the man said, taking the beer mug from Caspian's hand. "The bathrooms are downstairs. There's nothing for you here."

Caspian didn't resist and let himself be escorted down the stairs. He half expected to receive one or two jabs in the ribs as punishment for his poor behavior, but the man was polite and well mannered, and he ensured Caspian made it safely to the bathroom before leaving him be.

———

Under the watchful eye of the courteous but vigilant employee, Caspian exited the pub shortly after. Betting Aldrich had followed the same path he had the last few nights, Caspian took a shortcut that led him to a small grocery store on a street corner he knew was close to a specific point on Aldrich's itinerary. Caspian entered the store and purchased a pack of gum and an energy drink. He sipped his drink while browsing a magazine rack.

Caspian saw Aldrich first. The banker had lit another cigarette, and his pace was quicker than usual, which Caspian attributed to the cooler temperature.

*Unless he knows someone's following him.*

He started to count the number of pedestrians walking behind Aldrich. He got to eight before he spotted Ballcap. Caspian estimated the distance between the two men at just under one hundred meters. In his mind's eye, he brought up a map of Zermatt and merged it with the route he believed Aldrich would take to reach his hotel. Then he did the math.

*One. Average walking speed is three miles per hour, but Aldrich has picked up his pace. Let's say his speed is three point five.*

*Two. The distance between Aldrich and Ballcap is one hundred meters, which means Aldrich will be out of sight from Ballcap for as long as one minute five seconds. I'm gonna cut it down to fifty seconds to give myself a buffer.*

A few seconds later, Caspian had a plan, but before he could initiate it, he wanted to follow Ballcap for a little while, hoping to gather a few clues that would help identify him. Caspian left the corner store and gave Ballcap a lot of space. There was no point in tailing him too close. Given that Aldrich hadn't yet deviated from his regular route, Caspian assumed the banker would follow the same path he had in the past. This freed Caspian to spend additional time ensuring he didn't have a tail of his own and to confirm that Ballcap was indeed working alone. So far, he hadn't seen Ballcap talk on the phone or try to communicate with someone in any other way. But the distance between them was significant, and it was dark outside, so it was possible he had missed something.

The more he thought about it, the more Caspian believed that Ballcap was an intelligence officer, and that reminded him that he'd better check in with his handler before moving to the violent part of his plan.

# CHAPTER TEN

*New York, New York*

Liesel Bergmann was in the spare bedroom of her apartment, madly pumping the pedals of her stationary bike and looking like she'd been hosed down. The heat coming off the portable electric converter she had cranked way up combined with the warmth of the early afternoon sun blasting through the room's two large windows made the small space unbearably hot, which was exactly how she wanted it. She was a firm believer that a good sweat was psychologically beneficial.

She had gone out with people from work the night before and had eaten too much, drunk too many glasses of champagne, and come back to her apartment way too late. But that wasn't why she was pedaling her way to exhaustion. She didn't care about the calories. Her metabolism was firing and working at an optimal level, thanks to her workout habits. No, she was on her bike because it was the only way she had found to keep herself from checking her phone every damn minute to see if the email confirming that last night's operation had been successful had finally landed in her inbox. She had expected the email to pop up hours ago, and she was beginning to wonder if she hadn't made some sort of technical mistake.

*Stop speculating about something you no longer have control over,* she told herself, picking up the pace some more.

While she did have a good time with her team members, first at the Michelin-starred restaurant where she'd invited them for an over-the-top dinner to celebrate her team's acquisition of three über-wealthy clients in the last quarter, and then at the exclusive Fifth Avenue club where they drank expensive bottles of Dom Pérignon until the wee hours, her main objective for the night hadn't been to relax and socialize with them.

As was often the case with her—she was a spy, after all—Liesel had an ulterior motive.

That's why she was the one who had organized and paid for the entire outing of her four team members and their partners, which had cost well over $10,000. Though she had put the charges on her personal credit card, she would claim it all back, and she knew her superiors at the Bundesnachrichtendienst—Germany's foreign intelligence agency, or the BND—wouldn't bat an eye at the expense.

———

One of Liesel's team members, a trustworthy senior accountant named Danielle, had recently started to date a wealthy, down-to-earth software engineer named Rafael Ribeiro. Rafael was one of the founders of Edge Robots, one of the many start-ups Liesel's accounting firm had as clients. While Edge Robots wasn't in Liesel's team portfolio, she had met Rafael twice. The first time was during a New York Rangers hockey game. Rafael and Caspian, Liesel's boyfriend, had seemed to hit it off pretty well. They had been seated next to each other inside the suite her firm kept at Madison Square Garden, and Liesel had listened in on their conversation, which had been mostly about sports, cars, and, of course, politics. The second time had been at the office when Rafael had brought a take-out lunch—from Le Bernardin, no less—to celebrate Danielle's birthday and had invited Liesel to join them.

From what Liesel had observed at the hockey game and the discussion she'd had with him when they ate together at the office, Danielle's boyfriend wasn't only good looking: he was smart and funny as hell, and he treated Danielle like a princess. A week after the hockey game, and as per protocol, Liesel had filed a routine report to the BND mentioning the names and the workplaces of all the new contacts she'd made over the last month. Edge Robots and Rafael Ribeiro had made the list.

Edge Robots specialized in providing industrial automation solutions to medium and large businesses around the world. While this was true, intel collected by the BND eleven days ago through electronic surveillance in conjunction with another operation had revealed that Edge Robots was possibly a shell corporation for the Ministry of State Security—China's spy agency.

The intel had triggered a shitstorm of humongous proportions that had shot up to the president of the BND, then to the office of the German chancellor, then back down to Liesel's handler in less than two hours.

Once Liesel's handler had explained the problem to her, the gravity of the situation became all too clear. Eighteen months ago, believing Edge Robots would one day rival giant companies like Siemens and Honeywell, a large venture capital fund financed entirely by the German government had invested a significant sum of money into the start-up. The venture capital fund—a project championed by the chancellor himself—was part of the German government's effort to beef up its equity investments in order to get better returns for its pension plan, which was suffering from the shrinking number of workers relative to the number of pensioners.

Her handler, a man named Nicklas Drescher, who used to be a nonofficial cover—or NOC—operative before moving on and becoming a case officer, hadn't disclosed the amount invested, but, using the limited access she had through her office's internal server, Liesel had done a little digging into Edge Robots' finances. She had established that the venture fund from Germany had led Edge Robots' series C funding round with an investment of approximately €25 million. It was a staggering amount.

Unfortunately, there wasn't a whole lot more she could dig up on Edge Robots. As was generally the case with businesses that needed "special" considerations, the team assigned to Edge Robots did most of their work on site at the client's location, not at the firm's office, which left Liesel incapable of probing deeper into the start-up's corporate structure.

If the intel turned out to be valid, and her home country's public funds had been used to finance a Chinese intelligence operation on American soil, it could potentially cause the fall of the current government. In Liesel's opinion, it would at the very least send Germany into a major political crisis at the worst possible time.

Liesel didn't know much about automation, but, as a forensic accountant, she was pretty good with numbers. As intricate as Edge Robots' legal structure was, a qualified fund manager with an entire team of analysts at his disposal should have seen through the bullshit when they had done their due diligence prior to the transaction.

*Unless greed or corruption were involved,* she thought, knowing this was often the case when clients of Mellon, Borowitz and Associates— the firm in which she was now a senior partner—were involved.

Though the firm was highly rated and had gathered massive praise and recognition for its large charitable contributions to global health initiatives, there was a reason why Liesel had been tasked with infiltrating this specific firm when she'd first moved to the United States. In certain circles, Mellon, Borowitz and Associates had developed a reputation for using alternate accounting methods to facilitate financing that would otherwise be problematic to obtain.

When Liesel had been accepted into the elite unit of the BND tasked with deep cover operations on foreign soils, she had imagined that with her golden skin, dark hair, and language skills—apart from German, she spoke three languages fluently, including Arabic—she would have been sent to the Middle East to break up terror networks and help prosecute members of extremist cells.

But it wasn't to be. She got New York instead.

After six months of arduous training, Liesel had been less than enthusiastic to learn she was going to Manhattan to infiltrate an accounting firm. While her life in New York was less exciting than the one she'd dreamed for herself working treacherous assignments in foreign lands, her superior officers at the BND were pleased with the results.

The intelligence she had provided to the BND over the years had allowed German spies to force several start-ups to share their trade secrets and signature technologies with them. These technologies were then shared with a select number of German companies to help them remain ahead of their foreign competitors.

It was corporate espionage at its best. At first, she hadn't been thrilled to spy on American corporations. Despite their many differences of opinion, the United States and Germany were staunch allies in countless areas, and it felt weird to spy on them, even though she knew the Americans were doing the same thing. Over the years, her feelings of guilt faded bit by bit as she came to understand that most of the corporations she spied on were dirty in some way or other. Heck, that was why they were doing business with her firm.

When the BND was ordered by the chancellor to find out if Edge Robots was indeed a front for Chinese intelligence, the BND had initiated a search for anyone within its ranks who possibly had access to Edge Robots. The report Liesel had filed about the start-up and Rafael Ribeiro was instantly flagged by the algorithm.

"The software engineers over at the Innovative Technologies Division will have the application ready by tomorrow," Nicklas had told her. "I'll have someone hand deliver it to you. This is now your priority, Liesel. Understood?"

She had met with the courier—a short man with thick black eyebrows—two days later at a restaurant in Queens.

"They couldn't come up with a wireless solution given the short turnaround," the courier had informed her between two bites of his grilled cheese sandwich. "You'll have to physically insert the device into his phone."

The man had wiped a greasy hand on his pants, then slid a SIM card across the table.

"How long will it take to download?" Liesel had asked as she dropped the SIM card in a special compartment of her purse.

"I was told ten to twelve minutes. And they need that done yesterday," the courier had said, tapping an oily finger on the table to make his point.

Liesel nodded. She understood the urgency, but corporate espionage was a dangerous game. Maybe not as dangerous as taking down terror cells, but certain things couldn't be rushed. Still, she didn't argue with the courier. There was no point. Her mind was already focused on finding a way to get to Rafael's phone.

*Twelve minutes.*

Nowadays, with the average American checking his phone every nine to ten minutes, it was going to be tricky to access Rafael's device for at least twelve minutes without him noticing.

The courier was yet to finish the second half of his grilled cheese sandwich when she had an idea. She scrolled through the photos stored on her phone, found the ones she'd taken of Danielle and Rafael at the hockey game, then zoomed in on a picture in which Rafael was holding his phone.

Liesel's next step had been to purchase the same phone and protective case Danielle's boyfriend had. With that done, she had scheduled a get-together with her team to celebrate the acquisition of the three wealthy clients, making sure to select a date Danielle and Rafael were available. Then it had been a question of picking the right moment to make her move.

Liesel had just ordered two more oversize bottles of Dom Pérignon when one of her intoxicated team members accidentally knocked a champagne flute off the edge of the table and onto herself. Rafael, always the gentleman, had quickly gone to the bar to pick up some napkins. Noticing Rafael had left his phone behind, Liesel deftly made the switch. With the man's phone in her purse, Liesel had insisted on helping her drunk colleague to the ladies' room.

The two women had returned to the table thirteen minutes later, laughing and smiling. No one had given them a second look. It wasn't until much later that Rafael had noticed he had the wrong phone. To Liesel's delight, he had apologized profusely to her for *his* mistake, swearing he hadn't even realized he'd erroneously taken her phone at some point during the evening.

Liesel, playing the drunk, gracious host, had laughed it off as if it was no big deal.

———

Now that Liesel's share of the operation was almost complete, with her having done everything Nicklas had requested of her, the only thing left to do was wait for the email that would confirm that Rafael had brought his hacked phone to work and connected it to the start-up's Wi-Fi network.

As she embarked on the home stretch of her workout, Liesel reflected on what she had accomplished the previous night. She had done a good job, work she could be proud of. If she was honest with herself, last night's operation had been the most exciting BND task she had ever participated in. It had felt good to be in the thick of things for once. Liesel hoped she would have another opportunity to partake in a similar operation in the future, but she wasn't going to hold her breath.

*What would Caspian think of me if he knew who I really was?*

The thought made her smile.

# CHAPTER ELEVEN

*Zermatt, Switzerland*

Caspian stood immobile in the dark next to a small loading dock fitted to accommodate tiny electric delivery trucks. From his location—a back street stuck between two commercial buildings—he had a clear view of a long stretch of road Aldrich would have to take to return to his hotel. Caspian had discovered this specific spot the first night he had tailed Aldrich and had categorized it as a possible ambush point. The fact that it had very few streetlights was particularly appealing.

In this part of town, there were no restaurants, no cute shops with attractive window displays blazing light to attract customers, and only a few low-key hotels. It was much quieter than the area around Bahnhofstrasse, and the foot traffic was suitably lighter—but not non-existent. Although he knew by now that Aldrich was clearly not an expert in countersurveillance, Caspian was convinced that Ballcap would recognize the important difference in the traffic density and give the American banker even more leeway. It was no great feat to detect surveillance when there were only a few pedestrians out and about, and if Ballcap was indeed an intelligence operative tasked with gathering basic information on Aldrich, Caspian was sure he wouldn't risk detection by following him too closely.

After adjusting the brightness of his screen to minimum, Caspian double-tapped an exercise app on his cell's home screen and pressed the up-volume button five times in quick succession before exiting the app. He counted to three, then tapped once on the logo of his favorite wine-rating application. Instead of the familiar display of the latest wine bottles he had scanned through the program, an encrypted chat window appeared.

Before he had the chance to type a single word, a message popped up.

**From Merlot32: About time, Elias. We have an urgent update for you.**

---

*Elias.*

The name had become Caspian's code name eight years ago following an operation in Lisbon, Portugal. Martim Sousa, a Portuguese investigative reporter working for a small but well-respected regional newspaper, had supposedly found a credible eyewitness to the double murder of two Belarus politicians who had been on a state visit in Portugal's capital city.

The eyewitness had sworn that the visiting politicians' assassin was none other than well-known Portuguese actor Duarte Elias Barros. While Sousa hadn't gone as far as writing that the actor was the actual killer, he had left the eyewitness's statement untouched.

The article had gone viral.

The only problem with the *credible* eyewitness's version of the event was that Barros hadn't visited Lisbon in more than two months. At the time of the murders, he'd been partying on a private yacht off the Amalfi Coast. More than a dozen people, including two Hollywood A-listers, had come forward and vouched for Barros's presence on the yacht.

Caspian—who wasn't a movie buff by any stretch of the imagination—had never heard of the actor before. But he didn't live under a rock either. He had seen the news on television. And he had to agree: Duarte Elias Barros did look like him. A lot.

Caspian doubted he and Barros could be mistaken for twin brothers in broad daylight, but from a certain distance during low-visibility hours, he could see why someone might think they were the same person.

With Barros's indirect involvement, Sousa's story had continued to thrive and gained momentum. The whole situation was getting messier by the hour.

Then, out of the blue, an obscure criminal organization based in Minsk had claimed responsibility for the murders. Caspian knew it was total bullshit.

He was the one who had killed the two politicians.

Worried Onyx would challenge him about the operation, Caspian had replayed the entire op in his head numerous times, trying to figure out when and where someone could have caught a glimpse of him. His conclusion had been that he hadn't made a mistake. Nobody had seen him pull the trigger. He was sure of that.

Knowing he hadn't been sloppy, it hadn't come as a surprise to him when the police ended the investigation without being able to link a single suspect to the murders. But Sousa had refused to let it go. Caspian had to give it to the man: he was a fighter, and he hadn't said his last word. Yet.

Sousa insisted that someone looking like Barros had committed the crime, not a shadowy crime syndicate from Belarus nobody had ever heard of. Shocking Caspian, Sousa had started to accurately link other political assassinations Caspian had committed to the ones in Lisbon, claiming they were the work of a single but very skilled assassin. And, with the blessing of Duarte Elias Barros—the actor had benefited from a serious boost in popularity on social media since the original story had been published—Sousa had given the assassin the nickname Elias.

Slowly, and with the help of the actor who used his considerable reach to promote the whole shebang, Sousa's stories began to gain traction. Again.

Then, a couple of days later, and only hours before he was scheduled to appear on national television alongside Barros, Martim Sousa committed suicide by shooting himself under the chin with a shotgun.

A letter left behind by Sousa, which was later found by the police, had explained the reasons behind the reporter's decision to take his own life. Afraid he was about to get fired by his employer due to his less than stellar performance, Sousa had concocted the Elias story hoping to revive his dying career. There had been no eyewitness. He had made everything up.

Three days later, in an unfortunate twist of events, Barros's plane—a four-seater Cessna 182—crashed into the Mediterranean Sea less than a mile south of Marbella, Spain. Barros was the sole occupant. His body was quickly retrieved from the sea by the Spanish authorities, and an autopsy was ordered by the magistrate. The postmortem of Barros's remains revealed that the actor had three times the legal limit of alcohol in his blood at the time of the crash. Traces of several illegal substances were also found, but Barros's legal team was successful at blocking any other details from being made public.

A few offshoot writers controlling websites known to promote over-the-top conspiracy theories had tried to resurrect the Sousa story, claiming Elias was real. Pointing at the lack of transparency in the investigation surrounding Sousa's death, they had argued that Sousa hadn't killed himself; he had been assassinated.

By Elias.

One of the websites had gotten excited about a post on social media insisting that there had been two people aboard the doomed Cessna when it had taken off, not one. One man, Barros, and one female, an attractive brunette.

The social media post had been written by a sixty-six-year-old bachelor who lived with his mother and who worked part time as a fuel technician at the airstrip where Barros kept his plane. The police paid the man a visit. After a quick interrogation, the officers had deemed him an unreliable witness. The fact that he had mentioned being captured by an alien spacecraft the week before had probably played a role in the decision.

Caspian's handler at Onyx, who had been silent since Sousa had first broken the Elias story, made contact shortly after.

"We don't know how you managed to pull this off, but you did," Laura had told him. "Congratulations."

"I didn't—" Caspian had tried to object, but Laura cut him off.

"We don't want to know. What you do on your own time is of no interest to us. Do you understand, *Elias?*"

That was the moment Caspian had realized two things. The first was that Onyx assumed he was the one who had killed Sousa and Barros. The second, which in his opinion was much more worrisome, was that they couldn't care less that he had killed two innocent men.

And that didn't sit well with Caspian.

He was under no illusions about who or what he was. Everybody had their own expertise, though his was undeniably different from most. Being good at tracking and killing people wasn't a skill set many people shared.

Fortunately.

But Caspian had never, ever killed indiscriminately. He didn't get a thrill out of it, nor did he consider it a sport. He was a professional doing important work on behalf of his nation. Caspian was operating in a world of complex threats that never stopped evolving, but every single act of violence he had done since joining the elite Onyx program had been to protect his countrymen and to preserve and uphold his country's prosperity and economic security.

*With honor and integrity, we will safeguard the American people, our homeland, and our values.*

That was what Onyx stood for, right? So why was it that Caspian couldn't shake the feeling that if he didn't play along with Laura, he would be the next one in need of an autopsy?

———

Caspian dismissed the memory only to realize he'd been staring at his screen. He hadn't typed his reply.

To Merlot32: What's the update?

From Merlot32: New timeline. Effective immediately. Another team may be in play. We believe their objective is to capture your target. Expedite.

To Merlot32: 1. How many players? 2. Friendly?

From Merlot32: 1. Unknown. 2. Negative. I say again: EXPEDITE.

Caspian acknowledged his handler's latest text and exited the encrypted chat window. He hadn't learned anything new from the update, except that the option of waiting until tomorrow to take out Aldrich was off the board.

That was fine. He knew how he was going to kill the banker.

# CHAPTER TWELVE

*New York, New York*

Rafael Ribeiro stood behind Beatriz—his top black hat hacker—as the young woman's delicate, well-manicured fingers danced across her keyboard as if she was a maestro playing the piano. Rafael stared at the two screens in front of Beatriz, stunned by the sheer volume of data and files scrolling in front of his eyes. The secure, powerful desktop Beatriz was using to run the data and link analysis worked independently from any of Edge Robots' three internal networks and wasn't connected to the internet.

"You've been at it for close to an hour," Rafael said, doing his best not to show his impatience, which required a herculean effort out of him. "Are you any closer to telling me what it is?"

Beatriz responded with one of her irritated, borderline rude half nods. Rafael clenched his jaw but knew better than to push her. He was a competent enough software engineer, but Beatriz was on a whole other level.

Rafael's phone buzzed. It was a text from Danielle.

You left early this morning . . . Wish you were here . . .

The phone buzzed again. This time Danielle had sent a picture. It was a selfie of her standing in front of a mirror, her naked body half-covered by a white sheet wrapped around her. Danielle was fun, always willing to try new things with him. He liked that. Danielle wasn't a demanding woman, and he had found that if he threw a little love and attention her way, she could be easily manipulated into doing his bidding. Small things at first, for sure, but, until last night, Rafael had seen a clear path for Danielle to one day become a valuable asset.

But thanks to Liesel Bergmann—Danielle's boss—Rafael wasn't so sure anymore.

Liesel was a smooth operator. A real pro.

*I need to find her angle.*

Rafael had noticed someone had taken his phone the minute he had come back to the table with the napkins. But he had played it cool. The encryption on his phone was hard to crack. Even with the best tools, it would take a talented hacker a long time to access the programs he had buried deep into its operating system.

At first, he had thought Danielle had orchestrated the switch, so he had studied her and analyzed her behavior as she interacted with her colleagues.

Had he misjudged her? Had he been the one being played?

No. It couldn't be.

If there was one thing he knew about Danielle, it was that her eyes never lied. He could always tell when she was nervous or excited, or when she was hiding—or wanting—something from him. Either she was the best actress he had ever met, or Danielle had no clue whatsoever about what had just happened at the club.

When Liesel had come back from the bathroom with Danielle's other coworker, he had switched his focus to them. Though he'd had more than a few drinks too many, his boozed-up brain was still functioning and capable of analyzing data.

Because Liesel was the team leader and high enough in the Mellon, Borowitz and Associates hierarchy to know the real reason why Edge Robots had hired them to audit their operational business activities, she'd become Rafael's prime suspect. But, to her credit, Liesel hadn't given him any hint or even a single microexpression to confirm his suspicion.

And what about the way she had laughed it off at the end when she'd admitted she had his phone?

*Worthy of an Oscar,* Rafael thought.

But Rafael had been in the game for a long time too. And he was a master when it came to tricking people. Still, her performance had been such that he had considered that the whole incident might indeed have been an honest mistake.

*Trust but verify, right?*

At his apartment, with Danielle fast asleep next to him, he had gone through his phone. Everything had seemed normal; nothing had changed. That was why he'd asked Beatriz to carefully probe his phone. He hadn't told her what to look for, because he didn't know.

It didn't matter. Minutes after she'd connected the phone to the desktop, she had given him a grunt—not one of her stupid half nods—which told him something was wrong.

He'd been waiting since then.

"I've got it," Beatriz said, pointing with her left hand at two different series of numbers while her right hand kept typing. "Sneaky. Very sneaky."

"I see the numbers, Beatriz. What do they mean?" Rafael asked, letting a touch of impatience seep through for the first time.

"It's a sniffing program, and whoever built it is good," the black hat said. "'Cause the little bugger slipped through several of my traps."

"So, it's collecting data?" Rafael asked. "Nothing else?"

"Too soon to say."

Rafael was painfully aware of what he had to do next. As unpleasant as he knew the call would be, he had no choice. He had to advise his superior officer at the Agência Brasileira de Inteligência—or ABIN—Brazil's intelligence agency.

"Let me know once you figure out exactly what the program was set up to do. In the meantime, is there a way for you to pretend to allow the sniffer program access to our system without actually doing so?"

Beatriz replied with a half nod.

"You sure?"

For the first time since he'd joined her in the secured basement office, Beatriz stopped typing, swiveled her chair in his direction, and looked at him, her deep blue eyes fixed upon his.

"You deaf or something? I said yes."

Rafael cocked his head to one side, studying the black hat hacker with renewed interest. "You're gifted, Beatriz, but your people skills suck."

She gave him a wry smile.

"You didn't always think so," she said without breaking eye contact.

Rafael rolled his eyes and left.

# CHAPTER THIRTEEN

*Zermatt, Switzerland*

Caspian pulled down his knit cap, making sure it covered his ears, then blew into his cupped hands to warm them up. He couldn't remember a time when his handler, Laura, had asked him to *expedite* a kill before.

After the Lisbon operation and the untimely death of the actor and the reporter, it had taken a while for Caspian to fully trust her—and the entire Onyx program, for that matter—again. But a difficult mission in Tijuana, Mexico, during which he would have been captured, tortured, and probably decapitated if it hadn't been for Laura's timely intervention, had convinced him she had his back. Putting her neck on the line, she'd forged an order from the deputy administrator of the DEA Operations Division authorizing the deployment of a nearby Special Response Team to Tijuana. It had been a daring rescue, and the team leader had gotten shot in the calf, but they had all made it back across the border.

Laura knew better than to ask Caspian to rush into action if he didn't feel as though the tactical situation permitted him to accomplish his mission stealthily and with a clear exit path. For reasons that were unknown to him, Onyx wanted Aldrich to die before whoever else was in play in Zermatt got their hands on him.

Caspian looked at his watch. He estimated he had twelve minutes before Aldrich showed up at the street corner. From there, it would take the American banker seventy seconds, more or less, to walk from the street corner to the next intersection. Aldrich would then make a sharp left turn onto a narrow walking path that would lead him down a not-so-gentle slope toward the Matter Vispa River.

That's where Caspian would strike.

To prevent an unfortunate accident due to the path's steep downward angle, local officials had built numerous sets of stairs to mitigate the risk of injuries. To reach his current hiding place, Caspian had climbed those very same stairs in the opposite direction and had noticed several patches of black ice on the steps. That had given him an idea.

Timing was going to be tight, but it could be done.

After a quick look around to make sure he was still alone, Caspian pulled out his SIG Sauer P229 pistol and attached a suppressor. Instead of putting the pistol back into the inside-the-waistband holster, he placed it in the right-hand pocket of his coat, having modified the interior of the pocket to accommodate the extra length of the pistol that came with having the suppressor attached. If all went well, he wouldn't need his gun, but it made him feel better to know he could pull it out and use it quickly if something came up.

A couple walked out from one of the boutique hotels, chatting and laughing. Though he was too far away to say for sure, Caspian didn't think they were past their teenage years. They sure weren't dressed for the cold weather. They were both wearing jeans, and the woman did have a sweater, but the young man wore only a white T-shirt, and he held a bottle of liquor in his hand. Caspian watched him take a long pull from the bottle before handing it to his female partner. As she took a drink, the man fished something from his pants pocket. Minutes later, Caspian recognized the distinctive, pungent odor of marijuana, a smell he had become accustomed to since he'd moved to New York. He watched helplessly as five more teenagers joined the two already outside. More joints were lit up.

*Ski bums,* Caspian thought, shaking his head.

Drugs had never interested him. He had a hard time understanding their charms.

What was the appeal?

Sure, he did enjoy the occasional drink or two, but he didn't relish the feeling of losing control over his mind and body. He wondered what Liesel's thoughts were on the issue. He was surprised the subject had never come up. He'd certainly not seen her use drugs, though it didn't mean she didn't.

*But she definitely likes to party.*

As he stood immobile waiting for Aldrich to show up, the cold gnawed at his hands and feet, and his toes started to feel numb. He pictured Liesel, dressed in lingerie, waiting for him seductively, sprawled across a warm bed. Catching himself, he tried to chase Liesel out of his mind, but she came reeling back.

What would Liesel think of him if she knew the truth?

*Stop it! She'll never know the truth! Focus!*

The sound of a bottle shattering followed by a loud squeal of laughter coming from one of the teenagers caught Caspian's attention. He willed the teenagers to get back into their hotel. He didn't want them anywhere close to where he planned on taking down Aldrich. When two of them walked back in, moments later, Caspian was optimistic the others would follow suit, but his enthusiasm was quickly crushed when the two teenagers who had gone inside the hotel came back out with not one but three liquor bottles.

As the minutes ticked by, the teenagers became louder and more agitated, shouting in French and English alike. The tactical situation was going from bad to worse. Given the choice, Caspian would have postponed until the next day, hoping for a more suitable environment. But his handler had been adamant.

*Expedite.*

He would have to adapt.

There was another location from which he could take Aldrich, but he would have to shoot the man from twenty or so meters. For Caspian, that wasn't a difficult shot, even with a pistol, but the kill wouldn't be as clean, and he would need to alter his exit strategy. But to make it to the location in time, he had to move now.

Decision time.

As Caspian was about to step out of the shadows, he heard crunching footsteps behind him. He wrapped his fingers around the pistol grip and turned slowly toward the sound, aware that from where he stood in the dark, he was invisible to all but the most discerning eye. Fifty meters away, at the opposite end of the alleyway, three men were headed in his direction. There was just enough background light coming from the streetlights behind the three men for Caspian to see that they were all wearing police uniforms.

Caspian's eyes narrowed. Were the officers here for him? Had someone spotted him and called the police to complain about the presence of a suspicious man?

Then it came to him. A resident must have called the police and complained about the out-of-control teenagers. These officers had been the closest ones, and they had been dispatched to respond to the incident.

To ensure he wasn't being boxed in, Caspian looked over his shoulder. He had another surprise waiting for him.

Leonard Aldrich had just shown up.

Caspian's body reacted instantly; his muscles tightened, and all his senses went into overdrive. Caspian knew he had no business standing in the dark in the middle of the alleyway. The cops would know it too. He feared that if he was to leave the shadows and walk away from them, the officers would challenge him to stop. And if he tried to walk past them, there was a strong possibility they would physically try to stop him and question him. In both cases, he would lose his only advantage: surprise.

The window of opportunity to take out Aldrich was closing rapidly, but it was still open. In his mind's eye, Caspian visualized what he would do next. Satisfied with his odds, he took one step back, deeper into the shadows, and waited for the three police officers to close in.

# CHAPTER FOURTEEN

*Zermatt, Switzerland*

Edgar increased his pace. He had lost visual contact with Aldrich when the banker had turned left at the next street. Unlike the banker, who had hugged the building when he had made his turn, Edgar planned on crossing the intersection before he made his. This would allow him to look for a potential—albeit unlikely—ambush before committing to his turn. If all looked clear, he would continue to follow Aldrich from the opposite side of the street.

A soft ping coming through his Bluetooth earpiece told him he had an incoming call.

"Wife and kids are back in their room," Laurent informed him.

*Finally,* Edgar thought, relieved.

The banker's family had lingered at the pool longer than he had expected. Another ten minutes and Edgar would have been forced to delay the operation, at least for the time being. He wasn't going to order his team to abduct Aldrich's wife and kids while in plain view of the other guests. But now that they were back in their room, it was time for Laurent and his team to move in.

"Go ahead, Laurent, but be discreet. And remember, no violence if you can avoid it," Edgar said as he crossed the street Aldrich had turned onto. "You have about five minutes before Aldrich reaches the hotel."

Edgar tapped twice on the earpiece to end the call and turned left onto the street he'd seen Aldrich disappear into. Aldrich was halfway down the block and to Edgar's left. The banker's head was turned to his right in the direction of a boutique hotel where a bunch of teenagers had gathered outside the entrance. They didn't seem threatening.

*Just kids having fun,* he thought.

Edgar asked himself if these kids' parents knew how lucky, and privileged, they were to have healthy children. Edgar cringed at his own thought, aware he had passed a snap judgment on kids he didn't even know. Truth was, there was nothing else that would make him happier than to see Sebastian enjoy himself like these kids. It had always been a major challenge for Sebastian to make friends. He'd been kicked out of so many schools Edgar had stopped counting. These days, even keeping him out of prison was difficult.

As Edgar got closer to the group of teenagers, he realized some of them appeared to be drunk or high on drugs.

*Probably both,* Edgar thought, catching a whiff of marijuana.

One of the kids, a young man no older than Edgar's son and wearing a pair of jeans with only a white T-shirt to protect himself from the cold, yelled some sort of obscenity at him. Edgar ignored him. In an effort to keep a fair distance from the drunk kid, Edgar crossed the street. The last thing Edgar needed was to get into a confrontation with an intoxicated and testosterone-charged teenage boy like T-Shirt. Luckily, Aldrich was yet to look behind him, and Edgar didn't think the banker had noticed him.

But that was about to change.

T-Shirt, clearly empowered by the thought that whatever he'd yelled at Edgar had forced him to retreat to the other side of the street, broke away from his group and began to walk in Edgar's direction. One of the girls tried to stop him by grabbing his arm. T-Shirt easily broke free, but not without dropping the bottle of liquor he had been holding, which caused him to turn toward the girl and raise his hand in the air as if he wanted to slap her across the face.

For a moment, Edgar thought T-Shirt was going to hit her, but another boy, who towered over T-Shirt by at least a head, stepped in front of the girl. A shouting match ensued between the two teenage boys.

The commotion must have reached Aldrich because the banker looked over his shoulder toward the kids. Then his gaze stopped on Edgar, but only for a moment.

While Edgar was sure Aldrich had seen him, the banker's eyes hadn't stayed on him long enough to conduct any kind of threat analysis. Edgar took it as a good sign that Aldrich hadn't quickened his pace.

But the good news ended there.

From what Edgar could see, T-Shirt and the other guy had come to some sort of agreement, because the two teenage boys were headed straight at him. And they looked pissed. Edgar figured that in their drunken states, he was the one to blame for the loss of their precious bottle of booze. If there was something Edgar could have told the two angry kids that would have made them reconsider what he knew they had in mind, he would have gladly said it. But the expression of barely restrained rage on their faces told him there was only one way this was going to end.

Edgar shook his head. He didn't have time for this, but he didn't see an easy way out of it either.

*Stupid kids! They have no idea what's waiting for them.* He found it ironic that only moments ago he had seen them as exemplary teenagers.

Hadn't they read *The Art of War*, by Sun Tzu?

*Of course they haven't.*

Edgar would make it quick. He had a schedule to keep, but he would take a few seconds to teach T-Shirt and his friend an important life lesson. One they would have already known had they read Sun Tzu.

*Who wishes to fight must first count the cost.*

"Hey, old man," T-Shirt said, grabbing Edgar by the elbow. "You owe—"

Edgar didn't let him finish the sentence. He spun to his right, and, using both the spin's momentum and his shoulder muscle to add some velocity, he brought his left elbow up. The teenager's head snapped back as Edgar's elbow connected with his jaw. Although Edgar had used less than half his strength, T-Shirt's knees buckled, and his eyes rolled back. T-Shirt's body hadn't yet traveled halfway to the ground before Edgar had already reversed course and lashed the second youth's legs right out from under him with a sweeping kick. The kid crashed onto the street, hard, then rolled onto his back, a low moan escaping his lips.

"Stay down!" Edgar warned him, before glancing at T-Shirt.

Edgar had knocked him unconscious, but he was still breathing. T-shirt would wake up with a nasty toothache, but Edgar suspected he was so drunk and high that he wouldn't remember how he got it.

*Too bad.*

It had taken Edgar under three seconds to neutralize the two teenagers. It took another twenty before one of the other kids gathered in front of the hotel summoned his courage and went to check on his two fallen friends. By the time he reached them, Edgar was already a good distance away.

Edgar had lost sight of Aldrich for a moment while he had handled the unpleasantness with the two teens, but he saw him now. The banker had hastened his pace considerably and had almost reached the next intersection.

Had Aldrich seen the altercation? If he had, he might be wary of Edgar.

Edgar watched Aldrich pull a phone from his pocket and bring it to his ear. Then Aldrich made a tight left turn and once again disappeared from view.

# CHAPTER FIFTEEN

*New York, New York*

Rafael Ribeiro entered his office and went straight for his safe, which he had set up behind a false panel in the wall, less for secrecy than for the clean look it gave to his working space. He punched in his eight-digit code and opened the safe. Inside were legal papers related to Edge Robots, a loaded pistol, $10,000 in US currency, and several burner phones.

Taking one of the phones, he dialed the number of a shell company run by Brazilian intelligence. Someone picked up on the second ring, and Rafael identified himself with an alphanumeric sequence. After a couple of clicks, he was put through to his boss.

"I didn't expect to hear from you for at least another week," Rafael's ex-wife said. "I know for a fact you don't miss me, so I guess you've run into another problem?"

Rafael cringed. *Another problem?*

He'd been working his ass off for years on this project, and, as far as he was concerned, especially for an undertaking of this magnitude, the number of serious problems he'd encountered had been negligible.

*She knows that. She just wants to push your buttons,* he reminded himself. *Don't give her the satisfaction. Not worth it.*

"You're right, Dolores," Rafael conceded. "There's an issue."

He spent the next five minutes briefing her and answering her numerous questions.

"Don't do anything that could jeopardize the operation," Dolores said. "Our next move should be to determine if Liesel Bergmann is probing into our business on behalf of the firm or if she's doing it for her own enrichment. I have a feeling she's on her own. The firm has way too much to lose and nothing to gain from making such a play."

"If Bergmann is alone, how did she get access to a sniffer program as sophisticated as the one she dumped on my phone?"

There was a small pause at the other end of the line.

"Valid point. Ask one of your black hats to forward us the program once it's been safely isolated. I'll have to bring this up with our Chinese friends. In the end, they're the ones who'll make the hard call about what to do with Bergmann. It's their operation. We're just lending them a hand."

"I understand," Rafael said.

"Keep monitoring the situation and let me know if there are any further developments."

"Before we hang up," Rafael said, "one thing I suggest you mention with our overseas colleagues is that the woman I'm seeing—"

"Danielle, right? The one who likes to send you naked pictures of herself?"

The venom in Dolores's words didn't bother him, but that she had continued to read his private communications after he had warned her not to infuriated him. It was getting harder and harder for him to keep his irritation in check, but he had to tread carefully. Dolores was ambitious, and it was no secret that she was aiming for the top job at the spy agency. She had already gathered a lot of political support from outside the organization to back her candidacy.

"As I was saying," he continued after a brief moment, "Danielle acts as Bergmann's right hand, so if the lady boss was to, let's say, step down permanently—"

"Your new girlfriend would be the one replacing her," his ex-wife said, completing his sentence for him. "I recognize how this could be seen as a positive development down the road, but what you're proposing comes with significant risks. It will take some time to get a decision on this."

"Of course," Rafael said.

He'd keep kissing the ring. For now.

# CHAPTER SIXTEEN

*Zermatt, Switzerland*

By the time the three police officers reached his hiding spot, Caspian had less than thirty seconds to neutralize them all. Typically, taking down three men wouldn't be a particularly difficult task for him. But this wasn't a normal situation. Caspian had a major constraint to deal with. He didn't want to permanently injure any of the officers.

In order to achieve the desired outcome, Caspian would have to use the speed and surprise of his own attack, along with the momentum of the three approaching officers. Caspian willed himself into silence and immobility. As he waited for the officers to get closer, he stopped breathing, worried the movement of the vapor of his breath would betray his location. When the officers were five feet away, he pounced.

Caspian sprang forward with such speed that the first officer didn't even react before Caspian's knee struck him between his legs. The man folded in two, and Caspian finished him off with a mighty downward elbow strike to the back of the head.

*One down.*

The second officer didn't fare better. During the second and a half he had to react, he had only managed to do two things. He had opened his mouth wide, and he had begun to angle his body toward the perceived threat. Caspian's jab was fast, more like a blur, really, and struck him on the nose. It was too dark for him to see if he had busted the officer's nose—he hoped he hadn't—but he hadn't put much force behind the blow. That was okay. The idea had been to freeze the man for an instant and to open his midsection for a follow-up strike. And it had worked perfectly. A heartbeat after his jab connected, Caspian delivered a powerful right hook into the officer's left kidney. In theory, it should have been enough to drop the man to the ground like a brick. But it didn't. The officer's body armor had halved the force of the blow. His next effort, a right uppercut that connected squarely on the point of the officer's chin, did the job, but it had cost Caspian a precious second.

*Shit. Two down.*

The third officer also had his mouth open, but at least he had tried to distance himself from the shadow who had knocked out his two colleagues faster than he could have counted to four. He had taken three steps back and was in the process of drawing his service pistol, which was almost halfway out of its holster, when Caspian grabbed his gun hand by the wrist in an iron grip and blocked any further movement. Using his momentum, he pushed the officer against the brick wall. The officer struggled and slanted his lower body to one side, probably thinking it would save him from getting a knee to his balls. It did, but in doing so he had offered Caspian one of his favorite targets.

The common peroneal nerve.

And Caspian didn't miss. He sent a well-aimed left knee straight into the man's upper thigh. The officer's legs instantly turned into rubber, and he began to slide down the wall, a flash of panic crossing his face. Wanting the freedom to twist at the waist, Caspian let go of the officer's hand and delivered a full-blown right hook to the man's jaw.

*Three down.*

He was pleased with the way he'd neutralized the three police officers, but they wouldn't stay down for long. He put the odds at 75 percent they hadn't seen his face, or at least not well enough to draw a sketch. Caspian briefly considered relieving the officers of their weapons and handcuffing them to each other, but there was no time.

Aldrich had just turned onto the walking path.

# CHAPTER SEVENTEEN

*New York, New York*

Liesel let the stream of hot water run down her hair and back for some time. Long, almost scalding showers relaxed her. She didn't know why, but even as a kid she had always preferred showers to baths. It was still true.

*Unless Caspian's here,* she thought, allowing herself to savor the feeling.

The way he rubbed her back, her shoulders, and the inside of her thighs every time they shared a bath together was . . . almost transcendent. Just thinking about it made her shiver in delight. Yes, Caspian knew how to ease the tension in her muscles and how to pleasure her, but it was so much more than that. He knew how to make her feel vulnerable and ecstatic at the same time, a feat no other man had been able to accomplish. She swore there was something magical in the way he touched her.

Liesel's pleasant daydreaming session ended abruptly when the water switched from near sizzling hot to artic cold in less than a second. She jumped in surprise, almost slipping on the slick tiles at the bottom of the shower.

*What the hell? Did I run out of hot water?*

She stepped out of the shower and checked her phone. There were no new messages, and the clock indicated she'd been in the shower for over twenty minutes.

She cursed out loud, blaming Caspian for the distraction.

Looking out the window of her twenty-third-floor apartment, she saw that everyone at street level was wearing coats and hats. It had snowed overnight, but the warmth of the afternoon sun had turned the beautiful white blanket of snow she had witnessed on the city streets the night before into a dirty slush.

Liesel didn't mind. She would walk to her office anyway. Just not in high heels.

She put on a small amount of makeup, then opened the drawer where she kept her jewelry, her gaze stopping on a small blue box. She took the box out of the drawer and lifted the lid, revealing a delicate pair of icy-blue aquamarine drop earrings.

She sighed.

The earrings were a gift from Caspian. He had given them to her when they had gotten back together after a very short—less than forty-eight hours—breakup. Unbeknownst to Caspian, she'd been about to leave him again last week when he had called her from the airport to let her know he was on his way to Geneva for work. Then, before she could say anything, he had told her that while he was in Switzerland, he would take some personal time to explore the region and maybe even try his luck on the ski slopes.

That had given her pause. Her biggest issue with Caspian was that he was a boring guy. It wasn't exactly a secret; she'd told him straight to his face.

Yes, Caspian was attractive—hot, even—but beneath his physical attributes and assuredness in bed—and in the bathtub—the man didn't do much else other than work and teach a Krav Maga class as a guest instructor once a month at the fitness club she trained at.

Caspian taking some time off to explore Switzerland on his own and to go skiing was something she hadn't expected from him. Was it a sign of progress?

*Could be.*

In the end, she had made the decision not to leave him. At least not until he was back from his trip. Who knew, maybe he'd come back a changed man?

Deep down, Liesel knew there was more to him than met the eyes. It didn't happen frequently, but on occasions, usually when they were intimate, Liesel was able to glimpse something in Caspian's eyes, a light, some sort of self-assurance he rarely exhibited when they were together in public. But the light never stayed on for long. It was infuriating. She knew Caspian could be so much more, but he needed to come out of his shell. She had tried to help him, to guide him, but the man was stuck in his ways.

Would his latest trip overseas change that?

Part of her hoped so. She liked him. Quite a lot, actually. Probably more than she should. But the way she felt about him wasn't the only thing weighing in the balance.

Her handler had given her permission to end the relationship.

———

Liesel had met Caspian the year before at the fitness club where he taught an advanced Krav Maga class she had registered in. She'd been impressed at how good a teacher he was, and, by the way he kept looking at her during class, she knew he had noticed her too.

Wanting to learn more about Caspian, she'd looked him up on social media. Clearly Caspian was a private man, because she hadn't been able to find anything about him. A Google search had spit out a ton of results, but the photos linked to the results weren't of the same Caspian Anderson she'd met at the fitness center.

She had reported the contact to her BND handler. The next morning, she had a response.

And a tasking.

Attached to her handler's reply, an encrypted PDF file contained everything German intelligence had on Caspian. It wasn't much, but at least it had confirmed he wasn't a pedophile or on any terrorist watchlists. Caspian worked at the United Nations as a translator. He was single, in his early thirties, and spoke five languages fluently, including German, which she thought was cool.

Though it was a low-priority tasking, Liesel's handler wanted her to bond with Caspian. If Caspian could climb up a few echelons at the UN, his access to certain files could be useful.

It was only a month later that Liesel saw Caspian again. The smile he had flashed in her direction at the beginning of the class had been a clear signal of how he felt about her presence. Later, she had waited for him outside. They had walked together for a while before stopping at a coffee shop. Dinner at a cozy Japanese restaurant had followed, then drinks at her place.

Then breakfast the next morning.

Even after the BDN had concluded that Caspian would never rise to the level where he could become a valuable intelligence asset and had given Liesel permission to sever the relationship if she wanted to, she had decided to stick with him a little longer. She had no regrets. She had enjoyed her time with him. Truth be told, she missed him.

Liesel was still holding on to the blue box when her phone pinged. A new message had come in. To anyone other than her, the message would have seemed like a spam email coming from a well-known online casino. She clicked a hidden link at the bottom of the page. A sign-in page appeared. She entered today's username and password. Only then could she read what Nicklas had sent her.

We're in.

She sighed. *About damn time.*
Her phone pinged again.

We'd like to ask you a few questions about your relationship with Leonard Aldrich.

# CHAPTER EIGHTEEN

**Zermatt, Switzerland**

The first thing Caspian noted was that Aldrich had sped up considerably, and it seemed that the only thing keeping the banker from going even faster was the steep slope down. The second thing of interest he noticed about the banker was that he was holding a phone to his right ear.

Was there some kind of emergency?

Caspian felt a tinge of guilt.

What if one of Aldrich's children needed his assistance? What if his wife had fallen sick?

*Then he should have thought of that before getting involved in a human trafficking ring,* Caspian thought, trying to justify what he was about to do.

After one last look at the three officers to make sure they weren't about to shoot him in the back, Caspian craned his neck to see if Ballcap was still tailing Aldrich.

He was. But Ballcap was slightly farther away than Caspian had anticipated. Which was great. What wasn't so great were the two people who lay immobile in the street behind Ballcap. Something bad had happened while Caspian had fought with the three police officers. But what?

Had Ballcap killed the two teenagers? And if Caspian hadn't stopped the officers, would the kids still have been alive?

The gravity of the situation hit him like a lightning bolt, and, for a moment, he wasn't sure what to do next.

*You're overthinking this,* he told himself. *Just. Do. Your. Job.*

Caspian took a deep breath; then he slipped out of the shadows and went to work.

———

He looked to his right and left as he stepped into the pathway. He didn't see anyone else, but there were at least four other alleys like the one he'd taken refuge in that led to the pathway. He would have to remain vigilant as he continued to close the gap with Aldrich, who was now less than forty feet away.

Caspian walked with a fast but measured tread, his right hand wrapped around the grip of his pistol. His left hand, though, was in the left pocket, and his fingers were feeling the length of the toxin injector.

Something was wrong. The injector's tip was bent, and the push button had somehow loosened.

*Damn it!* He couldn't risk using a malfunctioning injector. He would have to improvise.

Caspian witnessed Aldrich lose his balance twice in the span of a few seconds just meters before he reached the stairs. Clearly Aldrich was in a rush, and he wasn't paying enough attention to his footing while he hurried down the steep incline.

Caspian strained his eyes as he continued to search for potential threats. Many windows from adjacent buildings faced the pathway. Some were lit, with a pale yellow glow spilling out from behind their curtains, but he spotted no silhouette looking down in his direction.

With the teenagers no longer shouting, the night had gone quiet and peaceful, and the light snow from earlier had returned. Tiny snowflakes were now drifting silently through the air, carried by the breeze.

*Straight from the pages of some classic Christmas tale.*

For as long as he could, Caspian stayed in the center of the pathway, where his boots had less chance to crunch the thin layer of ice that covered it. When it got too slippery, he took the stairs and positioned himself slightly behind and to the right of the banker, wanting to take advantage of the fact that Aldrich was still holding his phone tight against his right ear while he held the wrought iron railing with his left. Not only did the phone and Aldrich's own voice muffle Caspian's approaching footsteps, but the way Aldrich held his phone, his right arm also impeded his vision.

Only when Caspian was within half a step of Aldrich did the banker finally turn his head toward him. What he saw in Aldrich's eyes wasn't surprise or shock, as he had expected, but pure, unadulterated terror.

As he reached the banker and used his left hand to grab Aldrich by the back of his coat's collar, Caspian wondered what had caused the panic he'd seen in Aldrich's eyes. Caspian was a master when it came to presenting a sensible, good-natured exterior. Even if his sudden appearance had stunned Aldrich, there was no way he was the reason behind the man's reaction. But with mere seconds before Ballcap reached the intersection, Caspian didn't have the luxury of delving into what had triggered Aldrich.

With his hand firmly on Aldrich's collar, Caspian yanked the banker back and kicked at the rear of the man's right ankle, sweeping his legs from under him. As Aldrich fell back, Caspian rotated to his left and placed the palm of his right hand onto Aldrich's forehead. In addition to using Aldrich's weight to help him, Caspian let himself fall alongside the banker for added downward thrust. A heartbeat before impact, his right arm shot out like a piston, smashing the back of Aldrich's head onto the unyielding surface of the stairs in a sickening crack. Aldrich's body spasmed once, then went limp, but his eyes stayed vacantly open.

Caspian got up on one knee and saw that Aldrich's phone had remained clutched in his hand. He couldn't hear clearly what was being said, but the volume was high enough that he could make out the stifled sound of a young girl sobbing in the background.

Then, out of the corner of his eye, Caspian caught the faintest movement up the pathway. Without showing too much of his face, he looked up, his hand instinctively reaching for the pistol in his pocket. Ballcap had just turned onto the pathway.

Caspian got to his feet and hurried down the steps, disappearing into the night.

# CHAPTER NINETEEN

*Zermatt, Switzerland*

Edgar was surprised when he didn't immediately spot Aldrich. But there were a lot of alleys and side streets of different sizes leading in and out of the pathway. It was possible Aldrich had taken one of them.

Edgar silently cursed, angry at the situation.

He and his team had been thrown into this operation without adequate preparation. He hadn't had the time to study the street map of Zermatt as well as he wanted to, which meant he wasn't familiar enough with the village's intricate alley system to know which one—if any—of these alleys led back to Le Clarion.

To make matters worse, there was no one but him to blame for his and his team's predicament. Edgar was looking forward to this operation being over. He couldn't wait to get back to Paris, even though he knew he would have a lot of personal stuff—most of it unpleasant—to straighten out with his wife.

Edgar was less than ten steps into the pathway when he saw two figures against the white snow. Two men. On the stairs. Sixty meters down the poorly lit pathway. One was sprawled on his back; the other was next to him on one knee. Edgar's first thought was that they were friends, and that one of them had slipped and had knocked down the other while trying to regain his balance. That theory went up in flames a second later when he recognized who the man slouched across the stairs was.

Aldrich.

Then the one who had been on one knee got to his feet and left, hustling down the stairs and leaving his companion behind. With the snow, the visibility wasn't the best, but Edgar had no doubt: the man who'd just rushed down the stairs was the same man he'd seen earlier on Bahnhofstrasse.

The Smoker.

*What the hell is going on? Was Aldrich ambushed?*

As the thought crossed his mind, Edgar drew his pistol and sought cover in one of the side streets. Head on a swivel, Edgar scanned his immediate area. Only when he was sure there were no threats to deal with did he take another peek at Aldrich.

The man hadn't moved, and, from where Edgar stood, he could see that a pool of blood was spreading under Aldrich's head.

Was the banker dead? Had someone done his job for him? If Aldrich was dead, then Edgar wouldn't be able to get the answers he needed from him. The client would be pissed.

*Well . . . fuck the client!* Edgar thought.

Maybe this was for the best. He'd go check to make sure Aldrich was no longer among the living, and, if that was the case, he'd call Laurent and order him and the rest of his team to stand down.

*Then we can all go home.*

Edgar stepped out of the side street and slowly made his way down toward Aldrich, looking over his shoulder every ten seconds while keeping his pistol tight against his leg. The pool of blood grew larger as Edgar got closer. At this rate, if Aldrich wasn't dead yet, he would be soon. When he reached Aldrich a few steps later, Edgar no longer had any doubt. The man was gone. Aldrich's lifeless eyes were open and staring at nothing. But even in death the banker had managed to hold on to his phone, which was still turned on and hooked to a call with whomever he'd been talking to when he died.

Edgar bent down, and, just as he was about to pick up the phone, a man shouted something in German. Edgar looked up and was puzzled by what he saw.

A uniformed police officer was standing twenty meters away, his face a bloody mess. He had a pistol in his hand, but it wasn't pointed in Edgar's direction. Considering the sad state of the cop's face and the scene in front of him, if Edgar had been in his shoes, he'd probably have his gun pointed at the man bent next to the guy whose head was leaking blood.

Edgar wasn't complaining. Who knew what was going through the officer's head? But there was one thing Edgar was sure of: the cop hadn't seen his gun. If he had, his demeanor would be much different, and his pistol would be pointed straight at Edgar's head. For now, Edgar was able to keep his weapon out of sight, but that could change at any moment. If the officer ordered him to move position, it was game on.

"*Je suis français, monsieur,*" Edgar said to the officer. "*Je ne parle pas allemand.*" I'm French. I don't speak German.

"English?" the officer asked, taking a few steps toward Edgar.

"*Anglais? Ah non. Je ne parle pas* . . . English. No," Edgar said, shaking his head from left to right.

Edgar considered the tactical situation he found himself in. The officer had the high ground, but Edgar was quick, and he had killed before. He doubted the officer had. With the element of surprise on his side, Edgar estimated he could fire at least three rounds into the officer before the man even realized what had happened.

Edgar hoped it wouldn't come to that. Maybe there was a way he could talk himself out of this? Apart from holding a gun in his hand, Edgar had done nothing wrong, right?

Then, just like that, another uniformed officer showed up, and the whole situation turned to shit.

# CHAPTER TWENTY

*Zermatt, Switzerland*

By the time Caspian reached the bottom of the pathway and turned right onto Vispastrasse, a small street that ran along the Matter Vispa River, his breathing had returned to normal and his heartbeat had settled. Without breaking stride, he took stock of his surroundings. The street was quiet and lined on one side by the river, with hotels, midsize chalet-style apartment buildings, and trinket stores on the other. Most shops were dark and closed for the day, but a few tourists were still around, like the group of four elderly couples ahead of him, walking and chatting among themselves. The snow was falling faster now, but the breeze was gone, leaving the large flakes free to fall almost straight down.

At his current pace, Caspian would walk past Le Clarion in less than two minutes. He would then make a left onto Sunneggastrasse and cross the river. On the other side, he would start a ninety-minute-long surveillance detection route before deciding what his future steps would be.

Caspian's next thoughts were of the three police officers he had knocked unconscious.

Had they come to? And if they had, had they found Aldrich?

By incapacitating them, he had effectively cut in half the police presence in the village. Zermatt, as well as the nearby communities of Saint Niklaus, Grächen, and Täsch, were all patrolled by members of the Valais cantonal police. In Zermatt itself, there was only one small police station, and on most nights, no more than six officers were on shift, though officers from neighboring communities could be called upon if needed.

Behind him a vehicle impatiently flashed its lights. The road was narrow, and Caspian, along with the four elderly couples, had to step to the side of the road to give way. One of the women slipped, but the man next to her grabbed her arm before she fell. The vehicle was an out-of-service eight-passenger electric taxi. Caspian kept to himself as it drove past him, but one of the men in the group kicked the e-taxi's tire and shouted an obscenity at the driver in German. From what Caspian understood, the street was closed to vehicular traffic at this hour, and the driver had no business forcing pedestrians out of the road.

Seeing the e-taxi's taillights disappear around the bend in the road ahead of him, Caspian remembered that while taxi service was available twenty-four hours a day, the pitfalls of hiring one could be many. If the police were to call for a roadblock before Caspian reached the town of Visp, some twenty miles away, he'd be caught on the only road out of Zermatt. That road had very few exits and was flanked by beautiful yet inhospitable mountainous terrain.

Chartering a helicopter was another possibility, but it would have to wait until the next morning. Doing so now would only single him out. Since his arrival in Zermatt, he'd never seen a chartered helicopter flight take off from the heliport after sundown.

The Zermatt train station wasn't far, and with eighty-three trains per day departing from Zermatt, there were at least a dozen departures left before the station closed for the night. Then again, was he willing to take the chance? What if someone had seen him kill Aldrich? And even if nobody had witnessed the takedown, what about the cops? They hadn't gotten a good look at his face, of that he was sure, but had they seen enough to share a general description of their attacker with their colleagues?

*Probably enough to get me stopped and questioned at a police checkpoint.*

If the Valais cantonal police decided to shut down the tracks between Zermatt and Visp, Caspian would find himself in a very difficult situation. By all accounts, his best chance was to head back to his studio apartment, check in with Laura, and lie low until the next morning. At that time, and with Onyx's help, he would try to learn what the police knew about Aldrich's death and the assault on their three officers. From there, he would figure out a new exit strategy.

As Caspian neared Le Clarion, a small commotion outside the hotel's entrance caught his attention. He slowed his pace and analyzed the situation. The out-of-service e-taxi was parked in front of the hotel. The driver's side window was down, and a man was seated behind the wheel. A blonde woman was holding the rear passenger's side sliding door open while a short man with a fierce look and a bushy mustache steered two young girls toward the e-taxi.

Caspian recognized the girls. They were Aldrich's daughters.

While they weren't physically resisting, he could see they were crying. It was clear they weren't following the short man willingly. Five steps behind the girls, a well-built man of medium height with a ruddy face exited the hotel. He had one hand wrapped around the upper arm of Aldrich's third and oldest daughter, while the other was holding Aldrich's wife's hand. The man's lips were moving, but Caspian was too far away to hear what he was saying. Caspian guessed he was uttering nonstop threats to the mother and her children. Aldrich's wife looked terrified. Caspian's eyes moved to the oldest daughter. She wasn't crying. Her face was wary, and her body was tense, but she appeared to be in control of her emotions.

*She's gonna try something.*

This looked like a private security team escorting Aldrich's family out of harm's way. Though Caspian was sure that was how these people would sell it to the hotel staff—and even maybe to Aldrich's family—he knew this was bogus. Aldrich hadn't come to Zermatt with a security detail. This wasn't some sort of rescue.

Aldrich's family was being abducted.

Were these three or four people—Caspian didn't know if the driver was part of the team or not—in any way linked to Ballcap? If they were, and if Caspian was right about Ballcap, that meant they were intelligence operatives.

Just then, he spotted another man. This one was scanning the street, his hands crossed in front of him. He was tall, athletic, and dressed like an outdoorsman, with cargo pants, hiking boots, and a light brown jacket. He was standing in the shadows, a good twenty feet away from the hotel's entrance. From his position, the man had a clear view of the street and the action around the e-taxi.

Caspian, now less than one hundred feet from the parked e-taxi, watched the short man with the bushy mustache shove the two young girls into the vehicle. The mother tried to intervene, but the short man turned toward her and thrust a finger into her chest.

"*Toi, ta gueule!*" the short man shouted at them, loud enough for Casper to hear. Shut up!

Though French was one of the four official languages in Switzerland, Zermatt was a German-speaking town, and Caspian hadn't expected to hear the man speak French. None of the four or five team members he had spotted looked like Swiss police officers. Their demeanor was way off, and the way the short man had almost lost it with the mother hinted they weren't intelligence officers either.

The short man's outburst had quieted Aldrich's wife, but his threat had fallen on deaf ears when it came to the oldest daughter. With a speed that surprised Caspian, she used her free hand to slap the short man hard across his face. Her captor, the well-built man, grabbed her by the hair and jerked her head back. The young woman howled in pain and dropped to her knees. Her mother pleaded for the man to stop, but the man just pushed her away. While he did that, her daughter, who was still on her knees, reached for something in her back pocket.

Caspian guessed what it was before he even saw the small knife come out. And, from the look on the face of the tall man dressed in the light brown jacket, he saw it too.

As the girl stabbed her captor in the forearm in an upward thrust, the man with the light brown jacket unzipped his coat and reached for something inside. Before she could stab him again, the girl's captor punched her twice in the face with his uninjured arm, shattering her nose with a wet crunch.

The girl collapsed in a heap.

The sight of her daughter on the ground, with her face bashed in, must have flipped a switch inside Aldrich's wife's brain, because the primal, guttural sound Caspian heard next belonged to a possessed woman. Aldrich's wife charged at her daughter's captor, her hands extended in front of her, going for the man's eyes.

The next moment, the man with the light brown jacket pulled a gun from inside his coat.

Caspian's heart sank. The situation had spiraled out of control. In his mind, he could hear Laura's voice pleading with him to walk away, reminding him this wasn't his fight and that Aldrich's family wasn't his responsibility.

True, maybe. But how could he, in good conscience, walk away from this? He couldn't. Not when three young women's and their mother's lives were in peril. Caspian had no way to know who these men and the blonde woman were or who they worked for, but he didn't care. Not anymore. Whoever they were, they weren't with the good guys. That much he knew.

There was something else he knew. That whatever he chose to do, he was fucked. And Caspian was fine with that.

The good news was that the tall man with the light brown jacket wasn't the only one with a gun in his hands. Caspian had his, too, and he was aiming the suppressed SIG at the man's torso. So, when the man extended his arms in a two-hand grip and pointed his pistol at Aldrich's enraged, yet unarmed, wife, Caspian pulled the trigger.

Caspian's round hit him in the upper chest and knocked him a step back. Then the tall man's legs seemed to collapse from under him and he fell face first, his head connecting awkwardly with the ground.

Half a beat later, Aldrich's wife reached her daughter's captor at full speed, but the man simply threw her over his shoulder, sending her flying into the air.

Caspian, now in a combat crouch, took careful aim and squeezed the trigger, dropping the oldest daughter's captor with a bullet to the side of the head; a silver automatic pistol the man had just pulled from a holster landed in the slush next to him.

Caspian hated the tactical situation he was in. He had no cover or concealment and still had a minimum of two bad guys to deal with. To add a degree of difficulty to an already chaotic situation, he couldn't allow a single round to go astray—not with four noncombatants, three of them children, close by.

But he had to keep going, and fast, because if he didn't end this soon, he feared the kidnappers would kill Aldrich's family.

It had been three seconds since Caspian had fired his first shot, and that was the time it took for the blonde woman who'd been holding the door of the e-taxi to realize she and her crew were under attack. The muffled spits of the suppressed SIG pistol—compared to the much louder bang of an unsuppressed weapon—had given him a few extra seconds of partial stealth.

Caspian, his pistol aimed at the blonde woman, started to apply pressure to the trigger when the woman ducked behind the e-taxi.

Caspian lost sight of the woman, but he had a clear view of the short man with the bushy mustache, who was in the process of drawing his weapon from a shoulder holster. Unfortunately for Caspian, the only way he could engage the short man was to fire through the windows of the e-taxi, which wasn't an option given the two young girls trapped inside.

Caspian swore. He had no shot, he was completely exposed, and there was no doubt in his mind that the woman and the guy with the mustache were about to open fire.

Time wasn't on his side.

Twenty feet away, Caspian spotted two large concrete flowerpots. Two more were a bit farther away. The flowerpots weren't tall—under two feet—but they would have to do. He sprinted toward the first set.

Then, when he was five feet from the first flowerpots, the e-taxi driver did something Caspian hadn't expected. He fired through his door. Either the driver was a damn good shot, or he had simply gotten lucky: the bullet he'd fired through the thin metal door of the e-taxi grazed Caspian's right triceps.

Caspian dived headfirst behind the flowerpots, as if he was a baseball player attempting to steal second base, and landed on his stomach, the tiny layer of snow doing nothing to lessen the impact. He stayed hunkered down as more rounds hit the flowerpots, sending bits of concrete and puffs of masonry flying. His right arm was bleeding, and it hurt like hell, but it was still functioning.

And, at the moment, that was pretty much the only thing going for him.

# CHAPTER TWENTY-ONE

*Zermatt, Switzerland*

Edgar had ten, maybe twelve seconds left to make his decision. The gig would be up the moment the second police officer saw the pistol he had managed to keep against his leg, hidden from view.

Edgar had been able to buy some time by claiming he didn't speak German, but it was a losing battle. The officers had ordered him several times to get on his stomach and to spread his arms and legs, but Edgar had remained on one knee next to Aldrich and replied in French, pointing at the pool of blood next to the American banker's head.

Edgar had stolen a few glances at the officers. While the older officer had a busted nose, the younger one kept touching the area around his groin in an odd way. Edgar didn't think it would be wise to ask for the specifics of what had occurred, but a rapid verbal exchange between the two officers about the health of one of their colleagues who was still unconscious hinted they had been jumped by a lone assailant.

The Smoker?

*Can't afford to spend too much brain width on that right now.*

His options were limited. Either he surrendered to the officers, or he opened fire on them. The second option was more in his style. He could easily take at least one of the officers—preferably the second one—before his partner could get a shot off.

But surrendering would allow him to see his son again.

Edgar wondered what kind of jail sentences Swiss judges handed to foreigners found guilty of carrying an unlicensed pistol in their country. If he managed to contact Laurent and order him to abort before it was too late, Edgar thought his odds of seeing Sebastian before his son turned twenty were pretty good. If he didn't find a way to contact his brother, the police would eventually find out Edgar was involved in the abduction of Aldrich's family. In that case, the number of years he'd have to spend behind bars would go up significantly. Not something to look forward to.

"*Compose le numéro de Laurent,*" Edgar said, loud enough for his Bluetooth to pick up. Dial Laurent's number.

The second officer didn't appreciate the few words Edgar had spoken without his authorization and began to scream at him again. Edgar noted the officer's finger wasn't on the trigger guard but on the trigger itself.

*Not good.*

Since the second officer's arrival, things had gone downhill for Edgar. While the first cop—who was older by at least a decade—had been reluctant to aim his service pistol at Edgar, the second hadn't hesitated.

Quite the contrary. The younger cop seemed to relish it. And the sentiment was contagious apparently, because the other, more mature officer had changed his mind and was now pointing his pistol at Edgar too.

The young officer seemed to be itching for a reason to shoot him.

Through his earpiece, Edgar heard his phone connecting to Laurent's.

*About damn time.*

"Hold on for a sec," Laurent said in French. "Hey! You! What are you doing—"

"No! Abort! Abort, Laurent!" Edgar cut in, pleading with his brother. "Our target is dead."

The next sound to come through Edgar's earpiece sent a shiver down his spine. It was a low, pain-filled moan that seemed to last forever. And it was coming from his brother.

What the hell was happening at Le Clarion?

"Laurent? Laurent?"

Something serious had happened to his brother, and his team needed him. Edgar felt it in his gut, and, for an instant, he lost concentration. That's when the young officer slammed his boot into Edgar's back, propelling him forward, the strength of the blow ejecting the earpiece out of his ear.

Edgar was done playing nice.

Instead of letting himself fall flat on his stomach, Edgar spun his body to the left a heartbeat before he touched the ground. The young officer was three feet behind him, holding his pistol in a two-hand grip, but he hadn't had time to readjust his aim after he had kicked Edgar. Based on the barrel's position, the young officer's first round would go to the left of Edgar's shoulder—if he even managed to get a round off. But there was no time to lose; there was another officer to contend with after he dealt with this one.

Edgar, who had already bent his arm at the elbow, fired his pistol from an awkward position at the same moment his upper back and right shoulder hit the ground. His round hit the officer just below the chin, a tad lower than intended, but it was good enough to blow a chunk of the man's face off. The officer fell where he stood, and by the time his body made contact with the snow, Edgar had already rolled twice to his right and acquired the older cop in his sights. The officer was swinging his pistol in Edgar's direction. Edgar fired twice at the man's torso, part of him hoping the cop was wearing body armor. The man fell backward and stopped moving.

Edgar's objective hadn't been to kill the officer but to stop him from killing *him*.

It was time to go. Now.

Not only did his brother and the rest of his team need him, but the gunfire had undoubtedly attracted attention. If more cops weren't already on their way to the scene, they soon would be.

Edgar got to his feet, cleared his immediate surroundings, and started toward Le Clarion, praying he wasn't too late.

# CHAPTER TWENTY-TWO

**Zermatt, Switzerland**

"Go right! Go right!" a woman shouted in French. "Flank this asshole, Luc! We'll cover you. Understood?"

"Got it!"

Despite the dire situation he found himself in, Caspian's lips turned into a tight smile. He'd just found out what the enemy planned to do. Although his ears were ringing, at least his SIG P229 had a suppressor attached to it. The bad guys weren't using suppressors. In the last fifteen seconds, Caspian estimated the three remaining abductors had fired a total of at least thirty rounds. So, if his ears were ringing, theirs were on fire. That meant they needed to almost yell at each other in order to communicate.

This provided a great tactical advantage for Caspian.

Caspian continued to flatten himself to the frozen ground, but he edged forward to his left until he could peek from behind the flowerpot. After a quick look, he scurried back a few inches. The driver was no longer in the vehicle. Was he the one who'd just been ordered to flank Caspian? Or was it the short man with the bushy mustache? It was one or the other, because the order had been given by the woman.

If they wanted to flank Caspian by moving to their right, he had to be ready to repel an attack from his left flank. They couldn't hit him by shooting from behind the vehicle. The angle wasn't right. Of course, he couldn't score a hit either, but it didn't matter.

Not if he had understood their plan correctly.

Caspian's new position offered him a direct line of sight to the trajectory he hoped one of the men would take. Forty feet to the left of the e-taxi there was an outside flight of stairs leading to the hotel's ski lockers. The stairs were protected on two sides by a waist-high brick wall. It was the perfect spot. From there, a shooter could fire at Caspian without breaking cover.

*C'mon! Go for it. What are you waiting for?*

The blonde woman had ordered the flanking maneuver only fifteen seconds ago, but to Caspian it felt like an eternity. All his senses screamed at him.

*It's taking too long. Something isn't right.*

*Shit.*

Had he misread their plan? On a whim, he rolled onto his back, and pointed his pistol in the opposite direction.

Nothing.

The only people he saw were the four elderly couples. They, too, had flattened themselves to the ground. One of the men was covering his wife's body with his own. Caspian hoped none of them had been hit by a stray round.

Caspian returned to his previous position, his mind racing. He was missing something, but he couldn't put his finger on it.

Then he understood, and he swore, knowing he had only seconds to live.

# CHAPTER TWENTY-THREE

*Zermatt, Switzerland*

Florence Aldrich opened her eyes, but only enough to confirm nothing had changed in the last half minute. Everything had happened so fast. She wanted to scream, not so much for the pain she felt all over her face but for what these assholes had done to her two little sisters and her mom. Three men had barged into their hotel room and muscled them out into the hallway without explanation. Her mom had resisted at first, but one of the men, the tall one wearing a light brown jacket, had punched her in the stomach. Her mom hadn't made a sound, but Florence had seen the tears in her eyes.

Her mom had given her a do-as-they-say-and-everything-will-be-okay nod. But Florence hadn't been duped. At nineteen, she was no longer a child. She knew when adults lied to her. Especially her mother, who—unlike Florence's father, who had mastered the skill—had never been good at it.

Florence moved her eyes toward the tall man in the light brown jacket. He'd been the first to get shot, and he hadn't stopped moaning since. The man was obviously in excruciating pain, which Florence thought was ironic since he was the one who had sucker punched her mother. Right after he got shot, the man had fallen at a weird, almost comical angle. His butt was up, but his face and knees were on the ground. There was a pistol less than an inch from his right hand, but he hadn't tried to reach for it.

Florence didn't speak French, but ten seconds ago, she'd seen the man who'd been driving the taxi run back inside the hotel, gun in hand, after the blonde woman had shouted something. The blonde woman was now squatted behind the taxi next to the short man Florence had slapped across the face. She didn't regret doing it; it had felt so good.

At least her mom was safe. For now. The blonde woman had picked her up from where she'd fallen, then pushed her inside the vehicle. Florence's heart broke when she thought about her two little sisters. They hadn't done anything wrong. Florence didn't understand what or why this was happening to them, either, but at least she was old enough to think, and to defend herself. They weren't.

As much as she'd acted on a whim when she'd slapped the short man, the stabbing had been a premeditated move. The minute they'd been abducted from the apartment, Florence had known she was going to use the small knife at some point.

She'd seen the rage in the man's eyes when he'd realized what had happened. She'd honestly believed she had the time to plunge her little knife in him a few more times, but he'd reacted too quickly. She hadn't even seen his fist. But she had felt it. Twice.

Though the two punches to her nose had broken it—of that Florence had no doubt—she hadn't lost consciousness. The blows had stunned her, but not enough to prevent her from witnessing the head-shot that killed her captor.

She didn't know who was out there slaying her family's kidnappers one by one—though it couldn't be her dad, since he'd told her he had never fired a gun in his life—but she was grateful. Alas, it had been a while since their guardian angel had killed one of their abductors.

Had he been shot? The blonde woman and the short man had fired an awful lot of rounds.

*I have to do something. I can't play dead forever.*

The woman and the short man hadn't looked at her in a while. Florence could tell they were nervous. They kept peeking at something, or someone, on the other side of the taxi.

*Do they think I'm dead?*

Florence tasted blood in her mouth. She didn't dare touch her face, but she was sure that if she were to look at herself in a mirror, she'd scare herself silly.

The tall man was still moaning, but it now sounded more like the whine of an injured animal. His gun was so, so close.

Like her dad, she had never fired a gun, but she had watched a ton of YouTube videos on how to do it. It wasn't that complicated. Most pistols were point and shoot, right?

*If I hurry, I can probably get to it in less than two seconds. But if I make any sudden moves, they'll see me. And I'll die. But if I go too slow and they look in my direction, they'll realize I'm still alive. And I'll die. Just fucking great.*

Florence wished she could take a few deep breaths to calm her nerves, but she didn't dare make a move. Not until she was ready. She thought about how scared her two little sisters had been when the men had violently shoved them into the taxi. Then she thought about the man who had punched her mom.

When the rage building inside her threatened to burst, Florence moved.

# CHAPTER TWENTY-FOUR

*Zermatt, Switzerland*

Caspian knew that if he didn't move in the next few seconds, he was going to die. He couldn't stay behind the concrete flowerpots. His brain had finally connected the dots. The reason he hadn't seen anyone rushing toward the outside flight of stairs was because whoever had been chosen to flank him was going to do so by moving through the hotel. Earlier this week, he had reconnoitered the interior of Le Clarion. From the lobby, the guests could go down a flight of stairs and access the ski lockers. Instead of having people bump into each other in a single staircase with their skis, boots, and poles as some guests climbed up and others climbed down, the owners had built an exterior staircase to help with the flow.

It hadn't taken him long to get to the outside staircase from the lobby. If one was to hurry—and Caspian was pretty sure that whoever sought to kill him wanted to do so as soon as possible—one could go from the lobby's entrance to the outside staircase in about thirty seconds.

At any moment now, the two shooters behind the e-taxi would begin firing at his position to pin him down. That meant he was out of time. He couldn't stay where he was.

He could either sprint toward the river, jump over the railings, and leave Leonard Aldrich's family behind, or he could go all in and run as fast as he could, hoping to get to the outside staircase before the other man did.

*And maybe even surprise him,* Caspian thought, knowing the odds of that were slim to none. Still, abandoning the family was simply not an option.

Staying as low as possible to benefit from the cover offered by the concrete flowerpots, he took a second to prepare himself mentally, then risked a peek in the direction of the e-taxi to get a quick overview of the situation.

And it wasn't a good one. In fact, it couldn't have been worse.

The blonde woman and the short man had each taken good firing positions on opposite sides of the e-taxi they were using as partial cover. The woman was near the front of the vehicle, while the man had positioned himself close to the rear bumper. Unlike Caspian, who only had his head out of cover, the woman's entire right side was exposed, but both of her arms were outstretched in front of her. She had her gun aimed at Caspian, who still needed three-tenths of a second before he could bring his own gun to bear. The short man also had him in his sights.

*Shit.*

Before he could duck back behind the flowerpots, Caspian heard the crack of a pistol. The short man yelled in pain, his body arching forward. The blonde woman spun sideways just as Caspian brought the rear sights of his pistol into alignment with the front sight post, which was already on the woman's head. He pulled the trigger.

---

Florence had made it to the tall man's pistol without getting shot. Now on her knees, she picked it up. It was so much heavier than she thought it would be. Glancing to her right, she saw the blonde woman. She and the short man had just moved to new positions. The woman was fifteen feet away, and Florence could only see part of her.

Too far. Too small a target.

A little voice in Florence's head told her that one shot was all she was going to get. She refused to dwell on what that meant for her.

The short man was much closer, no more than five feet away. He had his back to her.

She could make that shot. She *would* make that shot.

Then she saw her mother. And her two sisters. They were in the taxi, looking down at her. Her mom was shaking her head. Florence looked away, refusing to meet her mother's gaze.

Holding the gun with both hands, she pointed it at the short man. Keeping both eyes open, like she had learned from a YouTube video, she brought the front sight to the center of the man's back. Only then did she start to squeeze the trigger.

Pulling the trigger was physically harder than she had expected. In fact, she had to use her two index fingers. Even then it was difficult. And it seemed to take forever before the gun finally fired.

And then it did, and the short man yelled in pain as he was struck in the back.

She had hit him!

But the short man was still alive. Should she shoot him again?

Then her mother screamed her name. She jerked her head to the right.

*Oh my God!* The blonde woman.

Florence had all but forgotten about her. Florence tried to swing the pistol toward the woman, but she was too late.

Way too late.

The woman's gun was already pointed straight at her heart.

Then the blonde woman's head snapped sideways, and she dropped to the ground.

———

Caspian still had no clue who had shot the short man, but he was grateful for the assist. The short man had fallen to his knees, but he was now twisting to his left, trying to raise the pistol still in his right hand. Caspian fired twice, sending two more rounds into the man's back, one of them finding its way to his heart. The man collapsed onto his side, and, as he did so, Aldrich's older daughter appeared. She'd been kneeling behind him, a gun in her hands.

Caspian's eyes met hers, and the look that passed between them only lasted for a fleeting moment, but it was enough for him to determine the girl was going to be all right. He allowed himself a small smile. There was steel in the young woman's eyes, a defiant, fearless determination to do whatever it took to stay alive and protect her family.

*Yeah . . . this one is gonna be just fine.*

# CHAPTER TWENTY-FIVE

*Zermatt, Switzerland*

Florence didn't know what to think of the man. There was something commanding about him that she found frightening and yet very reassuring. His eyes, which seemed to be a direct conduit to his soul, held a weightiness she had never seen before. She wondered what this man had seen and done. And then he smiled. Florence couldn't tell if it was meant for her, but his smile was surprisingly warm.

The cry coming from one of her two younger sisters broke the short spell, and she rushed to the e-taxi. She opened the sliding door.

"Let's go, guys! Out! Out!" she said, prompting her mother and sobbing sisters to come out.

"I don't want to," one of them said.

Florence took her hand. "I understand. I'm scared too. But we need to go somewhere where we'll all be safe."

"Where's Daddy?" asked the other one.

"He'll be back soon. I promise," Florence replied.

"Your sister's right, girls," her mom said. "Daddy will be here in a few minutes. Now, let's go."

Florence saw her mom's eyes move to the gun in her hand, but her mom only nodded.

Florence was the first to enter the hotel's lobby, which was empty except for the receptionist cowering behind the front desk. Florence was still debating where to go, uncertain if she should lead her family back to their room, when the door of the staircase leading down to the ski lockers burst open. Florence stepped in front of her sisters and raised the pistol. She lowered it an instant later, recognizing the hotel's owner and his wife. Both were in their late sixties but looked a decade younger. Both tall and wiry. They were hardly ever still. Florence had seen them numerous times helping the cooks at breakfast, pouring wine during dinner service, and even polishing glasses in the bar area. And they always did it with a smile.

But they weren't smiling now. They were both panting, their faces white with shock. The husband held a baseball bat. His wife had a shotgun. They seemed startled to see Florence but didn't say a word about the pistol in her right hand.

"Are you all right?" the hotel's owner asked. "I'm sorry. I'm . . . that was a stupid question."

"No . . . no, that's okay. We're . . . we're actually fine, I think," Florence said, looking at her mom and sisters. Her voice, like her legs, had become shaky, and it took a conscious effort to keep her emotions under control.

"We have no cameras inside the hotel, but we do have some outside and in the ski locker rooms. We saw everything," the owner's wife said. "We called the police immediately. They should be here soon."

Florence looked at the baseball bat, then at the shotgun.

"I don't know why, but one of the men who tried to kidnap you and your family was in the locker room," the owner said. "He tried to open the door leading to the outside staircase, but the door is locked electronically every night at eight o'clock sharp. When we confronted him, he had already shattered the lower part of the glass door and was busy kicking the pointy shards away. We weren't going to let him come back to the lobby and threaten any more of our guests."

"Or let him get away with what he had done," the owner's wife added, her tone glacial. "Somehow, and even though we'd been careful, he heard us coming."

"I wanted to use the baseball bat, you know," the owner said, "but when he turned around, he had a gun in his hand."

"Good thing I had my shotgun pointed at him," his wife said. "I shot him in the chest as soon as I saw his gun. He won't harm anyone ever again."

"My God . . . ," Florence's mom whispered. "I . . . I don't understand any of it. Why? Why did these people come after us?"

"I'm sure the police will want to talk to you about this," the owner said.

"But in the meantime, if you want, we'll take you back to your room until they get here," his wife proposed.

Florence didn't know how to respond, so she simply nodded, wondering what her father would say about the night's events.

# CHAPTER TWENTY-SIX

*Zermatt, Switzerland*

Caspian didn't waste a single second. He had none to spare. While Aldrich's older daughter helped her family out of the e-taxi, Caspian, using an attack angle that minimized his exposure, sprinted in the direction of the outside stairway, his SIG Sauer pistol in front of him.

He was perplexed as to why the other shooter hadn't yet shown up. It didn't make sense. Just before Aldrich's daughter had saved the day, the blonde woman and the short man with the bushy mustache had been about to open fire on Caspian's position in order to either provide a distraction or cover the other shooter's approach.

Caspian, back in a combat crouch, crept forward along the brick wall, keeping his pistol up. When he reached the corner, he waited and listened for a moment. On the other side of the brick wall was the flight of stairs leading down to the ski lockers. His ears were still ringing, but he thought he'd heard a strange gurgling noise. He did a quick peek around the corner and pulled back his head immediately. Then he looked again.

The man who'd been driving the e-taxi lay on the landing at the bottom of the stairs. Half of his body was still inside the ski locker room. He had a giant, gory wound to the chest, but he was still alive. The man opened his mouth to speak, but the only thing that came out was a dreadful croak.

Caspian raised his pistol and fired a merciful round into the man's mouth.

Caspian inserted a new magazine and pocketed the other. He decided to keep the suppressor attached and placed the pistol back into his modified coat pocket.

Caspian looked around him. The gunfight had scared most, if not all, of the pedestrians off the streets. He guessed that the few people he did see had come out to the streets after the gunfight had ended, or from far enough away that the surrounding buildings had hindered the sounds of the battle. To his relief, the four elderly couples were nowhere to be seen. Caspian hoped that meant none of them had been struck by a lost round.

In the distance, somewhere in the direction of Täsch, police sirens wailed. Caspian's internal clock told him he'd fired his first shot about ninety seconds ago. Now that Aldrich's family was no longer under immediate threat, it was time for Caspian to vanish.

Tradecraft dictated a long SDR, but Caspian's analysis of the situation told him otherwise. He didn't know how many people had seen him fire his gun. There were the four elderly couples, the Aldrich family, and probably a few other pedestrians. Now wasn't the time to linger in the streets. It was too risky. His rental apartment was the safest place for him right now. Furthermore, he needed to clean his wound. The pain radiating from the back of his right arm was getting worse, and while his dark winter coat helped to camouflage the wound, Caspian could feel blood trickling down the length of his arm.

Just as he had originally planned, Caspian made a left on Sunneggastrasse. His pace wasn't fast enough to make it look as if he was fleeing from a crime scene, but it wasn't like he was on a leisurely stroll either. He was almost halfway across the bridge when he looked back toward Le Clarion. A few people had started to gather outside, probably trying to make sense of what had happened. Caspian had yet to see an ambulance or another emergency vehicle, but the sirens were closer now. They would be at the hotel soon. Not that it would change anything.

Unless he was mistaken, there was no one left to save.

# CHAPTER TWENTY-SEVEN

*Zermatt, Switzerland*

Edgar wasn't out of breath, but his heart was pounding. He had been a few meters away from Vispastrasse when he had first heard the gunshots. His brother was the first member of his team Edgar had tried to call back. When Laurent hadn't picked up, he had called Luc, their driver for tonight's operation. Luc hadn't answered either.

Now that he had Le Clarion in sight, he pocketed his phone. He wanted to have two hands on his pistol. As Edgar moved, he swung his head from left to right, scanning for any threats, his pistol in front of him and ready to fire. There was always the chance he'd get shot in the back by a police officer, but he had no choice but to keep going forward at a good pace, fully aware that his pistol would attract some attention.

If anyone was to challenge him, Edgar would show a stolen French Gendarmerie police badge and a forged ID card. Most civilians had no idea what a police badge truly looked like. As long as Edgar showed them a piece of shiny metal and a plasticized card with his photo and name on it, they would buy it. Anyone crazy enough to challenge him would be told he was on an Interpol operation. Any further digging would buy that foolish person a bullet to the head.

Edgar glanced toward the main entrance of Le Clarion and immediately noticed Hubert, the newest member of his team. Hubert lay face down on the pavement, close to the rear bumper of the e-taxi his team had stolen. A fine layer of snow had already collected on his back.

Edgar's worst fears were now confirmed. His team had come under attack by an overwhelming force. His throat tightened with guilt and anger, but he had to be careful. He couldn't allow himself to suffer from tunnel vision. As much as he wanted to run to his fallen team member and look for the rest of his team, he had to be cautious. Threats could come from anywhere.

Edgar was about to step onto the hotel grounds when he caught sight of a lone person walking across the river on Sunneggastrasse. Edgar strained his eyes, trying to make out the details. The man was maybe forty meters away, and two-thirds of the way across.

Edgar's heart skipped a beat.

*Motherfucker. The Smoker.*

This was no coincidence. This man was part of a team that had derailed his operation and killed one of his men. Edgar raced to the railings that prevented pedestrians from falling into the river and used it to provide him with additional support. In a best-case scenario with perfect visibility and no wind, Edgar would easily make that shot. But it was dark, the snow had picked up again, and Edgar had a hard time shaking the feeling he was about to get a bullet in the back. Still, the FN 509 Tactical was a fantastic pistol, and it had an effective range of fifty meters. To hit his target, Edgar simply needed to concentrate and forget everything else around him.

Edgar took a long breath and steadied his aim, and for the next couple of seconds his entire world narrowed down to the front and rear sights of his FN 509 Tactical and the smooth but steady pressure he was applying to the pistol's trigger.

The gun bucked once in his hands. Edgar readied himself for a second shot, but it wasn't needed. His target was down.

Edgar was about to turn around when the unmistakable sound of a pump-action shotgun being racked behind him froze him in place.

# CHAPTER TWENTY-EIGHT

*Zermatt, Switzerland*

Caspian's body didn't even have the time to flinch before a bullet slammed high into his left shoulder, his brain registering the crack of a gunshot a millisecond later. The impact spun him around, and Caspian let himself fall, knowing that the partial cover offered by the heavy and intricate guardrails bordering both sides of the bridge was his only chance to get away from the shooter's direct line of sight.

Caspian felt as if he'd been hit by an iron mallet. The shot had come from behind and to the left, just about where Le Clarion was located. It didn't matter if the police or someone else had fired the shot; the outcome was the same. The blinding pain in his left shoulder wasn't going anywhere. His entire left arm was numb.

Where had the bullet gone? Had it entered through his left shoulder and run down his arm, or had it deflected and lodged itself in his back or chest? The pain was such that it was impossible to say. Caspian rolled onto his back, winced as he opened his winter coat, and touched his wound with his right hand. A jolt of newfound pain blurred his vision as his fingers explored the damage. Warm blood oozed from where the bullet had pierced his skin, but he had the impression the wound was a through-and-through. The bullet had torn through his winter coat, his clothes, and his flesh, and had exited a half-inch higher on the shoulder.

Caspian needed to get off the bridge and find a place where he could at least stop the blood loss. He groaned in agony as he got to one knee. Once he was sure he wasn't going to pass out, he half walked, half jogged toward the other side of the bridge, staying as low as he could. Behind him in the snow, a trail of fresh blood followed his progress.

———

Caspian reached the busy part of town a few minutes later. He took a few moments to find what he was looking for, then headed toward a busy bar that had numerous pairs of skis still resting on a wooden rack outside. He entered the bar and was glad to see a communal coat rack next to the bathrooms. As he walked past it, he grabbed a dark winter jacket he thought would fit and continued toward the bathrooms.

Caspian locked himself in a stall and slowly removed his coat and shirt. He needed to get a better look at his shoulder. His wound was a mess of flesh and blood. It wasn't pretty, but the damage wasn't as bad as he had thought. The bullet hadn't nicked an artery or hit a vital organ. A deep cleaning of the wound, stitches, and a few weeks of physical therapy would hopefully do the trick. For now, though, he had to find a way to stop the bleeding. He had everything he needed to treat the wound in his medical kit, including antibiotics, but it was back at his rental place.

Caspian tore off the sleeves of his shirt with the help of his knife and used them to hold in place the wad of toilet paper he had applied to the wound. He tied the knot under his arm as best he could with one hand. Bitching in silence about the pain, he put on the coat he'd taken from the rack. With luck, his makeshift bandage would hold until he reached his rental and would prevent most of the blood from leaking through the winter coat. Caspian emptied the pockets of his previous jacket, removed the suppressor from his pistol, and holstered his SIG back into his inside-the-waist holster. He exited the stall, shoved his old winter jacket in the garbage bin, and washed his hands thoroughly using the lavender soap provided.

To get back to his rental studio, Caspian didn't take the shortest or fastest route. Preferring to stay out of view as much as possible, he used the side streets and smaller alleys, which offered him more protection. Half a block away from his rental, he stopped briefly to observe the activity around his apartment building. Not seeing anything that aroused his suspicion, he crossed the street and entered the building.

# CHAPTER TWENTY-NINE

*Zermatt, Switzerland*

Without knowing what kind of threat he faced, Edgar wasn't about to do anything that the person behind him holding the shotgun might in any way interpret as a threat.

"I'm a French police officer," Edgar said calmly in German. "I'm here on behalf of Interpol and in collaboration with the Valais cantonal police. Can I please turn around?"

"Go ahead, but no sudden movement," a woman replied. "Because if you do, I'll blow your head off. Police or not."

Edgar slowly turned toward the woman. She was ten feet away from him, an expression of arrogant defiance plastered on her face. She was an older woman, but her shooting stance and the way she had her shotgun leveled at him told Edgar she knew how to use it. This was someone who wouldn't hesitate to fire a full load of buckshot into his torso. There was something familiar about her.

Yes, Edgar knew who the woman was. She and her husband were the owners of Le Clarion.

"Who did you just shoot?" she asked, her eyes drilling into him.

"One of the suspects," Edgar replied. "He's one of the men responsible for what happened here tonight. I need to go secure him."

"I saw him fall. He's not going anywhere," the woman said. "Now, slowly holster your pistol, and show me your credentials."

Edgar did as he was told, but the sirens he'd been hearing were getting closer. He had three, maybe four minutes before they arrived. While it was true that he wanted to go check on the man he'd just shot, he needed to find out what had happened to his team.

The woman glanced at the stolen police badge, then eyed him suspiciously. Edgar felt she was about to question him some more, so he took charge. He needed to hurry up the process.

"I did what you asked," he said, heading toward the hotel but raising his hands in mock surrender. "Now, please let me do my job, will you?"

He could see the older woman was still unconvinced.

"Let's go! Show me what you got," he said as he walked past her.

*Either I get shot or I don't. But I need to check on my team and get out of here before the real police show up.*

Still breathing a dozen steps later, Edgar deduced the woman wouldn't use the shotgun on him. Whatever relief he felt about this didn't last long. The closer he got to the hotel, the more he felt sick to his stomach. He'd already seen Hubert on his way in, and now he'd just spotted Jenny. She'd been shot in the head.

*Where the hell is Laurent?*

"It's a bloodbath," the woman said, catching up to him. "I called the police, but the dispatcher said they're sending officers from nearby towns. Apparently, the five officers on duty in Zermatt tonight are otherwise occupied."

Edgar had an idea or two about where the officers were, but he wasn't about to share his thoughts with the hotel owner.

"For God's sake, I can't think of anything more urgent than what we have here," the woman continued. "Anyway, I'm sorry for earlier. I'm glad you're here. Even if you're French."

Edgar was barely listening to her. The only thing he was interested in was finding Laurent.

"What happened here?" he asked.

"I can't say for sure, but my husband and I believe four men and a woman tried to kidnap four of our guests."

"Really? Why?"

"You're the police. You tell me why," the woman replied.

"I saw two dead bodies. One man and one woman," Edgar said, trying to keep his voice calm, despite the panic stirring inside him. "Are there any other victims?"

"Oh yes. There are three more."

Edgar's entire body stiffened. "Three more, you said?"

"Yes. Maybe I should have said so earlier, but all five kidnappers are dead."

Edgar's knees buckled, and he had to steady himself against the e-taxi.

"Are you okay, Officer?"

"Show me."

"They're just there. On the other side of the taxi," the woman said, leading the way.

Edgar followed her, and truthfully considered shooting her in the back when she kicked Hubert's body after she almost tripped over him rounding the rear of the e-taxi.

Then he saw Laurent, and he forgot all about her.

*Please, God,* Edgar thought, as he knelt next to his younger brother.

His brother rested on the ground in a grotesque way, a pose very similar to the balasana in yoga. His forehead, knees, and feet touched the ground, but his hips were up. A pool of blood had collected under him and melted a patch of snow.

"This one moaned for a long time," the woman said. "He was the first to go down."

Edgar flinched at the woman's words, once again considering shooting her, but this time in the face. Edgar closed his eyes and checked his brother's pulse. The woman had said Laurent was dead, but Edgar wasn't going to take her word for it. His brother's neck was still warm.

Then he felt it. His brother had a pulse. It was weak, but at least his heart was beating.

"This man is alive," he said, looking at the woman.

"What?"

"He's fucking alive! Get an ambulance!" Edgar shouted.

The woman looked at him strangely. Then she took three steps back but kept the barrel of her shotgun pointed down.

*Get a grip. You're no good to him if you're dead.*

"There are ambulances on the way. I'll call their central to let them know one of the kidnappers is still alive. Maybe they'll get here faster," the woman said, slowly backing away.

Edgar's mind was reeling in different directions, but he was conscious that his cover story was getting thinner by the second.

*She knows something's not right.*

Edgar ran his hands slowly over his brother's back and sides. No blood. No exit wound. Though he knew he shouldn't move Laurent, Edgar rolled his brother into the recovery position.

*Oh God. There it is. Bullet hole. Slightly off center. Upper chest. Three inches below the neck. Shit. Shit. Shiiit!*

Edgar felt the blood drain from his face. Though he'd known he would eventually find the entry wound, to see the actual hole in his brother's chest didn't make it easier to accept. Behind him, the first ambulance had arrived, the glow of its emergency lights reflecting against the hotel windows.

It was time for him to leave. There wasn't anything else he could do for his brother. Not now, anyway. He took one last look at Laurent, then was about to turn away when his brother blinked.

*I was wrong. There's something I can do for him.*

Despite the obvious pain he knew this would inflict on his brother, Edgar picked him up with a grunt, then started walking toward the ambulance, his arms shaking under the strain of his brother's weight. The hotel owners eyed him as he passed in front of the sliding doors of their lobby.

Edgar carried Laurent to the rear of the ambulance, where two paramedics were in the process of unloading a collapsible wheeled stretcher from the ambulance.

"Hey! I need help!" Edgar shouted in German. One of the paramedics rushed to assist him.

"I'm a police officer," Edgar said, continuing in German. "This man has a gunshot wound to the chest, but he's breathing. You need to take him to the hospital immediately."

To their credit, the paramedics jumped into action without hesitation. Within moments, Laurent was placed on the stretcher and loaded into the back of the ambulance.

When the ambulance's doors were closed, Edgar turned away and headed toward the bridge where he had shot The Smoker. He was still a few meters away from the intersection when he saw two ambulances and a police car turn onto the bridge. He kept an eye on them as they drove the entire length of the bridge without even slowing down.

Edgar shook his head in frustration.

*The Smoker's no longer there. The cops would have stopped, or at least slowed down, if they had seen a body in the middle of the road.*

Edgar was able to confirm his assessment a few steps later as he crossed the intersection. The bridge was empty. The Smoker was gone.

Edgar was tired and frustrated, and felt a mixture of hot and cold aching misery wash over him. There was an anger boiling inside him, an anger that was about to transform itself into an explosive, unstoppable, and mindless killing rage.

Edgar willed himself to keep it together for just a little while longer.

He needed to keep his head straight until he was out of Zermatt. Out of Switzerland. Then he would find The Smoker, and he would break every bone in his body.

Only then would Edgar allow him to die.

# CHAPTER THIRTY

*Zermatt, Switzerland*

Caspian closed the door of his studio apartment behind him and locked it. If someone was waiting for him here, he would be easy prey. His reserve of adrenaline depleted, he could barely walk. Just getting to the bathroom required every bit of strength he had left.

Good thing it was only two steps away.

At the faucet, Caspian opened the medicine cabinet behind the mirror and grabbed his small medical kit. He had a bigger one in the duffel bag he had stashed under the double bed, but he didn't think he could make it there without passing out. His building had no elevator, and the climb to his fourth-floor studio had exhausted the last of his energy.

He removed the toilet paper he'd used to control the bleeding and sanitized the open wound on his left shoulder with wipes and antibiotic ointment. He then folded the gauze from the med kit into a thick, uneven square and placed it atop the wound. He took a deep breath, then applied pressure with his fingertips.

Caspian groaned out loud. The pain was exquisite. He looked at his reflection in the mirror. His face was contorted in agony, and tears were running down his cheeks. Using the medical tape, he secured the gauze—which was already flooded in red—by looping the tape around his armpit.

Caspian examined his dressing. It didn't look nice, but it would have to do for now. Raising his right arm, he used the mirror to assess his right triceps. The bullet had carved a tiny tunnel in his skin. The wound was still bleeding, but at least it wasn't gushing out. This was good news, because with his left arm practically useless, he was incapable of treating it.

A wave of chills suddenly racked Caspian's entire body. Completely worn out and knowing he was too tired to do anything of value, he tottered from the bathroom to the bed. Though it was only ten steps away, he almost didn't make it.

As he flopped onto the bed, he closed his eyes and let his mind roam free. Expecting to be brought back to Le Clarion to relive the gunfight, Caspian was surprised that the first image to pop up in his head was of Liesel. He welcomed it.

How could he not?

If one of the two bullets that had struck him had been one or two inches more to the left or right, odds were that Liesel would have never known how much she meant to him.

All in all, he'd been lucky. It wasn't as bad as it could have been. His speed, his surprise, and his precise aim had allowed him to walk away from a five-against-one gunfight. But that wasn't entirely true, was it? Without Aldrich's daughter's assistance, the outcome could have been different.

*Would have been different,* he corrected himself.

He'd been in tough spots before, but the firefight he'd just been through at Le Clarion was unlike anything else he had experienced. Caspian was still in brilliant shape. His strength and stamina were just as good as, if not better than, when he had completed the Onyx training pipeline. And the last hour had proven he was still lethal and capable of doing the job he was trained to do, didn't it?

*Yeah. Maybe. But for how long?*

Although Caspian found it was taking more work with every passing year to maintain his level of physical fitness, he was still faster and fitter than most men in their twenties. But he wasn't duped. Life would catch up to him at some point. Eventually, he would have to pull the plug.

But would he be smart enough to recognize when to do it, or would he stay on with Onyx too long, until his life was ended abruptly at the hands of an operative younger and better than him?

And even if he was to leave Onyx in time, what then?

He didn't have any real friends, and his whole professional career outside of Onyx was built on a lie.

*Stop it! Nobody forced you to do that, remember?* Caspian reminded himself, not for the first time.

But his mind refused to let it go.

As much as he felt validated by his work, wasn't there something else he could do that would give him the same sense of fulfillment? It wasn't the first time he'd thought about changing gears and asking for a transfer out of Onyx. He could live with the nightmares and the occasional vivid flashbacks. He still had control over them, though he would be lying to himself if he didn't acknowledge they were starting to scratch at his psyche. Just as with his fitness level, it took more and more work every year to keep the demons at bay.

What had always frightened him to his core, though, was the *after Onyx*. That used to terrify him. But it didn't anymore.

Not since he'd met Liesel Bergmann.

Little by little, Liesel had changed his perspective on life. It wasn't long after they had started to date each other seriously that Caspian had begun to question his life choices. He knew it wasn't healthy to do so. Not in his chosen profession. But no other woman had ever infused him with such deep passions.

Caspian had even caught himself—more than once—fantasizing about how nice it would be to spend the rest of his life with her away from the violence. It was crazy to think like that. He knew that too. But he couldn't help it.

The sad truth, though, was that Caspian had the impression the feeling wasn't mutual.

If he didn't do something about it soon, he was going to lose Liesel.

# CHAPTER THIRTY-ONE

*New York, New York*

Liesel entered her apartment and locked the door behind her. She kicked off her black leather boots, replaced them with a pair of comfy slippers, then tossed her coat over the sofa as she made her way to the kitchen. She took the leftover spaghetti bolognese she had made two days ago from the fridge and warmed it in the microwave. While her pasta was being nuked, she grabbed a bottle of her favorite Barolo from her ten-bottle wine fridge and uncorked it. She poured herself a generous glass and took a tentative sip, and then a much longer one.

*Perfect.* This was exactly what she needed to unwind after the tedious—and unexpected—two-hour-long meeting she'd been forced to attend at the office.

Liesel poured a bit more wine into her glass and brought it to the dining table along with the plate of spaghetti. She grabbed the TV remote from the coffee table and tuned in to a news channel, something she rarely did when sharing a meal with Caspian, unless she wanted to annoy him on purpose. Caspian was old school when it came to these kinds of things. For him, dinnertime was precious, and watching television while eating made him cringe. She enjoyed teasing him about it, but, deep down, she thought it was cute.

Liesel took a sip of her wine, then rolled a mouthful of spaghetti around her fork, her eyes glued to the television. She brought the fork to her mouth and instantly burned the roof of her mouth and tongue in the process.

*Damn it!*

Angry at herself for not being more careful, she went back to the kitchen and took an ice cube out of the freezer. She sucked on it for a few seconds and spit it out into the kitchen sink. As she returned to the dining table, a news flash caught her attention. She turned up the volume.

*What? Leonard Aldrich is dead?*

Liesel was shocked. Was it a coincidence that earlier in the day, her handler, Nicklas, had asked her about her relationship with Aldrich? Nicklas's questions were based on an after-action report she'd filed three years ago that had mentioned the presence of Aldrich during an official firm function.

Her handler hadn't shared with Liesel the reason why German intelligence was looking into Aldrich, but that wasn't uncommon. She'd learned over the years that her handlers—she'd had three of them before Nicklas—liked to keep their cards close to their vests, even with their assets in the field.

Liesel had told him everything she knew about Leonard Aldrich. It wasn't much.

She had met Aldrich in person only once, and it had been during a charity event organized and sponsored by her firm. Aldrich and his wife—who Liesel thought was very charming compared to the dull banker—were among the guests. She'd shaken Aldrich's hand during the predinner cocktail hour, shared a laugh or two, but nothing more. Later, at the banquet, Aldrich and his wife had been seated at a different table than her, so she didn't remember all his table companions, but she did recall one: Ambassador Claus Eichberg, the permanent representative of the Federal Republic of Germany to the United Nations.

Eichberg was a difficult man to forget, and not only because he was representing her home country to the United Nations. Eichberg towered above everybody else—he was at least six foot six—and had bright steel-blue eyes and a head full of thick, wavy white hair. It was well known within diplomatic circles that Eichberg was a close friend of the chancellor of Germany. He was wealthy and well connected at home and abroad, and his influence at the United Nations was considerable, and growing.

Liesel's after-action report of the event to German intelligence had mentioned the presence of Aldrich and his wife at Eichberg's table.

During today's exchange with her handler, Liesel had also shared that she'd spoken on the phone with Aldrich on a few occasions. It was no secret that her firm often partnered with him. Aldrich was a financial fixer. Her firm dealt with him mostly when one of the start-ups they did business with needed to raise funds to grow, or when an established business needed funding for reasons regular banking institutions didn't lend money for.

Liesel's eyes were still glued to her television screen as she continued to watch the news report in horror. Not only was Aldrich dead, but his family had narrowly escaped an alleged kidnapping attempt at their hotel.

*Madness!*

And that wasn't all. If she was to believe the reporter, and she had no reason not to, Aldrich's body had been found next to a dead cop. Liesel's mind was reeling with the new information.

A dead cop? The attempted kidnapping of his family?

Leonard Aldrich wasn't on the straight and narrow. She knew that. The man had committed fraud, forged documents, lied in court, and had a long list of shady players with whom he kept in touch, but she doubted he was capable of murder.

Next to the TV remote, her phone pinged.

She logged into her online casino account. Her inbox had one new message, and it was a short one.

Take the call

# CHAPTER THIRTY-TWO

*Zermatt, Switzerland*

Caspian awoke, gasping for air.

Disoriented, with his entire body clammy with sweat, he sat upright in bed, his heart pounding. He had lost track of time. Had he fallen asleep, or had he passed out? The bedsheets, tangled in a knot at his side, were soaking wet. Was it from sweat or blood? Caspian didn't know. The room was dark, save for the light he had kept turned on in the bathroom.

His left shoulder was burning. The pain hadn't subsided one bit. In fact, it had become almost unbearable. Slowly, he got up and padded his way toward the light. The bathroom tiles were spotted with blood, and so were his clothes and the towels he had discarded. The wound had been too large for self-made stitches. He'd done his best to clean it with what he had found in the medical kit, but it wasn't enough.

*I need a doctor,* he thought, which reminded him he hadn't updated Laura.

It took Caspian longer than it should have to remember where he had left his phone. When he finally found it in the jacket he'd stolen at the bar, it was almost out of battery life. Caspian needed his third and final attempt to log into his encrypted chat window. Laura had left several messages.

*I've been out of it for almost six hours,* Caspian realized, glad the police hadn't yet burst through his door.

He didn't have the mental capacity to read through all Laura's messages or the strength to type numerous replies, so he sent a single text.

**To Merlot32: Call me. 49234**

49234 was the prearranged code to let his handler know he wasn't under duress. His phone vibrated. Caspian took the call. There was a soft buzzing sound followed by two clicks and a momentary silence; then Laura came on the line.

"Elias, confirm your location," his handler asked, her tone neutral.

"Still in Zermatt. At my rental," he said, noticing at once how hoarse and bone tired he sounded.

"Confirmed. I have you on my screen."

"I need medical assistance."

"How bad is it?"

"I took a round in the shoulder. It's a through-and-through, I think, but I lost a lot of blood, and some pieces of burnt clothes were forced into the bullet hole and I can't remove them. I'm afraid the wound is getting infected since I can't sanitize it properly."

"Anything else?"

"A graze on my right arm."

"Noted. The situation in Zermatt is challenging at the moment. It will be hard to get you the help you need," Laura said, her tone all-business. If she was worried about Caspian's health, she wasn't showing it. "Are you able to make your own way to Visp or Sion?"

Caspian almost said yes, which was often his go-to answer when someone asked him if he could do something. This time, though, he took an extra moment to truly assess his condition. His eyes were hurting, his vision had become misty, his entire body ached, and his already high fever had kicked up another notch. He was past exhaustion, almost too frail to stand. There was no way he was going to make it to the train station, and even if he did by some miracle, his weakened state would draw too much attention. No one wanted to stand or sit next to a sick person.

"No . . . I can't make it," Caspian said as a wave of nausea swept through him.

"I see. I'll call you back," Laura said and ended the call.

Caspian looked at his phone.

*What the hell? Did she really hang up on me?*

His conversation with Laura left him perplexed and frustrated. This was the first time he'd been injured during an operation. He'd never needed medical assistance in any shape or form prior to today. He understood the problem in getting a doctor into Zermatt. The authorities had probably placed the village in lockdown, or at least severely restricted the ins and outs. Nevertheless, he had expected more from his handler.

Caspian, needing to use the toilet, tried to get up on his wobbly legs, but his headache flared up and put his skull into an iron vise. A savage jolt of pain brought him to his knees, and a cry squeezed from his lips.

*Get up! Get up, or you'll die. Get up!*

He got back to his feet, slowly, but stumbled again and fell to his side before rolling onto his back. And this time, he didn't get back up.

# CHAPTER THIRTY-THREE

*New York, New York*

Leonard Aldrich's death had shaken Liesel. Her brain hadn't stopped racing since she'd watched the news, trying to catch up with all the new information. And now, her handler wanted to speak with her. She had no doubt it was about Aldrich.

Liesel hadn't seen Nicklas face to face in more than two years, and she could count on two hands the number of times she'd spoken to him in the last year.

And never had she received from him a text as abrupt—or exciting— as Take the call.

*Something is up.*

When her phone rang, she answered on the first ring.

"Hey! Is Jenny around?" Nicklas asked, initiating the predetermined code.

"There's no Jenny living here," Liesel replied.

"I'm sorry. I must have dialed the wrong number."

"Well, the previous owner's name is Penny. Could she be the one you're looking for?" Liesel asked, completing the code and confirming she was free to talk.

"Identity confirmed. This is Blackjack, and I'm secured," Nicklas said.

"Identity confirmed. This is Poker," Liesel replied.

"Are you familiar with the current situation in Zermatt?" Nicklas asked.

"I've been watching the news, but I don't have any privileged information or insights to share at the moment," Liesel said.

"I didn't expect you to. But tell me what you think you know."

Liesel spent the next minute regurgitating what the reporter had said on television.

"Here's what hasn't been made public yet," Nicklas said once she was done. "Beyond the death of the one police officer you already know about, another cop was shot. The only reason that officer is still breathing is because the two rounds the assassin fired struck his body armor."

"The assassin?" she asked. It was a weird term to use.

"Bear with me," Nicklas said. "There was also a third officer who was found on a side street less than seventy meters away. That officer is in a coma. This hasn't been confirmed by our source, but the working theory is that the three officers were initially surprised and assaulted by one man."

"One attacker? The assassin you mentioned? And they think it's Aldrich?" Liesel asked, confused. "It . . . it doesn't fit what I—"

"No!" Nicklas snapped. "They know it wasn't Aldrich. They think the three officers surprised the assassin while he was waiting for Aldrich to walk by."

"Okay . . . and . . . why didn't they arrest him, or at least detain him?"

"That's unconfirmed, too, and I doubt we'll ever know the details, but whoever that man is, he managed to disable the three police officers in a matter of seconds. And without firing a single shot."

Liesel frowned. She'd been a Krav Maga practitioner for twelve years, attending as many classes as her busy schedule allowed. Three-on-one fights were notoriously difficult to win. Despite all her training, she didn't think she could neutralize three armed cops.

*And in seconds? That's just nuts.*

But something in what Nicklas had said didn't make sense.

"What do you mean by 'without firing a single shot'?" Liesel asked. "Didn't you say two officers were shot?"

"Yes. That part gets blurry. The officers who were shot were fired upon shortly after they were physically assaulted. Maybe the assassin thought they would stay unconscious for longer? I can't give you a clearer picture than that for now."

She appreciated being read in, which didn't happen often enough, in her opinion, but Nicklas wasn't sharing all this intel without a reason. In Liesel's relationship with her handlers, the intel usually flowed from New York to Berlin, not the other way around.

"And there's more," Nicklas said. "The attempted kidnapping of Aldrich's family ended in a bloodbath."

Liesel gasped. *Please, no. Not the kids!*

"Thankfully Aldrich's wife and three daughters are safe," Nicklas continued. "But four of the five kidnappers were shot dead. The fifth has been admitted to the ICU."

Liesel relaxed slightly, glad Aldrich's family was unscathed.

"The police killed them?" Liesel asked.

"That's where things get confusing. There were only five officers on duty in Zermatt at the time, and three of them were incapacitated, remember? The police dispatcher had to call in reinforcements from nearby towns. When the cops arrived, the gun battle was over."

*What?* This was getting weirder.

Liesel was aware that in Switzerland, despite its being one of the countries with the highest rates of gun ownership in the world, deaths from gun violence were minimal. Four dead bad guys, plus one more in the ICU, all of them shot without the police being involved, was unheard of.

"The firefight was over? I'm not following," she confessed. "If the police weren't there, who shot the abductors? Good Samaritans with guns?"

"Again, this is unconfirmed," her handler replied, "but someone showed up while the kidnappers were forcing Aldrich's family into a vehicle. That person fired two shots. One round neutralized the guy that's now in the ICU, the other blew another kidnapper's brains out."

"Jesus Christ," Liesel whispered to herself. "And the other three?"

"One of Aldrich's kids managed to get hold of a gun and fired at a bad guy, injuring him."

"Holy shit!"

"Then the person who shot the first two bad guys once again jumped into the fray by drilling a round into the side of the fourth abductor's head before finishing off the kidnapper the kid had injured."

Liesel shook her head in disbelief. "And the fifth?"

"The hotel is owned by a well-respected couple in their sixties. One of them fired a shotgun at the last kidnapper at very close range, hitting him in the chest."

"So, one of the owners killed a bad guy. Good."

"Yeah, maybe. Possibly."

"What do you mean?" Liesel asked. "The crook is dead or not?"

"Oh, he's dead now. But that crook, as you put it, was also hit through his mouth by a small caliber round. And my guess is that once they're done examining the bullet, their conclusion will be that it came from the same weapon that killed the three other abductors and sent the fifth to the intensive care unit."

"A mercy killing?" Liesel said, thinking out loud before she asked, "And you said that all of this is unconfirmed? Why is that?"

Nicklas seemed to hesitate for a moment. "All I can share with you is that German intelligence has a very good working relationship with the Swiss authorities. You get what I'm saying?"

"Of course," Liesel replied, though she didn't really understand.

Did the German spy agency and the Swiss police have such a fantastic bilateral relationship that the Swiss automatically shared everything they had on an investigation the moment the BND asked for it? And vice versa? Liesel didn't think so. The odds were higher that her organization had broken into Switzerland's telecommunication systems and her service was now spying on them.

"Good. Then there are two things I need from you," Nicklas said.

Liesel took a deep breath. She was about to learn why her handler had shared all these insights with her.

"A report you filed mentioned you'd seen Leonard Aldrich and Ambassador Claus Eichberg share a table during a charity event held by your firm," he said. "I'd like you to dig further into the kind of relationship they had, if any."

Liesel winced. Spying on German citizens was strictly verboten.

"Let me be crystal clear about this, Poker. We are not, I repeat, we are not ordering you in any way, shape, or form to spy on Ambassador Eichberg or any of his family members. To do so would be against German laws. You understand?"

"I do. I'd never—"

"Good! As long as we understand each other."

Ambassador Eichberg was one of her country's top diplomats, and he had a direct connection to the German chancellor. Regardless of what Nicklas had just said, what he was asking of her was borderline illegal.

*And he fucking knows it!*

*If anything goes wrong, I'll be the one they throw to the wolves.*

*Or push in front of a bus . . .*

Suddenly, Liesel wasn't so sure becoming a NOC operative had been a good career choice. In order not to end up in a German—or American—prison, she'd have to be very vigilant.

"While I'm digging into Aldrich, is there something in particular I should be on the lookout for?" Liesel asked.

"Here's the deal. We suspect Edge Robots is playing with us and has somehow found out we tried to hack into their system."

Liesel's face turned red. "What?"

"Relax. I said 'we suspect,' not 'we know.' With that said, I believe you should keep in mind that the possibility exists that Rafael Ribeiro knows you broke into his phone."

That was unfortunate, but she could deal with that. Ribeiro knew her firm often colored outside the lines. That's why they were doing business together, after all. Liesel was a very good liar, and she often impressed herself with the quality of the bullshit she came up with on the fly. She'd be okay.

"Anyhow," Nicklas continued, "the techies told me that before our sniffer program got shown the door and thrust into what we *think* is a never-ending loop of bogus data points, it was able to extract a contact list from Ribeiro's phone."

"Let me guess," Liesel said, "Ambassador Eichberg's number was on it."

"No, not the ambassador's number," Nicklas corrected her. "His wife's. Ribeiro had the private contact information of Catharina Eichberg."

# CHAPTER THIRTY-FOUR

*New York, New York*

Liesel had crossed paths with Catharina Eichberg only once, but like her much older husband, Catharina was hard to forget and easy to spot in a crowd. Liesel had bumped into the couple as they were exiting a Brazilian steak house on Fifty-Third Street. Not surprisingly, the ambassador hadn't recognized Liesel, but Catharina, smartly dressed in a fancy summer dress that clung to her curves like a second skin, had looked at her, studying Liesel in a brief perusal from head to toe, as if she was deciding whether she should feel threatened by her. Liesel, with her humidity-flattened hair and sweaty jogging attire, hadn't warranted more than a three-second look before being dismissed.

Liesel remembered thinking at the time that not too many women, including her, could pull off carrying herself with the gait befitting a princess like Catharina did. She was an elegant, beautiful woman with an olive complexion and dark shining eyes.

But how was she connected to Rafael Ribeiro?

"They could be friends," she said to Nicklas.

"I'm sure of it," her handler agreed. "In fact, by the number of text messages they've sent to each other in the last four days, they're probably best friends, or lovers."

*Yeah, I can see how he could be attracted to her. Most men would be.*

"How many texts are we talking about?" she asked.

"More than one hundred messages were sent from or received by Ribeiro's phone."

"Are we able to read them?"

"I'm afraid not," Nicklas replied. "The moment the raw data was extracted, it became gibberish. The techies are working on it, but they aren't hopeful."

"I admit this sounds strange, but there could be a simple explanation for this," Liesel offered.

"I pray to God there is."

Nicklas didn't need to say it out loud. Liesel understood the stakes. If Edge Robots was indeed a front company for Chinese intelligence and Ribeiro one of their assets, it would put Ambassador Eichberg in a delicate, maybe even untenable, position if it became known that his wife had a personal relationship with Ribeiro, as innocent—or not—as the relationship might be.

At these levels of government, appearances were everything.

"You said there were two things you wanted me to do," Liesel said. "What's the second one?"

"I need you to tell me where Caspian Anderson is."

Liesel sat straighter in her chair. This inquiry had come so far out of left field that Liesel wondered if she hadn't misheard. *Caspian* and *Anderson* were the two words she had least expected to hear coming out of her handler's mouth. Seconds ago, they'd been talking about a potential threat to the national security of Germany, and now Nicklas wanted to talk about . . . Caspian?

"Why in the world would you need to know where Caspian is?" she asked, realizing as she said the words that her mind had shifted from shock and disbelief to actual defiance.

"I'm sorry?" Nicklas said, clearly challenging her.

*Careful, Liesel,* she warned herself, baffled at how protective of Caspian she was.

"In Switzerland. Geneva, to be more precise," she said. "It's a work thing. I reported it."

"You did," Nicklas said. "When was the last time you talked to him?"

For some reason, she was suddenly uncomfortable sharing personal info about Caspian with her handler. This was a new feeling for her. And it felt weird. Why did she care? She shouldn't.

*Caspian is just a job, right?* she asked herself, although she knew it wasn't the case.

"A while," Liesel said.

"The conference he attended ended five days ago," Nicklas said, somewhat accusingly. "Did you know that?"

"Yes, I did," Liesel said. Then, feeling the need to defend Caspian, she added, "He's taking some personal time to go skiing. Honestly, I fail to see how this is of any interest to you. Aren't you the one who told me I could end the relationship if I wanted to?"

"Do you want to?"

Liesel hesitated, unsure how to answer the question. "I thought I did," she said after a moment, "but I'm not so sure anymore. Again, why does it matter?"

Instead of answering her question, Nicklas asked one of his own.

"Two months ago, you mentioned in a report that Caspian went on another work trip. You remember that?"

"Yes, of course. He went to Kowloon to—"

"I know what's in your report, Poker," Nicklas cut in. "And what about last November?"

"If you know the damn reports so well, why do—"

"He was in Lagos, Portugal. And four months prior to that?"

"Where in hell are you going with this?" Liesel asked, no longer caring if her annoyance with her handler was seeping through. She wanted him to know she was about done with his bullshit. "What is it that you're not telling me? Because if there's a point to all this, I sure would like to know what it is."

"Four months before his trip to Portugal, Caspian was in Vancouver."

"I'm about to hang up," Liesel said, meaning it.

"Does the name Elias ring any bells?"

"Who? Elias? No, I never heard that name before," Liesel said, beginning to wonder if her handler had lost his mind. Nicklas had stopped making sense and jumped from one topic to the other.

*Maybe the pressure is too much for him?*

Liesel didn't know what had pushed Nicklas into transitioning from being an undercover asset to a case officer. She'd never asked him, and he'd never shared, but she knew mental breakdowns were common in her profession. Case officers weren't in constant danger, but the pressure was still enormous.

When Nicklas started to speak again, though, Liesel knew her handler hadn't lost his mind.

But she almost did.

# CHAPTER THIRTY-FIVE

*Andorra la Vella, Andorra*

Ambassador Claus Eichberg sat across from Bilal Amirouche, a former general in the Algerian army who still yielded plenty of influence in the former French colony. They were the only two people seated at a dining table that could easily accommodate twenty. Catharina and Amirouche's wife, a model and a former Miss Namibia, had left the property minutes ago and were on their way for what Eichberg had been told was a shopping spree.

Bilal Amirouche was of medium height, but stockily built. He was bald as an egg, and he had a large goatee shot through with streaks of white and gray and a set of ivory-colored teeth Eichberg thought was too big for his small mouth.

While Amirouche was well liked and a popular dining guest among the influential people of his adopted country—his jovial manner and easy smile were quick to put people at ease—a close observer would detect something about the former general's dark eyes that might contradict their first impression.

Eichberg and Amirouche had known each other for a long time and had been doing business together for over two decades, since the time Amirouche was a muqaddam—or lieutenant colonel—in the 104th Operational Maneuvers Regiments, an elite unit within the Algerian Land Forces.

But now, Eichberg was forced to admit that their friendship—though the term *business arrangement* was probably more accurate—was under a great deal of pressure.

Last week, in the port city of Durrës, Albania, a shipment of ten women and four children coming from Haiti had been pinched from under the noses of a corrupt UN team answering to Eichberg. After cutting the throats of the three UN workers on the docks, a local criminal group had moved the cargo to Tirana, Albania's vibrant capital city, and had gotten themselves intercepted by a team from RENEA, Albania's leading counterterrorist organization.

The firefight that had ensued hadn't lasted long, with the RENEA team killing all but one of the six criminals. When the container in which the cargo was secured was finally opened by the police, all fourteen souls inside were dead. Asphyxiated.

While most people wouldn't dare place a monetary value on a human life, Eichberg had no such quandary. The death of these ten women and four children had incurred him a net loss of approximately €900,000.

Even more problematic was the warning he'd received from Amirouche, who had acted as the broker for that deal. Amirouche's clients had been upset when he hadn't been able to deliver the promised goods and had threatened to stop their business dealings with him.

"There are plenty of other people I could go to, Claus," Amirouche had said at the time. "But I chose you. Don't make me look bad ever again."

To make amends to Amirouche, and to replenish his own pockets, Eichberg had come up with an ambitious plan. He would kill two birds with one stone. He would eliminate Leonard Aldrich, and he would deliver the man's wife and children to Amirouche's clients.

And it had almost worked.

But in the business he was in, almost wasn't good enough.

Eichberg had no idea what had gone wrong.

"You've put us in a very difficult position, *mon ami*," Amirouche said, pointing a steak knife at Eichberg's chest. "*Très difficile.*"

"I'd love to apologize to you, Bilal, but I wouldn't know what to apologize for," Eichberg said. "I'm baffled as to what happened in Zermatt. If I could only—"

Amirouche interrupted Eichberg by raising his hand and holding a finger to his lips in a shushing gesture. "I'm hungry," the former general said.

Two waiters arrived at the table. One was carrying a silver tray of hors d'oeuvres filled with olive tapenade, stuffed mushrooms, and maaqouda—a type of potato fritter—while the other had four huge lobsters split in half. The waiters left the dishes on the table, but in a way that made them accessible only to Amirouche, who immediately tossed a couple of the mushrooms in his mouth.

One of the waiters came back for the wine service, but only poured a little red wine—a Château Ausone Grand Cru 2012—into Amirouche's glass. The former general shook his head and signaled he wasn't interested in tasting it.

"There's no need for that. The bottle is good," he said in French.

As the waiter poured a more generous amount, Eichberg thought that the only thing waiter-ish about the man was the way he was dressed—black pants, black shoes, and a white shirt. Everything else about him—his crew cut, his athletic frame, and the pistol holstered at his waist—screamed military.

"Should I pour a glass for your guest?" the waiter asked Amirouche in the same language.

Amirouche waved his hand. "No. Just water."

Eichberg was starting to get annoyed, but he was in no position to complain. This was Amirouche's domain.

He and Catharina had arrived in Andorra feeling like conquerors, convinced the operation in Zermatt had gone without a hitch. Amirouche hadn't been there at the time, apparently busy with other matters, but his staff, informed in advance of their arrival, had welcomed them. Although Catharina and Eichberg had access to most of Amirouche's gigantic property—a luxurious estate perched high in the Andorran mountains—and the house's staff were courteous enough with them, Eichberg quickly realized that his and Catharina's access to the internet had been restricted and that he wasn't allowed to step outside the property's borders.

It wasn't until two hours ago that Eichberg had learned about the debacle in Zermatt. As Amirouche continued to munch on the appetizers, Eichberg was restless to get the conversation started.

The waiters returned, this time bringing what Eichberg assumed were the mains. The plates were covered with silver cloches. The waiters removed the cloches, and Eichberg noted that the piece of meat—if it even was meat—on his plate didn't look anything like the perfectly cooked filet mignon in front of Amirouche.

"Bon appétit!" Amirouche said, reaching for two pieces of lobster.

While a wicked smell emanated from whatever was on Eichberg's plate, Amirouche's steak was tender enough that the former general only needed to use his fork to cut through it. Amirouche took his time chewing, his eyes never leaving Eichberg. After he'd swallowed, he emptied his wineglass in one gulp and motioned for his waiter to pour some more.

"You're not hungry?" Amirouche asked.

"I lost my appetite," Eichberg replied.

"Don't be disrespectful, Claus. Being impolite doesn't suit you. And it's a special treat. Just for you."

Eichberg forced a smile. Whatever Amirouche's chef had cooked for him, it wasn't beef. It wasn't even the same color.

Eichberg sighed and looked at Amirouche. "You've made your point."

"Not yet."

Amirouche leaned forward, grabbed a small porcelain carafe, and poured some thick grayish sauce all over Eichberg's plate.

"You want to know what happened in Zermatt? Eat your fucking food."

The meat was hard, gray, and dry, and tasted like a discarded truck's tire with gravy. It was revolting, but it was clear that the former general wouldn't say a word about what had taken place in Switzerland before Eichberg had eaten it all. Midway through, a sickening thought crossed Eichberg's mind, and he immediately began to feel unwell.

*What am I eating?*

He looked at Amirouche, a thin film of perspiration building on his forehead. The former general was fixing him with a hard stare.

"You're not done," Amirouche warned him.

By the time he finished his plate, Eichberg felt nauseous, and sweat had also now broken out on the back of his neck. He didn't dare ask what he had just been fed. He didn't want to know.

Amirouche owned him. Of that Eichberg had no doubt. In fact, he'd known since the general had introduced him to Catharina, an officer for ABIN—Brazil's intelligence agency—six years ago. What had started as a loose affiliation between Amirouche, Brazil's spy agency—which was really just a puppet for the Chinese MSS—and Eichberg, then the United Nations high commissioner for human rights, had morphed into a business agreement where Eichberg was no longer pulling the strings. At some point, Amirouche had turned the tables on him. Still, his understanding with Amirouche and ABIN had made Eichberg a very wealthy man, and Catharina had been a decent side benefit to their agreement. You didn't get to become as rich as he was on a politician's salary or by walking the straight and narrow.

Eichberg had had no regrets. Until now.

Amirouche's dark eyes were still on him. A crooked smile had materialized at the corner of his mouth.

"*Mon cher ami*, aren't you curious to learn what you ate?" Amirouche asked.

Eichberg swallowed hard. It didn't matter if he said no. Amirouche was going to tell him anyway. He closed his eyes, fearing the worst.

"My chef cooked for you a Namibian warthog anus," Amirouche said, beaming at Eichberg. "A true delicacy from my wife's country of birth."

It took a few seconds for Eichberg's brain to register what Amirouche had said.

"What?"

"I'm no monster, Claus, but I needed to know you were still committed."

Eichberg reminded himself to stay calm. Losing his temper would do him no good. He needed to keep his mind sharp.

"I'm committed."

Amirouche nodded and poured some wine for Eichberg, who until now had only been allowed half a glass of water.

"Four of the six members of your team were wiped out in Zermatt," Amirouche said. "One is at the hospital in Visp, but thankfully the leader, who is our best man, survived and escaped."

Eichberg was immediately worried about the man who had been admitted to the hospital. Not because he cared about his health but because he wasn't dead.

"I know what you're thinking," Amirouche said. "But you shouldn't worry. The man at the hospital is no longer a threat."

"He died?"

Amirouche took a sip of wine and shook his head. "No. But leave it to me. If it becomes necessary to send someone, I will."

"And the team leader?"

"He made contact. He isn't sure what hit them. He thinks it could be the work of a single man."

"One man? No, that's impossible," Eichberg said. "This team is good. They never let us down."

"This team *was* good," Amirouche said, correcting him. "They're no longer operational. And there's one more thing I haven't mentioned yet. More bad news, I'm afraid."

Eichberg winced, not only because he was anxious about the additional bad news but because his stomach growled with pain and his shirt collar, damp with sweat, seemed to have gotten tighter. Eichberg loosened his tie, unbuttoned the top button of his shirt, and used his cloth napkin to wipe his forehead.

"What is it?" he asked.

"I haven't heard anything from the two UN contractors in Zermatt. The ones who were supposed to escort Aldrich's family to our doctor. Do they know anything about me?"

"They don't even know about me, Bilal, so they certainly don't know about you," Eichberg said.

"You sure?"

"Yes!"

Amirouche stared at him for a long moment.

"All right," he finally said. "If they don't make contact by tomorrow, I'll have to assume the worst. Give me the contact details of the person who handles them."

There was no point in arguing with the former general. The man was right. The person Eichberg employed at the UN to manage the contractors was high enough in the organization that he would be offered a deal in exchange for his testimony. A testimony that could help put Eichberg in prison for a very long time.

"What else?" Eichberg asked.

"The buyer who wanted the eight kidneys, the heart, and the two lungs is a high-ranking officer of the SVR," Amirouche said. "And he's asking for retribution."

Eichberg swore. He disliked the SVR, Russia's foreign intelligence service. They were a bunch of unsophisticated, violent thugs.

"Okay. I'll figure something out. I'll get him what he needs. Kidneys aren't that difficult to—"

"No, my friend," Amirouche said, shaking his finger at Eichberg. "It's too late for that. The client no longer needs them. The heart was for his niece, and she died yesterday."

Eichberg's heart sank even deeper. He didn't care about the dead girl, but he knew the Russian would demand hell. Eichberg felt as if he had aged an extra decade in the last hour.

"It's not even my damn fault!" Eichberg shouted, slamming his fist on the table.

Amirouche frowned from across the table. "Are you done?"

Eichberg took a long, deep breath, but it didn't help. He still felt like shit, which kind of made sense, since he'd just eaten a warthog's anus.

"What does he want?" he said.

"Access."

Eichberg raised an eyebrow. "Access? To whom?"

"To someone in the United States who can replace Leonard Aldrich," the former general said. "And by the way, they're ticked off that he's dead."

"I had no choice, Bilal. He was going to release a dossier about our business dealings in Haiti," Eichberg said. "I'm not sure how Aldrich found out, but he did."

"I understand Aldrich represented a danger to you, but Chinese intelligence trusted him. And now, that side business of yours, as lucrative as it is, made them . . . unhappy. And so are the Russians."

Eichberg tensed. "Please tell me you didn't say it was us who—"

"You mean that it was *you* who had Aldrich killed?" Amirouche said. "Of course not. They don't know about these . . . extracurricular dealings of yours."

"You're involved too," Eichberg said.

"I'm merely a broker, Claus. I find people who want to buy what you're selling. I'm a facilitator of sorts. Nothing more."

They both knew this wasn't true, but Eichberg had no leverage.

"Why does your SVR client need access to an American financial fixer?" he asked.

"As I'm sure you've noticed, the Russians and the Chinese are getting along well these days. I can only assume the MSS talked to the SVR about the great work you've been doing for them through the Brazilians. And they want in."

"It's not that easy," Eichberg said. "It took years for the Chinese to build their network in the United States."

"I'm told the Russians have teams in place, and there are half a dozen start-ups actively looking for funds. The groundwork is done, Claus. They just need to lock in the right investment funds."

"So, they've been searching for a while, then?" Eichberg asked.

Amirouche shrugged. "I don't have the answer to that. But what I do know is that the Russians were about to make Aldrich a business proposal."

Eichberg thought about it for a moment. Russia's economy was in total freefall due to all the severe sanctions imposed on it by the West. As powerful, violent, and deranged as he was, the Russian president wouldn't be able to hang on to power for much longer if his country's economy continued its downward spiral. One way to stop these sanctions would be to influence the elected decision-makers in the American Congress and Senate.

American decision-makers were no different from their counterparts in other countries: they either voted with their wallets—which included straight-up bribery—or through coercion. If the Russian SVR could get their grip on a few influential members of those two chambers, it would be a major coup for the Kremlin and could eventually turn the tide for Russia's embattled economy.

In recent years, though, it had become harder to buy an American senator or a congressman through campaign donations. Sexual scandals were also a thing of the past. A large portion of the American electorate no longer cared about the sexual orientation of their politicians. That in itself had been a major blow to foreign agents trying to blackmail their way into a politician's decision process.

But there were still ways one could get one's hands on high-ranking members of the American political establishment. One just had to know how.

*And I do.*

Eichberg conceded that his number of solid connections to fund managers with whom the top politicians were invested wasn't as impressive as Aldrich's, but he had a few. If he could find a way to position himself as Aldrich's replacement, Eichberg could become a power broker in his own right, which in turn would go a long way in guaranteeing his safety. People tended not to want to kill you when you provided them with an essential service.

He would fly back to New York with Catharina in the morning and set the wheels in motion.

"The Russians are brutes, but they're not stupid," Amirouche reminded him. "They'll eventually figure out what happened to Aldrich if you give them time to investigate. If I were you, I'd fly home and start working on the problem."

Eichberg didn't feel the need to share with Amirouche that he'd already found a solution.

"Buy me a couple of weeks," Eichberg said. "I'll get them someone."

"Don't make me regret this, Claus. We've known each other for a long time, but my patience has its limits. Do you understand?"

"Of course."

"And with that we come to our other arrangement. Do I need to remind you that you aren't the only supplier I can go to?"

"I might not be the only supplier you have on your roster, Bilal, but who else has the UN secretary-general or the German chancellor on speed dial?" Eichberg replied, his self-assurance returning.

Amirouche laughed, but it only lasted an instant. Then he grew serious again. "They don't. But you better get your things in order, because having these people on your speed dial won't be enough to keep you alive if you keep fucking up."

# CHAPTER THIRTY-SIX

*Zermatt, Switzerland*

Caspian woke up. There was a fuzzy figure hovering over him. He tried to sit up but couldn't. His body didn't respond. He could feel a cold compress on his forehead.

"Take it easy, Elias," a woman whispered in his ear as she gently stroked his hair. "I'll be here when you wake up. Now rest, my love."

Caspian felt a small pinch in his right arm.

*My . . . love? Am I dreaming?*

*Liesel was here, in Zermatt?*

*No. She can't be.*

Caspian rolled his head toward the sound of the woman's voice. He blinked a few times, trying to bring the woman into focus. She was in her mid- to late thirties and had shoulder-length brown hair, devilish tawny eyes, and a beautiful, easy smile. And her name was Amy.

Caspian knew her well. *Very* well, some people might say. They had trained together at the Onyx facility in Montana, and, for a while, prior to her abrupt departure, they had had a little fling together.

Caspian fought to keep his eyes open, but his mind was numbing. He felt himself drifting away. Amy's face began to fade, replaced by the rolling hills and flat grass-covered valleys of Montana. The place where it had all started.

———

Though Caspian wouldn't learn this until he had made it through the long, grueling pipeline Onyx had set up to train its assets, Onyx had had an eye on him since he was in college pursuing a bachelor's degree in applied languages. Caspian, an athletic, straight-A student who had earned a black belt in Brazilian jujitsu, was fluent in five languages.

Driven from a very young age by his two loving parents to be the best he could be in everything he did, Caspian had always wanted to pursue a career in federal law enforcement, preferably with the Federal Bureau of Investigation.

During his senior year in college, he had applied to the FBI, the Department of Homeland Security, the Drug Enforcement Administration, the Secret Service, the National Security Agency, and even the CIA. It was DHS who had come knocking.

After an initial stint of six months at the Federal Law Enforcement Training Center in Glynco, Georgia, where he successfully completed the Criminal Investigator Training Program and the Homeland Security Investigations Special Agent Training with flying colors, Caspian was sent to the HSI—Homeland Security Investigations—office in Washington, DC, for six weeks of field training. Then one day, and without notice, he was pulled from his bed by an HSI Special Response Team. Unaware this was all part of his training, Caspian had fought back, incapacitating three SRT members before being taken down and gagged. With his hands tied behind his back and a black cloth bag thrown over his head, Caspian was hurled into the back of a panel van and driven to a private airfield outside DC. From there, he was flown to a training facility somewhere in Montana.

There were nine other candidates with him in the unheated wooden barracks. Three of the candidates were females; the others were males. It didn't take long for Caspian to realize that, like him, they had no freaking idea why they were there. A quick inspection of the barracks confirmed there was no hot water and no electricity. The interior was occupied by half a dozen aluminum bunk beds with thin, dirty mattresses. Even bedsheets and pillows were a luxury the candidates weren't entitled to.

The next morning, as the ten candidates stood smartly at attention, Laura had made her first appearance.

"As HSI special agents of the International Operations Division, your job is to identify and combat transnational criminal and terrorist organizations before they threaten our country," Laura said as a cluster of hungry mosquitoes attacked Caspian's neck and arms.

"Most agents do so by assisting foreign governments in collecting the necessary evidence to prosecute these organizations. Don't get me wrong, folks, what they do is important work. Vital. But sometimes it's not enough. Sometimes arresting the head of a crime syndicate or throwing a terror cell leader behind bars at a black site aren't the right solutions to a specific problem. I'm here to offer you a chance to make a real difference."

Then Laura warned them that the road to join her team wasn't easy, and that based on previous groups, most of them, maybe even all of them, would quit within a week. There was no shame in that. Despite the best efforts of her office's psychologists to select and bring in the right candidates, the type of work she offered wasn't suited for everyone.

"What's the actual job, if you don't mind me asking?" the candidate next to Caspian had asked.

"I'm afraid I'm not at liberty to share that with you until you've signed the nondisclosure agreement," Laura had replied. "And it's a lengthy one. But I'll be honest with you all, it's perilous work, and you need to volunteer for it. If you think the way you've been treated in the last twenty-four hours was harsh, then I suggest you leave this place at once."

Nobody had.

They were all given thirty minutes to read through the nondisclosure agreement and sign it. Two candidates refused to do so. They were gone the next hour.

For Caspian and the remaining seven candidates, the training started the next morning. There were small-arms training, memory exercises, and hand-to-hand combat courses, among other types of instruction. The small cadre of instructors pushed them from dawn to late at night for fourteen straight days, and with just enough food and water for them not to pass out. At the end, only four bruised, exhausted candidates remained, one of them Caspian. Another was a woman from Arizona named Amy. While their relationship began as something purely physical, a way to deal with the pressure and stress of the training, Caspian could see Amy wasn't completely satisfied with the arrangement. He wasn't, either, but the training regimen was simply too intense to consider anything else.

The remaining candidates were given five days to rest and heal their wounds. Caspian and Amy spent three of those nights together in a quaint, cozy bed-and-breakfast.

Then the first phase of the real training began. During the next eight months, Caspian was schooled in demolition, marksmanship, individual and small-unit tactics, combat medicine, and tactical communications. All of it had come easily to him. He felt as if he had finally found his true calling.

The second phase of training was less physical. Weeks were spent learning the etiquettes of foreign cultures, lock-picking skills, the art of disguise, and, most important of all, surveillance and countersurveillance techniques. At the end of that phase, only Caspian and another candidate were left standing. The two others, one of them being Amy, had failed to meet the high standards required to pass the surveillance segment of the training. Though he'd been sad—and somewhat surprised—to see her go, Caspian had quickly forgotten her.

Laura, who Caspian hadn't seen in months, had come to congratulate him and the other candidate in person. It was then that she had first spoken to them about Onyx and the true nature of their work.

It had only confirmed what Caspian had already figured out.

He was to become an assassin.

"The rationale behind Onyx's creation is that our enemies aren't playing by the rules, so why the hell should we?" Laura had said.

The hardest, most brutal, and sometimes emotionally draining phase of training had come next.

"We can teach anyone how to kill. That's the easy part," an instructor had said to Caspian at the beginning of the third phase. "But killing someone without being seen or caught is an art. That's why Onyx doesn't recruit from Special Forces or Navy SEALs. These guys are great at what they do, and they play an important role, but the moment you take them out of a war zone, they have a hard time blending in.

"They're blunt instruments," the instructor had explained. "They break stuff. They make noise. But you won't. Once I'm done with you, you'll know how to kill someone with a feather in the middle of a crowded ballroom without anyone noticing. I'll give you the greatest of gifts: I'll teach you how to become invisible."

And that he did. The instructor—a man with sensitive features, calm eyes, and the aloof demeanor of someone who didn't care—had taught him how to become unremarkable, how to disappear, and Caspian had mastered the skill better than any trainee before him.

Or at least, that's what he'd been told.

———

When Caspian woke up, his throbbing headache was gone.

"Good, you're awake," Amy said, beaming at him, the two charming dimples that had once made his pulse quicken revealing themselves. "The drugs are starting to wear off, but you're still feeling the effect of the muscle relaxant I injected you with. Your movements will be restricted for another ten, maybe fifteen minutes. It's completely normal, so don't panic."

Caspian couldn't reply. His throat was too dry, and his mouth tasted like the bottom of an old garbage can, or at least what he thought the bottom of an old garbage can would taste like.

Amy must have seen him struggling to speak, because she reached behind her for a glass filled with ice chips.

"Open your mouth," she said. "These will help."

She placed a couple of chips in his mouth. The ice melted on his tongue, and the cold water felt good against his parched throat.

"Thanks, Amy from Arizona," Caspian said, after swallowing the cold water.

"I'm happy to see you remember me," she said with a radiant smile.

"You're a hard woman to forget."

Amy's eyes sparkled, and her grin grew even wider. "I'm sure women say the same about you all the time."

"Not really," Caspian said. "I'm apparently boring."

Like a bolt of lightning on a dark, hot summer night, a flash of anger cut across Amy's face; then her smile returned.

"Laura sent you?" Caspian asked, studying Amy's face.

"When I got here, I thought you were dead, and not only because you stank," Amy said, forcing a laugh. Her dimples were still there, but Caspian could see her smile was strained. Amy was concerned.

"In all seriousness, you weren't a pretty sight," she continued. "You were passed out, your pulse was weak, and you had lost a considerable amount of blood. What worried me the most, though, was what seemed to be the beginning of a serious infection in your left shoulder. It's better now, but I had to clean the wound, remove the burnt clothing the bullet had forced into it, and give you antibiotics through an IV. Pills would have taken too long."

"How long was I out for?" Caspian asked, as Amy checked his wound.

"I'd say you were out for about twenty-four hours when I got to you. And that was two days ago. You've been drifting in and out of consciousness since then. I've kept you nourished, changed your dressings, and administered the antibiotics at the right time, but it was your body that did most of the work. Good thing you've kept yourself in decent shape."

"Decent?"

"Okay, more than decent," she said.

"Thank you," Caspian said, meaning it. "How . . . how did you get here?"

"That was the fun part," Amy said, sitting down close to him, her thigh touching his side. "Zermatt was almost closed off for twenty-four hours, so I had to think this through. Have you skied on the Italian side? Because if you haven't, it's worth the extra cost. I'd be happy to show you around sometime, you know?"

Amy's eyes were burning with a rare intensity, and they were locked on him. Caspian understood this wasn't a rhetorical question; she actually expected him to answer.

"Sure," he said, without much conviction.

Caspian's brain was set to survival mode. Skiing in Italy with Amy wasn't even on his radar. He doubted it ever would be.

Amy grinned at him and didn't seem to read too much into his one-word reply.

"Did you know the Italians have heated seats on their chairlifts?" she asked. "It's fantastic. You'll love it."

Caspian's head was still fuzzy, and it took him a second to realize Amy had skied her way into the village. She had crossed into Switzerland using the slope that linked the Cervinia ski resort to Zermatt.

*Smart move.*

They didn't talk for a few minutes as Caspian let Amy do her thing. After she was done cleaning his wound, she used a small mirror to show him the work she had performed on his left shoulder and right triceps while he was passed out.

Amy had done a good job with the stitches. The wound on his shoulder was still red and warm, but the antibiotics had worked as advertised and stopped the burgeoning infection from getting worse. And, as an added bonus, no green pus was oozing out.

"I'm glad you're here," Caspian said. "I can't thank you enough for coming."

"You and me . . . we've been through a lot together. And I know you would have done the same for me, right?" she asked, gently placing a hand on his forearm.

"Of course," he said, a weird feeling creeping inside him.

"And coming here gave me the opportunity to see the famed Matterhorn," she said with a wink. "My first time."

Caspian hadn't seen Amy in ten years, and he found it strange that she was being so familiar with him. Yes, they'd had a few good months together during training, but it was a long time ago, and, in the end, they had both agreed that it had been nothing more than a way to release some steam from the massive pressure they'd been under.

"Listen, Amy, I have to ask—"

"Why did Laura send me, right?" Amy said, reading him correctly.

He nodded. "I didn't think you were still with . . . you know, with us," Caspian said, not sure how much Laura had shared about Onyx with Amy.

"Right. Well, I'm not an operator, if that's what you mean," Amy replied. "But yeah, I'm with Onyx too."

"And . . . in what capacity?" he asked.

"Well . . . despite my obvious shortcomings during training, Laura figured I could still be of some value to the program. You might not remember this, but I was a registered nurse before I applied to Homeland. I was about to sign my release documents and some additional NDAs when Laura asked me if I'd like to stay on and become a doctor."

"Obviously you accepted," Caspian said.

"It was an offer too good to pass up," Amy said. "Who says no to med school when someone else is footing the bill?"

"Right."

"The rest is history, as they say," Amy continued. "I've been helping Onyx operators like you for the last four years."

Caspian nodded. Was it possible he'd been too quick in judging Laura's response to his plea for medical assistance? Laura had found a way to send help to him without breaking his cover or putting him in additional danger.

"I'll have to extend my thanks to Laura, then," Caspian said.

"It would have been a shame to let you die after what you've done," Amy said.

"What I've done?"

"Laura knows it was you at Le Clarion. She's beyond pissed, by the way."

"Oh. That. I couldn't—"

"Hey," Amy said, cutting him off as she began to stroke his hair. "You don't need to justify yourself to me. Like ever, okay? For what it's worth, I would have done the same thing. But what I think won't help you with Laura, I'm afraid."

"It will be fine," Caspian said.

He was getting more and more uncomfortable at how Amy seemed to continually invade his private space.

"I . . . I think I'm done," he added.

Amy cocked her head sideways and removed her hand from his hair.

"What do you mean?" she asked.

"You said you've been doing this for four years, right? So, tell me this, how many operatives like me have you helped during that time?"

Amy's dimples vanished, and her eyes turned cold. "I don't think that's something Laura would—"

"What?" Caspian said, cutting her off. "Not a statistic she'd like me to know?"

"Something like that, yeah," Amy said.

"I've been doing this for ten years," Caspian said. "And I'm starting to think there might be something else for me out there, you know?"

Amy's smile returned, curiosity in her eyes. "Okay, I'll play," she said, once again invading his space by leaning toward him. "Like what? Tell me what's out there that will satisfy a man like you as much as what you're doing now?"

"I'd like to patch things up with Liesel—"

"Liezzel? Who the fuck's that?" Amy asked, straightening back up.

Caspian cocked a challenging eyebrow at her and said, "Her name's Liesel, and don't tell me Onyx isn't keeping tabs on me, because I'm calling bullshit."

"I haven't been read into your personal life, Caspian," Amy said bluntly. "Who is she?"

Although her last sentence made her sound like a jealous girlfriend, Caspian knew it couldn't be the case. They hadn't been together for ten years, for goodness' sake.

No, it had to be because Amy had been genuinely taken aback by his wish to leave Onyx and find something else to do with his life. If Caspian had been in Amy's shoes and had failed to graduate from the Onyx training pipeline, he, too, might have been curious about why someone who had sacrificed so much to live this life now wanted to quit it.

Although her demeanor today raised some questions, Caspian had seen what Amy was capable of during training. Amy might be lovely to look at, but seeing her solely as eye candy would be a grave mistake. She was a tough woman, a true winner, and an overachiever. No one could finish the punishing selection course they had been through without possessing an iron will. In Caspian's mind, it was Amy who had taken the role of leader during that very first portion of their collective train-ing. She'd been the one to rise to the top and help the other candidates navigate the two-week selection course.

During the next phase of training, Caspian remembered thinking that it was as if Amy had gone through the training before. She'd been a natural. And yet, to his surprise, she'd been deemed not good enough to progress to the final stage of training, despite having given her all. Amy hadn't been able to become a field asset, but she had had a taste of what that life could be.

*And she has probably never wanted something as bad as to live that life.*

"Caspian," Amy said urgently, bringing him back to the here and now. "I want to know who Lisa is?"

"Her name's Liesel, not Lisa," Caspian replied, aware he was correcting her for the second time. "She's someone I care about very much."

"Your girlfriend, then?" Amy said, smoothing her hair.

"Yes. For now."

"What does that mean, 'for now'?" Amy asked, making air quotes.

"I . . . I don't know."

Amy's face froze in scorn. "You're certainly not thinking about getting married and having kids, are you?"

"I mean . . . maybe?"

"Wow. Honestly, Caspian, that's the last thing I expected from you," she said, with a dismissiveness that Caspian found disconcerting.

"Really? Why is that? You haven't seen me in ten years. How could you possibly know what I want? Don't you have someone you share your—"

"None of your business," Amy hissed, her eyes turning dark.

*Okay . . . clearly a sensitive subject.*

Amy raised her hands, and a tiny smile appeared at the corners of her lips.

"I'm sorry about that," she said, her tone matching the newfound softness in her eyes. "I didn't mean it the way it came out. I've been under some stress recently, and sometimes I let it get to me. And I've been very—almost over-the-top—inquisitorial with you, so you had every right to push back and ask me the same questions I did. It wasn't fair of me to snap at you."

Caspian managed to manufacture a smile. "There's no need for an apology. I'm not sure if I'd still be alive if you hadn't shown up. In my book, Amy, I owe you."

Amy took a deep breath and let it out in a loud sigh, as if what he had just told her had brought her enormous relief.

"Okay, so let's say you do get out, and you marry that woman of yours. Then what?" she asked. "How would you make a living?"

"The truth? I'm not sure," Caspian admitted with a chuckle. "I haven't thought this through just yet."

"Yeah, I get that, but you've clearly given it some consideration. Please tell me you're not thinking about joining one of our competitors?"

Caspian's eyes narrowed. "A competitor? You mean the CIA?"

"Yes, the CIA," Amy said. "Or the private sector."

"I'm not a gun for hire, Amy," Caspian said, his voice stern. "Everything I've ever done was—"

"Of course! I know that," Amy said, cutting him off. "I'm just glad to hear you say it."

They remained silent for a few minutes; then Caspian cleared his throat and said, "You know, there's a fishing camp I like in Maine—"

"A fishing camp?" Amy asked, her dimples back on full display.

Caspian closed his eyes and smiled as he let his mind transport him back to the fishing trips he'd taken with his dad, which were some of his best childhood memories.

"I'm originally from Maine, and a few hours' drive from my parents' house there's that fishing camp my dad used to take me to during the school breaks. It's on Nahmakanta Lake. You know the one I'm talking about?"

"I'm from Arizona, remember?"

"Right. Anyway, it's a beautiful lake, surrounded by mountains and forests, and the perfect spot to catch brook trout and landlocked salmon, if you're into freshwater fishing, of course."

"I've fished a few times, but it was offshore," Amy said. "But I can easily see myself enjoying being on a lake. Peace and quiet. What's not to like, right?"

"I wouldn't mind finding work as a bush pilot for a camp like that, you know?" Caspian said. "Flying clients in and out of—"

Caspian stopped talking when he saw Amy's face screwed up into a knot.

"What?" he asked her.

"Oh, that just makes total sense," Amy said, her voice dripping with sarcasm. "Elias-the-bush-pilot."

Caspian ignored her. "Or I could go work for my father. He still owns his small trucking company."

"Even better," she said, rolling her eyes. "Please tell me you're not being serious."

"You can mock or laugh at me if you want to, Amy, but I'm dead serious," Caspian said. "I've been in the field for ten years, and I never complained. Not once. I chose this life, I'm aware of that. But now might be the time for me to pass the torch to someone else."

"Pass it to whom?" she asked, giving him a helpless shrug and making a show of looking around her. "You're the best we have."

"What do you mean? The best? And I'm not the only asset in the field, you know that. Is Onyx still running the same training program I went through a decade ago?"

"The . . . yeah, of course," Amy replied. "You're right."

Caspian felt that Amy was trying to be nonchalant about it, but her tense shoulders told another story.

Had Onyx stopped developing new field assets?

*Well, either they have or not. It's not my problem.*

"Anyway," Amy said after a beat, "I'm gonna go out and get us some dinner. Any special request?"

"Nope, but thanks for asking. I'm famished, though, so I'll eat anything."

Amy nodded.

"Okay," she said. "Don't move a muscle. I shouldn't be more than forty-five minutes, then I'll cook you something," she said.

Amy scooped the keys from the dining table.

"Keep your phone handy," she said. "If I feel something isn't right and need to get on a long SDR, I'll let you know. Don't you worry about me, okay?"

He nodded and waved at her. And then she was gone.

# CHAPTER THIRTY-SEVEN

*Visp, Switzerland*

Edgar, using one of his forged IDs, checked out of his hotel using the online app and walked to the taxi stand across the street. He climbed into the lone taxi waiting at the curb and asked the driver to take him to the Visp hospital. Edgar didn't see the point in running an SDR. If someone had given his description to the police and he'd become a suspect in the murder of a police officer, the cops wouldn't waste their time following him. He'd be arrested—or shot—on the spot by armed officers.

Edgar was hungry, tired, and in a very foul mood. Following the chaos at Le Clarion and his inability to find The Smoker, the man he had shot on the bridge, Edgar had gone into hiding for three days, changing hotels every night and spending his time watching the news.

Passing himself off as a French police officer attached to the International Affairs Division of the Swiss Federal Office of Police, Edgar had learned through his numerous phone calls that his brother, Laurent, ended up being flown to the hospital in Visp some thirty kilometers north of Zermatt to be treated at its trauma center.

When the taxi pulled into the semicircular driveway of the hospital and Edgar paid the fare, Edgar thanked the driver and climbed out of the cab but didn't immediately enter the hospital. Edgar looked up at the towering beige-colored building in front of him, not knowing what to expect once he walked through those doors. His phone rang, and Edgar looked at the screen.

It was his wife, Juliette. Edgar sent the call to voicemail, just as he had done at least a dozen other times during the last three days. He wasn't ready to talk to her. Not yet, and not on the phone. Their next conversation would need to be in person; her latest texts had seen to that.

The previous night, before going to bed, he had sent Juliette a short text letting her know he was fine and that he'd be back in Paris shortly. His wife's reply had been instantaneous and filled with questions he didn't know how to answer.

The police hadn't released the names of the dead police officers or the names of his deceased team members. They hadn't mentioned Laurent, either, but Edgar knew that his brother—contrary to Edgar's explicit order against it—had shared with his own wife where he was going. Like Juliette, Laurent's wife had been angry at the sudden changes in her husband's schedule, and, to appease her, Laurent had told her he was headed to Zermatt for a few days. And since the two women talked to each other several times per week, Edgar wasn't naive enough to believe the information hadn't been passed on to Juliette. He hadn't replied to any of her messages and had made the conscious decision to power off his phone. He needed to rest, and there were already too many things on his mind. As if the events in Zermatt weren't troublesome enough, Edgar knew Juliette was worried about something else: her own safety.

Following the stabbing incident with Sebastian the month before, Juliette had begged him to go to the hospital and see a doctor, but Edgar had flatly refused. There would be too many questions, he'd explained to her. The police would need to be involved, and their son would be arrested. Edgar could have lied to the police, of course, and could have said he'd been mugged or ambushed by a bunch of drunk kids, but such accusations would have brought unwanted attention.

Not something Edgar could afford. Ever.

His chosen career required him to remain anonymous, below the authorities' radar. On a more personal level, calling the police on Sebastian wouldn't do anything to repair the broken relationship he had with his son. Edgar wanted to fix things with his only child, not make things worse, and sending Sebastian to a youth detention facility would annihilate any lingering hope of doing that.

Edgar and Juliette rarely agreed about anything anymore, and this held true when it came to what they believed was best for their son's health. Edgar felt that Sebastian, who was suffering from chronic schizophrenia, wouldn't benefit from being incarcerated. Juliette disagreed.

Edgar had promised his wife he'd work with her on finding a permanent solution. A solution he was yet to identify.

Prior to him leaving for his latest assignment, Juliette had made it clear to him she didn't want to be left alone with a rebellious, violent teenager who had grown stronger and taller than her.

"He's dangerous! I love him, but I can't control him. Our son needs help, Edgar. He needs to be admitted to a psychiatric hospital."

"No! The best thing for Sebastian right now is to be home with you, his mother," he had insisted. "He stays with you. And that's final!"

But now, after reading Juliette's pleas for help, he didn't know what to think anymore.

*Fuck.*

Edgar pushed out of his mind everything not related to Laurent and entered the hospital through the sliding double doors. A burst of thick, suffocating heated air immediately hit him in the face. Edgar unzipped his coat and walked into the brightly lit lobby. A receptionist, a middle-aged woman with short gray hair, was seated behind a glass window off to the left. Edgar walked to her and showed his French police badge and ID card.

"Bonjour, monsieur," the receptionist said in French, catching Edgar off guard.

Although Visp was a German-speaking town, it was still in the Swiss canton of Valais, a bilingual canton with both French- and German-speaking regions.

"*Et bonjour à vous aussi, madame,*" Edgar replied in the same language. "I'm looking for—"

"Laurent Augustin, yes?" the receptionist said with a knowing smile. "I recognized the badge. You're with the gendarmerie?"

"I am," Edgar replied. "I'm new here, though. I'm a liaison officer with Interpol on a temporary assignment to fedpol in Bern."

"How nice," the woman said. "My husband's French, and our son is with the gendarmerie too. Maybe you know him?"

"It's a big organization, ma'am. We're over one hundred thousand—"

"I know, I know," the receptionist said. "But who knows, right? His name is Gabriel Bernard . . ."

Edgar made a show of thinking about it for a few seconds, then said, "I'm sorry, the name doesn't ring any bells."

The receptionist shrugged. "It was worth a try, yes?" she said. Then, looking at her computer, she continued, "So, for Mr. Augustin, he's on the third floor. Room 310. I'll let the officer guarding him know you're coming."

Edgar gave the receptionist a warm smile. "That's very kind of you. Thank you."

"The elevators are down the corridor and to your right."

Edgar followed the receptionist's directions to the elevators. On the third floor, the doors slid open onto a busy hallway. A tall, older, but still very fit uniformed officer was waiting for him, an unsympathetic look on his face.

"You're the French cop?" the officer asked in German, without offering his hand.

"Yes, and I'm here to speak with Laurent Augustin," Edgar said, showing the cop his credentials.

"Nobody warned me you were coming," the officer said, not bothering to look at Edgar's badge.

"I'm very sorry about that, but I have to say, I'm not surprised," Edgar said, shaking his head, and giving the Swiss cop what he hoped was a sympathetic smile. "We've had a bunch of good people retire in the last few months, and the new hires don't have a clue how it's done. Would you prefer I come back later?"

The officer sighed, but at least he didn't shove Edgar into the waiting elevator behind him.

"Why do you want to see the suspect?"

"Apparently Paris is considering asking the Swiss government for the extradition of Mr. Augustin," Edgar said. "But before they get started on what we all know will be a lengthy application process, an informal request was made through Interpol to see if this is even an option considering the suspect's health."

At the mention of a potential extradition, the cop seemed to relax. "Okay, then," he said, with a nod. "Follow me. He's in room 310. Don't expect him to speak with you. He has opened his eyes only once since he got here."

Edgar swallowed hard.

*This doesn't sound good,* he thought as he walked past a nursing station where three people in medical scrubs chatted together.

"How is he?" Edgar asked, petrified about what the officer might say next.

"You'll have to speak to the doctor for a more accurate picture, but I've been told the surgery didn't go as planned. They couldn't remove the bullet lodged in his spine. Too dangerous. Odds are that he'll never walk or move his arms again. He'll shit and piss in a tube for the rest of his life. If it was me, I'd rather die."

The officer's words hit Edgar hard, and it took everything he had to keep walking in a straight line.

*Laurent has a bullet stuck in his spine?*

The officer stopped, and Edgar almost bumped into him.

"You're okay?" the cop asked. "You look pale."

"Yeah," Edgar said. "Just thinking about the paperwork I'll have to fill out has me scared."

The Swiss cop chuckled. "I know the feeling, but between you and me, I don't think it will be complicated to extradite this asshole."

It took Edgar an insane amount of willpower to keep a straight face. "Why is that?"

"It's costing a fortune to keep him alive. The sooner we can get rid of him, the better. Anyway, sign here," the officer said, tapping his finger on a logbook. "I'll be by the elevators."

———

Edgar closed the door behind him and took a few steps toward the bed where his brother lay. Laurent had several tubes running in and out of him, and his entire torso was wrapped in white bandages. The color of his brother's skin that wasn't covered by the bandages was a clammy bluish white, and the only sound was the humming and beeping of the medical equipment as it did the breathing for him.

Edgar walked to his brother's side and watched helplessly as the ventilator kept cycling to the next mechanical breath. Edgar couldn't bear seeing his brother like that.

Should he simply unplug the machine and be done with it? Would Laurent want that? The Swiss cop had said Laurent would never be able to use his arms or walk again, hadn't he? That he would need to piss and shit in a tube? The thought of it sent shivers up and down his spine.

That wasn't a life worth living. If the situation was reversed, Edgar hoped his brother would have the courage to pull the plug and not be a coward like him. The worst part was knowing that Laurent's condition was his fault. Edgar would have to live with the horrors and the consequences of his choices for the rest of his life.

*I'm the one responsible for taking that contract. No one else.*

They all accepted the risks and dangers that came with the job, but agreeing to that last-minute operation in Zermatt was on him. He should have said no. He should have gone home.

*We should all be home now,* he thought, his eyes moist.

Edgar knew he was coming unglued, and he forced himself to get control over his emotions. He spent another five minutes at his brother's side, then headed for the door.

With his hand on the door handle, Edgar looked back and said, "I love you. And I'm sorry, my brother."

Laurent's only response was a slow hiss coming from the breathing ventilator.

# CHAPTER THIRTY-EIGHT

*Alexandria, Virginia*

Laura Newman, holding a bowl of popcorn in one hand and a can of Diet Coke in the other, retook her place on the sofa and cuddled up next to Christopher, her husband of thirty-nine years.

Prince—a copper-colored golden retriever who'd kept a watchful eye on Laura as she made the short trip back to the living room in case a kernel was to fall from the bowl—stood in front of her, his tail wagging so fast his entire back end was swaying along.

"Did you give him any?" her husband asked.

"Of course not," Laura lied, tossing a piece of popcorn at the dog. Prince caught it in midair. "Good catch!" she said, lobbing another.

"He's getting fat," Christopher warned her as he powered on the TV. "That ain't good for him, not with the amount of butter you're putting in this thing."

"He's almost twelve, for heaven's sakes. Can you give him a break?"

"Hey, I'm just repeating what the vet said, okay?" Christopher said, kissing Laura on the top of her head. "You wanna watch a movie?"

"Why do you think I brought the popcorn over?"

Laura took a long sip of the Diet Coke and offered one to her husband.

"You know I don't drink that stuff," he said, scooping up a handful of popcorn. "But I'll get some of that."

As her husband began to scroll through the list of movies, Laura's phone vibrated.

"I'll be right back," Laura said, as much for the dog's benefit as her husband's.

She left the living room and looked behind her to see if Prince had followed her. He hadn't. He had stayed behind, with the popcorn bowl. Before pushing the green button to accept the incoming call, Laura entered an eight-digit code that would encrypt the conversation and any data sent or received by the two phones.

"This is Laura. I'm secured," she said.

"This is Amy, and I'm secured."

Laura closed her eyes for a moment, composing herself. She had been anxiously awaiting this call. Zermatt had turned into a nightmare, and that was before she'd learned that Elias had gotten himself shot.

"How is he?" she asked.

"He's doing fine," Amy replied.

Laura breathed a sigh of relief. "You sure?"

"Yes. I mean . . . physically, he is. I'm glad you allowed me to go to Switzerland. His health was deteriorating at an alarming rate when I finally got to him. As I said, physically he's fine, and in case of an emergency, Elias could potentially be operational as early as tomorrow, but I wouldn't recommend it. He needs to rest for a while for his wounds to heal properly. It will take some time for him to get back to his normal—"

"How long?" Laura asked, cutting in.

"Two weeks should do it, maybe three. But now that the infection is well under control, his wounds aren't what I'm worried about. They're painful, that's for sure, but they're also superficial."

*I should have known there was a but coming,* Laura thought, clenching her teeth involuntarily in anticipation of what Amy was about to share with her. As soon as her mouth closed and pressure was applied, a sharp pain filled her whole head.

*Damn it! I really need to get that molar looked at.*

"Go on," Laura growled, massaging her jaw with her fingers. "Rip the Band-Aid, Amy. What's wrong with him?"

"Elias wants out," Amy said.

"Say that again?"

"He wants to become a bush plane pilot or a truck driver. He said his father owns a trucking company?"

"Yeah, up in Maine," Laura replied, but her mind was somewhere else, looking for an explanation.

Where the hell had that come from? Caspian had always been reliable and steadfast even in the worst of circumstances. Laura had detected some friction with the whole Elias saga in Portugal, but she had won him back. She had a hard time accepting he was considering leaving because of what had happened in Zermatt.

He got shot. So fucking what? He survived, didn't he?

"What else did he say?" Laura asked.

"He mentioned a woman. Liesile, or Liesel. I'm not sure."

Laura sat up straighter in her chair. "Her name's Liesel."

"You know who she is?" Amy asked.

"I'm asking the questions, Amy," Laura said, her voice hard. "What did he say about her?"

"He said he wanted to patch things up with her, and that he cared about her," Amy replied.

Laura couldn't believe what she was hearing. Was Caspian Anderson . . . in love?

*Jesus Christ!*

# CHAPTER THIRTY-NINE

*Zermatt, Switzerland*

Caspian powered on the television as soon as Amy stepped out of the studio apartment. Amy had told him he had been out for three days, so Caspian wanted to know what had happened since then and if any progress had been made regarding the shoot-out investigation.

The evening news had just started, and Caspian had no difficulty finding a local station that talked about the shooting in Zermatt. In fact, from what Caspian deduced by scrolling through the different TV channels, the violence that had racked Zermatt wasn't only local news; it was on all the news channels, even the international ones.

Caspian sighed.

*No wonder Laura's pissed off . . .*

After ten minutes, Caspian had a pretty good idea of what had happened since the shooting. If the police were making any progress, they were being tight lipped about it.

But the witnesses, not so much.

Caspian's stomach tightened into a hard knot when he learned that two police officers had been shot right next to where he'd killed Leonard Aldrich. One was still alive, but the other had died. A third one was in a coma, which ratcheted the knot in Caspian's stomach up another degree.

*Shit! This one is on me.*

Caspian didn't think he had hit the officer that hard, but it was obvious he had misjudged the strength with which he'd struck the back of the officer's head with his elbow. Unfortunately, there wasn't anything he could do for the injured cop. As for the other two officers, Caspian had a pretty good idea who had shot them.

*Ballcap.*

If Ballcap had shot the cops, could he be the one who fired at him too? In his mind's eye, Caspian could see how this whole thing could have played out.

*Ballcap, standing next to Aldrich's body, is surprised by the cops. Gunfire erupts in the distance. Ballcap knows his teammates are in a jam. Ballcap shoots the two officers and sprints toward the hotel. He gets there too late, but he spots me as I'm crossing the bridge and takes his shot. Yeah, that's a plausible explanation.*

There were two pieces of good news, though. The first was that Aldrich's family was safe. Caspian had been afraid a second wave of kidnappers would storm the hotel, but his fear hadn't materialized. The second was that his picture wasn't on any of the news sites.

*Maybe there's a way out of this after all . . .*

Caspian was about to turn off the TV when a reporter announced that the exclusive interview he had done with the surviving members of the Aldrich family, a piece that had already aired earlier in the day, would be shown again after a short commercial break.

This wasn't something Caspian wanted to miss, so he kept the television turned on. Aldrich's wife was seated in the middle of a large sofa with her two youngest daughters seated on her left and the other—the one who had helped Caspian—to her right.

He was startled to see that none of the four ladies seemed to be in distress. With what they had been through only a few days ago, it would have been normal for them to be upset and agitated. Caspian, who had been trained to detect telltale microexpressions—facial expressions that lasted for a tenth of a second and often manifested themselves when a person was lying—studied each of the four ladies, one at a time. He didn't spend a lot of time on the two youngest ones. As far as Caspian could tell, they didn't really understand what was going on.

Aldrich's wife was hard to analyze. The angle of the camera wasn't always right, and he had a hard time evaluating her based on her facial cues. But there was something off with the woman. Of that Caspian was sure. Although she was clearly furious, even enraged, when speaking about the shooting at the hotel, she betrayed none of the sorrow and misery Caspian expected to see from a grieving widow. When the reporter asked her specific questions about her late husband, her answers were thoughtful and included all the right words, but they didn't ring true. This wasn't a woman devastated by her loving husband's death.

As he moved his attention to Aldrich's oldest daughter, who the reporter had introduced to his viewers as Florence, Caspian's eyes were instantly drawn to her left hand. Her index finger kept tapping on her thigh in a steady but erratic rhythm. Because the cameraman often zoomed in and out, he couldn't keep a constant watch, but he recognized it for what it was. Florence was tapping a perpetual SOS in Morse code.

Aldrich's daughter had adapted the international distress signal—familiar and easily decipherable with its three short, three long, and three more short sounds—by tapping three quick times on her thigh, then doing it again three more times at a slower pace and completing the sequence with three rapid taps.

Focusing on Florence's eyes, Caspian noticed they still possessed the same iron determination he'd seen in them after the shooting. Was the distress signal meant for him? Did she need help? His help?

Then the reporter asked Florence a question, and Caspian listened attentively, noting that while she spoke, she was no longer drumming the SOS on her thigh.

*A hotel guest I interviewed yesterday who witnessed parts of the abduction attempt told me in no uncertain terms that your mom and sisters owed you their lives. Is that true, Florence?*

*I'm . . . I'm shocked anyone would say that . . . I'm . . . I'm not sure why someone would say that about me. I . . . I didn't do anything heroic, I think. In fact, I panicked, and . . . and I really don't remember much of what happened. The only thing I remember, even though I really wish I didn't, is that I stabbed the man who hit my mother.*

*I think—and I know everyone who's watching us will agree—that you're a very, very brave young woman. But I have to ask you this, Florence. Is it true that you were able to subdue one of your kidnappers, steal his gun, and fire at another of your abductors?*

Caspian watched as Florence's mother started to berate the reporter, only to see Florence turn toward her and place a gentle hand on her shoulder.

*It's fine, Mom. It's okay. Really.*

Once her mom had calmed down, Florence faced the reporter and said, *I'd be happy to answer your question, but I think you'll be disappointed.*

*Why's that? Are you denying the eyewitness account—*

*I'm . . . I'm not denying anything, okay? But I have no memory . . . none whatsoever of holding a gun in my hand. What I do recall, though, is that someone, and . . . listen, I'm not even sure if it was a man or a woman, but that person is the real hero. Not me. And I really wish I could thank that person. Whoever he or she is.*

Caspian's heartbeat sped up as he listened to Florence. He had the feeling that her last comment was directed at him. Not only had she looked directly into the camera when she spoke, but she'd also started tapping SOS on her thigh again.

On the television, the reporter had regained control of the narrative and was explaining to his viewers that the police were also looking for the person who had intervened during the shoot-out but that no progress had been made in identifying the person.

While there were probably a handful of persons who'd seen him at the scene, he doubted any of them could identify him well enough to provide a breakthrough for the police, apart from Florence and the four elderly couples who'd been walking close to him on Vispastrasse.

With any luck, the elderly couples had already left Zermatt and would remain quiet about what they saw. Only time would tell.

*She wants me to contact her. I need to find a way to do that.*

It didn't take him long to figure out how.

Caspian got up from the sofa. Once on his feet, he slowly moved his arms and was glad he could do so without hurting too much. The pain was still there, but it had decreased tenfold compared to the day he'd been shot. He slid the wardrobe door open and unlocked the room safe. He took out one of the three prepaid phones he had in the safe and powered it on. Caspian skipped the Wi-Fi provided with his rental and connected to the internet using the data he had purchased with the phones. After he had created a new email account, he used it to generate a new profile on Instagram.

Two minutes later, he had found Florence Aldrich.

Florence didn't have a crazy number of followers, but her account was private. For Caspian to view the activity on her profile, he needed to send her a follow request, which he did.

Caspian headed to the small kitchen and poured himself a glass of water. He'd only drunk half when his phone pinged.

Florence had accepted his follow request.

# CHAPTER FORTY

*Zermatt, Switzerland*

Florence had stopped counting the number of follow requests she'd received since she had appeared on television. She hadn't accepted any of them and was slowly coming to terms with the fact that the man who had saved her family hadn't understood her message, hadn't seen the interview on TV, or simply didn't care enough to contact her.

Though she did her best not to show it, Florence was a mess. It had come as a surprise to her that she hadn't had difficulty dealing with what she had done to the short, mustached man. In her opinion, the bastard deserved every bit of the pain he felt before he died. And she felt the exact same way about the man she had stabbed in the forearm. He'd taken his revenge on her, breaking her nose with two punches to the face, but, in the end, it was he who had gotten his brains blown out, not her.

*Another X in the win column,* she thought.

No, what had really messed her up was what her mother had shared with her about her father. Florence had always suspected her dad was a crook, but never in a lifetime could she have imagined the monster he really was.

There was a vibe about him she'd never liked, but he had always been nice to her and her sisters, so she had come to accept it as part of life. And, if she was honest, the benefits of having a criminal for a dad had far outweighed the drawbacks, at least until the past few days.

It was because of her father that her family was so wealthy. It was her father who paid for her boarding school in the Alps, bought her a new car when she turned eighteen, and brought the entire family four or five times a year to the exotic places Florence had become accustomed to vacationing in.

But now that Florence had learned how her father had made his money, she felt the sharp and continuous sting of guilt ripping through her. Just thinking about it made her feel sick. She, too, had enjoyed the benefits that had come from her father's appalling dealings, and for that she was sure she was going to hell, if such a place existed. And if it didn't, God would create it so that everyone who had ever benefited, willingly or not, from her father's dealings would rot there until the end of days.

Despite all this, she was glad to have forced her mother to share that heavy burden with her. Florence couldn't imagine what her mother had endured in the last few months, since she had discovered the truth.

*Now I know why she's always sad and depressed.*

When her phone chirped with a new notification, she literally jumped out of her seat. It had been a few minutes since her last notification, and she had fallen asleep. Her two sisters were looking at her, smiling.

"You almost fell off your chair, Flo," one of them said, in between two bites of a chocolate cookie.

Florence looked down at her phone and read the name attached to the account that had sent the Follow request. Then every single muscle in her body tensed.

SOSZerSOSMatt

It had to be him. How could it not?

"I'm going to the bathroom," she said to her sisters, who didn't even look up from the tablet they had in front of them.

Florence locked the bathroom door behind her and sat on the toilet. She clicked on the profile name. The account was public, and SOSZerSOSMatt had zero followers and followed only one account.

Le Clarion's.

Florence accepted the follow request and immediately typed a message.

From Flo: Is that really you?

From SOS: It depends who you think I am. Agree?

*Shit. He's right. I should have thought about this beforehand.* Then she had an idea.

From Flo: What color was the taxi? White, gray, or light blue?

From SOS: It was black.

From Flo: Where did you take refuge?

From SOS: A set of flowerpots.

From Flo: The black plastic ones next to the curb?

From SOS: No. The concrete ones in front of you.

From Flo: At the end, when I waved my hand at you, how many fingers was I holding up?

From SOS: You never waved your hand at me.

From Flo: Holy shit! It's you. Can I trust you?

From SOS: You shouldn't.

From Flo: Thank you.

This time, the response wasn't immediate as it had been for all the others.

*He's thinking.*

From SOS: You shouldn't thank me.

Now it was Florence's turn to ponder what to say next. What did she want from the man? Why was she doing this?

*Because you want the truth,* she told herself. But to get to the truth, she had no choice but to share things with him too. Things she'd sworn to her mother never to reveal. But as inexplicable as it was, Florence couldn't deny she felt a connection to this man. They had shared a moment together. A violent one, for sure, but that moment had forged a bond between them.

*Or am I just crazy, stupid, and naive to believe that?*

*No,* she told herself. *You're not crazy. He wouldn't have contacted me if he didn't feel it too.*

From Flo: I have something important to tell you. It will change everything.

# CHAPTER FORTY-ONE

*Zermatt, Switzerland*

Caspian was aware he was breaking most of—if not all—the rules he had been taught by the training cadre at Onyx. His decision not to walk away at Le Clarion had been the catalyst of the situation he found himself in. Still, he could have called it quits and let Florence and the rest of Aldrich's family fend for themselves, but seeing Florence on TV had made it impossible for him to turn his back on them.

He didn't know why, but the young woman trusted him. And for a reason he still wasn't completely sure about, Caspian didn't want to break that trust, though it felt stupid, since he was the one who had killed her father. Still, if Florence needed someone to speak to, he would listen and do his best to understand her needs.

*Even if I'm the least qualified person on earth to do so. Seriously, what could she tell me that's so important that it would change everything?*

Caspian typed his reply and hit the send button.

From SOS: What is it?

From Flo: My mom killed my father.

Alarm bells started going off in his brain the instant he finished reading Florence's message. Was she trying to pry something out of him? Had the police set an elaborate trap for him with Florence as the bait? Did this mean that there were police investigators following the exchange blow by blow? If this was indeed the case, it meant they were already tracking his phone, and a SWAT team was about to hit his location.

A burner phone, like the prepaid one Caspian held in his hand, was nearly impossible to track down or listen to if the police didn't have its number and it was used only once or twice. But once the burner was used to communicate with either a landline or a cell phone that was monitored or known by the authorities, it could be easily tracked and its conversations listened to.

Caspian had already made the decision that if the Swiss police were to bust in his door, he wouldn't resist, though he wasn't naive enough to believe that by raising his hands he would be safe. The Swiss police were in general seen as a professional force with a high level of integrity, with almost no corruption within its ranks. But the officers were still human, and when faced with the individual they believed had killed one of their own, shot another, and put a third in a coma, Caspian knew their gloves would come off. In most other countries, he'd be shot on sight and a gun would magically appear by his side. In Switzerland, his odds of survival were higher, but he still expected to be roughed up.

Caspian's phone buzzed in his hand, but he refused to look at it. Wouldn't he be better off just throwing the damn thing away? He sat at the small dining table and thought of Laura, wondering what her reaction would be the moment she found out one of her top assets—a man who the US government had spent a fortune to train—had been outplayed by a nineteen-year-old girl. Caspian chuckled despite the gravity of the situation.

The phone buzzed again, and this time he looked at the messages.

From Flo: Are you still there? Hello?

From Flo: Was I wrong about you?

Caspian took a long deep breath and shook his head in surrender. Either the police were coming or they weren't. If he wasn't about to be put in handcuffs, then his initial reasoning about helping Florence and her family was still valid.

From SOS: You're wrong about me. But not for the reasons you think.

From Flo: Okay . . . I don't care. I think you're a good person.

Caspian was about to type back that he wasn't, but he took an extra second to think about it. He was a good person. Had he colored outside the lines once or twice to get the job done? Yes. But his purpose had always been to do good, at least in the grand scheme of things. He didn't think his victims would see it that way, though. Did Liesel think of him as a good person? He hoped so. She deserved someone good, someone honest, and someone with whom she could build a future. Could he be that man?

*Not if I'm arrested for murder,* he thought.

From SOS: I try to be.

From Flo: And I wasn't lying. My mother did kill my father. She told me.

From SOS: She told you? She confessed to killing your father?

From Flo: Well . . . Not really. She admitted that she hired someone to do it. My dad was a very bad person. A monster. I understand why she did it. My mom also told me the person that was hired was supposed to work alone, not in a team. She doesn't understand what happened.

There were so many questions popping into Caspian's head that he didn't know how to classify them all. The effects of the drugs Amy had injected into him were still lingering in his system and slowing down his entire thought process, making it virtually impossible to find the answers he was looking for. Despite his foggy brain, he had a bad feeling about where this was headed, and for the second time during his decade of service for Onyx, a little voice in his head was warning him about the organization he was working for.

From SOS: How did your mother contact the person she hired?

From Flo: She didn't. Her brother is some sort of spy in Israel. He's the one who contacted him.

From SOS: Did she tell you the name of the man she hired?

From Flo: Yes. But she was crying when she told me. It sounded like Isaias, or something similar. Elias, maybe? Are you familiar with the name?

Caspian's gut turned sour, and he tasted bile rising in his throat. Then the world around him began to spin, and the walls of his studio apartment seemed to be closing in on him.

*Enough! Think!* Caspian ordered himself.

Now wasn't the time to stand still. He had to find a way to clear the heavy fog of paralysis out of his brain because at the moment, he couldn't get a handle on anything, and every single time he tried to fit two pieces together, his mind became even more murky.

The little voice in his head, the one that kept telling him to watch his back with Onyx, was now screaming. While Caspian didn't want to believe Laura had betrayed him, what Florence had shared with him forced him to at least consider it. The idea that Onyx would sell its services outside of the US government was insane.

Or was it?

Could it be just Laura and not the entire Onyx program that was dirty?

*Stop it! You're jumping to conclusions.*

Caspian wouldn't have the mental capacity to delve further into Onyx's and Laura's loyalties until the drugs had completely worn off, but that didn't mean he was going to stay idle either. He had to ditch his Onyx phone, and he needed to move out of the studio. But, on the odd chance that Onyx had become the enemy, he had to warn Florence first.

From SOS: Are you and your family safe?

From Flo: I think so. There are two police officers outside our door. Why?

From SOS: I think you should leave Zermatt.

From Flo: They told my mom we were leaving tomorrow.

From SOS: I think you should leave now.

From Flo: You're scaring me.

From SOS: You don't seem like the type of person who's frightened easily. Don't be scared but try to convince the police to move you to another location.

From Flo: I'm not worried about me . . . Only for my mom and sisters. I'll talk to my mom.

From SOS: Don't mention me.

From Flo: I don't intend to. Can I tell you something else?

From SOS: Yes.

From Flo: Before we leave tomorrow, I'll leave something for you in one of the concrete flowerpots. They removed the set that was damaged but left the other. It will be inside a small plastic bag.

From SOS: What's in the bag?

From Flo: A flash drive. Everything that's on it I copied from my mother's laptop.

From SOS: Why are you giving this to me? We've never met.

From Flo: We did meet. And you saved my sisters, my mom, and me. After what happened here, my mom is too scared to do anything. So maybe you'll find a way to make it all stop. I hope you will.

From SOS: Stop what??

From Flo: The atrocities my dad and his friends did. Are still doing.

The target package he had received from Laura had specified that Leonard Aldrich was directly involved in human trafficking. In Caspian's book, this was one of the worst offenses one could do. There wouldn't be a lot of tears shed for Aldrich's death. Even his own wife had wanted him dead.

From SOS: Don't give this to me. Give it to the police. I'm not a cop. There's nothing I can do for you.

From Flo: I know you're not a cop, but I have a pretty good idea who you are.

Caspian read the last message twice. Florence was a smart young woman, but he didn't think she had enough information to figure out who he was. Florence's next text forced him to reassess that belief.

From Flo: After my mom talked to me, she showed me the stuff she had uncovered on my father's laptop. Though my mom doesn't understand what's going on, I think I do. There were two parties going after my father in Zermatt. I think you're one of them. That's why I was hoping you'd reach out to me.

Caspian swallowed hard. Before he could think of a reply, Florence sent one last message.

From Flo: I've got to go. The police are here. Don't know why.

# CHAPTER FORTY-TWO

*Alexandria, Virginia*

Laura was still stunned by what Amy had just told her. It was a shocker. *He wants to patch things up with her. He cares about her,* Laura mumbled to herself. *Elias in love? What the actual fuck?*

"What did you say?" Amy asked.

"Give me a sec. I'm thinking about what you said." Laura tried to think how to best move forward.

Laura had taken Caspian in, trained him into one of the most efficient assassins alive, and now he wanted out because he was in fucking love?

The more she thought about it, the more it pissed her off.

Laura had known about Liesel from the early days of her relationship with Caspian. Caspian himself had told her about the pretty accountant and how he had met her. Laura had checked her out, just to be sure. Liesel was a German expat and a green card holder, and she had never married. She had no kids and paid her taxes on time, and the only big-ticket item she'd purchased in recent years was a motorcycle, a black Kawasaki Ninja. Her only vices were a bit of online gambling and a couple of expensive bottles of wine every week.

After a few additional inquiries, Laura had confirmed that Liesel had been a member of the fitness club way before Caspian had started to go there to teach Krav Maga.

It wasn't as if Liesel had set a trap for him. How could she have known Caspian would one day show up? She couldn't, so Laura had cleared her. Truth be told, Laura considered herself a practical woman. She had seen Liesel as the perfect sexual release for Caspian. A win-win. Until today.

The only way Laura could explain Caspian's situation was that he had somehow suffered a mental breakdown and that whatever was going on in his head prevented him from prioritizing the things that were important over those that weren't.

"You told me he needed two or three weeks to heal, correct?" Laura asked Amy.

"Yes. What do you have in mind?"

"You know as well as I do that Elias is by far our most productive and lucrative asset. I would much prefer to keep him than to retire him. You understand that, don't you?"

"I'm aware of the math, Mother," Amy replied bitterly. "This is my business as much as it is yours. So yeah, I get it. To remove him now wouldn't make economic sense."

"Right," Laura said, taken aback by her daughter's tone. "As I said, not my first choice, but Elias isn't the kind of operative you can let loose once you're done with him."

Laura heard a loud sigh.

"I know," Amy said after a beat.

"Better him than us," Laura said. "Did you ever stop for a minute to think what he would do or how he would react if he was to find out the truth?"

"Just about every second I spent with him," Amy said. "I know what he's capable of."

"You're just as capable, Amy," Laura said. "Don't sell yourself short. I don't like when you do that. When you take your meds, you're his equal."

"The meds slow me down," Amy said.

"No. They keep you focused," Laura said, suddenly worried. "Are you taking them, Amy?"

"Yes."

*Fuck. She's off her meds. Did I send her back in the field too soon?*

"Okay. Good," Laura said, knowing now wasn't the time to talk with Amy about her meds, a very touchy subject. "Remember, Amy, what you accomplished in Portugal all those years ago was nothing short of exceptional. You were incredible, as I knew you would be. You covertly taking out the reporter and the actor allowed me—allowed us—to build the Elias legend faster than we had anticipated. You're a brilliant operative."

It took a little while for her daughter to reply, which was a testament to how good Amy was at reading between the lines.

"You'd like me to step into Elias's shoes," her daughter said matter-of-factly. "It's a big fucking ask."

"I'd only ask you to do this if we were to get rid of Caspian. And it wouldn't be for very long," Laura said. "A few years. Four tops."

"I don't know," Amy said. "I looked at the contracts he's taken on in the last few years, and some of them were off-the-chart risky. There are at least a couple I don't think I would have been able to pull off."

"Well, a way to mitigate that, if you were to step in, would be to be more selective when it came to choosing what we take on."

"It's easy for you to say that while seated behind a desk," Amy said. "I take all the risks, and you reap all the rewards. I know you, and I know how you think, Laura. We fabricated the Elias legend from the ground up so that we could maximize profits. And the only way to do that is to accept a large quantity of projects the other brokers don't want anything to do with. I have a hard time imagining you saying no to lucrative deals for my sake."

Though they were thousands of miles apart, Laura could feel Amy was angry, which wasn't good. To manipulate her daughter into doing her bidding, Laura needed Amy to be in a better mood and be more receptive. There was no point in continuing this over the phone. Laura's objective had been to get a feel about how receptive Amy was to the idea of taking over the Elias alias.

*I have my answer.*

Amy needed more time. Her mind wasn't there yet, so Laura would have to walk on eggshells and not mention Elias for a while. Amy had never been what any psychologist would deem stable. While she was undeniably a talented field asset and her medications—when she actually took them—kept her focused, she was an emotional basket case. It was better not to stir the pot too much.

Laura's thoughts moved on to Caspian Anderson. The last four days had tested her in ways she wasn't accustomed to anymore. Onyx had been officially terminated by Homeland eight years ago, a little over two years after Caspian had completed his training. Laura had known from the start that the whole shebang was going to end at some point, but she'd been hopeful that she would get a few more years out of Caspian before he was killed or put out to pasture by Amy.

Laura had taken a lot of risks in creating the Elias legend, and although it had turned out to be lucrative, it had taken longer than she thought to gather $3 million. She was still quite a long way from her initial goal of $10 million. The operational expenses were high, and the profit margins weren't what they used to be. If she was to lose Elias, she'd probably be forced to shut down the business. Apart from Amy and Caspian, she had only one asset left.

Laura had to be careful how she played her cards, especially with her daughter, who seemed to enjoy second-guessing her at every opportunity.

"I hear you, Amy," Laura said in response to her daughter's comment. "I disagree about the part where you said I wouldn't turn down a well-paid contract, but based on some decisions I've made in the past, I understand why you might think that way. But remember, darling, my objective is to keep Caspian in play for as long as possible, not for you to take his place."

"I get that," Amy said. "I feel the same way as you do about this, but I want you to understand that if Caspian dies, I'll be the one who decides if I take over Elias or not. It won't be you."

Laura pursed her lips, then bit her tongue. It was better to remain quiet than to say what had crossed her mind.

"Of course," Laura said. "For now, I want you to give Caspian some leeway. Let's allow him to think he can get out whenever he wants. We'll give him the time he needs to heal, and when the moment is right, we'll reel him back in."

"And how do you intend to do that?"

"I don't think we should worry about this now," Laura said. "We'll formulate a plan together when it's appropriate."

"Anything else?" Amy asked.

"As a matter of fact, yes. Something came up."

"Aldrich's wife, yes?" Amy said.

Laura smiled. She had to give it to her daughter. When it came to strategizing a way out of a problem, Amy was ahead of the game.

"You watched the news?" Laura asked.

"I did. When Caspian was still out. It didn't matter which channel I tuned in. They all aired the same interview."

"So, you agree with what needs to be done?"

"I can see how Aldrich's wife has become a problem. The woman is clearly shaken and afraid for the safety of her kids."

"You think she'll talk to the investigators?" Laura asked.

"It's possible. The Swiss are thorough. She doesn't know who we are, but she could give them the details of our client in Tel Aviv."

"It's her brother," Laura said.

"That complicates things, doesn't it? Should we wait until she's back in the US?"

"No," Laura said, disappointed Amy couldn't see why this wasn't a viable option. *I guess she still has things to learn.*

"Once in the United States, she'll hire a private security firm," Laura continued, "which will make it harder for us. And she has the money to hire a good one. But there's another reason why we should neutralize her while she's still in Zermatt. Do you know what it is?"

"Because there's more than one player involved," Amy said. "Our Israeli client won't dare accuse us of turning on his sister unless he's absolutely sure it's us. If his sister dies in Zermatt, the first suspect on everybody's mind will be whoever was behind the well-publicized kidnapping attempt."

Laura smiled, satisfied and proud. Then she asked, "Have you learned anything about the kidnappers?"

"Other than them being French, no. Should I pursue this further?"

"Leonard Aldrich made a lot of enemies over the years. It could be anyone. I want you to focus on his wife. And the quicker you move, the better. I don't expect them to remain in Zermatt for much longer."

"I'll find a way to get to her," Amy said.

"I know, dear. You always do."

# CHAPTER FORTY-THREE

*Zermatt, Switzerland*

Caspian closed the door of the apartment behind him and locked it. He hurried down the back stairwell of the building and exited into a narrow street, stepping into the cold and drizzly night air for the first time in days. Amy could return any moment, and Caspian wanted to be as far away as possible when she did.

After the final text exchange with Florence, he had written a quick note to Amy letting her know he was heading back to the United States. He hadn't disclosed his itinerary to her, but he did mention he would let Laura know once he was back stateside. Caspian had then gathered his most important belongings and shoved them into his backpack, and, after performing a factory reset on the device and breaking it in half, he had thrown his Onyx-issued phone in the toilet and flushed it down.

His pistol, though, was back in its inside-the-waistband holster, and he had placed the suppressor and an extra magazine inside the pocket of the winter coat he had "borrowed" from the owner's wardrobe.

Before he had destroyed the prepaid phone he had used to communicate with Florence, Caspian had used it to book a room in a hotel right across from Le Clarion. It was on the other side of the Matter Vispa River, but the room he had selected would give him a direct line of sight to the hotel's facade.

As Caspian began his SDR, a cold, biting wind hit him in the face and made him shiver. His fever was down, the infection in his left shoulder was under control, and the invisible vise he had around his head was no more, but he was still a long way from being back to full efficiency. His left shoulder and right triceps still throbbed with pain, but that, too, had lessened and was now manageable.

Caspian's training had taught him to operate by himself for extended periods of time. Before today, he'd always known someone was watching over him. From thousands of miles away, maybe, but watching nonetheless. Despite the minimal interaction he had with Onyx and the fact that he had spent the last ten years in the field, either on a covert overseas mission or in New York, living the life of a UN translator, Caspian's conviction about the righteousness of what was demanded of him had remained strong due to his knowledge that he had the entire apparatus of the Department of Homeland Security backing him.

But now, Caspian wondered if it had been a mirage. As he walked alone under a dark sky and against the cold wind, racking his brain as he tried to make sense of what Florence had told him, he felt abandoned and isolated, more so than he had ever experienced during an operation. His only comfort came from knowing he'd get a shot at fixing things with Liesel. He had a hard time getting the image of her out of his mind.

Tomorrow, after he had picked up what Florence had left for him in the flowerpot, he would head back to New York, buy a gigantic bouquet, and tell Liesel the truth.

*Maybe not the whole truth.*

Fifteen minutes after Caspian had left his studio apartment, he made a conscious decision to shut his mind off from everything related to Amy, Laura, Onyx, and Liesel. He had to get his head back in the game and concentrate on his personal safety. Making sure he was doing a proper SDR before heading to his hotel room was a good first step.

*Because I'll never see her again if someone blows my brains out onto the pavement.*

Caspian saw a crowded corner souvenir shop with two exits a bit farther down and to his left. After he made the left turn at the intersection, he ducked into the shop and slowly headed back toward the exit he had originally bypassed while staying alert and on the lookout for anyone he might have spotted earlier. His next stop was at a grocery store, where he purchased two water bottles, three made-to-go sandwiches, and a few dispensary articles he needed to continue treating his wounds.

Fifty minutes later, satisfied he wasn't being tailed, Caspian hailed an electric taxi and asked the driver to take him two street corners away from his new place of residence.

———

The hotel room was more luxurious than Caspian had anticipated based on the pictures he had quickly scrolled through before booking it, but he couldn't care less about how well appointed the suite was. The only thing of consequence was the room's floor-to-ceiling windows, which gave him a perfect view of Le Clarion's facade.

After taking a quick shower and wolfing down two of the sandwiches, Caspian turned on the second of his prepaid phones. He then set up his surveillance equipment, which consisted of a pair of binoculars, a spotting scope, two cameras, and a night-observation device. Once everything was ready, he switched off all the lights of the suite, opened the heavy blinds, and made final adjustments to his night-observation device before settling down for a long, boring night.

# CHAPTER FORTY-FOUR

*New York, New York*

Liesel leaned forward and told her Uber driver she would be climbing out at the next intersection.

The driver looked at her through his rearview mirror.

"In this rain? Are you sure?" he asked her. "It's only a few blocks away, you know?"

"Yeah, I'm sure," Liesel said. "A friend texted me. I need to catch the subway. But don't worry, buddy, you'll get a five-star rating from me."

"As you wish," the driver said as he pulled over to the curb. "Have a good day, miss!"

Liesel stepped out of the Uber at the intersection of Seventh Avenue and Twenty-Third Street, opened her white-and-blue umbrella, and began to walk north. This had been her second Uber ride of the last hour, and she'd do at least one more before she got to her final destination. She'd left her apartment almost two hours ago, and she estimated she had another hour or so before she was done.

It was one of the longest SDRs she'd done since she came to New York, but it wasn't every day—even every year—that her handler from the BND wanted a face-to-face meeting in her city. While SDRs weren't part of her day-to-day life, she still remembered how to do them.

Liesel made a left at the next street and entered a busy drugstore. She closed her white-and-blue umbrella and walked all the way to the back of the store, where she removed her gray raincoat, reversed it, and put it on again, this time as a dark blue raincoat. The switch was going to get her clothes wet, but there was nothing she could do about it. She could live with the brief discomfort.

Liesel hooked the wet umbrella to the interior of her raincoat and pulled out an extendable black umbrella from her purse. A minute later, she exited the drugstore and turned right, walking in the opposite direction she'd come in while keeping her umbrella over her head as low as she could. The black umbrella wasn't as large as the other one and wasn't as efficient at protecting the lower part of her body from the downpour, but it was the perfect tool to help her blend in with the impressive number of pedestrians who were also hiding under black umbrellas.

For today's meeting with Nicklas, she was going to leave nothing to chance. During her training, she'd been taught to expect every moment of her undercover life to turn into a potential life-threatening situation. She was taking this advice to heart.

*And I sure hope Nicklas is doing the same,* she told herself, thinking about her last conversation with him.

The last three days had been hard on Liesel's psyche. What Nicklas had told her about Caspian had left her literally speechless. She had listened to everything her handler had said, and when he'd asked her if she had any questions, she'd simply disconnected the phone and finished the entire bottle of red wine she had opened for dinner. She had gone to bed right after she'd drunk the last drop. But she'd barely slept. Her drunken thoughts had tormented her.

Was it true? Was Caspian an assassin? A killer for hire?

She didn't believe it. She didn't want to believe it either.

Who would believe such crap?

*Mm-mm. Not me.*

There had to be another explanation. Caspian was surely not the only man who had visited all the places on the dates Nicklas had mentioned. Liesel had asked him during their follow-up call the next day.

"That was one of the first things we looked at," her handler had replied. "You're right, he wasn't the only one. But there were only three other people who were at these exact locations on these dates. One is a travel blogger, the other two are airline pilots."

"Okay, but you can only track people who actually passed through regular border controls, correct?" she'd asked.

Nicklas had reluctantly agreed.

"So then, it's all circumstantial."

"For now, everything's circumstantial. But we'd like you to stay with him a little longer, if you don't mind?"

She didn't mind at all. But she did inquire why. That's when Nicklas had told her he was coming to New York to meet her.

"I need to give you something. In person."

"You're not going to send one of your couriers?"

"Not for this. I'll see you soon."

Liesel was about to use her phone to reserve her third Uber of the day, but she changed her mind. Instead, she walked two blocks east and hailed an incoming yellow taxi. She hopped in the cab and gave the driver an address that was a five-minute walk from the restaurant Nicklas had picked for the meeting.

Confident she hadn't been followed, Liesel tried to reach Caspian for the sixth or seventh time in the last three days.

Direct to voicemail. Again.

*Shit! Why can't you pick up your damn phone?*

She had tried to text him too. But her messages weren't even being delivered anymore. She still didn't believe Caspian was the assassin Nicklas had told her about, but she was beginning to run out of excuses not to take her handler seriously. She closed her eyes, pushed her head against the backrest, and exhaled loudly. She suddenly felt very tired.

*Aren't you the one who wanted a little more excitement in your life?* Liesel asked herself. *Well, you got it, girl. You won the excitement jack-fucking-pot.*

# CHAPTER FORTY-FIVE

*Zermatt, Switzerland*

Amy climbed the stairs toward Caspian's floor with a paper bag filled with groceries and two bottles of wine in her arms, replaying the conversation she'd had with her mother. She was relieved her mom hadn't asked her to kill Caspian. It would have thrown a wrench in her plan.

Amy honestly didn't know what she would have done. Her mother seemed to find a way to piss her off at every turn.

Amy had always been a bit infatuated with Caspian. He was a handsome man: not underwear-model hot, but good looking enough to turn heads if he wanted to. But his good looks weren't what turned her on. She could have any gorgeous man she wanted.

Though Amy was a firm believer that most men could be easily conquered and manipulated by any woman with a brain, she was ready to admit that the process was even more simplistic for gorgeous, smart, and witty women like her. She had heard many people say that men held all the power in this world; she strongly disagreed. Nobody was going to hand you their power, money, and influence willingly, but it was all there for the taking.

You just had to grab it and, sometimes, kill for it.

As for Caspian Anderson, her fondness for him had grown in step with the number of his kills. He had an impressive career. The man had killed so many people over the last ten years, and he had never been caught, even though some of his victims had been high profile and well protected.

*That* was hot. *That* turned her on.

It was thrilling to be in the same room as him. His unequivocal success, combined with her knowledge that Caspian was one of the most dangerous people in the world, made his presence electrifying.

She was very much looking forward to cooking for him tonight.

Amy reached the last landing and let out a light giggle, mostly at herself, as she remembered what she'd done. She had taken the liberty of sleeping in Caspian's bed, and had even cuddled with him a little, when she had been tending to his wounds. She had snapped a few selfies too. Some of them were a bit suggestive. She would send the best ones to Lysol, just to poke the bear a little.

*Lysol? That's a cleaning product,* she thought. *Why in hell can't I remember that woman's freaking name?*

Amy was curious, and excited, to see how the night would go. She had already made the decision that she wouldn't settle for just a cuddle. She wanted more. Much more. But it might take more work than she had thought. Most men looked at her with eager, hungry eyes, but she hadn't seen that thirst in Caspian's. That was fine. She loved a good challenge. She was confident she could change Caspian's mind about Lizette—or whatever the fuck her name was—and have him forget everything about that damn accountant.

Hadn't he said he'd love to come to Italy with her? That was a good first step, wasn't it?

Amy hadn't shared her plan with her mother, but her long-term objective was to take over the business. One of the best ways to do that would be to recruit Caspian to her cause. They could work together, as a couple. Elias could become a two-person team.

*Amy and Caspian. Caspian and Amy.*

She thought it sounded nice. It rolled off the tongue, didn't it?

And, contrary to her soul-sucking parasite of a mother, she would be happy to share the spoils with her man. It maddened her to no end that her mother was collecting all the payments of Elias's contracts without even risking a freaking sunburn. Amy made a mental note to mention the money aspect of the business to Caspian in her pitch.

It was getting harder and harder for her to hide her disdain from her mother, especially when Laura kept asking her if she was on her meds. It didn't matter how many times she'd told her mom the meds slowed her reaction time. Laura didn't care and kept insisting she take them.

*Amy, did you take your meds?*

*Amy, darling, we talked about this, you really need to take your medications.*

*Bullshit. Bull-shit!*

Amy shook her head violently, forcing her mother out of her mind. She didn't want to think of her while she was with Caspian. It would ruin everything.

As Amy approached the studio apartment's door, she decided to refrain from saying "Honey, I'm home."

It would be too soon.

Amy opened the door and immediately felt something had changed since she had left. She couldn't place what it was, but the vibe wasn't the same. She dropped the grocery bag, shattering one of the two wine bottles, and reached for her pistol.

*Caspian needs me.*

Amy cleared the apartment, her heart beating faster and faster in her chest as it became obvious she wasn't going to find him.

Her Caspian was gone. Someone had taken him.

———

Amy sat at the dining table with Caspian's handwritten message in one hand, a wet tissue in the other. Scowling, she read the note again. When she was done, she walked to the sink and burned it.

She didn't know what to think. Had she misread his signals? Didn't Caspian understand the bond they shared?

His odd little note, addressed to her as if she was a stranger, was cold and contained no warmth and no apology for his early departure. It was just a plain, uncaring statement to let her know he had decided to head back to New York and that he would contact Laura upon arrival.

Amy cocked her head to one side. Was Caspian playing hard to get?

*Of course he is,* she thought, chastising herself for not seeing this earlier. *I'm so silly.*

She was feeling better already.

Once she was done here, she would make her way to New York and join him. Amy turned her head toward the grocery bag. It lay on the floor, a mess of broken eggs and red wine. The bottle of white, which had rolled out of the bag and now rested against the baseboard, was still intact.

She was going to cook something nice for herself and drink a glass of wine or two, and then she would start to work on her plan for tomorrow.

She had an entire family to kill.

# CHAPTER FORTY-SIX

*New York, New York*

The restaurant Liesel's handler had picked was located inside a small boutique luxury hotel set on a serene side street of Midtown Manhattan. While the hotel was only a short walk away from Bryant Park and the theaters of Broadway—two of Liesel's favorite spots in the city—it still allowed its wealthy guests to spend quality time in a quiet environment away from all the bustle of that touristy part of town.

After a uniformed doorman took care of the door for her, Liesel entered the sophisticated confines of the lobby. Liesel didn't spend hours per week reading architecture magazines, but she did like to browse through them while waiting in line at the grocery store. Even with her limited understanding of everything related to interior design, she was impressed by how well the hotel had managed to maintain, through what must have been several renovations, its historic charms and architectural integrity while providing its guests with all the modern comforts they could want. Although the facade of the hotel screamed early 1900s, the public spaces' furniture was mostly neoclassical, with a few contemporary pieces thrown in. A weird mix, but she liked it.

The restaurant's entrance was across the lobby and to the left. Sitting at the back, beneath a small glass chandelier, was her handler, Nicklas. There were only three other patrons in the restaurant. Two women in their forties were seated next to a window, munching on a common salad, and a bottle of wine was chilling in a stand-up wine cooler next to their table. An older, well-dressed gentleman was seated by himself reading a newspaper, a pen in his hand and a coffee carafe within reach. He briefly looked at Liesel as she walked across the restaurant to Nicklas's table, then returned to his crossword puzzle.

Liesel's handler was an unremarkable man. He was of medium height, with a medium build, although Liesel did notice Nicklas's waist had suffered a little since she'd last seen him. Nicklas's eyes were neither green nor brown and had a deceptively vacant look. He was dressed in a suit but wore no tie, and his white button-down shirt was open at the top. Nicklas's only memorable attribute, if it could be called such, was that his left hand was missing its ring finger.

Nicklas rose when Liesel reached the table, but he didn't smile.

"Thank you for coming," he said in perfect English while he motioned for her to sit. "Any problems on your way in?"

"No," she said. "No problem."

"Would you like to eat something?" he asked her.

"Are you having anything?"

Her handler called over the lone waiter with a small wave of his hand.

Liesel looked quickly at the appetizing but simple menu and ordered a vegetarian omelet and a small bottle of sparkling water. Nicklas ordered chicken soup and a glass of chocolate milk.

Once the waiter had left them, she looked at her handler and asked, "Chocolate milk?"

He shrugged. "My wife won't let me have any at home." He touched his midsection. "So that's what I drink when I'm traveling."

"Is that why you flew all the way to New York? To drink chocolate milk?" Liesel asked, only half joking.

"I came to give you these," Nicklas said, pushing a flash drive and a single dull metal key toward her.

Liesel took the key and examined it. It looked like a regular house key. She turned it over a couple of times.

"It's just a key," Nicklas said, his voice flat.

"What does it unlock?" she asked, adding the key to her key ring and dropping the flash drive in her purse.

"I'll let you know when it's time."

"Can you at least give me a hint?" Liesel asked, trying to lighten the mood.

"This isn't a game," Nicklas said, his voice a threatening hiss.

Nicklas's rebuke stung, which startled her.

"I honestly didn't think this was possible," she said after a moment.

Nicklas raised an eyebrow. "What's that?"

"You're even less fun in person than you are on the phone. So, if we're done here, I think I'll head home," she said, pushing her chair away.

"You're not going to eat?" Nicklas asked.

Liesel stared at her handler; then her eyes moved to his left hand.

"What happened?" she asked.

Nicklas's eyes hardened, and his cheeks flushed red.

"This," Liesel said, pointing a finger at Nicklas. "This is why this will be my last operation."

"My hand?"

"Stop playing dumb with me," she said, shaking her head. "I was once told you were one of the top guys in the field. You know exactly what I meant. I'm done with the one-way flow of information."

"That's how it works," Nicklas said, moving his right hand over the four remaining fingers of his left. "I don't make the rules. You know that."

Liesel nodded. "Okay. I get it," she said, rising. "Enjoy your chocolate milk."

"Wait," Nicklas said, reaching out to hold her wrist lightly with his disfigured hand. "Please."

Liesel hesitated. Her handler's eyes weren't pleading, but she could see a change in his demeanor. She sat back in her chair.

Nicklas opened his mouth to say something but stopped when the waiter arrived with their meals. Her omelet, puffed up and perfectly presented with some freshly cut fruits and roasted potatoes, smelled delicious. Liesel thanked the waiter and took a bite. It tasted even better than it looked.

*Fluffy, well seasoned. Very nice. At least I'll get a good meal out of this.*

"Listen, I know this sucks," Nicklas said, stirring his soup with a spoon. "I was once in your shoes, like you said."

"I really do get it, you know?" Liesel replied. "But it just doesn't work for me anymore. It's as simple as that."

Nicklas took a small sip of his soup from his spoon, then said, "I can't share with you how I lost my finger, but I can tell you what happened to my leg."

"Your leg? What's wrong with your leg?"

"It's a prosthetic," Nicklas said as he extended his leg under the table. "Look."

She did, and he raised his pants.

Liesel swore under her breath and suddenly felt guilty about her attitude toward her handler. Nicklas was correct. She had no right to demand anything from him. Clearly the man had been through some tough shit. She had never noticed Nicklas had a prosthetic leg. He must have spent months in rehab. Then she realized that in one sentence, Nicklas had successfully put her back in her place and reminded her that she was a small cog in a very big machine.

"I'm sorry. I didn't—"

Nicklas raised his hand. "I don't need your pity," he said. "You play an important role, and I'd be disappointed if you were to leave, but you must understand that I'll never be able to share everything with you. It's not how this thing works."

"I know," she said as she cut a small piece of omelet with her fork.

"Good. But I promise I'll make an effort too. I tend to keep everything close to the vest nowadays. I learned the hard way what can happen when too many people have access to privileged information," he said with a sad smile.

Liesel nodded.

"I lost my leg in Venezuela four years ago, working on a joint operation with our American partners."

"Operation Gideon?" Liesel asked, talking about the failed attempt by Venezuelan dissidents to infiltrate the country and remove President Nicolás Maduro from office. "German intelligence was—"

"No, we weren't part of that op. The only reason you know about this operation is because it was a fiasco for the Americans, even though they weren't as actively involved as some claimed they were. Our most successful intel ops are rarely talked about," Nicklas said. "That's the way it should be."

"Rubicon was highly successful," Liesel said.

"Successful, yes, but also pivotal to what we've become as an organization. We have maintained a very special relationship with the Americans because of Operation Rubicon. I won't claim the op I was part of in Venezuela was as significant, but it was successful. Then I got shot."

"What happened?"

"It was our last day in Venezuela," Nicklas said, a sorrowful expression clouding his features. "We had just come out of our safe house and were about to climb aboard our vehicles when two motorcycles raced past us and opened fire with automatic weapons."

"I'm sorry, this is terrible."

"No, it's the job," Nicklas warned her. "We all know the risks, but we still do it, right?"

Liesel met her handler's eyes, and said, "Yes, we do."

Nicklas gave her a warm smile.

"The key I gave you unlocks the front door of Claus Eichberg's house in New York," he said. "The house belongs to the German government, so we can access the alarm system and the exterior cameras."

Liesel's heart skipped a beat, and what was left of her appetite vanished. She continued to chew on a potato, but it might as well have been a piece of cardboard.

Hadn't they talked about this?

*Shit.*

"I thought—" she started to say, but Nicklas cut her off.

"Yes, I know what I said about you not spying on the ambassador," he said. "But the report on Aldrich's activities you sent before our follow-up call changed everything."

"It did? In what way?" she asked.

The morning after their initial conversation about Eichberg and Elias, Liesel had returned to her office and done a deep dive on everything her firm had on Leonard Aldrich. She hadn't been in the mood to do a thorough analysis of the information she had collected, her mind powerless to distance itself from the possibility that the man with whom she was sharing her bed could be an assassin. But she had sent everything to the BND for further analysis. She hadn't thought about it since.

She'd been so sure this meeting was about Caspian that she hadn't even considered there could be another reason.

"Do you remember when I mentioned to you that it was through electronic surveillance in conjunction with another op we were running that we found out that Edge Robots could be a shell corporation for the Chinese?"

"Yeah, I do."

"Okay, so here's the deal. When we fed your report into our system, the AI quickly matched an IP address from your report to the operation from which we first heard about the link between Chinese intelligence and Edge Robots."

Liesel pushed her plate away and leaned forward, crossing her arms over the table.

"Do we know who the IP address belongs to?" she asked.

"We do now, thanks to you," Nicklas said, sweetening the words with a rare smile. "That specific IP address led us to a service provider in New York, which in turn led to an email account that belonged to Leonard Aldrich's wife."

Liesel frowned as she tried to make sense of what Nicklas had said. "Were we keeping tabs on Aldrich's wife?"

"No, but I can't tell you who we're eavesdropping on," Nicklas said.

"Someone in China? C'mon, give me something. You said it yourself, without my report you wouldn't have made the connection."

Nicklas let out a light chuckle.

*Wow. A smile and a chuckle. Not bad.*

"It took some doing, but we believe the recipient is in Israel," Nicklas said, bringing his glass of chocolate milk to his lips. "She's in constant communication with someone in Israel."

"Do we know who?" Liesel asked.

"No. Not yet. And I'm not sure we will. We're unable to crack the Israelis' codes. We're only able to break into the communications originating from that specific address. Not the other way around. Anyhow, one of the messages we intercepted led us to believe that Ambassador Eichberg has in his possession documents that could be detrimental to our country's interests."

Liesel could feel her pulse quickening. Nicklas wanted her to break into Eichberg's residence and search for these documents.

*Documents we're not even sure exist.*

Liesel was starting to doubt this was still about Edge Robots. Breaking into a German citizen's residence—let alone the house of an influential ambassador—in a foreign country was asking for a world of trouble. One thing she'd learned was that as certainly as flawed intelligence could cost lives, hasty efforts to acquire intelligence were sometimes equally perilous. To warrant the kind of risks the BND was asking her to take, the situation had to be dire.

"We're no longer talking about Edge Robots, are we?" she asked.

"We're not," Nicklas said.

"Okay," Liesel said. "What does the timeline look like?"

"There's still a lot of work to do on our end before your op gets green-lighted, if it ever does," Nicklas said. "You wanted more clarity, now you have it. You know as much as I do."

It was a lot to take in, but her conversation with Nicklas had revived her belief in what she was doing. Maybe she'd been a little too self-centered of late and had forgotten why she had been sent to the United States in the first place. She would have to do better in the future.

She didn't know if the BND would ever order her to break into Eichberg's house, but if they did, she would be ready.

# CHAPTER FORTY-SEVEN

*Zermatt, Switzerland*

Caspian yawned and stretched. As it was often the case with surveillance, it had been a long, boring night. He considered reaching out to Florence again but opted to wait a little longer. He had stayed up all night, hoping to catch the young woman dropping the plastic bag into the flowerpot. But he hadn't seen her. He wasn't worried, though. He knew Florence and the rest of her family were still there.

Why else would there be two police officers stationed on their floor?

Since the hotel elevator had a glass wall facing the river, Caspian was able to see who was coming up and down. Earlier that morning, around seven o'clock, he had seen two fresh cops relieve the officers who had been on duty overnight. Now, each time the elevator door opened on Florence's floor, he caught a glimpse of the officer stationed next to the lift. He couldn't see the second cop, but he assumed the officer was standing close to the Aldriches' family room.

Apart from the marked police vehicle—a hydrogen-powered Hyundai Nexo—parked in front of the hotel, Caspian hadn't detected any additional surveillance or security. The officers currently on duty had started their shift five hours ago, so Caspian didn't expect to see them being relieved for at least another hour or two.

It was the perfect time to go check the flowerpots. It was conceivable that Florence had dropped the plastic bag last night before he reached his observation post. She did specify in one of her messages that she would do it in the morning, but Caspian's plans changed all the time, and he expected the same was also true of Florence's.

Before heading out, Caspian adjusted the two cameras. He set the first at an angle that would capture the entire facade of Le Clarion and the side entrance and fine-tuned the second by zooming in on the elevator. He wished he could have an eye on the staff entrance located at the rear of the building, but it was impossible with the equipment he had on hand.

Caspian left the hotel and walked across the very same bridge where he had gotten shot. When he passed the exact spot where he had fallen, an uneasiness crept over him. His mouth turned dry as he vividly remembered the searing-hot pain in his shoulder, the blood, and the fear that had washed over him. Caspian shook the feeling away.

It had been a close call, but he had pulled through. He still didn't know what to make of Onyx, Laura, and Amy. The information he'd learned from Florence had shocked him, but there were many other variables to take into consideration. Part of him didn't want to believe Onyx had made him a mercenary. It seemed so improbable. Black program or not, weren't there checks and balances to prevent these sorts of things from happening?

Once in New York, he would search for the answers to his questions. But he would tread carefully, because if Laura, or the entire Onyx program, had turned mercenary, his search for the truth could become dangerous real fast. You didn't need Einstein's IQ to understand how far some people would be willing to go to keep Onyx out of the news or out of a congressional investigation.

Caspian reached the end of the bridge and turned right. He glanced to his right, toward the river. There were a few pedestrians crossing the bridge, but none of them grabbed his immediate attention. He was getting close to the flowerpots. They were a mere five steps away now. Caspian had tried to locate the plastic bag from his room using his spotting scope, but he hadn't been able to. For his first pass of the day, he wouldn't stop. He would pass alongside the set of flowerpots, keep his left hand close to their edges, and use his eyes to scan.

He was still a couple steps from the first flowerpot when he spotted the small plastic bag. The way Florence had positioned it made it impossible to detect from his hotel room. The bag rested against one of the walls of the second flowerpot. He picked up the bag without slackening his pace and kept walking another three blocks before he started an abbreviated surveillance detection route that would take him back to his hotel.

———

The first thing Caspian did after locking the door behind him was to watch the footage his two cameras had recorded while he'd been gone. The ins and outs from both the side and main entrances were minimal. Two different guests had arrived by taxi and entered holding shopping bags. Half a dozen more had returned from a morning on the slopes, wearing their ski boots and holding their skis. Caspian zoomed in on two men that had looked out of place but cleared them when he watched them exit the hotel a few minutes later, each holding two pairs of skis. He couldn't say for sure where they were going, but he had the impression they were employees of a nearby ski shop. It wasn't uncommon for ski shop employees to drop and pick up rental skis for the hotel guests at the beginning and end of their stay.

Done with the first footage, Caspian was about to begin watching the second when, from the corner of his eye, he caught movement coming from the elevator. He put the camera aside and picked up his spotting scope. A uniformed maid had entered the elevator with her cleaning cart on the second floor. She now had her back to Caspian, who hadn't reacted quickly enough to watch her step into the elevator.

Right away he knew there was something off about this maid.

Through his spotting scope, Caspian studied her, looking for the little thing that had triggered the warning bells in his head. It didn't take him long.

*Yep, there it is,* he thought as he consulted the detailed notes he'd taken.

Contrary to the other maids he'd seen, this one didn't wear the same footwear. While the others wore black shoes or boots that matched the rest of their uniforms, this particular maid wore brown hiking boots.

The elevator stopped at the fourth floor, and two young children and their dad entered the elevator. With the maid, the cleaning cart, and the three newcomers, the lift was getting crowded. To accommodate the new arrivals, the maid moved half a step to her left and rotated her body slightly to the right. Caspian adjusted his scope and focused on the profile of the maid's face. As soon as he got a clear view, his heart caught in his throat.

Seeing Amy dressed as a maid in the elevator confirmed Caspian's worst fear. Onyx had gone off the rails, and they had taken him along for the ride.

Caspian felt a stab of anger but pushed the feeling away. Now wasn't the time. He pulled his second prepaid phone from his pocket and typed three short messages to Florence.

From SOS: DO NOT open the door of your room.

From SOS: The maid is a trained killer.

From SOS: I'm coming.

# CHAPTER FORTY-EIGHT

*Zermatt, Switzerland*

Amy entered the hotel through its front door. She had spent an hour shopping for a cute ski outfit, a helmet, and a cool pair of ski goggles. She hadn't bought the skis or the boots, though. She'd stolen them from a hotel guest from a nearby establishment who hadn't bothered securing her stuff in the lockers provided by the hotel.

Amy knew that the guests of Le Clarion weren't allowed to walk inside the hotel in their ski boots. The only two exceptions were the lobby and the ski lockers. Not wanting to attract undue attention, Amy took the stairs down to the lockers. She left her stolen skis on one of the racks and removed her ski boots. From her large ski backpack, she pulled out a pair of hiking boots. She organized her ski equipment in a manner that would allow for a quick getaway, if needed.

From the locker room, Amy took the stairs to the second floor, her backpack tightly secured over her shoulders. She would need her two arms free for what she was planning to do next. As soon as she exited the stairwell, she found what she was looking for: a cleaning cart. It was parked across the hallway, three rooms down. Amy waited, her phone in hand, pretending to text someone. Less than two minutes later, she heard the door open. Amy pocketed her phone and began to walk toward the cleaning cart, trying to time her approach. A maid exited the room and crossed the hallway, then grabbed four clean towels from the cart. The two women made eye contact. Amy smiled at the maid and waved her hand. The maid smiled back.

"Good afternoon," Amy said in German.

"And to you, ma'am," the maid replied, as she walked back into the room with the four plush white towels in her arms.

Amy scanned the length of the hallway and glanced behind her. Satisfied there were no other guests or hotel staff, she quickened her pace and slipped behind the maid, following her inside the room before the door automatically closed behind her. With her rubber-soled hiking boots almost silent on the hardwood floor, Amy reached the maid in three quick steps. The woman had no idea Amy was there until it was too late.

Amy, who was shorter than the maid by a couple of inches, kicked the back of the woman's knee as her left hand reached around for the maid's mouth. Amy yanked the woman's head to the left and used her right hand to slide her knife deep into the side of the maid's neck. As Amy felt the woman's body stiffen, she guided her to the floor and used her weight to keep the maid from fighting back. Amy wished she could simply sweep her knife across the woman's throat to cut through the trachea and be done with it, but there would be too much blood. Not that Amy cared about the hotel's floor. She needed the maid's clothes, preferably not too bloody.

It seemed to be taking the maid a long time to die. At some point, the woman's eyes met hers, and they stared at each other in silence until the maid's eyes clouded and she died. Not wasting time, Amy took off her backpack and changed into the maid's clothes. The name Heidi was stitched in white letters above the left breast pocket. There was nothing she could do about that. Amy grabbed the master key, which hung on the lanyard the maid kept around her neck. The woman's clothes were two sizes too big, but they would have to do.

Amy went to the bathroom, washed her hands and face, then stared at her reflection in the mirror. She wasn't ashamed of who was looking back at her. Amy didn't see herself as a criminal or a degenerate but as a skilled professional doing a demanding but necessary job. She gave herself a large smile.

*Never a dull moment, is there?*

She wondered how Caspian would have done it. Was there room for improvement? Absolutely. There always was. But overall, she was proud of her kill. It was a good one. Caspian would approve.

Amy took three long, slow breaths to clear her head. Rejuvenated, she grabbed her backpack and cracked open the hotel room door. She listened for sounds signaling the presence of a guest or an employee but didn't hear anything. She exited the room, placed her backpack on the top shelf of the cleaning cart, then began pushing the cart toward the elevator. When the elevator doors slid open, Amy backed into the lift, keeping the cleaning cart in front of her. She had seen the marked police car parked out front. The vehicle had been unoccupied, which led Amy to believe that the officers were inside the hotel. She had been confident that she would see one in the lobby and another on the sixth floor standing next to the Aldriches' room, but it hadn't been the case.

Were they both on the sixth floor?

She was ready to take them both, if necessary, but she'd prefer if there was only one officer on the sixth floor. Recent events had the officers on edge. Amy was sure of it. It wasn't a secret that nervous cops were more prone to using their firearms. She was surprised when the elevator stopped to pick up three hotel guests on the fourth floor. She had been in her zone, thinking about how to handle the officers, so it took her a moment to realize she needed to step to the left in order to leave enough space for the two kids and their dad. The younger kid, who couldn't be more than six years old, pressed all the buttons of the elevator while staring hard at Amy, his eyes challenging her to say something.

*Little prick!*

The father looked at her and gave her a contrite smile, as if to apologize.

Amy shrugged, as if it was no big deal, but, in her head, she was seriously considering putting a round in each of their skulls.

How could Caspian even consider having kids? They were such a nuisance. She and Caspian would have to talk about that too.

*He's probably gonna insist on having at least one, but I'll hold my ground on this one. There'll be no offspring in our house.*

"We're going to the fifth floor," the dad said in English, startling her. "My parents have their own room. We tried to book the four-bedroom suite on the sixth floor, but it wasn't available. So, we have two rooms, you know?"

*Nod and smile, nod and smile,* Amy thought, acting as if she didn't speak the language. *Why does he think I care?*

Once the family was gone, Amy slid her ski backpack closer to her but kept it on the shelf of the cleaning cart. Having unzipped the bag, Amy slipped her hand inside to make sure her pistol—a Walther PPK/S on which she had attached a Sparrow suppressor—was easily accessible. Amy loved the little pistol. Some shooters complained about its lack of stopping power, but Amy disagreed. Loaded with .32 ACP caliber rounds, the PPK/S was the perfect tool for jobs at close range. Its only drawback, in Amy's opinion, was that when it was loaded with the .32 ACP, the pistol's magazine only held a maximum of eight rounds.

Amy readied herself as the elevator doors opened onto the sixth floor. She had just begun to push the cleaning cart out of the lift when she saw a very tall, broad-shouldered police officer standing against the opposite wall. The man's uniform clung tight against his body. She offered him her warmest smile, but the stern-faced officer didn't return it.

"You can't come this way. There's no cleaning on the sixth floor until further notice," the cop said in German, his intense blue eyes turned down toward her. "You should have been informed of this."

"Oh. Really? I'm new here. Nobody tells me anything," Amy said, pouting her lips, trying to appear as helpless as she could.

The officer looked at her suspiciously, then glared over her left breast. When his eyes met Amy's, she could see something had clicked in his brain. The cop took a step back, and his right hand moved to his holster.

The officer had spotted the name embroidered in white on the uniform. By the way he reacted, Amy assumed that the officer had crossed paths with Heidi before.

Amy believed she could still talk her way out. Heidi was a popular name, and the officer wasn't about to shoot her because two maids shared the same first name. The officer's hand was resting on top of his holster, but nothing more.

"What's your last name, ma'am?" the officer asked.

"Hmm . . . yes. It's Teucher. I'm Heidi Teucher," she said as she sidestepped to her left to keep the cleaning cart between her and the cop. "What's going on, Officer?"

"There are traces of blood around your collar, ma'am. Could I see your hotel identification, please?"

"I'm . . . I'm sorry," Amy said, her hand reaching into her backpack. "I'm new here, and they haven't—"

A door at the end of the hallway opened, interrupting her. This was the door to the Aldriches' family suite. The cop next to her swung his head toward the noise while Amy's hand wrapped around the grip of her pistol. An officer appeared in the doorframe, looking at his phone. He was yet to see Amy. This was her chance.

"Just received a flash warning from the guys who took—"

The officer closest to her must have sensed a change in dynamic because he yelled a warning to his colleague even before Amy's pistol was in full view. Startling Amy, who had expected him to create some distance between them by backing up, the officer sprang forward and pushed the heavy cleaning cart into her. The cart toppled, but Amy was quick and was able to step back to avoid being stuck under its weight. What she couldn't do was stop the beefy cop from slamming into her with the force of a linebacker making a tackle in an open field as he jumped over the fallen cart. The impact knocked Amy to the floor, her pistol clattering out of her hand.

A millisecond later, the cop landed on top of her, pinning her down.

The only limb she was free to move was her right arm. Her hand went to her belt, reaching for the same knife she'd used to kill the maid a few minutes earlier. The knife came free, but the cop cracked an elbow to the side of her head. Amy saw stars, and it was only through sheer force of will that she didn't pass out. She felt the officer's powerful hand grab her shoulders. The sturdy man was now squatted on top of her, straddling her.

He was going to roll her onto her stomach and handcuff her.

The cop, though, didn't know Amy had a knife in her right hand, so when he spun her, she used the momentum to plunge the knife into his side, just below his body armor. Amy ferociously twisted the blade as she pulled it out of the man's flesh. The officer grunted in pain, and the confidence that had blazed in his blue eyes only a second ago was replaced by fear and horror. The officer's hands moved to the gushing wound at his side.

It was a fatal mistake.

Amy used her abdominal strength to do a half sit-up, then stabbed the cop three times in the throat so fast that it almost took a full second for the cop to realize what had just happened. Then his eyes opened wide, and his hands moved from his side to his neck. Having left her knife embedded in the man's throat after the third stab, Amy pushed herself from under the legs of the officer and started to go for her suppressed Walther PPK/S—she could see where it had skidded after hitting the tiled floor of the hallway—but realized too late that she didn't have the time. The other cop was almost on top of her, but from the shocked look on his face and the fact that his pistol was still holstered, the scene in front of him hadn't been the one he had expected to see after he had run around the toppled cleaning cart.

Amy had to give the cop credit. While he had only four-tenths of a second to make his decision, the officer had come to the correct conclusion. If he was to stop running and go for his gun, the woman in front of him would have the time to empty half the magazine of her small silenced pistol that lay three feet away from her before he could even aim his weapon at her.

So, the officer did the only thing that gave him a chance. He kept running. Unfortunately for him, Amy was well versed in hand-to-hand combat.

The officer hadn't been the only one to calculate his odds. Amy had too.

Unable to get out of the way of the attack, she angled her body to face the oncoming cop. As he lunged at her, she dropped backward toward the floor. The officer's mouth opened in surprise, and he tried to change his trajectory, but it was too late. He was committed. Amy reached out with her legs and gave the officer a push as he flew above her. She immediately rolled to her right in the direction of her pistol. She grabbed it, got to one knee, and aimed it at the officer.

The cop landed on his stomach six feet farther down the hallway. The man was quick, and he was already facing her, with the barrel of his pistol two inches from being free of the holster, when Amy fired two rounds into his chest. Then, using the light muzzle rise of her pistol, she followed up with shots to the neck and face.

Amy spun around, fired two rounds into the first officer's head, then scanned for more threats as she tried to catch her breath. Seeing there was no imminent attack coming her way, she pulled her backpack from under the cleaning cart and dug into it, looking for the two spare magazines. After inserting a fresh magazine into the pistol, she dropped the other one in a pocket of her uniform.

She glanced at her watch. She'd been on the sixth floor for fifty-one seconds.

*Shit. Too long, and too much noise.*

*Now move!*

It was time to pay a visit to Aldrich's wife and three daughters.

# CHAPTER FORTY-NINE

*Zermatt, Switzerland*

It took less than one minute for Caspian to pack his things from his room. He was halfway down to the lobby when his phone vibrated. He looked at the screen. It was Florence.

From Flo: Don't worry. We're not at the hotel anymore.

From SOS: You're no longer at the hotel???

From Flo: No. They moved us last night. Right after we chatted. That's why the police were there. We're being flown out.

Caspian sighed in relief. A huge weight had been lifted from his shoulders. There were so many things he wanted to say to Florence, but he didn't know how to. At least Florence, her mom, and her two younger siblings were safe. That was the only thing that mattered.

From SOS: I'm glad you're okay.

From Flo: Did you find my plastic bag?

From SOS: Yes.

From Flo: And?? Did you look at it?

From SOS: Not yet.

From Flo: Do it. Now.

From SOS: I will. Goodbye, Florence.

Caspian powered off the phone before he could see Florence's next message, afraid she was going to tell him where they were flying her and her family to. Caspian didn't want to know. For their sake. He removed the battery from the prepaid phone and destroyed the SIM card. He would dump the phone in a garbage container a few streets away.

As he walked out of the hotel's lobby, Caspian prayed that the two police officers posted on the sixth floor of Le Clarion had made it through their encounter with Amy, but he wasn't hopeful.

*They're probably dead,* he thought, shaking his head.

Caspian couldn't imagine why Onyx had sent Amy to kill the rest of Aldrich's family. What Caspian did know was that the organization he'd given everything to for the last ten years wouldn't rest until they were all dead. Onyx had the resources to find them. Wherever the family was headed next, it wouldn't be far enough.

Caspian didn't have the heart to do nothing. How could he stand still when he knew trained assassins were coming after Florence? If something was to happen to her or her family and Caspian knew he had turned his back on them and stayed on the sidelines like a coward when they needed him, he would live with an immense guilt for the rest of his life. He would never be happy again. He had to see this through.

And he knew exactly what he needed to do. But first, he was going to buy a laptop.

———

A little over two hours later—and one hundred and fifty-six Swiss francs poorer—Caspian stepped out of the gondola on Italian soil. His one-way journey had started in Zermatt, where he had boarded the first of six gondolas and cable cars that would take him all the way to the Italian village of Breuil-Cervinia. Despite everything weighing on him at the moment, Caspian had enjoyed the ride.

It would have been impossible not to.

The fabulous, wild, and unspoiled beauty one could see at an altitude of 3,821 meters from Klein Matterhorn—the highest cable car station of the Matterhorn Alpine Crossing—was mind blowing. But for Caspian, it was the awe-inspiring engineering of the newly constructed pylon-free one-mile link between the Matterhorn Glacier Paradise and Testa Grigia that had taken his breath away. Caspian marveled at what the workers had been able to accomplish while constantly battling the snow, the endless wind, and the very thin air that reigned at almost four thousand meters. But now that his feet were back on solid ground, Caspian had to hurry. He had a lot of work to do.

While it was possible that Amy had lied to him about how she'd managed to get to Zermatt, Caspian believed she had been telling the truth. He was also inclined to think that she would take the exact same route back to Italy. If Caspian's assessment of the situation in Zermatt was correct, Amy would want to get out of the village as soon as possible. He didn't think she would risk spending another night in Zermatt.

Since the closest train station to Breuil-Cervinia was almost a one-hour car or bus ride away, Caspian assumed Amy had rented a car from whichever airport she had flown into. Prior to the beginning of this operation, Caspian had not only studied the map of Zermatt but also familiarized himself with all the different options available to him in case his primary and secondary routes of exfil were impeded. From the Italian side of the border, the two closest international airports were in Turin and Milan. Since most rental cars had stickers or license plate frames that indicated which rental companies owned them, Caspian would be able to easily differentiate personally owned vehicles from those owned by the rental companies.

Caspian looked at his watch and gauged how long he had before Amy showed up. Whether she had made a mess or not back at Le Clarion, Amy would without doubt conduct an SDR before getting to the first gondola. The question was, How long would it be? Worst-case scenario, Caspian estimated he had thirty minutes to find Amy's vehicle.

The walk from the gondola to the first parking lot was short, but the lot was small and all but one of the vehicles were free of snow. Since it had snowed quite a lot since Amy had parked her vehicle, Caspian could rapidly dismiss a lot of cars and SUVs from his search.

Caspian took a closer look at the lone snowed-in vehicle. It was an expensive Porsche SUV, not the type of rental a field asset would get for an operation. He walked to the small booth where a lone parking attendant, who seemed old enough to have fought in World War II, was smoking a cigarette while watching an Italian soap opera on a miniature TV that looked as ancient as its owner.

Feigning that he couldn't remember where he had parked his car, Caspian asked the elderly man where the other parking lots were. The attendant looked at Caspian, took a long drag from his cigarette, then blew reeking, bluish smoke toward Caspian's face.

"*Questa non è la Germania, idota! Questa è l'Italia!*" the man said in rapid Italian, which wasn't one of the languages Caspian spoke.

Either the parking lot employee didn't speak German or he didn't want to.

Caspian asked the question again, this time in French.

"*Bien sûr, pardonnez-moi, monsieur. Voudriez-vous m'indiquer où se trouvent les autres stationnements? Vous seriez bien aimable.*"

The old man studied Caspian for an instant, then pulled a coffee-stained black-and-white map of the village from a drawer and slapped it on the counter with a grunt. Before Caspian could thank him, the old man slammed the small window of the booth shut.

There was only one other public parking lot, and it was several times larger than the first one. Thankfully, when he arrived there, Caspian counted only thirty-one vehicles that were snowed in. Eleven of them belonged to a local rental company that had its office at one of the nearby midsize hotels. Without a second thought, he dismissed these rentals and five more vehicles that were painted in flashy colors. Four more were small cars that looked like they'd been there since the beginning of the winter. They were dismissed too. Of the four remaining vehicles, three had French license plates. The last vehicle, a blue Volvo XC40, had an Italian license plate. Caspian used his gloved hand to remove the last of the snow from the plate. The letters *T* and *O*—which stood for *Torino*, the Italian translation of Turin—were printed in white on the right side of the metal plate against a blue background.

Caspian smiled. He had found Amy's rental car.

———

Twenty minutes later, Caspian walked out of a nearby hotel with the keys of one of the eleven rental cars he had earlier dismissed in his hand. The rental came with unlimited mileage, but he wasn't planning on driving it more than a few hundred feet. In fact, he wouldn't take it out of the parking lot.

Caspian hadn't wanted to steal a vehicle if he could avoid it. There were too many windows facing the parking lot. Standing by himself in the cold wasn't a viable option either. He needed a car, so he rented one.

Caspian cleared the snow from the edges of the door with his hands and unlocked the car. He found a snow brush on the rear seat and used it to remove the snow from the roof and hood. The car wasn't a beater, but it was far from new, which explained the cheap rate he had paid for the week. But, to Caspian's relief, it started on the second try. Once he was sure the car engine wouldn't stop, he drove the vehicle to a spot three cars away from Amy's vehicle and turned off the engine.

Caspian attached the suppressor to his SIG, then placed his binocs on the seat beside him. He glanced at his watch. It was five past three. He had been in Breuil-Cervinia for forty-four minutes.

*The ski lifts close at four. I'll know soon enough whether she's coming or not.*

Caspian powered on his third and last prepaid phone. The only person he would communicate with on this one would be Liesel. It took a while to connect to the network, but when it did, Caspian sent a text to Liesel letting her know he'd lost his phone and was now using a local one he'd bought at the store. They hadn't spoken or texted each other since the day before he'd gotten shot. She wasn't the type to be jealous, but she'd be curious about the bounced texts. She would also wonder why he hadn't reached out to her earlier. He'd stop by a store to buy more burners.

Caspian checked the local news, anxious to know if there was any mention of an incident at Le Clarion. His heart sank when he read the headline.

**Another shooting at Le Clarion. One employee and two police officers murdered in cold blood.**

*Goddammit to hell!*

The news article didn't mention the job description of the hotel employee, but Caspian knew the employee was a woman and was part of the housekeeping staff. The poor woman had been Amy's first target. The maid's only crime had been to wear a uniform Amy had needed.

Caspian's eyes remained dry and his face stoic, but a violent anger mixed with guilt and remorse was brewing in the pit of his stomach. Two more cops and a civilian were dead.

Could he have done more? Could he have saved the cops? Had he made a selfish decision by not running to Le Clarion?

Deep down, he knew his intervention wouldn't have saved the maid, or the cops, but he still felt guilt ridden by their deaths. It wasn't healthy to think this way, but his subconscious refused to give him a break. He was exhausted, and he needed rest, but he had to deal with Amy first. And for that, he needed to be sharp.

Caspian brought the binoculars to his eyes and scanned the pedestrian entrance to the parking lot. A steady flow of skiers were loading their ski equipment into their cars and leaving for the day. The lot was still two-thirds full, but at this rate, there wouldn't be many vehicles left by four o'clock.

Not a bad thing for what he had in mind.

Caspian pulled out the new laptop he'd bought in Zermatt and powered it on. It took a few minutes to set up, but since he wasn't importing any data from another device, it was a straightforward process. He opened the plastic bag and looked at the thumb drive Florence had left for him. He inserted it in the USB port. An instant later, a USB drive icon appeared on his laptop screen. He clicked on it. A single unnamed file folder appeared. He clicked on that too.

The file contained dozens of PDFs and pictures. He opened the first picture. Someone had taken a photo of white numbers and letters against a green metallic background. Caspian didn't understand what it meant until he opened the second picture, where a shipping container filled the entire frame.

The third thumbnail icon he opened wasn't a picture but a video. He clicked on the play button and watched a man open the green shipping container. Moments later, several women and teenagers—both boys and girls—walked out, shielding their eyes from the bright sunlight with their hands. They all looked exhausted, and their clothes were torn and dirty, but they didn't seem malnourished. It was impossible for Caspian to determine exactly from which country the video had originated, but the man yelling at the confused people who had walked out of the container was doing so in Albanian. Caspian didn't speak the language, but the tone of the man's voice, and the punch he delivered to the solar plexus of one of the teenage boys, told him the man wasn't there to rescue them.

Florence had told him her father was involved in human trafficking. She'd been right.

*And so did the target package I got from Laura. At least that much was true.*

After taking his time to observe the parking lot to see if Amy had shown up, Caspian scrolled through a few of the PDF files. He was puzzled to see that many of the pages had the official UN letterhead. Something circled in red grabbed his attention. He zoomed in on it.

Claus Eichberg.

His phone buzzed between his legs. It was Liesel. She'd texted him back with the short but famous four-word message everyone just loved to receive from their partner.

We need to talk.

# CHAPTER FIFTY

*New York, New York*

Liesel woke up rested and reinvigorated with a new energy. She had stayed away from wine the night before and had gone to bed early, knowing a good night's sleep was the best way to sharpen her mind and fine-tune her reflexes. She didn't know when, or if, she'd get the nod for the operation, but she saw it as part of her job to be physically and psychologically ready if she was called upon.

Rolling to her side, she scooped her phone from the nightstand and looked at the time.

*Oh my God, I slept in.*

She sat up in bed and clicked on the mail app and waited for the emails to load. Most of the messages in her inbox were about an important file she was working on at the firm. Her team seemed to be handling everything, as she was only cc'd to the emails. She noticed that a few texts had come in late the night before, but since she'd silenced her phone for all calls, texts, and emails coming from anyone outside a very small group of people to whom she had granted twenty-four-hour access, she hadn't read them until now. Looking at the time stamp, she saw that Danielle and her boyfriend, Rafael Ribeiro, had pleaded for her to join them at a Brazilian nightclub on Fifty-Eighth Street a few minutes before midnight.

Liesel was in no rush to see Rafael again. She wouldn't have gone to the nightclub even if she'd read the message in time. She wondered if the request had come from Danielle or if it had been Rafael's idea.

Another text had recently come in from a number she didn't recognize. She was about to delete the message when something caught her eye. She looked at the phone number again. Her heart began to pound in her chest.

*+41. That's Switzerland! Caspian!*

She hadn't heard from him in almost four days. Excited, but also worried the number belonged to a hospital, she clicked on the message.

Hey Liesel—So sorry I didn't reach out earlier. I lost my phone. Just got a new one. I hope you weren't too worried. I miss you. A lot. I'll be back soon. C.

Liesel wasn't sure how to respond. There was nothing wrong with the message per se, but it didn't appear to be well thought out. Caspian was the kind of guy who enjoyed writing emails or texts that were fun and cute and often made her laugh. This one, not so much. It felt like an afterthought. She began to type her reply but stopped midway. She thought about everything Nicklas had shared with her about Elias, the assassin.

She rolled her eyes. This was so far fetched, right?

"Damn it," she said between tight lips.

She exited the message app. She would reply to Caspian all right, but she was going to link up with Nicklas first.

———

Liesel was impressed at the speed with which Nicklas and German intelligence had reacted. Within minutes, they had broken into Caspian's phone. She was now waiting for its location, which Nicklas promised he would have momentarily.

"We got him," her handler said. "He's in Italy."

"In Italy? Are you sure?" she asked, puzzled.

"He's just across the border," Nicklas explained. "He's in Breuil-Cervinia. Do you know where it is?"

"Yeah, I do," she said.

"And do you—"

"You don't need to say it," Liesel said, interrupting her handler. "It means he could have been in Zermatt when Aldrich was killed."

"What will you say to him?" Nicklas asked.

"He doesn't know we know where he is, right?" Liesel said, thinking out loud. "The first thing I'll do is establish if he's gonna lie about where he is. We'll see from there."

"All right. Good luck. We'll talk again . . . Would you wait for me a minute, please?"

"Sure."

She didn't have to wait long to hear Nicklas's voice again.

"There's been a development. There was another shooting in Zermatt. Same hotel. Le Clarion."

"When?" she asked.

"A few hours ago. Two cops and one hotel employee are dead."

*Not again.*

Liesel closed her eyes. A cold shiver ran down her spine. She thought about Caspian, and she just couldn't imagine him gunning down two cops and a civilian.

"You think it's Elias," she said matter-of-factly.

"Too soon to say," Nicklas replied. "But I'll say this: based on the intel we have, Elias has never killed on two separate occasions in the same city. So, keep that in mind, okay?"

Liesel ended the call and took several deep breaths to calm her nerves, then reopened her messaging app and typed her message.

*If he cares about me, that should prompt him to reply,* she thought, pressing the send button.

Liesel brought her phone with her into the bathroom as she used the toilet and brushed her teeth. She was halfway dressed when Caspian called.

"Hey you," he said.

"Hey. Thanks for calling me back so quickly," she said, pacing the length of her bedroom. "So, you lost your phone? How did that happen?"

"Yeah, of course. No problem. Listen, I'm . . . I'm so, so sorry, Liesel. When I first realized I didn't have my phone, I was on the slopes and thought I had forgotten it at the hotel. Then, when the mountain closed, I went out and had a few drinks with some guys I met, and I forgot all about it. I fell asleep as soon as I got back to my room. I slept like a log."

"You had too much to drink? That doesn't sound like you, Caspian," she said, letting out a light chuckle.

"I know, right? Well, I guess Swiss beers must be stronger than the ones we brew in the US."

"Were you okay the next morning?" she asked, making sure to sound appropriately worried.

"Yes, totally fine. And I had a great time on the slopes too."

"Oh. Good. Glad to hear that," she said. "But what about your phone? You didn't find it?"

"I didn't, and I was shocked at how hard it was to find another."

"Really? They don't sell phones in Switzerland?"

"No, no, they do, but I didn't want to buy an expensive one and get into a contract with an overseas service provider. So, to keep the cost down, I bought a prepaid one."

"Yeah, yeah, of course," Liesel said. "Makes sense."

It was hard to know for sure, but to her, Caspian sounded honest.

"How are things with you?" he asked. "Anything new?"

"Yes, kind of, mostly work related. But really, Caspian, I'm just happy to hear your voice. I missed you. I've been thinking a lot about us in the last few days."

"Same here, Liesel. This trip has been a real eye-opener for me. On so many levels."

"Oh yeah? Well, that's great, then."

"It really is," he said.

"And Caspian, I want you to know that I'm thrilled you're having such a blast in Switzerland. Where are you, by the way?"

"I'm in Italy, actually. Breuil-Cervinia, to be exact. It's right across the border from Switzerland."

"Oh my God, that's right across from Zermatt, isn't it?" Liesel said. "Did you hear about the shooting?"

"Yeah, I know. Horrific. Just . . . awful. But I'm afraid it's *shootings* now, with an *s*. There's been another one earlier today."

"What? Another? Do you know what happened?" she asked.

"Only what I read in the news. The police aren't sharing a lot of details, but apparently a hotel employee and two cops are dead."

"I can't believe this is happening while you're there," Liesel said. "Please tell me you're coming back soon?"

"I am. In a few days."

"Okay," Liesel said. "I'll see you then, but let's not wait four days before we talk again, all right? I know the minutes are probably costing you a fortune, but we can text, right?"

"I'll keep this phone open as long as I have data left," Caspian said.

Liesel smiled. Getting Caspian to keep his phone open had been one of the objectives of the call.

"And Caspian?"

"Yes?"

"Watch your back."

There was a small pause, then Caspian replied, "Always."

She ended the call and pondered if she hadn't said one thing too many.

# CHAPTER FIFTY-ONE

*Paris, France*

From across the street, Edgar watched his wife and son as they entered their luxury apartment building. He had missed them so much, but he knew the feeling wasn't mutual. His wife loathed him, and he assumed his son did too.

*Sons who love their father usually don't stab them.*

It was a weird feeling to know he was the only one of his team to make it back home. During the one-hour flight from Geneva to Paris, Edgar had considered not returning to his Paris apartment. He could make a large deposit in Juliette's account and leave.

They would probably be better off without him, anyway.

But it didn't feel right. He had too many loops open. He couldn't just disappear.

Edgar had never forgiven his father for walking out on him and his mother when he was seven years old. One day his dad was there, having dinner at the family table inside their small one-bedroom apartment, and the next he was gone. Edgar never did learn why his dad had left, and he had never seen or heard from him again, though his departure had wrecked his mother's life. She hadn't been the same since, and even now after so many years had passed, she still blamed Edgar and Laurent every chance she got for his departure.

Edgar had sworn he wouldn't be like his father.

After crossing the street, he entered the apartment building and took the stairs. Should he call Juliette beforehand to warn her he was coming?

*No. It's my apartment too. That would look so, so weak. Man up!*

Edgar stopped in front of his door and looked down at his right hand, which was holding the key to his apartment. It was shaking. His palms were sweaty, and his urge to bolt had never been greater. He couldn't remember the last time he'd been so nervous. There was no question about it, the whole situation was ridiculous, but the apprehension he had about how the reunion with Juliette and Sebastian would go was real.

Edgar pressed his ear to the door, listening for any sound that would give him a clue as to the current mood inside the apartment. He heard some footsteps, but they weren't near the door. Then his wife shouted something unintelligible, but it prompted an immediate, angry response from Sebastian.

And this one Edgar had no difficulty hearing through the door.

"Shut your damn mouth!"

This wasn't the mood Edgar had hoped for, but it was time for him to show his face. Edgar used his key to enter the apartment, and, as he took his first step, someone slammed a door shut so hard that the walls shook.

"Come back here, you little puke!" his wife screamed in French as she ran out of the kitchen with a frying pan in her hand.

Then Juliette saw him, and she stopped dead in her tracks, her eyes wide with shock.

"You?" she said, taking a threatening step toward him. "You?"

Edgar felt as if he was in a combat zone. The note of near hysteria in Juliette's voice had sent all his senses on high alert. The prospect of the peril lurking ahead was real, but this time, instead of facing off enemy combatants wielding machine guns, he was facing his wife and a frying pan.

"How dare you show up here after you've ignored me for days!"

"I know, Juliette, I know," he said, showing open palms. "I'm so sorry. It's been a very, very difficult few days."

Juliette took a few more steps in his direction. "Difficult few days, you said?"

Edgar could tell his wife was furious and hurt, but when she spoke next, her voice came down several notches with no apparent anger in it. "Where were you?" she asked, her free hand on her hip.

"In Switzerland," he said. "Listen, I need—"

"Were you in Zermatt?" Juliette asked, her big green eyes now shimmering with tears. The intensity of her gaze made Edgar want to take a step back, but his back was already touching the wall.

Edgar nodded.

"I didn't hear you," Juliette snapped at him.

"Yes. I was in Zermatt," he said after summoning his strength.

Juliette's tears were flowing freely now, and she looked at him with anguish.

"I told you not to go, but you didn't listen," she said, shaking her head. "I told you not to go!"

"You did tell me, and I should have listened to you," Edgar said.

"Did you kill those cops, Edgar? In Zermatt? Were you the one who murdered them?"

"What? Of course not," he lied.

Edgar's muscles tensed as he asked himself how much of what had happened in Zermatt Juliette knew. He didn't have to wait long for his answer.

"I watch the news, you know? Did you know that the younger of the two officers who were killed had a child named Sebastian?"

Edgar didn't know that. It could only mean one thing. The Swiss police had begun to share additional details about the events.

"Did you hear what I said? The cop had a kid named Sebastian."

Edgar felt sick to his stomach. He remembered the exact moment he'd pulled the trigger and the sound the officer had made when Edgar's bullet had ripped off a portion of his face.

"Was that your plan all along? To go kill people? Is that what you've been doing since you left the Foreign Legion?"

Edgar stayed silent, frozen in shock.

"Answer me!" Juliette yelled at him. "Answer me, goddammit!"

"I . . . I don't kill people, Juliette," Edgar said, his voice strangulated. He was aware he was doing a very poor job of lying.

His words hung in the air for what felt like an eternity.

"You fucking liar!" Juliette shouted as she hurled the frying pan at his face.

Edgar ducked in time but decided not to block Juliette's slap to his face or the punch that followed, which cracked his bottom lip. Edgar looked at his wife in disbelief, but she wasn't done. She telegraphed her next one, and this time Edgar caught her fist in his hand.

"Enough!"

"Let go of me!"

Edgar did, and she yanked her arm back.

Juliette took a few steps away from him, then leaned against a bookcase. She was shaking.

"On the news . . . they said . . . five people tried to kidnap a woman . . . and her three children," Juliette said, sobbing. "Children, Edgar. Children."

Edgar's mind raced to come up with an answer. If he could find something to say to Juliette that would convince her he wasn't a bad man, he would.

"We were hired to protect them, Juliette," he said a moment later as he took cautious steps toward his wife. "I'm not supposed to tell you this, but you've earned the right to know."

He scrutinized her eyes, trying to gauge if she was buying what he was saying, but her face remained deadpan.

"Laurent and the rest of the team . . . they're heroes, Juliette. Heroes," he said.

She scoffed and fixed him with a hard stare.

"Heroes? Really? It sounds to me like you're trying to convince yourself," she said as she wiped her tears with her forearm. "Laurent looked up to you. He trusted you. How could you lead him down such a path?"

"It wasn't supposed to go down like this," Edgar said, seeing an opening. "We were supposed to escort them to a safe house, but we were ambushed."

"Oh yeah? A safe house? And what were you doing while your brother and the rest of your team were being 'ambushed'?" Juliette asked, making air quotes with her fingers. "Because you sure weren't fighting alongside them, were you?"

Edgar was starting to feel more confident. Juliette seemed to have bought into the protection-detail gig. Why else would she be pissed at him that he hadn't been with his team during the fight at Le Clarion?

*Better for her to think I'm a coward and a poor leader than a killer.*

Now was the time to seal the deal.

"I was at the safe house, Juliette, making sure everything was ready," Edgar said, visualizing in his head the story he was telling, hoping to make it sound more credible. "I had just completed a reconnaissance of the route they were going to take. And honestly, I felt like the five of them was a strong enough presence to deter any attack. Obviously, I was wrong. I made a terrible mistake."

Juliette had calmed down. Edgar could see she was processing everything he had told her. This was another encouraging development.

"The safe house . . . Where was it?" she asked. "Was it far? Is that why you couldn't get to Laurent in time?"

"Yes. It was in Zermatt, but completely on the other side of the village."

Juliette nodded and managed a weak smile.

Edgar's entire being yearned to touch her, to stroke his wife's hair and her porcelain skin, but he didn't want to push his luck. He didn't feel they were quite there yet. So, when Juliette levered herself off the bookcase she'd been leaning against and started toward the living room,

Edgar resisted the urge to grab her by the wrist and pull her into his arms.

No, Edgar was going to wait until Juliette invited him to join her in the living room. Then, hopefully, she would invite their son to join them. The thought brought the ghost of a smile to his cracked lips.

And then it got even better.

"Dad?"

Edgar spun toward his son. Sebastian had come out of his bedroom. He was smiling and seemed genuinely happy to see him. The big noise-canceling headphones around his son's neck had prevented Sebastian from hearing the quarrel between him and his wife.

"Hey, Sebastian. How are you? Come here, my man."

"Good . . . I'm good, I guess," Sebastian said, hesitant to get closer to his dad.

"I'm glad to see you, son," Edgar said, fighting back the tears welling up in his eyes.

To Edgar's left, the sound of a hammer being cocked had the effect of a cold shower. He slowly turned his head toward the sound. Juliette was pointing her revolver at him. Edgar noted she was holding the weapon in a two-hand grip and that her arms weren't shaking. But it was the cold resolve in her eyes that told him she would shoot him if he did anything she wasn't happy with.

"Mom? What are you doing?" Sebastian said. "Mom?"

"Get away from him, Sebastian. Now!" Juliette shouted.

Edgar looked at his son and nodded. "Don't worry, Seb. We'll work this out, I promise. But for now, do as your mother says, okay?"

"I'm not going anywhere! Tell me what the fuck is going on here!" Sebastian yelled. "Is this because of me? Oh my God, it is!"

"Stop, Sebastian! Just . . . stop!" Juliette shouted back. "It has nothing to do with you. Nothing! Your dad is . . . your father is a murderer. An assassin!"

"What? Are you mad? Why would you say something like that?" Sebastian said, his voice quavering.

"Tell him, Edgar. Tell him, or I will," Juliette hissed.

Edgar looked at his son. He didn't like what he saw. Sebastian was getting agitated, shifting his weight from one foot to the other. If the mood in the room didn't change real soon, Sebastian would lose control. If that happened, all bets were off.

Edgar ground his teeth. He'd been so close. Or at least he'd thought he was. Had Juliette played him from the beginning? It was evident she knew more than she had let on.

"I'll leave now, Juliette, okay?" he said. "There's no need for that gun. Please lower it."

"Fat chance of that, Edgar. You haven't watched the news recently, have you?"

Edgar felt beads of sweat building on his forehead. He hadn't watched the news in the last few hours. Had something come out that could compromise what he had just sworn to Juliette was the truth? Something incriminating? Something that would prove beyond any doubt that he was indeed a killer?

"You know the safe house you mentioned, Edgar?"

"What about it?"

"Minutes before you walked in here and started bullshitting me with your lies, I was watching the news on TV. Did you know that the Swiss authorities arrested two people with a direct link to human trafficking the night of the shooting? The images . . . the things these associates of yours have done . . . I had to send Sebastian to his room!"

Edgar stiffened. *Human trafficking?* This couldn't be. This had to be a mistake. Switzerland had nothing to do with Haiti.

"By the fucked-up face you have, I guess you didn't know your buddies had been arrested."

"Juliette, please, you have—"

"Shut up!" his wife said, walking toward him, the gun still pointed at his chest. "Before you start piling on more of your lies and excuses, you should know that the Swiss police found the address of the house they raided programmed into the GPS of your getaway car."

The wheels inside Edgar's head were spinning so fast he thought he might lose his balance. Nothing made sense. His contact, General Bilal Amirouche, had been the one who had given him the address where to drop Aldrich's family. None of his team members would have been dumb enough to enter the address on a GPS.

*Shit. Maybe not dumb enough, but tired enough?*

"You're addicted to the violence, Edgar. You're an animal. You hear me? An animal!" Juliette screamed at the top of her lungs. "Get out! Get out!"

Edgar looked over at his son. Sebastian was confused. His eyes were moist with tears as he continued to shift his weight from left to right.

"I'm sorry, Sebastian. I really am," he said. "Be kind to your mother, okay? She loves you very much."

Edgar pulled out his key from his pocket and showed it to Juliette. He then placed the key on the bookcase and left the apartment without another word.

# CHAPTER FIFTY-TWO

*Breuil-Cervinia, Italy*

Amy was already in a sour mood when she spotted a lone snowboarder in her peripheral vision. She was carving down the mountain at a high rate of speed, but the snowboarder was going even faster. Amy gave the snowboarder a lot of room to maneuver, but he suddenly veered to his right and lost control. He rammed into her left leg at full speed, sending them both over the edge of the trail and toward the rocks ten feet below.

Amy lost both of her skis during the collision but landed on a patch of packed snow between two big rocks. The impact took her breath away, but apart from a twisted knee, she was all right, her backpack having softened the blow considerably. Amy found her ski poles and used them to reach the snowboarder twenty-five feet higher. The snowboarder was clearly in immense pain, and there were tears in his eyes, but he began to yell insults in Russian at Amy the moment he saw her.

*Really? What an ass. To hell with him.*

Without saying a word, Amy changed direction and began to climb back toward the ski run, stopping to pick up her skis. The lifts were about to close, and with any luck, the man wouldn't be found until the next morning.

Amy reached the bottom of the hill four minutes later. She removed her skis, winced in pain as she picked them up, and placed them against the ski rack. What a shitty day this had turned out to be. It was hard to understand the clusterfuck it had become.

And yesterday had started so well!

Even now, as she walked with a slight limp toward the parking lot where she had left her rental, Amy could still feel the aftershocks of the rush of emotions she'd experienced when Caspian had finally opened his eyes. She'd been so happy.

And then, when their eyes had met, she'd thought she was going to melt. Just thinking about that moment again brought a delightful warmth that threatened to overtake her entire being. She shared an undeniable bond with that man. She just knew it.

And then, after she'd spent a considerable amount of time choosing the freshest of ingredients for their first meal together—an occasion she'd been thinking and dreaming about for so long—Caspian was gone. He had left Amy behind with only a cold, impersonal note to explain his decision. She understood the little game he wanted to play with her. She wasn't mad at him for that, but his timing had sucked. Big time.

For Christ's sake, she had nearly died at Le Clarion! That big cop had surprised her with his speed and agility. If Caspian had stayed with her, they could have gone after Aldrich's wife and her three kids as Elias. It could have been their first successful Elias op together. Maybe Caspian should have thought of that before leaving?

*What a waste.*

And what if she had been killed in Zermatt? What then? What would he have done without her?

Now that the two of them were about to get back together, Amy wasn't sure Caspian could have continued—or even wanted to continue—to live if she was gone.

*Not a chance,* she thought. *Not with the brutal guilt that would have assaulted him upon hearing I was dead. The poor thing would have slashed his wrists wide open.*

Amy shivered at the thought.

*We'll need to have a long, hard talk about all of this,* she said to herself, not for the first time.

Amy's phone vibrated in the front pocket of her ski coat. She thought about letting it ring, but she knew who it was. At some point she would have to take her mother's call.

Laura was still the boss. For now.

Amy removed her helmet and ski goggles and answered.

"I'm sorry I missed your previous calls," she said, after going through the authentication process.

"Are you okay?" her mom asked.

"I'm all right, but it turned out Aldrich's family was already gone when I got to their room."

"Damn it! That's what I feared. When they didn't mention their names in the news, I knew something had gone wrong."

"Do you know where they are?" Amy asked, looking for her car. She couldn't remember where she had left it.

"No. But I'll find out. Now, tell me about Caspian. Is he with you?"

"He isn't, but we ate together last night, and I'm pretty sure he never seriously considered leaving us," Amy lied as she looked for her car keys.

"What makes you say that?"

"Listen, Mother, I took the call just to let you know I was safe and on my way to Turin," she said. "Book me a flight to New York, and make sure it's in business class this time."

"Why do you want to go to New York?"

"Caspian and I agreed to meet there in two days' time. I'll update you then."

Amy ended the call and dropped her phone into her backpack. Car keys in her hand, she unlocked the vehicle.

"Oh, c'mon," she said, realizing her car was covered in snow. "What a fucking day."

Amy opened the door and sat in the driver's seat. She looked behind her for a snow brush that wasn't there. She started the car, its engine turning over on the first try. She closed the door. There was no point trying to remove the snow now from the windshield by activating the wipers; they were frozen in place. Amy turned the defrost blower on high and selected maximum heat. It was going to take a while to warm up the car.

Amy closed her eyes and began to massage her left knee, wondering if the injured snowboarder she'd left tangled amid the rocks had been found . . . or if he was going to freeze to death overnight.

Then the rear passenger door opened.

# CHAPTER FIFTY-THREE

*Breuil-Cervinia, Italy*

Caspian replaced the binocs on the seat next to him and replayed his conversation with Liesel in his head. Overall, he thought he'd done a decent job. Liesel hadn't asked too many pointed questions, which was good, and he'd stayed as close to the truth as he could.

The *Watch your back* at the end, though, had caused him to pause. It was somewhat out of character for Liesel to say something like that. Still, it had been a small blip in a largely positive chat.

At the other end of the parking lot, the flow of incoming skiers had slackened.

He did another pass with the binocs. An athletic woman with a slight limp caught his eye. She had just entered the parking lot with one of her arms deep into her backpack. The woman was still wearing her helmet and ski goggles, but Caspian knew it was Amy. This was confirmed moments later when she removed the equipment to take a call. Caspian stayed immobile, not wanting Amy's eyes to catch any movement coming from inside his vehicle.

Caspian wondered if she was talking with Laura. It would make sense, since her operation had failed. The call was short. Amy looked angry. Then the lights of her rental car flashed.

*Okay. Get ready. The car's unlocked.*

Caspian's plan was to use the right side of Amy's car to make his approach, since all the windows on that side were heavily covered in snow. He would then get in by the rear passenger door, but he was mentally prepared to rush to the other side of the car if the door handle or the door itself was frozen in place.

Seeing Amy easily open the driver's door attenuated his apprehension. When Amy disappeared into the vehicle, Caspian moved. There were ten, maybe twelve people in the parking lot, but Caspian didn't linger and covered the distance rapidly, keeping his suppressed SIG Sauer along his right leg.

His fingers found the handle, and he tried the door. It opened with a creaking sound, the heaviness of the snow weighing on its hinges, and Caspian slid into the rear seat, closing the door as soon as his right leg had cleared the frame.

"You move, you die," Caspian said, loud enough to ensure Amy heard him above the blower.

Amy's head spun, and she looked at him, her eyes open wide, her mouth hanging slack with shock.

"Two hands on the steering wheel. Now!" Caspian ordered her.

Amy's right hand moved to the wheel, but her left hand remained hidden. Caspian fired one round two inches below Amy's right thigh. The round entered the seat cushion and exited underneath the chassis.

"Both hands, Amy! Both hands! Next round goes in your neck," he warned her.

She gave him a warm smile. "I was just massaging my left leg," Amy said as she complied. "A maniac on a snowboard knocked me over midrun. I twisted my knee."

As Amy talked, Caspian could see she was assessing the options available to her.

*What would I do if the roles were reversed?* Caspian asked himself. *I'd try to smooth talk my way to a more advantageous position. Then I'd strike.*

Caspian had the upper hand, but if he was right, Amy's claim to have gone to med school was false. Caspian had a feeling that, like him, Amy was a pro, a seasoned assassin.

"Whatever you're thinking about doing, Amy, I'm thinking it too. So don't," he said.

She chuckled, her right dimple making an appearance. "I'm not thinking about anything. Honestly, Caspian, I'm just relieved, and so happy to see you. We have so much to talk about."

"That we do."

"And, oh my God, I can't believe you're actually sitting right there! Like, honestly, mind blowing!"

"Hands!" Caspian shouted as both of Amy's hands went to her head.

"Jesus! Have you gone mad? Did you forget I'm the one who kept you alive for three days? Please, Caspian, I beg you. Help me understand what's going on, okay? Whatever it is, we'll figure it out. Together. Like we used to. Remember?"

Despite his best effort, Caspian couldn't detect any indications that Amy was lying. There were no microexpressions to suggest she was telling anything but the truth.

The dynamic was very strange.

"I'll ask you a series of questions, and you'll answer them without thinking about your answers. If you lie, I'll know, and I'll hurt you. Understood?"

"Yes! That's all I'm asking. An honest dialogue between two friends. But I have to say, Caspian, what you just said to me is tactless and inappropriate. Because I would never—"

"Did you go to medical school?" Caspian asked, cutting her off. He'd had enough of her verbal diarrhea.

"I didn't, and I'm sorry I lied to you about that," Amy said. "This is so embarrassing. Listen, I . . . I just wanted you to feel safe, okay? Like . . . anyway. Enough said. I'm sorry."

"Did you at any time complete all the phases of the Onyx training pipeline?" Caspian asked.

"Yes. Two years before you did."

"Why were you on my selection course?"

Amy hesitated before she answered. Not long enough for Caspian to warn her, but he could see she wasn't happy to talk about that subject.

"Because of Laura. She wanted me to befriend as many future operators as possible, but rest assured, she never forced me to sleep with you." Amy kept her voice low, her eyes boring into his. "Sharing my bed with you was all me. My body, my choice, right?"

Caspian couldn't think of a reason why Laura would want a talented operator like Amy to waste her time befriending future Onyx operatives. Unless . . .

"What was Laura's objective in having you—"

"You're not gonna like my answer, Caspian," Amy said, interrupting him. "But I think it's important for you to know that my job at Onyx was to finish off injured operators."

Now it was Caspian's turned to be shocked as he realized the reason Amy had been sent to Zermatt.

"Laura sent you to Switzerland to kill me," he said.

"That was an option, yes," Amy confirmed.

"Why?"

"Because Laura doesn't trust you anymore."

Caspian stopped breathing, not because of what Amy had said but because of the way she had said it. Compared to her other answers, this one had come off as rehearsed. He focused on Amy's face and thought he detected a tell.

"Really? Why?" he asked, pressing his point.

"I wouldn't know. Laura doesn't share everything with me."

Now Amy was telling the truth again. He would circle back.

"Why was I sent to kill Leonard Aldrich?"

"You won't like this one either," Amy said, shaking her head.

"Answer the damn question," Caspian growled.

"Because somebody paid Laura a lot of money to get him killed," Amy said with a shrug. "There you have it. The truth."

"Are you saying Onyx has become a mercenary outfit?"

"Kind of. Yes."

Caspian's blood was boiling. While he had reached the same conclusion by himself after reading through Florence's messages, it was still difficult to hear. Caspian knew his emotions were getting the better of him, but he had a hard time controlling his anger.

How many of his kills had been work for hire?

He had so many questions. And Amy was going to answer all of them.

# CHAPTER FIFTY-FOUR

*Breuil-Cervinia, Italy*

Amy was sweating. She didn't know if it was due to the mounting heat inside the car or because of the negative vibe she was getting from Caspian. It was all wrong. She was no longer feeling the tenderness he'd shown her the day before.

Why had he lied to her about going back to New York? Did he want to make her look like a fool in front of her mother?

And then Amy understood, and her breath stuck in her throat. It was as if a large snake had wrapped itself around her neck and had begun to squeeze.

*They're plotting against me. Laura and Caspian.*

What else could it be? How could Caspian have found her car if not for her mother giving him the info?

*I've been such a fool.*

"Amy!" Caspian's voice shook her. "Answer the questions."

Amy blinked. She'd lost track of time for a moment. But she had a new purpose now. She had to find a way to destabilize Caspian. It was her only shot at getting out of the trap he and her mother had set up for her.

"What questions?" Amy shot back. "What questions?"

Caspian frowned at her and said, "How long has this been going on? Why did you go to Le Clarion this afternoon? Who wants Aldrich's family dead?"

"Why does it matter so much to you? Why? Killing for the star-spangled flag is cool, but when it's for money it isn't? You're a hypocrite, just like the rest of them. I thought you were different. I believed in you. Can't you see that? You macho men with the American flag tattooed over your heart are all the same. You're jokes. You look at your reflections in the mirror and you see yourselves as heroes, but you're not. You're pawns. Pawns!" Amy shouted.

And then, either due to the vibrations caused by her voice or the constant heat being pushed through the vents, a big chunk of the previously frozen snow on Caspian's window fell off, drawing his attention.

The instant Caspian's eyes were no longer on her, Amy pounced.

———

Startled by the sudden light coming in from the window next to him, Caspian's reaction was to distance himself from the next threat by tilting his body to his left—toward the middle of the car—and to whirl his weapon to his right. It took him less than half a second to realize there was no danger coming from his immediate right, but by the time his brain connected the dots, it was too late.

Amy, who had already propelled herself over the center console, landed on him, her right knee crashing and digging deep into his thigh while the fingers of her left hand encircled the wrist of his gun hand. An excruciating pain tore through Caspian's thigh, but Amy wasn't done. Her right arm was free. Caspian knew what was coming next and managed to tuck his chin in just as Amy's fist began to slam into the left side of his face again and again. Caspian saw stars, but the strength of her blows was drastically reduced by the poor position she was in. He sucked up the pain and was about to free his gun hand when Amy switched tactics and started to pummel the top of his injured left shoulder with powerful downward swings of her elbow. He tried to fight off the pain, but it was so intense that it overwhelmed his senses. He was in total agony and out of breath, and a blackness crept into his vision, threatening to overcome him.

Caspian willed himself to stay conscious. If he passed out, Amy would finish him off.

Then, surprising him, Amy used her left leg to push herself off the floor, and, as she came down, she thrust her right knee into his exposed groin.

Caspian howled as Amy crunched his balls under her knee. The pain, electric, shocked his nervous system and loosened his grip on the pistol. But since Amy was busy destroying his shoulder with her right arm, she didn't have the extra hand to snatch it away.

Caspian drove his head forward, trying to butt Amy's face, but due to the headrest inches behind him, he wasn't able to coil his strike as much as he wanted. Amy, who must have felt the strike coming, whipped to the side. His forehead hit the side of her jaw, causing no damage, except maybe to his own skull.

Caspian was desperate to create some distance between them. He didn't know how many more elbow strikes he could sustain before his arm became useless. Although he knew this would cause him a world of pain, he shoved a vicious open palm into Amy's solar plexus. As his palm sunk into Amy's midsection, he heard a hissing sound as the wind exploded out of her lungs.

But Amy was a ferocious fighter, and she didn't let go of his wrist. Still, her elbow strikes had stopped, no longer being in range of his shoulder. Caspian took full advantage of the short window of opportunity he'd created for himself to strike again, this time using all his strength while aiming for Amy's nose.

There was a loud, bone-crushing sound as his palm intercepted and tore into the cartilage of Amy's nose as her head descended toward his face with lightning speed. Had her forehead connected with his head, the blow would have knocked him out cold. But it hadn't.

Instead, the momentum of her own attempt at headbutting him had turned against her. Amy's head snapped back as if it had been hit by the back legs of a horse. Amy let go of his wrist and looked at him with a crazed look on her blood-covered face. Caspian swung his pistol at her, but he didn't pull the trigger. Amy blinked once and tried to say something; then her eyes became vacant as blood began to run out of her ears.

Caspian watched her as she fell to her side in slow motion.

Keeping his pistol close to him and in a two-hand grip, he leaned forward and looked at Amy, whose body was now shuddering between the driver's seat and the rear seat. Her eyes had remained open, but her mouth opened and closed in rapid succession, an obvious sign of severe and permanent brain damage.

Caspian closed his eyes and sighed.

Then he put two rounds into his former lover's head.

# CHAPTER FIFTY-FIVE

*New York, New York*

Rafael Ribeiro wiped the sweat off his brow with the back of his hand and glanced at the timer on the treadmill. The timer, which had started at forty-five minutes, now read five minutes and ten seconds.

Despite his seven-minute-per-mile pace, Rafael wasn't breathing very hard. He would never be a threat to any professional athlete, but neither would he run out of steam during a lovemaking session with Danielle. Four days a week, following thirty minutes of intensive weightlifting at the Edge Robots gym, he would go back to his office and jump on his personal treadmill and run for forty-five minutes, alternating between interval training and linear speed runs. Although there were three treadmills and a bunch of other cardio equipment in the employees' gym, Rafael preferred running alone in his office. The view from his office window was much better, and it allowed him to clear his mind while he ran.

Contrary to Danielle, who was addicted to the variety of information she got from her smartwatch during her workout, Rafael didn't need fancy accessories to let him know his muscles were working the way they were supposed to, or that his heart was beating faster.

He was sweating, wasn't he? That was good enough for him. Rafael wasn't the kind of man to cheat himself out of a full effort anyway. Smartwatch or not, he always pushed himself until the very end.

With four minutes remaining to his run, Rafael prepared himself for the final stretch. At the two-minute mark, he would tilt the incline another three degrees up and accelerate to a six-minute-per-mile pace. Rafael didn't carry his phone while he ran, and his staff knew better than to disturb him during his near-sacred workout time. So, when his assistant entered his office, Rafael shot him a harsh look, reflecting his dissatisfaction. He was about to start his sprint; now wasn't the time to be bothered.

"What . . . is it?" Rafael asked in between breaths.

"I'm sorry, sir, but you asked me to get you if there was ever someone from Banco Cielo calling. Someone from the bank is on line two."

Rafael's irritation with his assistant was replaced by a rush of adrenaline. Banco Cielo, a small Brazilian bank with offices in Brasília and Rio de Janeiro, was a Brazilian intelligence front. His ex-wife and handler, Dolores, rarely called his office directly.

Rafael slammed the palm of his hand onto the treadmill's emergency stop button and jumped off the still-moving belt, grabbing his towel in the process.

"Thank you," Rafael said to his assistant. "I'll take it here. Close the door behind you, will you?"

Rafael unlocked his office safe and pulled out one of his burner phones before taking the call.

"Rafael Ribeiro," he said.

"Please call us back at your earliest convenience, Mr. Ribeiro. You know the number," a man said before ending the call.

Rafael indeed knew the number. A minute later, he was speaking with Dolores.

"You had a good workout?" she asked.

Rafael's sweaty face turned red. He didn't like to be reminded that covert surveillance equipment had been installed in all the public spaces and offices of Edge Robots. Rafael knew very well this wasn't common practice in other start-ups and shell companies run by his country's intelligence agency. Dolores had sworn it was the Chinese that had made the request for the enhanced security package, but Rafael knew this was a lie.

His ex-wife was a jealous bitch: she was the one who had ordered the surveillance equipment; her only objective was to keep an eye on him, he was sure of it.

"What can Edge Robots do for you?" he asked, reaching across his desk for a bottle of water.

"Ha. No preambles," Dolores said. "Can't say I'm surprised, honestly. You've never been very good at foreplay."

Rafael was about to reply with a nasty comeback of his own, but that would only show Dolores her insult had gotten to him. The best response was to keep his mouth shut and act as if he couldn't care less what she thought, which was . . . mostly true.

"Whatever you say," he said, putting his feet on his desk, knowing Dolores was watching him. "Someone from your office mentioned this was urgent."

It took Dolores an extra second to reply, and Rafael imagined her pondering whether she should send another salvo of insults his way or get on with the real reason she had reached out to him. She chose the latter.

"I wanted to let you know that my suggestion about what to do with your girlfriend's boss has been approved," Dolores said.

Rafael sat at his desk, fuming. It had been his idea to remove Liesel Bergmann from the equation. At the very least, his ex-wife should have had the courtesy to say *our* suggestion, but Dolores being Dolores, she had found a way to make it all about herself. That was fine; he was going to add this to his growing list of reasons why he was going to take her down.

*The closer to the top of ABIN she gets, the harder will be her fall from grace.*

"During our last call, you were under the impression it would take a while to get a decision. What changed?"

"Chinese intelligence put their top US team on her," Dolores said. "She was seen meeting with a man named Nicklas Drescher. I'm—"

"Who's he?" Rafael asked, cutting her off.

"Will you let me finish?" his ex-wife snapped at him, her impatience at his interruption evident in her voice. But then she smoothed her tone and said, "He's a German intel officer. Our service doesn't have anything on him, but the Chinese do. The last time he was seen was in Venezuela four years ago. Apparently, the Chinese didn't think he had survived his trip to South America, whatever that means. And before you ask, that's all I know about Drescher."

"I wasn't going to ask," he said.

Rafael heard Dolores snort at the other end of the line.

"Anyway, the Chinese surveillance team had to let go of Bergmann at some point," she said. "Their report indicated she had been running an SDR."

"Which is kind of telling in itself, isn't it?" Rafael said. "But if they dropped her, how did they—"

"I was coming to that," Dolores said, this time keeping in check the typical annoyance she had when he asked a question. "I asked them the same thing, and my contact said that Chinese intelligence had a second, albeit smaller, team on Drescher. It's him they followed. His SDR wasn't as thorough, I suppose."

"A second team? In New York? How many guys do they have in this city?" Rafael asked, astonished at the number of intelligence operatives the Chinese had managed to position in New York.

"Obviously, more than we do," Dolores said. "I wouldn't be surprised if they had dozens of agents, and that's not counting the plethora of paid informants they have spread across the US. Anyhow, the second team was activated when one of the paid informants warned them of the Drescher sighting at LaGuardia."

Rafael thought about what Dolores had shared with him. A former German operative meeting with Bergmann wasn't enough to conclude Bergmann was a spy. But the fact that she was able to have a top Chinese surveillance team pull back because of an SDR: that was damning. Partners at shady accounting firms didn't go through intricate SDRs before they met with their clients.

"What's the next step?" he asked.

"She needs to be taken off the board," Dolores said. "Permanently. With that said—"

"I know what you're going to ask," Rafael said, once again interrupting his ex-wife. "Before the Chinese take her out, you want me to find out how deep into Edge Robots she managed to get."

He heard Dolores chuckle. "Chinese intelligence won't take her out, my dear, not on American soil," she said.

Rafael, hardly able to sit still, said through clenched teeth, "Who then?"

"What is it? You don't remember how it's done?" Dolores asked with cynicism. "When I first met you, you were pretty good at these sorts of things, weren't you?"

Rafael chose not to respond. He had become an intelligence officer to get away from the type of work he used to do when he was with the Batalhão de Operações Policiais Especiais—BOPE—a special unit of the Military Police of Rio de Janeiro State. For five years, Rafael had been one of the unit's top operators during the violent drug war BOPE had waged in the favelas of Rio de Janeiro. Rafael, oftentimes operating alone for days, had become an expert at tracking and eliminating targets larger forces couldn't get to. His skills weren't as sharp as they had once been, but there was no question he could get the job done. But his ex-wife didn't need to know that.

"It's been ten years," Rafael said. "You can't ask me to—"

"Oh, calm down," Dolores said. "You'll oversee the operation, and I want you to personally question Liesel Bergmann, but you've been authorized to hire a third party. It goes without saying that the third party needs to be on the vetted list of contractors. Understood?"

"Yes," Rafael said, pleased with himself. He was going to pocket the fee. There was no need for a third-party operator to come in.

"And one more thing. I want you to officially request the assistance of Catharina for this op. She's becoming quite the princess, don't you think? She needs to be reminded who she answers to. A bit of actual fieldwork will do her some good."

For once, it had seemed that Rafael and his ex-wife had found something they could both agree on.

# CHAPTER FIFTY-SIX

*New York, New York*

Liesel walked down the stairs to the subway station and pushed through a turnstile using her monthly pass. She entered an already crowded subway car and looked for a seat. As usual, they were all taken. Holding on to an overhead strap, Liesel let her mind wander as the train carried her through the tunnel.

She had texted a couple of times with Caspian in the last few days, but every time she had tried to speak to him, her call had gone directly to voicemail. The last two texts she had sent him had remained unread. Curious of Caspian's whereabouts, she had asked Nicklas to let her know his location. Her handler's reply had left her unsatisfied. Caspian's phone hadn't moved in the last twenty-four hours. Its last known location had been a few kilometers outside Turin.

Liesel missed her stop and had to exit at the next one. Edging her way past dozens of people waiting to board the train, she made her way through a series of wide, low-ceilinged passageways and took the escalator to the street level.

The sky was dark, and despite the temperature being slightly above freezing, a light snow drifted lazily down to the busy streets and sidewalks, contrasting with the recent rain that had fallen on the city. Liesel stopped by a small Italian café and ordered a double espresso. She paid the waiter with a five-dollar bill and left the change on the table. She drank her espresso on the spot, Italian-style, and thought the coffee had been perfect. Even the shop itself looked like it could be a transplant from a café she used to go to in Berlin. Liesel told herself it might be a good idea to miss her train stop more often.

As she was about to leave the coffee shop, she bumped into a short man who was on his way in, causing him to drop his phone. She apologized and picked it up for him before he could react. The screen was unlocked, and she could see the man was about to text a picture of the coffee shop's facade to someone. The text was in Mandarin. Liesel gave the man back his phone, apologized again, and went on her way without looking back, her heart racing.

There could be a lot of reasons why a person would text a photo of a coffee shop to someone, but Liesel's gut was telling her not to dismiss it too easily. A week ago, she wouldn't have been so paranoid about everything, but since she'd talked about the MSS and Caspian to Nicklas, she was more aware of her surroundings than she'd been in a long time. With that in mind, she decided to run a quick SDR instead of heading straight home like she'd planned to do.

———

Thirty minutes later, and satisfied she wasn't being followed, Liesel turned onto her street. She was almost home, and she wished she was already there with a glass of red wine in her hand. It had been a long, boring day at the office, spent dealing with a minor crisis about a possible IRS investigation into one of her firm's clients.

But at least it had taken her mind off Caspian.

She entered her building and took the elevator to her apartment on the twenty-third floor. Someone had left a yellow sticky note on her door.

*I'm inside. Didn't want to scare you.*

*—C*

The instant she read the words, Liesel's pulse quickened as if she'd been injected with a shot of adrenaline. She was angry but wildly excited at the same time. She seriously considered calling Nicklas to let him know Caspian was inside her apartment but decided against it. Liesel took a deep breath to calm her nerves but realized that it was acceptable for her to be anything but relaxed.

Her boyfriend had just come home after being away for more than a week, hadn't he? For her to look cool and composed wouldn't be natural.

*You got this,* she told herself as she inserted her key into the door lock.

The moment she stepped inside her apartment, she was greeted with softly playing jazz music and the smell of onion, garlic, tomatoes, beef, and something else . . . Was it bread? Had Caspian baked his own bread? Her mouth watered, and the warm, hearty odors instantly drained the tension from her body.

She walked into the kitchen and spotted a bottle of red wine decanting on the table Caspian had already set for two. Next to the wine, the table held a huge bouquet filled with her favorite flowers: orchids and roses.

"Nothing too fancy, don't worry," Caspian said, standing at the stove. "Caesar salad and spaghetti, but the sauce is homemade. And so is the bread."

Liesel looked at him. His eyes, the color of rare emeralds, were on her, penetrating and self-assured. Something stirred inside her, as was always the case when Caspian looked at her this way. He was wearing a pair of jeans and a white long-sleeve shirt, with the two top buttons undone, under the apron she'd bought for him last Christmas.

Liesel walked into his open arms and closed her eyes. Whatever Nicklas thought of Caspian, this man was no murderer. He might have secrets, but she had hers too.

"Do you need to apologize for something?" she asked a minute later.

Caspian pulled back from her and cradled her face with his hand. "Do you?"

She was about to reply when her stomach growled, which made Caspian chuckle. He gave her a light kiss on her lips, then said, "Let's eat, then we'll talk."

# CHAPTER FIFTY-SEVEN

*New York, New York*

Caspian uncorked a second bottle of wine and poured Liesel another glass. He knew something was bothering her, but he hadn't brought up the issue while they were eating, not wanting to spoil a perfect dinner—and an awfully good spaghetti sauce.

Caspian grabbed the wine and motioned Liesel to follow him to the living room. They sat together on her sofa and cuddled for a while, remaining silent and slowly drinking their wine.

During his long drive from Breuil-Cervinia to Lyon, where he had boarded a flight to London and then to New York, Caspian had rehearsed countless times what he wanted to say to Liesel. There was so much he wanted to share with her, and he didn't know where to start. Part of him longed to tell Liesel everything . . . but sharing too much too soon was rarely a good idea.

Since he had destroyed his Onyx phone prior to leaving Zermatt, reaching his handler had become slightly more tedious. In order to contact Laura, now either he had to go through an intricate phone arrangement or he could type a message on a secondary encrypted instant message service using an eleven-digit alphanumeric code he had committed to memory. Caspian had chosen the latter. Wondering if Laura had found out about Amy's death, he had let her know he was back in New York, no longer had his Onyx-supplied phone, and that thanks to Amy, he had reconsidered his departure from the program and had decided to stay for the time being. He had also written that he was planning on taking three to four weeks off to heal his wounds and wouldn't consider another assignment until then. He had ended the message by thanking Laura for sending Amy his way and saying that he would check in again in a few weeks.

In Italy, Caspian had been careful not to leave too many breadcrumbs that could lead to him, and he hoped that his message would be enough to convince Laura he hadn't had a hand in Amy's demise.

Minutes before Liesel had walked in, Caspian had been mulling over another problem. He had had the time to review the entire file he had found on Florence's thumb drive. While it was undeniable that Leonard Aldrich was scum, combing through the documents had revealed to Caspian another angle, albeit one he was struggling to come to terms with. From what he understood, Ambassador Claus Eichberg was using his position at the UN to run an organ trafficking operation. While Eichberg's efforts had been concentrated in Haiti for the past year, Caspian believed Eichberg had plans to expand his dealings to Kathmandu, Nepal.

Florence's thumb drive had given him a hint about how Aldrich had uncovered Eichberg's dealings. Five documents—all of them with the letterhead of Mellon, Borowitz and Associates, one of the top forensic accounting firms in New York and the one in which Liesel was a partner—had contained the findings of a deep dive someone high up at the firm had performed on Eichberg's finances. Caspian believed Aldrich had hired the firm to probe into Eichberg's accounts to get a leg up on the ambassador in case their relationship ever soured.

Aldrich had turned greedy, though, and instead of keeping his discovery for future use—or doing the right thing by sharing his findings with the authorities—he had tried to blackmail Claus Eichberg.

A deadly mistake.

Whether Florence's mother had believed her husband had been the head honcho of the organ trafficking ring or simply complicit in it,

Caspian didn't know. But she'd been disgusted—and ashamed—enough to hire someone to dispose of her husband in a permanent manner.

The other team, the one that included Ballcap, had to have been there for the same reason Caspian had been. Neither Caspian nor the other team had known about the presence of the other.

Florence had told Caspian her mother hadn't expected a squad to show up. That meant she wasn't the one who had hired Ballcap's team of abductors. Had Ambassador Eichberg financed Ballcap's team? It was possible. It was something Caspian was planning to investigate.

Caspian had concluded that he wouldn't share with Liesel his suspicion about Eichberg. Not until he knew for sure what role her firm had played in this mess. Still, even if he didn't mention her firm's connection to Eichberg, the odds were that she was going to throw him out of her apartment. He had deceived her, and no woman liked to be lied to. And he hadn't misled her only once or twice but the entire time they'd been together. Their entire relationship was based on a big fat lie.

Liesel stirred against him and said, "This is nice."

It was nice, and Caspian wished they could stay like that for another hour, even though he knew doing so would only push back the inevitable.

After a while, she angled her head and looked at him. Her brown eyes, glistening with a moisture that wouldn't fall, were filled with so much raw emotion that it pulled at his heart. It took a colossal effort on his part not to simply lift Liesel in his arms and carry her to the bedroom.

"You asked me earlier if there was something I wanted to apologize for," he said.

"I'm not sure I want to know," she said, her voice a whisper.

He kissed the top of Liesel's head, finished his wine, then set the glass down on the small end table next to the sofa.

"I've thought long and hard about how this would go down," he said.

"By 'this,' you mean the chat we're having right now?" Liesel asked.

Caspian nodded, and Liesel returned to her previous cuddling position.

"Okay," she said.

"I care a lot about you, Liesel," he said, "and there's nothing I'd like more than to stay in your life, but I understand this might not be possible after what I'm about to tell you."

Caspian's heart felt like a jackhammer in his chest. Liesel must have felt it, too, because she gently placed a hand over his heart. She didn't say a word, but she leaned harder into his side.

"Although I'm really working as a translator at the United Nations, the job is a cover for something else I'm doing."

Caspian felt Liesel's body tense against him, but she didn't move away. He waited for her to ask a question, but when she didn't, he continued.

"Ten years ago, I joined the Department of Homeland Security, more specifically HSI, the department's investigative arm. I've been undercover at the UN since."

Liesel pushed herself off him and shifted her weight on the sofa, but Caspian noted she had remained close to him.

"So, you're some kind of federal agent?" she asked.

There was no anger stemming from her question, and Liesel's voice was calm and poised, a far cry from what he had expected.

"Yes," he said.

"All these places you've been to, were they business trips you took for the UN or something else?" she asked.

"Both," he said.

"What about Geneva?"

"Both," he repeated.

"No. You'll have to open up more than that, Caspian," Liesel warned him. "I'm done with your monosyllabic answers."

Caspian had always known it would come to this, but he was yet to decide what he would say to her when the moment came.

So, he told her the truth. Mostly.

"The Geneva part of the trip was for the UN, but Zermatt and Breuil-Cervinia weren't," he said.

Liesel swallowed the rest of her wine in one big gulp; then she took a long breath and exhaled slowly through her mouth.

"The bottle, please?" she said, pointing at the coffee table.

Caspian reached for the bottle of red and poured some wine into Liesel's empty glass.

"Thank you," she said.

Liesel didn't look as distressed as he had imagined she would, and he had a hard time understanding why. If he'd been in her shoes, he would have been livid.

"In Zermatt," Liesel said after taking one more sip of her wine, "there were two shootings. We briefly talked about them on the phone. You told me you didn't know anything more about them than what was in the news, but now that I'm looking at the shootings through different lenses, I think you might have lied to me. So, I'll ask you this: Were you involved in any way?"

This was the moment of truth. So far, Liesel had seemed to accept the fact he'd been an undercover federal agent. After all, working for Uncle Sam was an honorable profession, was it not? If this had been the end of it, Caspian knew she would eventually reach the conclusion that keeping his true identity from her had been a necessary lie.

But this wasn't the end of it. There was no way he could hide the two bullet wounds he had sustained.

What he was about to show her would shake her world.

And it terrified him.

# CHAPTER FIFTY-EIGHT

*New York, New York*

Liesel knew the wine had slowed her thought process, but she didn't believe her inebriated state was the reason why she hung on to Caspian's every word. The more he shared with her, the more she believed him.

It all made sense. And Nicklas would agree. He had to.

Her last question concerning the shootings in Zermatt hadn't seemed to make him shy away either. Nor had it shocked him. She had half expected him to instantly deny any involvement, but he hadn't. In fact, his green eyes still held the same intensity as earlier.

Caspian got up from the sofa and gestured for her to stay put. He slowly unbuttoned his shirt, and she wondered what he had in mind. If she was perfectly honest with herself, at that very moment, and with the intensity in which his eyes bored into her, she had only one thing in mind, and it wasn't conversation.

Then, when Caspian's white shirt fell in a heap at his feet, her breath caught.

"*Oh, mein Gott*, Caspian," she murmured, looking at his injuries.

"The answer to your question is yes," Caspian said. "I was very much involved."

Liesel set her wineglass on the coffee table and got up from the sofa. She stood next to Caspian, almost touching him.

"You're the man they're looking for, aren't you?" she asked softly. "You're the one who saved that family at the hotel."

"I wasn't even supposed to be there," Caspian replied. "I was there to investigate a man named Leonard Aldrich. It all happened so quickly."

Aldrich's name sent electric impulses into Liesel's brain.

*What? Caspian was there for Aldrich? Is the American government running an operation against him? Am I on their radar too?*

Now Liesel wished she hadn't drunk so much. She looked at Caspian for any sign of duplicity, but she didn't see any. Quite the contrary.

"Are you all right?" he asked, cupping her chin with one of his hands.

"I'm fine," she assured him. "It's a lot to take in."

"I know," he said, diverting a strand of hair away from her face.

"Why were you investigating Aldrich?" she asked.

He gave her a puzzled look, and she cursed herself for asking the question, but his eyes softened.

"We thought the guy was involved in human trafficking. But I'm not so sure anymore. I got to look at some documents," Caspian said, then paused for an instant, as if he was expecting her to say something. When she didn't, he continued, "I'm starting to think Aldrich had nothing to do with it. He certainly knew about it, but if I was a betting man, I'd say he was trying to use the information he had uncovered to blackmail someone."

Liesel could think of at least five questions she wanted to ask Caspian as follow-ups, but she bit her tongue, doing her best to remain in character. She would have to be patient, but she would circle back in a few days.

"Does it hurt?" she asked, tracing the edge of the wound on his left shoulder with the tip of her finger.

"A little."

"You know that I should be furious with you right now, yes?" she said, her hand moving to the back of Caspian's neck. "But I find this whole James Bond thing very, very hot."

Caspian smiled and said, "Is that so? And what about you? Do you have something you'd like to confess?"

Her heart skipped. Did Caspian know? And what if he did? Would it really matter? Was he giving her the opportunity to come clean and start anew? It was tempting.

*Careful, Liesel. That's the wine talking.*

She wanted to look into his eyes to find the answers to her questions, but his gaze was lingering on her lips, as if he was about to kiss her.

*No. He knows nothing,* she thought, or hoped.

"Promise me, Caspian. No more lies, okay?" she said, drawing him in. He nodded. "No more lies."

———

When Liesel opened her eyes the next morning and saw Caspian next to her, a genuine ear-to-ear grin appeared on her sleepy face. She propped herself up on one elbow and examined the wound on his shoulder as he slept. Later today, she was going to update Nicklas about Caspian, but for now, she wanted to enjoy her morning with him.

There was nothing Caspian had told her last night that exonerated him or proved beyond any doubt he wasn't Elias.

*And . . . I don't care,* she thought, slightly puzzled by her lack of concern. *I really don't.*

She snuggled her back against him, and Caspian stirred. A moment later, she felt his hand on her belly as he pulled her in closer.

Later, while he was in the shower, she received a notification on her phone. She logged in to her encrypted mailbox. Nicklas had sent her a message.

It's approved. In two days from now, C.E. is leaving for DC aboard chartered jet. See attached schedule and tail number for reference. Good luck. I'll update as needed.

# CHAPTER FIFTY-NINE

*New York, New York*

Eichberg waved at Rafael Ribeiro as the Brazilian intelligence officer walked into the restaurant. The place was packed with the professional lunch crowd. Eichberg had chosen the restaurant because Catharina loved its lobster bisque. Eichberg was partial to the Cobb salad. The wine cellar wasn't bad, either, and they were already halfway through a bottle of chardonnay.

When Ribeiro reached the table, he kissed Catharina on both cheeks and shook Eichberg's hand.

"Sorry I'm late," he said, taking a seat.

"Busy morning?" Catharina asked.

"You can say that."

Eichberg was about to pour Ribeiro some wine, but the spy covered his glass with his hand and shook his head.

"Not for me, and I hope this isn't your second bottle," he said, his voice serious. "Because you'll need a clear head for what I'm about to tell you."

Eichberg didn't like the sound of that. His nerves had taken a beating during his meeting with Bilal Amirouche, and he was yet to recuperate fully. Eichberg had spent the last two days setting up meetings in Washington, DC, with fund managers and elected officials.

Their waiter arrived with a basket of freshly baked breads and took their lunch orders.

"What's so important that it couldn't wait until we're back from DC?" Eichberg asked once the waiter had walked away.

"We?" Ribeiro asked. "I wasn't aware Catharina was traveling with you."

"I was just about to text you," Catharina said, breaking a piece of bread.

"She's pretty good at schmoozing, but you already knew that," Eichberg said. "We're leaving tomorrow afternoon. We should be there for a day or two."

Ribeiro made a face.

"What?" Eichberg asked.

"You might want to reconsider your trip," Ribeiro said.

"I don't think so," Eichberg replied. "I've got appointments, some of them critical to our operation, lined up almost nonstop. I had to call in a few favors to get these meetings, so I'm not about to back out of them, Rafael."

Eichberg felt Catharina's hand on his lap. "Let's see what he has to say, yes?" she said.

Ribeiro leaned in and said, "Does the name Liesel Bergmann ring any bells?"

"I've heard the name but can't seem to remember when or where. Why?"

"Same here," Catharina said.

Ribeiro pulled a phone from the breast pocket of his suit jacket and placed it on the table. Eichberg watched him scroll through a number of files, then click on one. Ribeiro turned the phone toward Eichberg, and said, "This is Liesel Bergmann. You recognize her now?"

Eichberg did. She was one of the forensic accountants working at Mellon, Borowitz and Associates. He'd never liked the firm, had always found them to be too nosy, but Aldrich had sworn by them. Now that Aldrich was out of the picture, Eichberg was going to switch firms.

Mellon, Borowitz and Associates weren't the only accountants in town capable of looking the other way.

"Who is she?" Catharina asked.

"An accountant," Eichberg replied; then, turning his head toward Ribeiro, he asked, "Why are you showing me this picture?"

"We believe Bergmann is with German intelligence and that she's presently investigating Edge Robots."

Eichberg felt the color drain from his face, and a band seemed to tighten around his chest. It couldn't be. Ribeiro had to be making some sort of mistake.

"What makes you believe that?" Catharina asked.

"She planted a sniffer program on my phone," Ribeiro said. "We believe we caught it in time—"

Eichberg exploded and slammed the palm of his hand against the starched white tablecloth, knocking off his and Catharina's wineglasses. "You believed?" he howled.

Ribeiro looked at him, his eyes like daggers. "Get yourself under control, you moron," he hissed.

"Rafael's right," Catharina said, squeezing his thigh. "Let's hear what he has to say, dear."

Eichberg slapped Catharina's hand away, then loosened his tie. She had no idea of the stress he was under. She hadn't been at the dining table when Amirouche had forced him to eat some sort of weird animal's anus. Eichberg was convinced he had ingested some kind of bacteria or bug because he hadn't stopped having diarrhea since.

As much as Eichberg hated to admit it, Ribeiro and Catharina were right: he had to remain in control. Eichberg risked a glance around the restaurant. Everyone was chatting, drinking, or eating, and they were all dutifully ignoring his table.

"My apologies," Eichberg said, forcing a smile. "Please continue."

"At first, we weren't sure if she was working on behalf of her firm or by herself. I ran it up my chain of command, and I learned that my message was passed on to our friends in China, who put a team on her. She was seen meeting with a known BND officer."

Eichberg massaged the bridge of his nose with his fingers, the band around his chest getting tighter. If German intelligence was aware that Edge Robots was a front for the Chinese, the investment of German public funds into the start-up would cause Eichberg to be recalled to Berlin, but he doubted he would ever face criminal charges. The chancellor would be frantic to close the case.

And anyway, how could they prove Eichberg knew the Chinese were pulling the strings at Edge Robots? They couldn't. He would claim innocence.

But what if the BND had investigated deeper into his finances and dealings at the United Nations? Eichberg had thought his accounts were well hidden, but Aldrich had managed to get his hands on some incriminating evidence, or so he had claimed. If the operation in Zermatt had gone according to Eichberg's plan, he would have learned how Aldrich had obtained the documents. But the op had failed, and now Eichberg was left pondering whether he wasn't being outplayed.

He looked over at Catharina. Had she told Ribeiro about his other dealings? Was Ribeiro aware that Eichberg was harvesting and selling organs? The worry on Catharina's face suggested she hadn't. She appeared to be in as much distress as he was, which made him feel better.

"What now?" Eichberg asked, looking once again at the photo of Liesel Bergmann.

"I'll have a little chat with Miss Bergmann," Ribeiro said, his voice just loud enough to carry across the table. "I'll find out what she knows, and then we'll adjust accordingly, depending on what she says."

"I'm sure you'll agree with me that she can't go back to Mellon, Borowitz and Associates," Catharina said.

Ribeiro nodded. "For that part, I'll need your assistance, Catharina."

"My assistance? With Bergmann?" Catharina asked.

"The home office was adamant about it," Ribeiro said. "Feel free to appeal their decision, but it wouldn't look good for you."

Eichberg, who had been scrolling through the different photos of Liesel Bergmann, suddenly stopped. Panic tightened his throat, and the pressure in his chest turned painful. He pushed the phone toward Ribeiro.

"Who's he?" Eichberg asked through clenched teeth, even though he already knew the answer to that.

"His name is Caspian Anderson. He's Bergmann's boyfriend. He's not a player," Ribeiro said.

Eichberg glanced at Catharina, but his vision had blurred as an opaque terror enveloped him, almost choking him. Eichberg commanded himself to breathe, and his vision returned, only for him to realize that Catharina's face had turned pale. She, too, understood the significance of Caspian Anderson's presence in Zermatt.

Caspian Anderson was a German intelligence officer. Always had been.

Eichberg's brain was bombarded by questions. How long had the German spy agency known about his activities? Why hadn't he been recalled? Was he currently under surveillance?

*Mein Gott! Of course I am!*

His whole world was collapsing around him. He was done. They were done.

"Are you all right, Claus?" Ribeiro asked.

Eichberg slowly nodded, his brain racing to find a solution to the mess he found himself in. He had already chartered a small jet to take him and Catharina from New York to Washington, DC, the next day, and he knew the private aviation company he dealt with had already filed a flight plan. The instant Eichberg returned home, he would call them to request a plane with more range. He wouldn't tell them why, and he doubted they would ask.

*As long as they're getting paid,* he thought.

Despite his instincts screaming at him to leave the country now, he knew it would be a foolish decision. If the German BND, and maybe even the Americans, was onto him, they would move on him the moment they knew he was leaving the country. Changing the flight plan too early was a bad idea. He would wait until the very last minute to do it. And truth be told, Eichberg didn't yet know where he and Catharina could go.

Eichberg's only remaining play was to find a country that hadn't signed an extradition treaty with the US or Germany—or even Brazil, if Catharina decided to join him—and the clock was ticking.

# CHAPTER SIXTY

*New York, New York*

Caspian stretched his legs as best he could, then moved on to his neck, spending a few seconds on each side. He'd been behind the wheel of his Toyota Camry for the last three hours. But the car hadn't moved. It was parked in a garage—which wasn't heated—near the corner of East Seventy-Third Street and Fifth Avenue, which was ideally situated, since it was less than a one-minute walk from Ambassador Claus Eichberg's lavish townhouse near Madison Avenue and East Seventy-Third Street. Eichberg's residence, which in fact had belonged to the German government for the last eight years, had been built in 1901 and had six bedrooms and five full bathrooms, and if Caspian was to believe the eight-year-old real estate listing he had found on the internet, it had high ceilings on all three floors and was *gloriously* light filled. Caspian didn't know exactly what the difference between a light-filled home and one that was *gloriously* light filled was, but he admitted it sounded nice.

Caspian hoped Eichberg had enjoyed his time in New York because if Caspian had anything to say about it, the ambassador's stint at the United Nations would soon come to an abrupt end.

Caspian glanced at the screen of his tablet, wondering if Eichberg and Catharina would go out for lunch. Earlier in the day, Caspian had installed three miniature sticky cameras near Eichberg's townhouse. He had affixed the first one at the back of a parking meter, the second on the side of a mailbox, and the third one to a fire hydrant. All three had zooming functionality and a thermal mode that could be activated by a quick tap on his tablet.

Sitting in his sedan, watching a screen, was a big step down from what he and Liesel had done together over the last two days, which they had both taken off. They had gone on long walks, visited a couple of museums, and even rented electric scooters.

Liesel had gone back to work that morning, and Caspian had taken the subway to the United Nations, but not to go to work like he'd told Liesel. Caspian had walked into his superior's office and had requested the rest of the week off. His boss had signed his request, since the workload at the office wasn't heavy, but he had reminded Caspian that two of his days off would have to be without pay as he had already burned through all his annual paid vacation time.

Not that it mattered. Caspian had no plan to go back to the United Nations and had quickly stopped by his desk to pick up the only personal item he cared about: a Montblanc pen his father had given him for his eighteenth birthday. An hour later, he had parked his Camry in the garage.

His objective was to establish a pattern of life on Eichberg and his wife. He wanted to know their schedules, who had access to the property, what car companies they used to travel within the city, and how many people actually lived in the townhouse. Once he had established that, he would move on to more intrusive measures and would look for an opportunity to access the property and install surveillance equipment inside the house. Aware the German government had video surveillance installed outside the property—Caspian had so far spotted two cameras—he would need to think long and hard about how he would do that. For now, the car service was the lowest-hanging fruit. Caspian didn't imagine he would have any difficulty tagging the chauffeur and the car assigned to Catharina and Eichberg with a listening device.

Caspian was watching the screen when a black Mercedes sedan stopped in front of Eichberg's residence. Caspian sat straighter in his beige fabric seat; it was the first interesting action of the day. A man in a driver's uniform exited the car and climbed the five concrete steps leading to Eichberg's front door.

A moment later, Eichberg opened the door and let the driver in, but he didn't close the door. Shortly after, the driver walked out with two large suitcases, put them in the trunk of the Mercedes, then repeated the process with two more suitcases. The only difference was that the driver, despite his best effort, had to put the fourth suitcase on the rear seat of the sedan because the trunk wouldn't close with it in the back.

When Eichberg was the only person to step out of the townhouse and climb into the Mercedes, Caspian cocked his head.

*Where's Catharina?* he asked himself as he watched the Mercedes pull away from the curb.

# CHAPTER SIXTY-ONE

*New York, New York*

Rafael Ribeiro looked over at Catharina and was glad to see she didn't look anxious. On the contrary, there was a light in her eyes he hadn't seen in a while.

"You're enjoying this, aren't you?" he asked in Portuguese.

She shrugged. "Not really."

Rafael smiled. She was lying.

"Is the alarm on?" he asked.

"Yes. Claus put it on before he left. Doors only. We can move around the house without triggering the alarm."

Rafael didn't ask about the surveillance cameras. He already knew they were off. Mere weeks after Eichberg and Catharina had moved into the house, technicians working for Brazilian intelligence had come in and rewired the antiquated system in a way that would allow Eichberg to turn off the exterior surveillance cameras without alerting the security officer monitoring them. When Rafael had entered the house the night before, the cameras hadn't recorded his arrival.

They were in Eichberg's impressive library on the second floor of the residence. Rafael, who had always been an avid reader, was fascinated by the number of leather-bound and first edition books lining the floor-to-ceiling oak shelves that occupied two of the four walls. The exterior wall had three large windows that were partially covered with full-length drapes, and a fireplace occupied the fourth. In the middle of the library, two three-person leather couches—with their appropriate end tables and reading lamps—faced each other, with a coffee table in between them. Despite its grandeur, the room felt cozy, and its smell—a mix of high-end tobacco, ink, and old varnish—reminded Rafael of his father's reading room at their ranch an hour away from São Paulo.

On the end table to his left, Rafael's phone pulsed. It was his Chinese contact at the MSS. The last time Rafael had received an update from him, it had been to let him know that Liesel Bergmann had finally returned to work after spending two blissful days with her boyfriend, Caspian Anderson.

"Bergmann has been on the move for the last hour," Rafael said after reading the new update. "They think she's running an SDR."

"Where do you think she's heading to?" Catharina asked.

"The fact that she's doing an SDR tells me she's either on her way here or about to meet with her handler," he said.

"I think she's coming here. The timing is right," Catharina said.

"It is."

Rafael was betting that Bergmann was somehow monitoring Eichberg's movements. The ambassador hadn't made it a secret that he and Catharina were on their way to Washington, DC, for a quick twenty-four-hour trip. If Bergmann was looking for ways to prove Eichberg's involvement in a financing scheme, making a stop at the ambassador's house had to be on her to-do list.

The directives Rafael had received for this mission were clear. He was to find out what Bergmann knew about the financial stratagem Leonard Aldrich had put together.

Eichberg had been an esteemed partner from the get-go. He had been a superb behind-the-scenes advocate for the foreign policies of Brazil and China. Eichberg had followed the script to perfection, convincing in private many people at the UN that an expansion of the BRICS—a group of leading developing countries in which China and Brazil were original members—wasn't to be feared, despite what the

Americans might say. And it seemed to have worked, because during the BRICS' latest three-day summit, dozens of nations—many of which had previously been nervous to declare their support for the group— had expressed an interest in joining the coalition. This was a major political win for the BRICS.

The current BND investigation had put Eichberg's future influence with the German chancellor in jeopardy, but not before Eichberg had managed to persuade the German venture fund into investing heavily in Edge Robots. That objective had also been accomplished: Germany was compromised.

And with these two successes, Eichberg's value to the operation had shrunk. There wasn't much else the man could accomplish for them. Although Eichberg didn't know it yet, Rafael had read the tea leaves: the ambassador's affiliation with Brazil's spy agency was coming to an end.

But one question kept nagging at Rafael: Which side was Catharina on? Was she with team Brazil, or Eichberg's? Rafael felt he was missing an important piece of the puzzle. He hoped Catharina would enlighten him.

"Everything all right with Claus?" Rafael asked.

"Where's that coming from?" Catharina replied.

"Well . . . How would you feel if you were ordered to leave him?" he asked, keeping his eyes on her, trying to get the slightest hint of a reaction. He didn't get one.

"Do you know something I don't, Rafael?"

If there was one thing that irritated Rafael, it was being answered with a question.

"This isn't an interrogation, Catharina," he said. "This is two friends talking."

"My question is still valid. Why are you suddenly interested in my marriage?"

Rafael scooted forward on the couch and reached for the carafe of water. He poured himself a glass and offered to do the same for Catharina, but she shook her head.

"You did a fantastic job bringing him in, Catharina," Rafael said. "You've gone up two pay grades since you married him six years ago."

Catharina chuckled. "I live in a ten-million-dollar townhouse in one of the most expensive cities in the world, Rafael. Do you think I care if I make an extra five thousand US per year?"

"That's the problem, Catharina. This house doesn't belong to you. This isn't your real life," Rafael said. "You're an intelligence officer, not a trophy wife."

"You're incorrect," she replied. "I'm legally married to Claus. Half of what he made since we are together is mine."

Rafael knew she wasn't wrong, but her superiors at ABIN headquarters wouldn't see it that way. Catharina served at their pleasure, not the other way around.

"Listen," he said. "I get it. I'm in the same boat. I'm living like a king here—"

"That's very rich coming from you, Rafael," Catharina said, giving him a dirty look. "You come from a wealthy family. You joined a special unit of the military police and then ABIN for the adventure and the thrills these jobs offered. I joined to get out of my miserable life. You, my friend, can pull the plug any time you want and go back to your racehorses and sports cars. I can't! I have nothing to get back to!"

It was obvious which team Catharina was now playing for, so Ribeiro held up his hands in mock surrender. He forced a smile and said, "You got me. I'd do the same thing in your shoes, but I think you should—"

His phone chirped again, interrupting him.

"The Chinese surveillance team is pulling back, but they think she might be on her way here," he said.

"We should get ready," Catharina said, getting to her feet. "How do you want to play it?"

"Just as we talked about. It is imperative that we find out exactly what she knows. I'm hoping she's still in the initial phase of her investigation. In the end, though, Liesel Bergmann isn't getting out of here alive."

# CHAPTER SIXTY-TWO

*Paris, France*

One block away from the Airbnb he had rented for the next three weeks, Edgar sat alone at the bar, nursing his beer. The last forty-eight hours had been brutal on his psyche. He had called his son several times, but Sebastian hadn't picked up. Edgar hoped that the reason Sebastian wasn't answering was due to Juliette confiscating his phone, not due to Sebastian's conscious decision to reject his calls. Edgar had left many messages, and now his son's voicemail was full.

He had tried to reach Juliette, too, mainly by texting her, but his messages were no longer being delivered.

*She blocked me.*

Edgar wasn't mad at her, though. He might have done the same if the roles had been reversed, especially if Juliette had been right about the two men the police had arrested at his supposed safe house in Zermatt. The day before, Edgar had reached out to his contact, Bilal Amirouche, to inquire about the two men. Amirouche had yet to respond to Edgar's query, and Edgar planned on nudging him if he didn't hear back from the former general by the end of tomorrow.

For now, all Edgar knew about the two men was what the police had shared with the public. The men, one American and one Serbian, who were now facing charges of human trafficking, were also wanted in several countries for the illegal sale of human organs.

*Human organs?* The news had left Edgar speechless and dumb-founded about his own role in such a wretched business.

Just thinking about it brought up a new wave of nausea.

Was that what he and his team had been doing for the general these past months? Were the poor people he had picked up in Haiti brought to Europe to be mutilated? That hadn't been part of the deal. If he had known about that, he would have never accepted. That was a line he wouldn't have crossed, no matter the amount of money offered.

And, to add misery to his already muddled mind, he had learned through a call he had placed to the hospital in Visp that Laurent's health had taken a turn for the worse. His younger brother wasn't expected to live past the next twenty-four hours.

Not being able to be by his brother's side saddened Edgar to no end. The enormous guilt, combined with the shame, was eating him up to the point where an hour ago, Edgar had thought about putting an end to it all. He had gone as far as putting his FN 509 pistol deep into his mouth. His finger had already been more than halfway through the trigger slack when an image of Sebastian had flashed through his mind.

What kind of example would he set for Sebastian if he took his own life?

Disgusted with himself, Edgar had holstered the pistol, then run to the bathroom to vomit in the toilet of his rental apartment. Three glasses of water later, he had walked to the brasserie where he was now drinking his second beer. His mind, which Edgar didn't seem to have control over any longer, once again forced him to think about The Smoker.

What had been the man's true role in Zermatt? Even if Edgar had not been aware of it at the time, one of his mission objectives had been to deliver Aldrich's family members to a two-man team who had been planning on selling their body parts. If Edgar was ready to admit that he and his team weren't the protagonists in this story, did that make The Smoker the good guy? It wasn't something easy for Edgar to concede, but if The Smoker hadn't intervened, Aldrich's wife and daughters would no longer have all their body parts.

*Putain de merde!*

*Juliette is right . . . I'm the biggest hazard in Sebastian's life. He'll do better without me in his life.*

Edgar understood that walking away would be following in his father's footsteps and that he would break the most important vow he had ever made in his life, but what if walking away was the right thing to do?

A few barstools away, a large man with a buzz cut was typing a message on his phone. This gave Edgar an idea. If he could borrow the man's phone, he could use it to reach out to Juliette and Sebastian, couldn't he? They wouldn't recognize the number, but they would see his text, right?

Sure, Juliette would eventually block that phone, too, but not before she had read, or at least seen, his message. It was important for Edgar that his wife and son understood that he was leaving not because he didn't love them or because he didn't want to face his responsibilities but to offer them a better life and a chance to live without his evil influence.

Edgar was pondering how much he should offer the man in exchange for his phone when his own phone chirped, announcing an incoming text.

A rush of adrenaline shot through him, and he rapidly pulled his phone out of his jeans pocket, praying for a response from Juliette or Sebastian. While he recognized the sender's number, the message hadn't come from his wife or his son, but from Amirouche.

In a fit of rage, Edgar hurled his phone over the bar and into the glass shelves holding the liquor bottles. His phone flew in between two bottles of cheap vodka and shattered the mirror behind them.

"Hey! What's wrong with you, asshole?" yelled the bartender in French, pointing a menacing finger at Edgar.

The man who had been typing on his phone a few barstools away stood up. He wasn't much taller than Edgar's six-one frame, but he must have weighed fifty pounds more, most of it muscle. His tight white T-shirt showed off his biceps. The bartender, a stocky man in his fifties, jumped over the bar and joined the heavyset man. Edgar could see the bartender was the kind of man who enjoyed a good fight.

A few other patrons set their beers on the table to watch the show. Edgar thought about leaving but changed his mind. He turned to face the two men and eyed the bartender, who had one foot out and the other back.

*Right handed,* Edgar thought.

Someone in the crowd started to shout "Da-niel! Da-niel! Da-niel!" and was quickly joined by the other customers. The heavyset man with the white T-shirt smiled and lifted an arm in the air in a victory sign.

"I guess that makes you Daniel, yes?" Edgar said in French.

With the crowd chanting the man's name, Edgar saw that Daniel's demeanor had changed. He was no longer studying Edgar; he was now looking for a way to drop his opponent with a single punch, probably to the head, to impress his drinking buddies. Daniel's hands became two massive square fists the size of bricks, and he attacked a heartbeat later with a one-two combination. Edgar easily bobbed away from the left jab before ducking under the telegraphed, but mighty, right hook that followed a flash later. The big man, who had put everything he had behind the punch, found himself off balance as his sizable fist flew over Edgar's head.

Edgar swung a hard right fist into the man's exposed left kidney. The big man yelled in pain. His mouth was still open when Edgar's left hook caught him on the chin. Daniel's legs gave out and he crumbled to the floor, as if all the muscles, tendons, and ligaments that held him upright had gone to bed for the night.

Edgar had to give the bartender some credit. Even though he'd seen the big man fall within seconds of the start of the fight, he didn't hesitate. As Edgar had expected, the bartender was a right-handed fighter and opted for a right hook the moment he got within striking distance. This time, instead of ducking, Edgar used his tremendous speed to step into the strike while raising his left elbow to the side of his head. The meat of his forearm and biceps absorbed most of the blow while Edgar delivered his own quick, vicious jab into the bartender's solar plexus. The bartender staggered back but remained standing, holding his stomach. His face was red, and his eyes were moist with pain.

Edgar knew what the bartender was thinking. He was looking for a way out. The bartender had been a bit slow to realize he was in over his head, but the jab to his solar plexus had opened his eyes.

"I'll pay for the mirror," Edgar said, offering the man an exit ramp.

The bartender didn't speak. He was still looking for his breath, but he nodded.

Edgar pulled a wad of euros from his pocket and left five €100 notes on the bar, then added two more, and said, pointing at Daniel, who was still out cold, "That's for him."

Edgar grabbed his coat, then walked to the other side of the bar to pick up his phone. The screen was scratched, but the phone still worked. Edgar walked to the exit, a few patrons nodding their appreciation by raising their beer mugs in his direction.

Edgar hadn't walked more than fifty feet when a black Maserati SUV with deeply tinted windows rolled to a stop next to him. Edgar turned to face the luxurious SUV, confident that if someone wanted to gun him down, they wouldn't stop the vehicle, nor would they do it aboard an expensive and highly noticeable brand like Maserati. The rear window of the SUV lowered, and Edgar was greeted by the grinning face of Bilal Amirouche.

"Join me, *mon ami*," Amirouche said. "We need to talk."

# CHAPTER SIXTY-THREE

*Paris, France*

Edgar walked around the back of the Maserati and climbed aboard, closing the door behind him. Edgar recognized the driver. He'd seen him before. He was one of the contractors assigned to Amirouche's security detail. A former Egyptian paratrooper, if Edgar remembered correctly. There was another man in the front passenger seat. He could have been the driver's twin if it wasn't for the missing half of his left ear.

The Maserati surged forward and merged with the light traffic, the deep purr of its Ferrari-built V-8 swelling through the warm, lavish cabin. Edgar unzipped his coat.

"Did you have the time to look at my offer?" Amirouche asked.

"If you're talking about the message that landed in my inbox ten minutes ago, then no. I haven't opened it."

"Busy night at *la brasserie*?" Amirouche asked with a crooked smile, hinting that he knew about the short fight Edgar had been involved in.

"Nothing worth mentioning."

It didn't surprise Edgar to know that Amirouche had tracked him down and had him followed. Edgar had made it easy for him to do so. Edgar hadn't run an SDR and hadn't switched phones since he'd arrived in Paris.

What would be the point? Edgar wanted out. He was no longer interested in working for Amirouche, or for anyone else for that matter.

If he couldn't be there for his brother, maybe he could be there for Sebastian? He wasn't super wealthy, but he had enough. He would make it work.

"I don't want to be the bearer of bad news, Edgar, but your brother passed away thirty minutes ago."

Edgar swore under his breath. He'd known it was coming, but it didn't make it easier to accept. He could feel tears forming in the corners of his eyes. Edgar fought them back. He couldn't allow himself to give in to grief. It was too dangerous a path. He'd seen where it had led him earlier. And if he was being honest, he had to admit that after seeing his brother at the hospital, he'd known death wasn't the worst outcome for Laurent.

"Thank you for letting me know," Edgar said after a moment.

Edgar hadn't shared his phone number with the hospital, which explained why he hadn't been notified. He wasn't in the mood to ask Amirouche how he'd learned of Laurent's death: it wouldn't change anything.

"Since you haven't read the offer yet, let us do that together now, shall we?" Amirouche said.

Once he had loaded the document, Amirouche handed the tablet and its stylus to Edgar.

"It's for an overseas op?" Edgar asked a minute later, trying to look interested.

"Indeed. The contract is in the United States, New York City to be specific," Amirouche said. "Look at the pictures."

Edgar tapped on the first picture with the stylus, then zoomed in. Edgar's heartbeat immediately jumped through the roof. The man in the picture was The Smoker. Edgar was sure of it, but he forced himself to keep a straight face, not wanting Amirouche to notice any changes.

Whoever had taken that picture had matched the angle perfectly with the one Edgar had had in Zermatt when he had first spotted the man smoking with the three restaurant employees.

"When was this taken?" he asked, his pulse pounding in his temples.

"Earlier this week," Amirouche replied. "I've been told a Chinese surveillance team took them, but there's no way to know for sure."

"Who is he?" Edgar asked, pointing at The Smoker.

"Your mark. His name is Caspian Anderson. He's a staffer at the United Nations, a translator of sorts."

*A translator my ass. What else is the general not telling me?*

He tapped on the next photo. Anderson was still in the picture, but this time there was an attractive woman standing next to him. She was in her early to midthirties, if he had to guess, and had golden skin and dark hair.

"Is she a target too?" he asked.

"No," Amirouche said. "Her name is Liesel Bergmann. She's a forensic accountant for a midsize firm in Manhattan. She has no monetary value, but she's acceptable collateral damage."

Edgar nodded but kept his budding disgust for what Amirouche was offering, and for himself, too, hidden.

*When was it that I became the general's go-to operative for contract killing?* Edgar asked himself. *You're a long way from Saint-Cyr, my friend.*

"Why is Caspian Anderson a target?" Edgar asked. "Any details about him I should be aware of?"

"Everything is in the package, including his address and the license plate of his car," Amirouche said, then placed his hand on Edgar's shoulder and continued, "Edgar, I want you to know that I'm doing this for you. I love you, and I want you to get back on your feet and in the fight as soon as possible. It's not good for you to stay on the sidelines for too long. You know that, right? Men like us, who are true warriors, we live for these ops, don't we?"

Then, and with a strength he hadn't yet experienced, raw, gruesome images of the young Swiss officer he'd shot in Zermatt flashed in front of him. Edgar closed his eyes and shook his head.

"Edgar, *mon ami*, are you okay?" Amirouche asked him.

When Edgar opened his eyes, the images were gone. For now.

"Yeah. And you're right. How much?" Edgar asked.

Amirouche grinned at him and said, "A good payday. One hundred thousand euros plus all the expenses."

Edgar nodded slowly, as if he was thinking about the proposition.

"Can I ask you a question?" Edgar said.

"Yes. Always."

"Back in Zermatt, my team and I were supposed to drop off Aldrich's wife and three daughters at a secondary location, right?"

Amirouche's grin vanished, the man's set of big ivory-colored teeth returning to their hiding place behind his thin lips. "What about it?"

"I'm curious, General. You never told me what was supposed to happen to them."

Amirouche looked at him, his eyes narrowing into slits, as if he was probing into Edgar's mind.

"Why is that important?" Amirouche said. "That operation is over."

"Yeah, I know. But I've been thinking a lot about it lately—"

"And that's why you need to get back in the field," Amirouche said. "You shouldn't dwell in the past, Edgar. It can be . . . dangerous."

*Here's my first not-so-subtle warning,* Edgar thought.

"I get that," Edgar said. "But men like us, warriors, as you so well put it, need to know that we can trust each other, right? So, tell me, were you aware that the two men that were arrested at the safe house, the ones that are now being charged with human trafficking, had outstanding warrants for the illegal sale of human organs?"

Amirouche snorted. "Your point?" he asked through clenched teeth.

Edgar was aware he was walking a very thin, very dangerous line. He couldn't afford to show Amirouche one hint of his anger and growing hatred—he had to keep his resentment to himself.

"My point is that you've been underpaying me," Edgar said, his unwavering eyes locked onto Amirouche's. "All these ops I've been running for you in Haiti . . . all these people I brought back, you were after their kidneys, hearts, and lungs, weren't you? And it was the same for Aldrich's family. His wife and three daughters, you had buyers for them, I assume?"

"What if I did? I still don't see your point, and you're deviating from your lane here. You seem to have forgotten your place, Edgar. You're an operator. An operator that gets paid handsomely for his services. The reasons why I'm contracting you for an operation, whatever they might be, shouldn't be a concern of yours. Is that clear?"

It was, but Edgar wasn't about to back off.

"Here's the deal. If you want me to take the Caspian Anderson job, you better pay up. One hundred thousand euros won't begin to cover my fee."

Amirouche straightened in the posh leather seat of the Maserati. Edgar could see the former general wasn't used to being spoken to the way Edgar had just done. Amirouche stroked his goatee a few times, and Edgar knew the man was pondering how to answer the question.

Amirouche touched his driver on the shoulder and said, "Please stop at the next corner. Edgar's time with us is coming to an end."

Then, turning his head toward Edgar, he hissed, "I would have thought the French Foreign Legion would have taught you to know your place, Commandant. Who do you think you are? What makes you think you have any leverage to negotiate with me?"

Edgar had heard enough. He knew exactly what his place was and what he was supposed to do.

As the driver stopped next to the curb, Edgar clutched the tablet solidly in his left hand and the stylus in his right and used his legs and abdominal muscles to propel himself forward and to his left. He rammed the edge of the tablet as hard as he could into the exposed throat of Bilal Amirouche. There was a crunching noise as the tablet connected with his thyroid cartilage.

A beat later, and after leaning even more to his left to clear his right arm for the strike, Edgar thrust the stylus toward the bodyguard's face, aiming for his left eye. But the bodyguard was fast, and he reacted quicker than Edgar thought possible. The man had already released his seat belt and was in the process of pulling his pistol out of its holster, his eyes on Edgar. Had the bodyguard thought about protecting himself instead of Amirouche, he might have blocked Edgar's strike. But he didn't, and the stylus entered the side of his right eye.

The man's scream was unlike any other Edgar had ever heard, but he didn't let that distract him. He still had the driver to take care of, and if the man was as fast as his colleague in the passenger seat had been, Edgar might already be too late.

Edgar rotated his torso to the left as he brought both his arms up. The driver, who was a lefty, had a pistol in his hand. Edgar's life was saved by the steering wheel, which had cost the man a precious half second to go around. By the time the driver brought his gun to bear, Edgar was ready. As the pistol swung his way, Edgar's right hand intercepted the barrel, and he wrapped his fingers around it, keeping the muzzle away from his face. Since the driver had rotated right in order to draw his firearm, his right arm was pinned against his seat, which gave Edgar a massive tactical advantage. Edgar clamped his left hand on the top of the pistol's rear sight and violently spun the gun counterclockwise and out of the driver's grasp. The man's eyes went wide with fear as he realized what had just happened. Edgar pistol-whipped the driver across the face twice, rendering him unconscious.

Returning his attention to the still-screaming bodyguard, Edgar hammered the butt of the pistol against the man's left temple.

Suddenly, there was silence inside the Maserati, apart from the low gurgling coming out of Amirouche's mouth. Edgar eyed the former general. The man had both his hands around his throat, his eyes bulging in shock. His breathing had become shallow, his face twitching. Edgar imagined placing his powerful hands around Amirouche's neck and squeezing until the man's windpipe collapsed. Another enticing thing was that Edgar knew he could take his time doing it.

The man gasping and wheezing next to him was the person responsible for Laurent's death. Caspian Anderson might have pulled the trigger, but the blame lay entirely on Amirouche. It was the former general—not Anderson—who had thrust Edgar and his team into the middle of an operation he would have never agreed to if he had known its true purpose. What if it had been Juliette or Sebastian instead of Aldrich's family? The thought sent his blood boiling. The rage in his belly had become a powerful force, and Edgar almost gave in to it.

But this wasn't the legacy he wanted to leave behind for Sebastian. He wasn't going to torture Amirouche.

That didn't mean Edgar wasn't going to kill him, though. Amirouche knew where Juliette and Sebastian lived.

*So . . . that kind of seals the deal, doesn't it?*

Edgar removed the suppressor from his coat pocket and pulled his FN 509 Tactical pistol from its holster while he kept his eyes on Amirouche. When Amirouche tried to open the door, Edgar hit him hard on the nose with the loose suppressor. Blood immediately gushed out.

"That wasn't smart, Bilal," Edgar said, shaking his head. "You can barely breathe through your mouth, and now your nose is broken."

Edgar attached the suppressor to his pistol, then aimed at Amirouche's right knee.

"Since when are you in the organ business, my friend?" he asked.

Amirouche mouthed something, but Edgar couldn't read his lips. There was too much blood. And since he wouldn't put it past Amirouche to bite him if he got too close, Edgar wasn't about to. Amirouche took another whistling breath.

Edgar sighed.

"I don't know if you were aware of this or not, Bilal, but the man you wanted me to kill in New York, Caspian Anderson, well, this is the guy who rescued Aldrich's wife and three daughters."

Amirouche's face contorted into a distorted circle, and the veins in his forehead bulged out.

"I know what you're thinking," Edgar said. "He's the guy who killed my team. Yeah, I used to think the same thing, but not anymore. You're the twat who killed my team."

Edgar took aim at Amirouche. The former general shook his head, panic rippling his face.

Edgar fired twice into the man's heart.

Edgar picked up Amirouche's tablet and looked outside the window. There were plenty of pedestrians, but the well-insulated chassis of the Maserati combined with the low growl of the idling V-8 and the suppressor seemed to have been enough not to draw attention. Edgar tapped a finger on the tablet to refresh its screen, hoping the device was still unlocked. It was.

He took a moment to study Caspian Anderson's face, committing it to memory.

Edgar climbed out of the Maserati, pulled the hood of his coat over his head, and jogged across the street before merging with the flow of pedestrian traffic. Four minutes later, he hurried down a subway entrance and bought a ticket. Hearing the train coming, Edgar rushed to the platform and slipped into a car just as the doors were closing.

Edgar found an empty seat next to an old lady. He gave the woman a brief but sincere smile, then looked straight ahead. That's when he realized he had nowhere to go.

With a sigh, Edgar closed his eyes and began to think about Caspian Anderson.

# CHAPTER SIXTY-FOUR

*New York, New York*

Liesel disembarked from the city bus and jaywalked across the street, zigzagging in between stopped vehicles that were waiting for the light to turn. It was a long SDR, but it wasn't every day that your handler asked you to break into an ambassador's home.

Moreover, an hour into her SDR, while she was coming out of a grocery store, Liesel thought she'd seen the same Asian man she had bumped into three nights ago at the café where she had stopped for a double espresso. Her possible watcher had been sitting next to a homeless woman and her dog across the street from the store's exit. She hadn't seen him again, though.

Liesel wished she had a team to support her, but she understood that running an operation outside of Europe was a daunting task for her organization. Not only was there a severe time constraint—the window of opportunity being less than twenty-four hours—but Eichberg would probably catch wind of a small contingent of German BND officers arriving in the United States. The man had eyes and ears in all spheres of the German government.

Liesel climbed into what she hoped would be her last taxi and asked the driver to drop her off one block west of Eichberg's townhome. She glanced at her watch. She had another four hours before her date with Caspian. Plenty of time to install two listening devices and plug a thumb drive into the computers she'd find inside Eichberg's residence.

The last two days with Caspian had been a blast. She felt like she was going out with a completely different man. The new Caspian had all the virtues she loved about the previous model but lacked all the glitches she didn't like. He had laughed when she told him that. Like her, Caspian had returned to work today. He had shared with her that he was no longer motivated, and that he would keep his eyes open for other opportunities.

For some reason, she kept putting off updating Nicklas about Caspian's status change. She'd convinced herself she would do it after the Eichberg operation, but now she wasn't so sure it was a good idea. It put her in a bind, because if the BND came to learn she hadn't been totally transparent with them, there would be hell to pay.

As much as she enjoyed her job, Liesel had never felt as complete as during the time she'd spent with Caspian in the last two days. The culpability she felt about not telling him who she truly was, was growing. It didn't keep her from sleeping at night, but who knew how she would feel in one, or three, or even six months from now? It could only get worse.

What would happen to her if she was to resign from the BND? Would she be allowed to stay in the US? Would he follow her back to Germany if she couldn't? Because she had thought about that too.

As the taxi came to a stop, Liesel willed herself to focus on the task at hand. For years this was the kind of mission she'd been hoping to be tasked with. Now that she was actually working a cool op, she couldn't wait for it to be over and to return home to get ready for dinner with Caspian.

Liesel paid the cabdriver and climbed out, the cold air contrasting with the heated interior of the taxi. She casually scanned her surroundings. It was a busy street with many commercial and apartment buildings lining both sides. The street was frantic with taxis, delivery vans, and private vehicles filling the air with the cacophony of their horns. The sidewalks were bustling with people, too, with a good mix of visitors, young couples with flashy baby carriages, and street vendors selling knockoff handbags and fake Rolexes to tourists.

*New Yorkers going about their daily lives.*

Liesel tilted her head down as she continued toward East Seventy-Third Street, walking past half-empty restaurants, bars, and shops hawking everything from high-end jewelry to donuts. On a whim she entered a cupcake shop and got herself a lemonade to go with a coconut cream cupcake. She stood by the window, sipping at her lemonade and looking for the Chinese man that she thought she'd caught a glimpse of exiting the grocery store.

She set the untouched cupcake on the bar-like counter fixed against the window and logged in to the encrypted chat on her phone. Nicklas had sent a short message to let her know that, due to technical difficulties, the surveillance cameras were presently out of operation, but that she shouldn't concern herself with that. The alarm system, though, had been set like they'd hoped, which confirmed that the ambassador and his wife had departed the property.

Liesel was cleared to proceed as planned. She typed a message to acknowledge reception and got an immediate reply from Nicklas letting her know the alarm system would be switched off in three minutes.

Getting herself ready to leave the shop, Liesel took a bite of the cupcake and quickly realized it was way too rich for her taste. She was about to spit it into the small pink napkin the cashier had given her when she noticed the baker, who was leaning against the door-frame leading to the kitchen, looking in her direction. She forced herself to swallow the overly sweet mixture, then gave the baker a dynamic thumbs-up.

She exited the store, finished her lemonade, and tossed the cupcake and the empty lemonade container into a trash can.

Sixty-one steps later, she turned onto East Seventy-Third Street. And that's when she felt the hair at the back of her neck stand up.

# CHAPTER SIXTY-FIVE

*New York, New York*

Caspian blew into his hands to warm them up. The temperature had dropped a few degrees in the last hour, and since the parking spot he had chosen didn't get any sunlight, the tips of his fingers had begun to feel numb. Thirty minutes ago, Caspian had lost a camera. He didn't know what had happened. One second it worked perfectly; the next his screen showed a blank spot where the feed of the second camera used to be. Although the first camera was still functioning properly, it had become useless the moment a full-size Range Rover had parked next to it. The only useful feed on Caspian's screen came from the third camera, the one he had set up on the fire hydrant. Unfortunately, this was also the camera that had the poorest angle of Eichberg's front door.

Caspian was rubbing his hands together when he saw a woman with a gray coat turning onto Eichberg's street. Her head was slanted down, so Caspian couldn't see her face, but he recognized her walk instantly.

*Liesel.*

What was she doing on the Upper East Side? Was she visiting a client?

When the woman climbed the five steps leading to Eichberg's door, Caspian's brain dismissed the notion that the woman was Liesel. It simply couldn't be. There was no explanation, none whatsoever, that could explain Liesel's presence in front of Eichberg's townhouse.

His stomach twisted into knots as he remembered the letterhead from some documents he'd read on Florence's thumb drive.

*Mellon, Borowitz and Associates. Liesel's firm.*

*My God!*

Caspian pulled his tablet closer, zoomed in, and watched as the woman inserted a key into the door lock.

*What? She has a key?*

Then, just as she was about to step into Eichberg's house, the woman turned and seemed to make direct eye contact with Caspian. His heart dropped.

*It's her.*

Caspian's heart was thumping so fast in his chest that he could feel the blood pumping in his neck. His temples began to throb. Never in his life had he been so confused. Even Laura's betrayal hadn't hit him this hard. This was personal. Caspian had been ready to give up everything for this woman.

*No! No! No! Think! This can't be.*

Caspian grabbed his phone, thought for an instant, then began typing.

———

Liesel closed the door behind her and stopped moving. She willed herself into silence and immobility. She was barely breathing, her ears doing all the work. After thirty seconds, she allowed herself to breathe normally.

Her eyes found the alarm system panel. The system had been disarmed, just like Nicklas had said it would.

Confident she was by herself and wouldn't need to exit in a hurry, she removed her boots. The gleaming cherrywood floor was spotless, and her boots were wet. Keeping them on would have left a hard-to-miss trail of her comings and goings inside the house.

Liesel was about to turn toward the main door to lock it when her phone chirped in her pocket. The surprise was total, and Liesel almost cried out in shock.

*Damn!*

She had turned off all notifications for the day, except the ones coming from Caspian or from her encrypted chat. She had made a mental note to remove Caspian before the operation was set to begin, but she had forgotten. Looking at her phone, she saw his text.

> Hey! Can I stop by your office? I'm a few minutes away. Would be nice to see you.

Shit. She had to reply. She had told her assistant that she was leaving early to spend the afternoon with her boyfriend. Caspian showing up at her firm was the last thing she needed. It would raise a lot of questions she didn't have the answers to.

> Sorry, C. I'm not at the office. See you tonight, okay?

Liesel powered off her phone, upset at her own lack of discipline.

The BND had confirmed that the German government was paying for the property's normal upkeep but wouldn't cover anything specific for the couple's day-to-day life. The BND did say that over the years, Eichberg had hired the services of housekeepers, gardeners, and personal chauffeurs, among others. The BND hadn't kept a log of their names or the usual times at which the staff could be expected to show up at the residence.

That meant she had to hurry up. Nicklas had mentioned that Eichberg's office was on the second floor, next to the library. That's where she would start. Heading toward the staircase, she walked past a well-decorated formal living room and an immense, immaculate kitchen with a large island with what seemed to be a quartz countertop. To her left was a pair of french doors, and Liesel guessed they led into a lavish dining room.

She climbed the stairs, taking each step one by one, making sure to listen every few seconds. The stairs opened directly onto a magnificent library. Farther down, a door had been left ajar.

*Eichberg's office, if Nicklas is right.*

Liesel walked toward the door, nudged it open with the tip of a finger, and was greeted on the other side by Rafael Ribeiro, who was aiming a suppressed pistol at her heart.

"Hi, Liesel," he said. "We were waiting for you."

# CHAPTER SIXTY-SIX

*New York, New York*

Caspian swore out loud when another text of his wasn't delivered.

This was a fucked-up situation, and Caspian knew he had to think this through and analyze the problem as if the person he had seen wasn't Liesel.

And he had to do it fast.

His gut was telling him this whole thing wasn't going to play out the way he wanted it to if he took too long to ponder his options.

What would he do if a woman he didn't know had accessed the property?

He'd write a detailed comment in his notepad that would include the time at which the person had accessed the property, how she was dropped off, her physical description, how she was dressed, and all other pertinent observations normally associated with a surveillance report.

What he wouldn't do was charge into a house whose layout he was unfamiliar with because his gut told him to do so.

But this wasn't someone he didn't know, was it? This was Liesel, the woman with whom he was considering spending the rest of his life.

Clearly, Liesel had kept from him some important details about herself.

*No more secrets, my ass,* he thought. Still, that didn't mean Liesel was a bad person or that she had anything to do with the illegal sale of human organs, though he admitted things weren't looking good at the moment.

If Liesel had indeed betrayed him, wouldn't it be better if he knew that now? And if she hadn't, was it possible she needed his help?

Caspian quickly put his tablet away, attached his suppressor to his SIG Sauer pistol, and climbed out of the car. One way or the other, he'd have his answers soon enough.

———

Liesel raised her hands, unconvinced she'd managed to hide the shock from her face. She took in her surroundings.

*Well . . . Nicklas didn't lie about the office.*

She was indeed in Eichberg's office, or at least what used to be his office. A printer was still plugged in, and so were two desktop monitors, but the hard drives were gone.

Liesel's least favorite part, though, was the eight-by-eight clear plastic sheeting covering the hardwood floor in the middle of the office space. An aluminum chair that had seen better days was in the middle of the plastic sheeting.

"Don't be shy. Come in, and have a seat," Ribeiro said, taking two steps back while gesturing toward the aluminum chair.

*If my butt hits that chair, I'm dead.*

Liesel heard footsteps behind her, so she only took a mincing step forward, a plan born of desperation budding in her head. When the muzzle of a gun was shoved in between her shoulder blades, Liesel wasn't caught by surprise.

"You heard him, move!" a woman shouted.

She took another small step, bowing her head, as if to admit defeat. The trick was to appear as submissive as possible while hoping the bad guys would underestimate her. Liesel felt more than she heard the woman behind her take another step in her direction. Knowing the muzzle would land in the middle of her shoulder blades a heartbeat later, Liesel sidestepped to her left while rotating counterclockwise as fast as she could. Her left forearm parried the pistol away. Liesel, using her momentum, continued her rotation and brought down her right hand in a knife-hand strike to the woman's radial nerve. The woman's hand opened involuntarily, and her pistol clattered to the hardwood floor.

Liesel, who knew the only reason Ribeiro hadn't yet shot her in the back was because he'd been afraid to hit the other woman while she spun 180 degrees, ducked under a lazily thrown left hook and pushed off with her legs, ramming her right shoulder into the other woman's stomach. Liesel's objective had been to get out of Ribeiro's line of fire by pushing the woman toward the stairs.

But her plan backfired.

One second Liesel's right shoulder was in the woman's midsection; the next Liesel was flying backward. To Liesel, the time she spent airborne felt like an eternity, though she knew it couldn't be more than half a second. When her back finally collided with the floor, the other woman landed on top of her, pushing all the air out of Liesel's lungs.

Gasping for breath, Liesel recognized her adversary.

*Catharina.*

Liesel's second realization was that Catharina knew how to fight, which was a serious problem, since Ribeiro was ten steps away and probably looking for a shot. Thankfully, Liesel wasn't out of options either. She encircled Catharina's waist with her legs, thrust herself up using her abdominal muscles, and delivered a perfectly executed elbow strike to the left side of Catharina's jaw. The snap was loud, and blood jetted out of Catharina's mouth. Liesel was sure she had loosened a few of Catharina's teeth.

But Catharina wasn't out of the fight. And she was still on top. Bright light flashed in Liesel's eyes as the other woman connected with a short right. Then there was another, and another. Liesel bracketed her head with her forearms, but the punches kept coming, faster and faster.

While some blows were absorbed by her arms, some made it through, and Liesel's vision became blurry.

*I must do something. Now. Or I'll die on this floor.*

Timing herself, Liesel abandoned her ineffective defense and grabbed onto Catharina's left fist as it connected with her forehead. Liesel saw stars, but at least she had her two hands on the other woman's fist.

Catharina must have sensed what Liesel wanted to do because she screamed just as Liesel managed to open Catharina's hand. Catharina delivered another punch, but it was poorly aimed and glanced off Liesel's scalp, just as Liesel bent back the other woman's index finger until it snapped. Before Catharina could respond, Liesel latched on to her pinkie and broke it too.

Catharina yelled in agony.

Pressing her advantage and trying to limit Ribeiro's angle of fire, Liesel once again thrust her upper body forward and wrapped her left arm around Catharina's neck while twisting her body to the right. Liesel, letting herself fall back, brought Catharina down with her and began to squeeze the life out of her.

# CHAPTER SIXTY-SEVEN

*New York, New York*

Rafael had rarely seen someone move so fast, and without fear. He admitted that the look of defeat he'd seen on Liesel's face had tricked him. He'd seen that face—that hopeless, beaten expression—countless times in São Paulo. So tonight, he had taken it for granted.

Danielle had mentioned Liesel was into Krav Maga, but he had dismissed it without giving it much thought. Maybe he shouldn't have.

The entire fight had started ten seconds ago, and now Rafael wondered who had the upper hand. The two women were now outside the ambassador's home office, and Liesel was holding Catharina against her chest, choking her. He could see Catharina's pretty face had turned crimson red. Rafael could get closer and fire a proximity shot, but his orders were to find out what Liesel knew, and what she had shared with the BND.

And if Rafael was honest, he didn't mind seeing the precious princess take a few hits to the face. Maybe it would remind her where she was from and who she answered to. Rafael would give it another ten seconds or so, and then he would fire a round into one of Liesel's knees.

Then Rafael's phone began to vibrate nonstop in his pocket. Four short pulses followed by two longer ones. Someone had walked through one of his ad hoc laser beams.

Rafael swore. They had a visitor, or visitors.

———

Liesel could see her choke hold wasn't perfect. Catharina was still able to breathe, though with some serious difficulties. But time wasn't on Liesel side, and at some point, Ribeiro would be coming for her. Just when Liesel thought Catharina was about to run out of stamina, Catharina delivered two solid hits into Liesel's ribs, which allowed Catharina to wriggle free.

Catharina was panting hard, her entire face was purple red, and her eyes were wild, as if she had gone feral. Then Catharina reached for something, almost losing her balance as she did so.

Liesel didn't waste her opportunity.

Bringing both of her elbows tight against her body, she planted her right foot on the hardwood floor and thrust her hip up, propelling Catharina off her. Liesel glanced to her right and left but didn't see Ribeiro. She was about to get to her feet when, from the corner of her eye, she saw Catharina slashing at her neck with a small tactical knife. Unable to duck or sidestep in time, Liesel blocked the strike with her left forearm, the razor-sharp blade easily slicing through her clothes and flesh. The pain shocked Liesel, and she screamed, but she didn't let up, knowing she had to take control of the fight. Before Catharina could strike again, Liesel clamped both of her hands around the other woman's fist, paying for it with a deep cut into the palm of her right hand. With blinding speed, and in a move she'd practiced countless times during Krav Maga classes, Liesel swung her entire body 180 degrees, using her left leg as an anchor. As she spun, her hands still clenched on Catharina's fist, Liesel bent forward, using her rotation speed and her hip to throw her opponent over her shoulder. As Catharina's back hit the hardwood floor, Liesel tilted the angle of the blade and fell forward on top of the ambassador's wife, using her weight to drive the tactical knife into the middle of Catharina's chest.

She stared at Liesel, her big brown eyes wide in disbelief. The women's faces were a mere four inches apart, and Liesel could smell

Catharina's freshly shampooed hair and brushed teeth. Liesel gave the small knife a sharp twist and pressed it down for a two count, Catharina's body wriggling underneath her. Liesel wrenched the knife out of the woman's chest and stabbed her in the neck twice in rapid succession. Catharina's right hand shot to her neck, trying to stop the blood from leaving her body with it.

That didn't work. Blood continued to spurt through her fingers.

Liesel glanced behind her, just as Ribeiro cracked her over the head with the butt of his pistol.

# CHAPTER SIXTY-EIGHT

*New York, New York*

Caspian was carrying his lockpick gun in his backpack, but he was glad he hadn't had to use it. He knew he had made the right decision the moment he had stepped into Eichberg's house. A woman had yelled something unintelligible, and Caspian was glad it hadn't sounded like it had come from Liesel. Five steps later, he had heard another scream.

*Sounds like Portuguese.*

There was a lot of noise coming from the second floor, but Caspian, who was in a combat crouch, knew he couldn't move too fast despite his eagerness to cover the distance to the stairs rapidly. Caspian peered around the living room corner.

*Clear.*

He crossed to the other side of the hallway toward a pair of french doors. Caspian turned the knob and pushed the door open. The door swung easily and quietly on its hinges. It was the dining room. Caspian stepped carefully over the threshold, sweeping his pistol from corner to corner.

*Clear.*

Caspian exited the dining room, moving as fast and as silently as he could, almost gliding on the impeccably clean hardwood floor. Caspian continued to clear the first floor, his brain searching, evaluating, and taking inventory of what he was seeing. So far, he had spotted two laser beams, and Caspian assumed he had missed at least one. Maybe more. *Just brilliant. They know I'm coming. Great work, Caspian.*

He had no idea how many threats he would face on the second floor, and he didn't know the layout, but he had to go. For all he knew, Liesel was in a fight for her life one level up.

Caspian reached the stairs. He had finished clearing the first floor and, being fairly optimistic he wasn't going to be surprised from behind, he began to slowly climb the steps, keeping his pistol steady in front of him in a two-hand grip. Ignoring the sound of a rowdy and still ongoing hand-to-hand fight just a few feet above him, Caspian focused on keeping his weight on the outside of each stair to minimize the squeaking of the boards. He thought he heard a couple of muffled words coming from a man, but he didn't stop. He had lost the element of surprise anyway. He had to keep going.

At the top of the stairs, Caspian froze. In front of him, Catharina lay flat on her back, a pool of blood growing on the no longer spotless hardwood floor. A bit farther, a man he recognized as Rafael Ribeiro had an arm wrapped around Liesel's neck.

———

Liesel hadn't lost consciousness, but the blow to her head had dazed her and sent a searing bolt of pain through her skull. The bloody tactical knife had slipped from her grasp. She had felt Ribeiro's arm wrapped around her neck, but she had been too weak to fight him off as he lifted her up from the dying Catharina as if she was as light as a feather.

Ribeiro was behind her now, tight against her back, using her as a shield. His left arm was still wrapped around her neck, her windpipe in the crook of his arm. She could feel his hard biceps and forearm on each side of her neck, and she was pretty sure that the stiff object jammed into her lower back and against her spine was the muzzle of a gun, not a part of Danielle's boyfriend's anatomy.

Liesel tried to speak, but Ribeiro clenched his biceps, and the words caught in her throat.

"Quiet, Liesel," Ribeiro whispered in her ears. "Be a good girl and you might walk out of here."

Liesel didn't believe him. Not after having seen the clear plastic sheeting in Eichberg's office. As her foggy brain slowly came back online, so did her aches. Her face announced its displeasure about all the punches it had absorbed from Catharina by providing her, free of charge, with excruciating pain. Liesel, who despite all her years of Krav Maga had never had any of the bones in her face broken, was convinced both her cheekbones had been shattered by Catharina's fists. She could feel her face beginning to swell on both sides. She closed her right hand into a fist and winced, blood seeping through her fingers from the cut on the palm of her hand. She tried to move her left hand. It worked. While the throbbing radiating from the cut on her left forearm had intensified, her tendons seemed to be intact.

And her nose appeared to be okay too. So, there was that.

Catharina was on her back a few feet in front of Liesel. She was dead, or soon would be. Deep cuts to the throat like that were unforgiving. As she continued to regain her strength, Liesel wondered if it was Nicklas who had sent someone to rescue her. She doubted it. Who would he send? It wasn't like German intelligence had tier-one operators ready to go in New York.

Then she saw Caspian. The odds of her surviving the ordeal had just gone up exponentially.

———

Caspian didn't see a gun or a knife, but he was certain Ribeiro had one or the other pressed against Liesel's back.

"Are there any others?" Caspian asked, knowing he'd probably have only one question answered.

"Don't think—" Liesel started to answer before Ribeiro flexed his biceps again and shut her up.

Liesel hadn't given him a definite answer, but it was all Caspian was going to get.

"Drop your weapon, Caspian," Ribeiro said, his voice calm and measured.

Caspian didn't. The only thing that would result from him lowering his pistol would be his and Liesel's deaths. Instead, Caspian sidestepped to his left, his hands tightening around the SIG pistol grip.

There was very little of Ribeiro that Caspian could shoot at. The man had managed to hide a good portion of his substantial frame behind Liesel. Still, his forehead was visible atop Liesel's head, and so was his left shoulder. An easier target would be Ribeiro's left knee. Caspian's finger began to apply pressure on the trigger. He knew that at this distance, he could place his round wherever he wanted. His aim wasn't the issue. The problem was that he didn't know what kind of weapon Ribeiro was threatening Liesel with, which made the situation dicey. A slight jerk of Ribeiro's hand or finger, or even a dying spasm, could result in Liesel's death.

"What's the deal here, Rafael?" he asked, keeping his eyes on Liesel in case she tried to communicate with him. "Any chance we can work something out?"

"I didn't expect to see you here," Ribeiro said. "UN translators aren't usually armed with suppressed SIG Sauer P229s."

Was Ribeiro trying to pass on a message to him? The man definitely knew his guns. Your ordinary Joe Blow wasn't able to identify a pistol just by looking at it once from a distance.

"Right," Caspian said, slowly closing the gap. "And software engineers do?"

"Do you like this woman, Caspian?" Ribeiro asked, his voice suddenly urgent. "If you do, don't take another step. Move again and I'll put a round in her spine."

"You do that, you die," Caspian said.

"Maybe, but you'll be the one living with the guilt."

Caspian stopped.

As much as he hated where this conversation was headed, at least he'd learned one thing. It was a gun, not a knife, that Ribeiro held in Liesel's back. Not the positive development he was looking for.

"Are you with the BND too?" Ribeiro asked.

The BND? Caspian had no idea what the man was talking about. The only BND he knew was . . . then it clicked in Caspian's brain. German intelligence. He looked at Liesel, and while he couldn't be sure, he thought she'd given him a nod.

Had Liesel just acknowledged to him she was a German spy? She'd been in the United States for so long . . . it didn't make sense. Unless Liesel was a NOC operative. But in New York? Why?

Then Caspian sighed.

*Because of me. No! I'm missing something.*

Liesel hadn't known about him being a federal agent. She had seemed genuinely taken aback when he'd spoken to her about him being with HSI.

"Oh. I guess you didn't know your girlfriend was a spy, then," Ribeiro said, managing a chuckle. "Your face, dude. Priceless. Really."

"What about you?" Caspian asked. "By your accent, I'd say you're either with Portuguese or Brazilian intelligence. Or you could just be a thug."

Ribeiro scoffed at him.

"My allegiance doesn't concern you," he said. "But anyhow, if you aren't with German intelligence, what the hell are you doing here? You look competent enough. And if you were a cop or a federal agent with any authority, you wouldn't have come here alone, and you wouldn't have a suppressor attached to your pistol."

Liesel couldn't talk, but she was moving her tongue in and out of her mouth. Her face was swollen, but Caspian saw that she could breathe.

*She's trying to get my attention.*

He briefly locked eyes with her. And she looked down.

"You're right. I'm not a cop," Caspian said, his mind spinning.

Was Liesel signaling for him to shoot Ribeiro in the leg, or was she telling him she was going to drop down?

*What would I do if I was in her shoes?*

He'd want her to kill Ribeiro, and you didn't kill a man by shooting him in the leg—at least not if you wanted him dead quickly.

"Is there anything, anything at all, I could say that would convince you to walk away from this one?" Ribeiro asked, but Caspian was just barely listening, focusing instead on his sight picture. "Because if there—"

Liesel bent her knees forward and slightly to the side, as if her legs had suddenly stopped supporting her. An extra two or three inches of Ribeiro's head appeared.

It wasn't much, but it was enough. Caspian didn't need a whole lot to make this work.

Caspian, who had already worked the slack of the trigger, applied full pressure. The round entered Ribeiro's left eye, splattering the white wall behind him with blood, bones, and pieces of his brain.

A follow-up wasn't needed.

Caspian rushed to Liesel's side. There was a lot of blood at her feet.

"Are you hurt?" he asked her as he patted her down with his left hand, looking for any sign of injuries.

"I got a laceration from a knife cut on my left forearm and another on the palm of my right hand."

"Okay. Any bullet wounds? Do you have any—"

Liesel stopped him by grabbing his wrist. "Casp, I'm good."

*Casp? This is a first.*

"Have you seen anyone else in the house?" he asked.

"I haven't, but I haven't checked the other floors."

Caspian nodded. "Do you need to?"

Liesel hesitated an instant, then said, "No. Do you?"

"I'm here for you, Liesel," he said. "I'm not looking for anything else."

"Eichberg is gone, and he's not coming back," Liesel said. "Listen—"

"Not now, Liesel," Caspian said, heading back toward the stairs.

They would have plenty of time to chat about what had happened in Eichberg's townhouse, but Caspian would prefer to do that outside a federal prison. He stopped at the top of the stairs and looked over at Liesel. She was taking pictures of Catharina and Ribeiro. He watched her as she pocketed their phones.

"Are you sure you want to bring—"

"Yes. I'm sure," Liesel said, catching up to him. "These people are monsters. That's bigger than us."

Caspian nodded.

"Yeah. I kind of figured that," he said, going down the stairs.

Caspian stopped by a bathroom and grabbed two towels and a medical kit.

"Use your right hand to keep pressure on your forearm," he said, tossing Liesel a towel.

As they reached the front door, he turned to face Liesel and said, "I don't need an explanation, but is there a team on their way here to clean this up?"

Liesel shook her head. "I . . . I honestly can't say for sure, but I'd be surprised if there was."

"Is there someone on their way to pick you up?"

"No . . . only you," Liesel said. "There's only you."

# CHAPTER SIXTY-NINE

*Near Plainville, Massachusetts*

Liesel grimaced as she moved the bag of ice away from her face. She looked outside the SUV window and saw a sign welcoming them to Massachusetts.

"If you're tired, go right ahead," Caspian said, giving her a small lopsided grin. "We'll stop in Portsmouth for gas and something to eat. I'll wake you up. Don't worry."

She nodded, then pressed the bag of ice against her forehead and closed her eyes. She needed to think. Her entire existence had changed in the last four hours. Although she trusted Caspian—he had saved her life, after all—there was so much she didn't know about him, and he about her, that it was driving her nuts.

She had remained mostly quiet as Caspian had gone through his exfil process. Their first stop had been to a large self-storage facility in East Bronx, a two-minute drive away from the I-95. They hadn't stayed for long, but Caspian had exchanged his old Toyota Camry for a much newer Jeep Grand Cherokee he had bought a couple of years ago.

Caspian's priority had been to take care of her wounds. They weren't life threatening, but they had required attention and more than a few stitches. Once he was done, he had loaded the back of the SUV with four full-size duffel bags and two Pelican cases. He'd also taken a minute to show her the two secured drawers that had been installed inside the cargo area of the Cherokee.

"Same key works for both drawers," he'd said, giving her a key. "Open it."

Inside the drawers was an assortment of pistols, magazines, suppressors, ammunition; a pair of night vision goggles; and a modified M4 rifle.

"Are we going to war?" she'd asked him, only half kidding.

"No. To Maine."

"What?"

"We're going to Maine. My father's there."

They hadn't talked much since then, both lost in their thoughts. The two phones she'd taken from Ribeiro and Catharina were in the glove compartment of the SUV. She had powered them off and removed the SIM cards, but Caspian had insisted she put them in a special box he'd pulled out of his storage unit. She hadn't talked to Nicklas either. Truth was, she had no idea what she was going to say. There was so much she didn't understand.

She sighed and opened her eyes.

"Are we fugitives?" she asked Caspian.

"I was asking myself the same question," Caspian said. "I don't think we are, though. At least not for now."

"You're not really with HSI, are you?"

"That's complicated," Caspian said as he stretched his neck. "I know how lame that sounds, by the way. If you'd asked me the same question a week and a half ago, I would have told you yes, I'm with Homeland."

"I'm not judging, you know," she said, meaning it. "Just trying to understand, so that I can start connecting the dots. Like you're doing, too, about me."

Caspian didn't speak for the next ten miles, and she didn't push it.

They made an unscheduled stop at a roadside coffee shop, and Caspian asked her if she wanted something.

"Coffee would be nice, and a cranberry muffin if they have some."

"You got it."

When Caspian came back ten minutes later, he gave her a paper bag and a to-go coffee cup.

"Careful with the coffee. It's scalding hot."

She thanked him and opened the paper bag. The muffin wasn't big, but it was warm and tasted delicious.

"Ask me anything," Caspian said, two minutes later as they merged back onto the highway.

"Really? Just like that?" she asked. "Don't you want to know who I—"

Caspian raised his hand and shook his head, interrupting her.

"I know everything I want to know about you," he said. "If you want to share more, I'm happy to listen. Also, I just left you for ten minutes alone in a running vehicle with a tank full of gas, with weapons in the back. If you didn't want to be with me, you could have left."

She looked at him, stunned. "That actually never crossed my mind," she said.

Caspian smiled and placed his hand on the tan leather center console. She thought about it, but just for a second. She slid her hand into his and gave it a light squeeze.

"Anything?" she asked. "You sure?"

"Yeah. Anything you want to know. Ask away," he said.

And she did.

# CHAPTER SEVENTY

*Kennebunkport, Maine*

Caspian opened his eyes. Liesel was already looking at him, her head against the fluffy pillow. The bed was one of the most comfortable he had ever slept in, and Caspian made a mental note to ask the innkeeper where he'd purchased the mattress.

Using one of the prepaid phones Caspian carried in his duffel bags, Liesel had found them a last-minute deal in a lovely inn in Kennebunkport, a peaceful seaside town in southern Maine. The inn was perched at the top of the village and offered fantastic views of the small but charming downtown area and its art galleries, cafés, and antique stores.

"Good morning," she said.

"Morning," he said. "Any news?"

"Not yet, but it's not even eight o'clock," she said. "Nicklas said to reach out to him at noon, remember? Patience, Casp. Patience."

"I know," Caspian said.

She gave him a kiss. "I'm going to take a shower. Care to join me?"

"I will, but go ahead," he said, rolling onto his back, feeling lighter and more rested than he had in years.

He heard Liesel turn on the water, but Caspian's mind was on the lengthy discussion he'd had with her the night before. He hadn't hidden anything from her. Not a single thing. She had listened intently and hadn't shied away from asking some pointed questions.

And he had done the same, after she had threatened to walk away if he didn't.

"Trust works both ways, Casp," she'd said. "I need you to know there's nothing off limits between us any longer."

Once they had arrived at the inn, they had walked to town and found a quaint restaurant to eat dinner, where they had continued their discussion. Later, after watching the evening news and changing the dressings on her wounds, they had both concluded that for now, the police weren't looking for them. After comparing their notes about the events in Zermatt and New York, they had decided that the best course of action was for Liesel to contact her handler and to brief him on what had happened, while keeping Onyx out of it.

Caspian knew this had been a huge gamble. While he believed the BND would take care of Liesel if any legal issues were to develop, Caspian had no idea what he would do. That wasn't entirely true, though. He did have an elaborate escape plan, but it was for one person.

And he had no intention of leaving Liesel behind.

True to her word, when Liesel had placed the call to her handler, she'd shared her set of earphones with Caspian. To his utmost surprise, Nicklas had been very receptive to what Liesel had shared with him, and he hadn't seemed distraught when Liesel told him that Caspian Anderson, a former HSI special agent, had saved her life.

But it was what her handler had said at the end of the call that had left Caspian speechless.

"It's two in the morning in Berlin," Nicklas had said. "The whole thing is a trainwreck, there's no other way to describe the situation. I mean, it's complete chaos. But with that in mind, let me work on this. Reach out to me again at noon tomorrow."

And then, a beat later, as if he knew they were both on the line, Nicklas had added, "It's a long shot, but I might have a solution. For both of you."

Caspian looked at the bedside clock. They had another four hours to wait. He swung his feet over the edge of the bed, got up, then made his way to the bathroom to join Liesel.

# CHAPTER SEVENTY-ONE

*Old Orchard Beach, Maine*

Caspian had accepted his fate. Whatever it was. Still, a not-so-small voice in his head told him he still had time, that it wasn't too late to change his mind, and that he could still drop Liesel at the next corner and leave.

But where would he go? He would have at least one major intelligence agency running after him. Caspian was good, but one day, when he least expected it, they would come for him, either with guns blazing or with a pair of handcuffs and a hood to put over his head.

But that didn't frighten him as much as imagining spending the rest of his life away from Liesel and wondering what might have been if he had stayed.

"Okay, Liesel," Caspian said, taking his foot off the gas pedal. "The I-95 is ending in less than a quarter of a mile. After that it changes into Ocean Park Road."

"I know, but I haven't received any other instructions," Liesel said, her eyes on the screen of her phone.

Liesel, as planned, had called back Nicklas at noon. The call had been brief, and Nicklas had said that Liesel had two options. She could make her way to Boston, where a business-class ticket was waiting for her, and board an 8:00 p.m. Lufthansa flight to Munich, then continue to Berlin after a two-hour layover. If she chose that option, she was expected at headquarters no later than 5:00 p.m. the next day. Nicklas told her there would be a long debrief.

"It could take months before you're cleared for duty again," Nicklas had said.

The other option, the one Liesel had chosen after exchanging a one-second look with Caspian, was to follow Nicklas's directions to a meeting place.

They'd been following directions for the last two hours.

"Okay. Got it. Continue onto Ocean Park Drive and enter the 7-Eleven you'll see at the first traffic circle."

Caspian spotted the 7-Eleven easily and parked the Grand Cherokee in the lot.

"They want us to enter the store and give our keys to the clerk."

Caspian was getting anxious. He had a lot of gear in the Cherokee, and handing over the key to his SUV to a kid working a cash register didn't seem like a good idea.

Liesel must have deciphered his dilemma because she looked at him and said, "Your call, Casp. I'm game for anything."

Liesel had told him more than once that she trusted Nicklas. That was good enough for him.

"Let's go," he said, opening his door.

Caspian entered the store first and scanned the interior. It wasn't busy, with only one other customer. He looked at the woman. She was in her late twenties, dressed in a dark green jogging suit, sporting a pair of headphones and dancing to a beat only she could hear.

Caspian walked to the cashier—a man in his early to midforties—and placed the car keys on the counter.

"Don't worry about your truck, sir. It's in good hands," the cashier said, passing a hand through his scraggly hair. "Now, please follow my friend."

Caspian turned, and the woman with the headphones waved at him. His eyes moved to Liesel, but she was already following the woman and heading toward the exit at the back of the store.

The woman waited for them at the exit door.

"There's a gray SUV waiting for you right outside this door," the woman said. "Please take the rear seats."

The woman pushed the door open. A gray Lincoln Navigator was idling five feet away. The SUV's windows were heavily tinted, and it was impossible to see how many people were inside. Caspian exited the store and followed the woman's instructions. He'd been following instructions all morning; he could do it one more time. Caspian opened the door and noticed right away how heavy it was.

This was an armored vehicle.

Caspian climbed into the SUV with Liesel following two steps behind. The rear of the SUV was like a miniature conference room. There were six swiveling chairs, all in black leather, and a rectangular wood-like table in the middle. Caspian and Liesel sat next to each other, facing the two other people—a man and a woman—who were already settled around the table.

From the front passenger seat, a man in his fifties was looking at them. Caspian noted the earbud in his left ear. The man was a bodyguard.

A nod from the woman at the table was all that was needed for the Navigator to surge forward.

"Casp, may I introduce you to Nicklas," Liesel said, gesturing to the man seated across from Caspian.

Caspian shook the man's extended hand.

"Nicklas Drescher. I'm with German intelligence, as I'm sure you know," the man said.

"Caspian Anderson."

"Samantha Ranger," the woman said, shaking Liesel's hand, then Caspian's. "Thank you both for coming."

The woman was in her early fifties, with long, wheat-blonde hair tied up on her head with a green band, which matched the color of her eyes.

"I doubt you're with the BND," Caspian said.

"I'm with the Defense Clandestine Service, Mr. Anderson."

Caspian looked at Liesel, who just shrugged.

The DCS was the small, clandestine arm of the well-known Defense Intelligence Agency and specialized in deep cover operations against high-priority targets. Caspian had never met anyone working at the DCS, but he had heard only good things about the organization. His previous feeling of apprehension had morphed into one of curiosity.

"I wasn't aware the BND and the DCS worked together," Caspian said.

"We don't have an official affiliation, at least not at the moment," Ranger said, looking at her watch, "but yes, we do work together. And when Nicklas called and told me about the two of you, I'll admit I was intrigued."

"May I ask how you two know each other?" Liesel asked.

Ranger raised an eyebrow at Nicklas and said, "I thought you told me you told her about Venezuela."

"Maybe not everything," Nicklas said, looking at his hands.

"Let me guess, Nicklas, you didn't mention the part where you saved my life? Am I right, Liesel?"

"He definitely skipped that part," Liesel said.

"Can I share with Liesel and Caspian what you did for me?"

"If you have to, Samantha," Nicklas replied, looking uncomfortable.

"As you know, we were working in Venezuela on a shared project, and we were about to leave for the airport when we were attacked. Nicklas knocked me to the ground when the lead motorcycle opened fire. If it hadn't been for him, the first salvo would have hit me at chest level. But Nicklas wasn't done. Knowing there was another motorcycle two seconds behind the other, he adjusted his body so that he would cover my right side. That's when he got hit. That's why he lost his leg."

Caspian took another look at the man, but this time, he actually paid attention.

Even though Nicklas had been seated in front of Caspian for well over five minutes, Caspian hadn't really noticed him. Nicklas was an unremarkable man of medium build, and his eyes didn't have the fire most intelligence officers possessed.

*That makes him the perfect spy.*

As Ranger continued, her eyes were on Caspian, and he could see she meant every word. "So you'll understand, Mr. Anderson, that when Nicklas called me late last night and asked for my assistance in regard to a delicate matter, I was happy to oblige."

Caspian wondered what kind of assistance Nicklas had requested, but he didn't ask. Instead, he said, "Absolutely."

"Samantha," Nicklas said, tapping a finger on his watch. "We'll be at Portland International in ten minutes."

"Right. So, here's the deal, Mr. Anderson," Ranger said. "I'm not sure how much you know about your former employer, but Onyx closed up shop eight years ago."

While Caspian had come to peace with the fact that he'd done a few hits that hadn't been ordered by the US government, never had he even imagined that he could have been duped for as long as eight years.

Ranger snapped her fingers. "Hey! Focus, Mr. Anderson. We're getting short on time, and I need to figure out ASAP what to do with you."

Caspian was taken aback by the woman's words, not sure if the *what to do with you* was a good thing or not, but he liked her style.

"I'm listening," Caspian said.

"Okay. Great. First question. Elias. It was you, yes?"

Caspian was glad he had told everything to Liesel, because if he hadn't, it would have placed him in an uncomfortable position.

"I guess you could say that," Caspian said.

"Explain."

And he did. For the next seven minutes, he told Samantha Ranger everything he knew about Onyx, and he didn't even care if Nicklas was there. Someone at Homeland had dropped the ball big time regarding Onyx, and Caspian was pissed off.

*I was left behind,* he said to himself.

Caspian briefly talked about his recruitment, his training, and a few of the missions he'd done, including the one in Portugal where the news reporter and actor were killed, and spent the last two minutes—with the help of Liesel—going through what had happened in Zermatt and New York and the last phone call he'd had with Laura.

When he was done, Ranger looked at her watch, then looked at Nicklas.

"What do you think?" she asked.

"It could work, Samantha," the German intelligence officer said. "He's qualified, and I vouch for her."

"You know she'll have to—"

"Hey!" Caspian said, cutting off Ranger.

Ranger looked at him, as if she was surprised Caspian was still there.

"I'm right here, and Liesel is right there," Caspian said, tapping his hand on the table. "It would be fun to be included in the discussion, don't you think? Especially since it seems to concern us."

"Deputy Director Ranger," the bodyguard in the front passenger seat said, glancing over his shoulder, "we're two minutes out."

Ranger gave him a thumbs-up.

The Lincoln Navigator drove past an open gate watched by two security officers and continued toward an idling Gulfstream G400.

"I'm looking for dependable people that can work independently overseas, or in the United States, for long periods of time," Ranger said while typing a message on her phone.

"To do what?" Caspian asked.

"Think a mix of what you did in Zermatt and New York," Ranger said, then looked at Caspian with a smile. "But this time, you would really be working for Uncle Sam, if you know what I mean."

"New York is unfinished business, I'm afraid," Liesel said.

Caspian caught Nicklas looking in Ranger's direction. She gave him a subtle nod.

"I wouldn't worry too much about him. He's about to . . . disappear," Nicklas said. "The BND is also working on a strategy to put the blame squarely on his wife, Catharina. We all agree it will take some work and that there will be some repercussions, but we've seen worse."

"Can you expand a bit more on his . . . disappearance? Does that mean you know where Eichberg is?" Liesel asked, leaning forward.

*Here's that subtle nod from Ranger again.*

"He's in Tunisia, about to be arrested," Nicklas said, smiling for the first time. "And the prisons in Tunisia . . . well, let's just say they're different. Justice will be done."

The Navigator rolled to a stop next to the Gulfstream.

"Let them know I need another two minutes, George," Ranger said to the bodyguard.

"By the way, Mr. Anderson, were you aware the woman you killed in Italy was Laura Newman's daughter?" Ranger asked as she gathered her things.

Caspian shook his head and crossed his arms over his chest. He couldn't help but to chuckle. "Nope. I didn't know that either."

"Is the name Bilal Amirouche familiar to you?" Nicklas asked. "A former general in the Algerian army."

Caspian thought about it for a moment. "Should it be?"

"It doesn't matter anymore. The man's dead. He was killed in Paris, shot twice in the heart at close range inside his luxury SUV. A man we assumed was his bodyguard was found in the front passenger seat, dead from a severe traumatic brain injury—"

"He also had a stylus embedded in his right eye," added Ranger.

Caspian shrugged, then said, "I didn't do it, if that's what you're insinuating."

"Yes. We know that. We think it might be the driver. We'll see where this leads," Nicklas said.

"Nicklas was simply asking because our friends in France shared with us the content of a tablet that was found in Amirouche's SUV,"

Ranger said. "Apparently, there was a one-hundred-thousand-euro contract out on you, Mr. Anderson."

"Do we know who the client is?" Liesel asked.

"Laura Newman," Ranger said, her hand on the handle. "I guess she didn't believe your story."

"Guess not," Caspian grunted.

Laura was going to be a pain in the ass.

"Is there anything that can be done about her?" Liesel asked, looking at Nicklas.

"You're not asking the right person. Eichberg is German. Laura Newman belongs to Samantha."

Caspian watched with interest as Ranger sat in her seat again.

"I can tell you straight up that Laura Newman will be very difficult to prosecute," Ranger said. "I'm not saying it can't be done, but a lot of people on both sides of the aisle will be nervous if this ever moves forward. It will cost the government a fortune and waste a lot of good people's time."

Caspian smiled.

"I have a hard time picturing you going to court, Deputy Director Ranger," Caspian said. "I have a feeling that most evidence you collect—and I doubt you collect any, but for the sake of argument let's say you do—well, it would be thrown out of court. Something about the way you collect it, maybe?"

"Maybe," Ranger agreed.

Caspian made eye contact with the three other people seated at the table.

"And to be completely honest, I have to say that the vibe I'm getting from this very pleasant meeting is that we all like to save taxpayers' money, don't we?"

"Who doesn't?" Ranger replied.

"What about Laura Newman? Would the US government like to save money on that specific case?"

"Mm-hmm. Very much so, I would say," Ranger said. "In fact, there might already be a cost-cutting measure in the works."

"Can I participate?" Caspian asked.

Ranger seemed to mull it over for a moment, then said, "Let's see how the cards fall on this one. But I'm not saying no."

# EPILOGUE

*Three Months Later*

*Daingerfield Island, Virginia*

Caspian's senses were honed to a razor's edge as he stood motionless in the night, tucked deep into the shadows of the trees, waiting for Liesel to confirm the sniper's arrival. Caspian, with the help of Liesel and his new team at the Defense Clandestine Service, had prepared for this moment for the last four weeks. Caspian didn't know how long he would have to remain in his position, but he didn't mind the wait, since it allowed him to become attuned to his environment.

A warm breeze rustled the leaves, carrying with it the sound of the not-too-distant city. The moon was high, and while it was partially veiled by a wisp of cloud, it still provided Caspian with sufficient visibility. If this was to change, the handheld thermal monocular camera in his left pocket was easily accessible.

Just north of Old Town Alexandria and close by the Mount Vernon Trail, the 106-acre Daingerfield Island wasn't an island but a peninsula on the shore of the Potomac River. Although most of the area was wooded, a marina and a restaurant could be found on site. Popular with joggers and cyclists during the day, at night it was mostly dog walkers who wandered the trails.

One of those dog walkers was Laura Newman. Three times a week, she took her dog out for a long walk along the Potomac, always stopping for a few minutes at the same place on Daingerfield Island.

Two months ago, when Ranger had reached out to Caspian to inform him that the funding for the new unit she was going to lead had come through, she had invited him to her office at the DIA headquarters.

"The Strategic Support Unit will have its own satellite office," she had told him. "But I wanted you to come in and see for yourself who you'd be working with if you were to accept the position."

Caspian had briefly met the team of technicians and analysts that would staff the SSU office. Some were in military uniforms; others wore civilian clothing. The liaison officer position had been approved. Liesel would need to go through a six-week indoctrination, but most of it was to confirm her qualifications. While at the DIA headquarters, Caspian had asked about Claus Eichberg.

"Nicklas handled the case, so he's the go-to person in regard to Eichberg, but the last time he mentioned Eichberg's name, it was to let me know that your friend Claus was in a prison cell with twenty-five other prisoners," Ranger had replied. "And keep in mind the cells are supposed to have no more than eight prisoners."

"Interesting . . . it will take a while for him to get used to this . . . cramped space," Caspian had said. "It's a big step down from his five-thousand-square-foot luxury townhouse in New York."

"Very true. The way the prison system works in Tunisia is a bit different than in the United States," Ranger had explained, a slight smile on her lips. "If the prison cell is supposed to be for eight prisoners, that means they prepare food for eight inmates, not twenty-six. Survival of the fittest, right?"

The conversation had pleased Caspian very much and had put him in a good mood for the rest of the visit.

Caspian had never worked as a member of a large team. His time with Onyx had been mostly spent working as a lone operative. It would take some time getting used to having someone in his ear, but the fact that the voice belonged to Liesel would help speed up the process. While the sensation of having several pairs of eyes watching his every move was unsettling, Caspian would be a fool if he refused to acknowledge all the tangible benefits of having a support team.

Establishing a pattern of life on Laura Newman had been a lot easier than if Caspian had done it alone. An unlimited access to micro unmanned aerial vehicles, infrared and thermal cameras, and other high-tech surveillance equipment had seen to that. It was one of those night-vision-equipped microdrones that had detected an immobile warm body hidden five meters into the wood line. The location, which had a direct line of sight to the spot where Laura stopped with her dog, had been identified and marked as a potential sniper hideout. A hypothesis Caspian had confirmed the next day while wandering the trails with a dog belonging to an SSU analyst. The sniper's nest was well done and would have been nearly impossible to detect without the drones.

Caspian's original thought on Laura was that she'd become sloppy with her tradecraft. Why else would she be stopping at the same place for five to six minutes three times per week?

Now he knew, and it had nothing to do with Laura being lazy. She had set a trap for him. Caspian's assumption was that his former handler had concluded that he had found out about the hit she'd put on him and that she was now waiting for his retaliation.

It had taken a few more days to confirm who the sniper was. Caspian had been stunned when he had discovered that it was Laura's husband, Christopher, who'd been one of Caspian's instructors back in Montana.

"Fabius, this is Sky," Liesel's voice came in through the wireless earpiece tucked in Caspian's ear.

"Go ahead, Sky."

"Sierra is on his way to his location," Liesel said, using Christopher's code name.

"Good copy."

Taking into consideration the last four trips and how long it had taken Sierra to walk from the marina parking lot to his sniper's nest, Caspian estimated it would take the sniper fifteen to twenty minutes to get in position. Then it would be another twenty to forty-five minutes before Laura showed up at her usual spot.

Caspian took advantage of the solitude to control his breathing. His nerves, taut as bowstrings, needed to loosen a little. He thought of Florence and the conversation he had had with her. It had been a risk to reach out to her, but he had done it anyway.

"Your father wasn't a nice man. He was a criminal, and nothing will ever change that," he had told her. "But I want you to know that . . . the thing we believed he was involved—"

"The illegal sale of human organs, you mean?" Florence had said, cutting him off. "I'm not afraid to say it. You shouldn't be either."

"He was never directly involved, Florence," Caspian had said. "He never profited from it. Never. Do you understand what I'm saying?"

"How sure are you?"

"I wouldn't say something like that if I wasn't sure," Caspian had replied. "It took longer to confirm than I had hoped, but now it's done, and I didn't want you to live the rest of your life thinking your father was worse than he actually was. He didn't commit these horrendous crimes. Others did."

It had taken a long moment for Florence to respond.

"I can't tell that to my mother," she'd finally said. "It will be my secret to keep. Goodbye, Elias."

Now, as Caspian waited for his prey to get in position, he wondered if he hadn't made a terrible mistake by sharing what he knew with Florence. He'd told her the truth about her dad to make her feel better, but had he simply added more weight to her already overburdened shoulders?

*Or did I do it to alleviate some of my own guilt? I'm the one who took her father—as crooked as he was—away from her and her sisters.*

"Fabius from Sky," Liesel said. "Sierra is in position."

"Good copy."

*Time to get your head in the game.*

———

It was thirty-two minutes later that Caspian heard from Liesel again.

"Horsefly is five minutes away," Liesel said, using the code name that had been assigned to Laura. "That's about how long it will take you to reach Sierra's position."

"Copy. On my way."

The wind had picked up since Caspian had first taken his position. Not by much, but enough to conceal the swooshing of the leaves being crushed under Caspian's soles. The clouds had moved on, and the moonlight was filtering through the foliage.

"Fabius from Sky," Liesel said with a tension that hadn't been there before. "The battery life of my drone is draining at a faster rate than expected. In forty seconds, I'll have a two-minute gap before the other gets on station."

"Fabius copy."

"You're now twenty meters away," Liesel said. "Sierra is slightly to your left and looking through his scope. You're still good."

As he continued to move forward, Caspian's eyes, sharp and unyielding, slowly scanned his surroundings with a predatory focus, making sure he hadn't missed anything. His suppressed pistol was out and in front of him, ready to fire.

"Stop!" Liesel's voice came in. "Sierra's moving."

Caspian obeyed, his senses on alert.

"Horsefly now in position," Liesel said.

Caspian didn't move a muscle. With Laura in position, her husband was probably scanning the area around her. Caspian doubted he'd looked behind him, but if he did, Caspian would shoot him. It would wreck the plan, but it was better than the alternative. Caspian had no intention of dying tonight.

"I'm blind, Fabius," Liesel said. "One minute and fifty seconds before the next drone arrives."

The next voice Caspian heard belonged to Ranger. He hadn't known she'd been listening in, but it made sense since it was their first operation.

"I know you can't respond, but it's your call, Fabius," Ranger said.

Caspian appreciated the vote of confidence. Ranger wasn't a micromanager, and she was letting him decide what he wanted to do. That was good to know. Having a team was great, but Caspian had years of being a solo operator under his belt. There was never a hint of hesitation about how this would go down.

Keeping his pistol in his right hand, Caspian used his left to draw the Taser on his belt.

It took him thirty seconds to cover six meters. When he was four meters away from Sierra, he could see the man hunkered behind his rifle.

The man was speaking. Caspian was convinced Laura and her husband didn't have a support team to talk to. That meant he was speaking with his wife. Caspian waited for a break in the conversation, then counted to four to make sure it was indeed over and that no replies were expected from the husband.

Caspian pressed the Taser's trigger. The barbed probes penetrated Christopher in the back and hit him with a surge of electricity strong enough to interrupt the man's neuromuscular system.

Caspian moved rapidly to the man's side and smacked him once with the butt of his SIG pistol. Playing it safe, he zip-tied the man's hands behind his back before looking for his radio. Like Caspian, he had a wireless earbud in his right ear. Caspian removed it and placed it in his own left ear before taking the man's spot behind the rifle.

He wasn't a fan of using a rifle he hadn't zeroed himself, but this time there was no alternative.

"Fabius, sitrep," he heard Liesel say through his right earbud.

He didn't reply, afraid it would also activate Christopher's mike. Then he realized it might not be a bad idea.

Caspian adjusted his aim, then said, "Elias is in position."

———

Laura Newman leaned against the railings, her gaze on the horizon. The loss of her daughter had hit her harder than she had thought. It wasn't hard to imagine what had really happened. Elias had seen through Amy's play, had followed her to Italy, and had managed to overpower her.

*Then he put two rounds in her head,* she thought, closing her eyes.

She'd seen the images the local police had taken of the crime scene. Like many before her, Amy had fought with Elias, and lost.

Laura had tried to get Caspian killed through a well-respected broker, but that hadn't worked out. She didn't know how Caspian had found out, but he had.

*And now he's after me,* she thought.

She let out a long sigh.

She'd hoped it would be done by now, but Caspian hadn't taken the bait she and her husband had set up for him. Would he ever show up? Was he here already, stalking her in the night? She was tired of looking over her shoulder.

"I'm here, L.," her husband whispered. "Nothing so far."

"I'll stay another five minutes, then I'll go," she said.

Where was he? Where was Elias?

She had betrayed Caspian's trust and had put a price on his head. She knew he wanted his revenge.

*He already killed the broker. I must be next on his list, right?*

Laura's entire strategy was based on her conviction that Caspian wouldn't just put a bullet in her head. No, he would want her to know he was the one who had won. That's what she would do if the roles were reversed. She would look Caspian in the eyes as she pushed a dagger in between his ribs and into his heart.

That's why she was here three times a week. She was giving him an opportunity to fulfill his vengeance.

*Take the bait, Elias,* she willed him. *Take it!*

Her husband might have been out of the game for almost a decade, but he was still an excellent shot. And at a distance of one hundred meters, he wouldn't miss. In the end, she'd be the one watching Caspian Anderson die.

She would be the victor. She glanced at her watch.

*One more minute.*

Then, startling her, a voice that didn't belong to her husband came through her earpiece.

"Elias is in position."

Laura froze, but only for an instant. She thought about running, even jumping into the Potomac, but what would be the point? Amy was gone, and her husband was dead, killed by the man he had helped to train.

Laura smiled. It was a fitting end. She rested her left hand on top of her dog's head, then closed her eyes for the last time.

———

Caspian pulled the trigger, sending a round to the base of Laura's neck. She pitched over the railing and fell into the Potomac. Her dog watched her go over, barked twice, then sat. For a moment, Caspian was afraid the dog would jump after Laura, but she had tied it to the railing.

"Horsefly down," he said.

"Good copy, Fabius," Ranger replied. "We'll look for her heat signature once we have a drone on station."

His attention shifted to Laura's husband. The man was still either unconscious or faking that he was. Caspian wasn't going to leave it to chance. Taking his suppressed SIG, he jammed its barrel into the man's mouth, breaking at least three teeth in the process.

Christopher's eyes opened wide in shock as he howled in pain. Or was it despair? Caspian didn't care.

"I knew you were faking it, asshole," Caspian said, then pulled the trigger.

He cut the man's zip-ties, then wiped the pistol clean before placing it into the man's right hand. It was a sloppy kill, but it would confuse the hell out of the authorities.

"Sierra is down," Caspian said.

"Well done, Fabius," Ranger said. "Sky will walk you through your extraction. See you at the office."

# ACKNOWLEDGMENTS

I'd like to start by thanking my readers. This is my twelfth thriller, and whether this is your first Simon Gervais book or you've read them all, it is important for me to let you know that I appreciate your support. I couldn't do this without you.

I'd like to thank my entire publishing team at Thomas and Mercer. *The Elias Network* is my seventh novel with them, and I can't imagine working with a more talented group of people. Special thanks to Liz Pearsons and Gracie Doyle. You are two very special people, and it's an absolute delight to work with you. Thanks, too, to Kevin Smith for his wise guidance.

Many thanks to the reviewers and podcasters who have supported me along the way. Ryan Steck, a.k.a. The Real Book Spy, and the team at Best Thriller Books have been amazing advocates for my books. Thank you!

Writing books isn't easy, and it's important to connect with like-minded writers with whom you can freely talk shop. I consider myself lucky to know such a bunch of writers. Thank you, Don Bentley, Connor Sullivan, Jack Stewart, David McCloskey, and Taylor Moore, for our almost-daily chat and laugh. Thanks, too, to Mark Greaney, Brad Thor, Marc Cameron, Brad Taylor, Brian Andrews, Jeff Wilson, Jack Carr, Kyle Mills, Joshua Hood, Steve Konkoly, Chris Hauty, and Steve Urszenyi for their support.

On the business side of things, I'd like to thank my literary agent, Eric Myers. Over the years, Eric has become a close family friend, and I know I can count on him to handle pretty much everything I throw at him. Also, many thanks to Debbie Deuble Hill and Alec Frankel, my two terrific film/TV agents in Los Angeles, for their excellent work. I'm amazed at the deals you've negotiated for me, and I can't wait to see what's next!

And as always, I sincerely thank my wife, Lisane—who's stood by me since I started in this business—and our two children, Florence and Gabriel, for their love and unconditional support. It means the world to me. Without you three, none of this would mean anything.

# ABOUT THE AUTHOR

*Photo © 2013 Esther Campeau*

Simon Gervais was born in Montréal, Québec. He joined the Canadian military as an infantry officer. In 2001, he was recruited by the Royal Canadian Mounted Police, where he first worked as drug investigator. Later he was assigned to antiterrorism, which took him to several European countries and the Middle East. In 2009, he became a close-protection specialist tasked with guarding foreign heads of state visiting Canada. He served on the protection details of Queen Elizabeth II, US president Barack Obama, and Chinese president Hu Jintao, among others. Gervais lives in Ottawa with his wife and two children. He's an avid boater, SCUBA diver, and skier. Visit his website at SimonGervaisBooks.com and follow him on Facebook @SimonGervaisAuthor, on Instagram @SimonGervaisBooks, and on X @GervaisBooks.